FRIENDSHIP

Also by Lars Saabye Christensen in English translation

LARS SAABYE CHRISTENSEN

ECHOES OF THE CITY II
FRIENDSHIP

Translated from the Norwegian by
Don Bartlett

MACLEHOSE PRESS
QUERCUS · LONDON

First published in the Norwegian language as *Byens Spor: Maj* by
Cappelen Damm AS, Oslo, in 2019
First published in Great Britain in 2021 by MacLehose Press
This paperback edition first published in 2023 by

MacLehose Press
An imprint of Quercus Publishing Ltd
Carmelite House
50 Victoria Embankment
London EC4Y 0DZ

An Hachette UK company

This translation has been published with the financial support of NORLA

ISBN (MMP) 978 1 52941 335 9
ISBN (Ebook) 978 0 85705 917 8

10 9 8 7 6 5 4 3 2 1

Designed and typeset in Scala by Libanus Press, Marlborough
Printed and bound in Great Britain by Clays Ltd, Elcograf S.p.A.

Papers used by Quercus Books are from well-managed forests
and other responsible sources.

TIME

The pigs do not seem to be overly concerned. In a little while they are going to die. They just do not know that they are. But how can Jesper Kristoffersen be so sure? Perhaps the pigs are fully aware they are going to die and there is no escape. That is why they aren't trying to make a run for it. They have given up. It could also be that they possess a certain style, in other words, they are pretending. Which only makes matters worse. One by one they enter the pen where a man in a blue smock is waiting for them. He places a pair of electric tongs over each animal's head. The stunning, which is the red carpet of death, occurs with immediate effect. As soon as the pig is on its knees, it is hoisted by a chain attached to its rear left foot and transported along the track under the ceiling, the legendary chain conveyor system, past another man who slits the pig's carotid artery with a gleaming knife. Jesper is dazzled by all the bright red blood spurting out in a jet that never appears to land. He can't bear to see any more. Yet he cannot take his eyes away. Now the pig is sucked into a rotating bristle remover, where it swirls around between the cylinders in a frantic ballet. The pig is a pig no more. It doesn't resemble one. The final shave awaits – for who would want to have such hair in their food? Another man stands poised with a bigger knife to open the steaming carcass. He slices down the belly, as easily as unfastening a compliant zip, unfolds the intestines as swiftly as others might clean their nails and hangs what will be eaten on the numbered hooks which slowly rumble down to an elderly gentleman wearing round spectacles and holding a pair of tweezers. It is impossible to bypass him. He is the Ministry of Agriculture's very own high priest. His job is to dissect, approve and stamp. Only then can these delicacies, the pig's vital organs, be sent on to the meat hall where the packers are waiting to load the goods onto lorries so that the drivers can ultimately deliver them to the town's many butcher shops, in which customers can buy chops and roasting pork, not only for a Sunday dinner but also perhaps for a very ordinary Wednesday lunch. These are good times. There is meat. Apprentice Jostein Melsom disposes of what remains. He lugs intestines and bones into the huge basins, hoses down the walls and scrubs the floors. Then, through the steam, he turns and waves. Jesper can't take any more. He makes for the nearest door and directly behind Oslo Slaughterhouse sinks to his knees and spews up. He vomits over his shoes and bag. He vomits over his hands and his new wristwatch, which says half past one. He vomits over the glockenspiel ringing out from the City Hall tower. He drowns the deep tones in gastric juices, snot and other mucus. Then, empty as an umbrella, he swivels around and rests on his back. The sky is in motion even if in all its blueness it isn't moving. There is a bright reflection on the black water at the mouth of the river Akerselva, or wherever it is, perhaps it is only the knives being sharpened again. Jesper has no idea. He is on the wrong side of Oslo, as far away from Fagerborg as it is possible to be. It is August, soon it will be September. Autumn is already a nip in the air out in the fjord. Jostein appears above him. He is having a five-minute break, lights a fag and grins.

"Wimp."

"Shh!"

"Why?"

"The pigs," Jesper says.

"What about them?"

"They're mooing."

Jostein flicks back his fringe.

"Cows moo."

"Cows?"

"Or bulls."

"I'm never going to eat meat again."

"Then you'll starve."

"Not if I eat cake instead."

"Cake? Have you got some cake?"

"I should never have come."

"What did you say?"

"Nothing."

"Why did you come then?"

Jesper gets up, wipes the bag with his forearm and takes the fag out of Jostein's mouth.

"Your hearing gets even worse when you smoke."

Jesper takes the last deep drag, spits out the butt and has to conduct an internal dialogue with himself.

"Why did you come then?" Jostein persists.

Jesper manages to re-focus his eyes.

"To invite you to a birthday party. If you wash your hands first."

"It's not your birthday."

"It's my mother's."

"How old is she?"

"You don't ask ladies."

"I'm asking you, aren't I?"

"Then I'll have to ask my mother."

"Don't you know?"

"At five-thirty."

Jostein tosses back his head and laughs.

"Are you as deaf as a post or what?"

"She'll be forty."

Then the glockenspiel is there again. It is already two o'clock. Wasn't it half past one a minute ago? Jesper is desperate. He is in a hurry. He will soon be fifteen and is pressed for time. It shouldn't be like this. You should have plenty of time when you are fifteen in August. You should have your whole life in front of you. You should have the rest of the day and the following one. You should at least have the next moment in front of you. But what makes him most desperate is that no matter where you are in this town sooner or later you end up in the acoustic shadow of the City Hall bell towers. It is inescapable. It is the same whether you are standing at the top of Blåsen Hill, have buried yourself in the Royal Palace Park, are asleep on Huk beach, swimming under the Bridge of Sighs or have been whisked off in a paddy wagon: you cannot escape. The two friends, Jesper and Jostein, as different as two peas in a pod, go their separate ways, except that Jostein has to go back to the pigs, or rather the pig offal, while Jesper runs off, bag tucked under his arm, like a discombobulated errand boy on a bike with no wheels. He crosses Youngstorget, where farmers vie to yell the lowest price loudest and headscarfed women haggle over and poke at all the vegetables on the groaning stalls that fill the square with a soft, yellow light that smells of rain and earth. There are pumpkins, sprigs of dill, tomatoes, cabbages and cucumbers, they are the fruits of the summer, what remained of it after the sun went down, but unlike the pig, which is a closed chapter, the summer rises from the dead. With the summer there is always more to be reaped. Yes, Jesper is going to stop eating meat and become a member of the turnip club: people who live off fresh air and potato peelings. Then he can become even thinner and perhaps the pallor of his skin will change. Although there is no need. Being pale is fine so long as he is thin, because he definitely doesn't want to be fat and pale. "Blackboard Jungle" is on at the Centrum cinema. Three girls are studying the pictures of Glenn Ford in the glass display case outside and don't notice Jesper, who certainly notices them. They have tight skirts, slender necks and weak knees. Up in Grensen, two police officers are helping a tramp into a Black Maria. Jesper stops for a moment. There is something familiar about him, about the unkempt, decrepit figure. Jesper has seen him before. But all tramps have fought in the same war and so they all look the same. Now he knows. He is the man who was walking in the water at Vestkanttorget some time ago. Jesper sprints down to Karl Johans gate, which at certain times is called Strøket or Stripa, depending on whether you live in the West End or east of the Akerselva. Today, a Tuesday, the name of the street is just Karl Johan. He goes into Musikkforlaget, squeezes past the seething mass of kids sharing two headphones out of which "Rock around the Clock" can be heard all the way to Færder lighthouse in the fjord, finds the classical section and utters the word he has come to town for:

"Satie."

The assistant, who looks like a grieving dog with oversized ears, leans across the counter and repeats the word:

"Satie? Erik Satie?"

"Yes."

"What do you want to do? Listen, buy or play?"

"Play."

"Let me guess. *Gymnopédies?*"

Jesper nods.

"One, two and three."

"Now you wait here like a nice young man and do not mix with the hoi polloi."

The assistant is gone for a while. Jesper waits. He has no intention of mixing with anyone and especially not with this lot. He turns his back on them. But unfortunately he cannot avoid hearing the driving beat in the floor. This is the well-worn path. It is tempting and superficial. It is dance music. It is ephemeral. But there is something else that strikes Jesper. It is sixteen minutes past two and he has missed the City Hall intermezzo. Is this where salvation lies, in Musikkforlaget? Is this where silence, or to be more precise, the absence of bell-tower chimes, is to be found? The assistant returns, places the music on the counter and gently blows the dust off the sheets. They are a thing of beauty, and fragile: *1. Lent et douloureux. D major/D minor. 2. Lent et triste. C major. 3. Lent et grave. A minor*. The dust settles again, somewhere else. It doesn't disappear. Jesper takes the money from one of his back pockets: two notes and a coin. It is the right amount. The assistant carefully rolls up the sheets of music and slips an elastic band around them. Jesper drops them into his bag, which doesn't become noticeably heavier. He can feel no difference. Music weighs nothing.

"Thank you."

The sales assistant extends a hand.

"My name's Åge. It's *I* who should thank *you*."

Jesper shakes the hand, which is dry and flaky.

"Jesper," Jesper says.

"You're Norway's hope for the future, Jesper."

Then Jesper has to walk past the crowd, who can't stand still and are deafer than Jostein. In Karl Johan light descends over the pavement in lustreless shades. Ibsen and Bjørnson guard the doors to the National Theatre, one with his coat wide open, the other as withdrawn as an embittered tortoise. Over in Pernille, the open-air restaurant, abbreviated to Nille, it will soon be the last round for this year. When the first leaves fall, the beer taps are turned off and the parasols are folded up and stored in the giant herbarium. However, the waitresses are still carrying trays of foaming beer in tall glasses and serving tables, where young men in tweed jackets are always waiting for someone. Outside Myhres Tobakk, Jesper collides with a man who is more interested in opening his blue packet of cigarettes than looking where he is going. The man immediately starts mouthing off, but fortunately he slips into a lower gear and keeps his foot off the accelerator.

"Jesper?"

Jesper nods.

"Jesper Kristoffersen?"

Jesper nods again. He feels ill at ease, almost embarrassed. This is like being caught red-handed. The man lights a short cigarette and the smoke that rises from the chimney is black-ish.

"I can see you don't recognise me," he says.

"Morning, Rudjord."

"Not bad! How are you doing, Jesper?"

"Fine."

"You haven't finished school yet, have you?"

"No. Why?"

"As you're wandering around here with a briefcase under your arm, I thought for a moment you'd become an office monkey."

"I haven't got that far yet."

"But time doesn't exactly stand still, does it?"

"Time tells, Gjensidige excels," Jesper says, quoting the insurance company slogan.

Rudjord laughs and the whole of Karl Johan inhales.

"How's your mother?"

"She's forty today."

"Forty? I suppose you're having a big party then?"

Jesper shrugs.

"Just us."

Rudjord drops his cigarette on the pavement and slowly grinds it out with his shoe.

"Haven't you got a satchel?" he asks.

"Yes."

"You're not skipping school, are you?"

"Got the last lesson off."

"Say hello to your mother. From me and everyone at Dek-Rek."

"OK."

"And by the way, can you ask her to give me a ring one of these days?"

Jesper doesn't hear the rest. Instead he runs through Studenter-lunden, a word from which Ewald, his father, made a scurrilous anagram, jumps on the Briskeby tram and jumps off at the bend. Soon there will be no more time. Soon time will have run out. There is everything waiting for him. It is waiting everywhere. He sets a PB down to Jørgen Moes gate and if he could have slid up the banisters to the second floor he would have done. His satchel, by the way, is under the staircase. He can grab it on the way out. He takes the stairs in three strides and presses the bell. He rings once again. After a couple of years, at twenty minutes to three, that is, Enzo Zanetti opens the door. He is still attired in a dressing gown and you can see the stubble growing on his face. He probably has to shave with a lawnmower more often than the City Hall bells ring.

"Have we got a lesson?" Enzo asks.

"Not until Monday."

"So why are you here?"

"I've bought Satie."

"Go home and practise. And *con calma*. The pianist who spends most time on Satie and never takes his hands off the keys wins. Do you understand?"

They are interrupted by a voice issuing from the bowels of the flat. There is always a woman calling – she sounds as though she has her mouth full of boiled sweets:

"Where are you, Tutti Frutti?"

Enzo's eyes begin to wander and he pulls the dressing gown more tightly around him. His toenails curl upwards, they are almost yellow.

"It's my mother's birthday today," Jesper says.

"Is it? Then say happy returns from me."

"If you like, you can come at half past five."

"And one more thing, Jesper. No-one calls me Tutti Frutti. Absolutely no-one. That includes you. Do you understand?"

Enzo Zanetti closes the door long before Jesper can say he has probably understood and, even if he hasn't, he won't call him Tutti Frutti anyway. Nor a drunk. He slides down the banisters, both thighs on the verge of smoking, and he imagines the fire engines in Briskeby racing out with ladders, hosepipes and parachutes. Then he slings his satchel over his shoulder and it is down the final straight to Majorstua School. She is standing at the gates. Her satchel is bigger than his; it is like a snail's shell on her back. Her hair is short and dark, but the long summer, the longest in living memory, has lent it a new glow. Some of the light has stayed with her. And this light, or its reflection, is held by a hairslide on the right-hand side, so that it doesn't fall into her eyes. She is wearing grey shoes, green stockings and a blue dress that reaches down to her knees. Jesper instantly knows what he should have bought his mother: the dress she tried on at Steen & Strøm. But perhaps it won't fit anymore. Perhaps her taste has changed, as so much has happened since then, it is a hundred years ago, at least. Or do we like the same things all our lives? Will Jesper wake up one morning and not like Satie? It is a staggering thought. It is a chasm. It is akin to death. Apart from her, the schoolyard is deserted. Only a pigeon is sitting on the edge of the drinking fountain. He stops in front of Stine, breathless.

"Have you been waiting long?"

"Only until you came."

Jesper laughs and takes her hand. But as they are about to set off, a man with a pronounced stoop passes the flagpole. He resembles a lonely crab at the bottom of an empty pool. It is Løkke, his old form teacher, who rode into the sunset and only half came back. Now Løkke sets the table in the school canteen every morning, serves the Oslo breakfast to his pupils and gives private lovesickness lessons. Too late. He has seen them, unfortunately.

"Well I never," Løkke exclaims.

Jesper thinks they are rid of him, but as always Løkke has more to say.

"Where do you go to school now?" he asks.

"Fagerborg."

"The food's not quite as good there, is it?"

"Just packed lunches."

Løkke stands rapt in thought for a while and the chances of sloping off are minimal. He seems to be blocking the way with all his anxiety and wisdom. He is a wall. He would be a boon to a handball team. He looks at Jesper again.

"Packed lunches? Ones you make yourself?"

"Yes. Or the old girl does it."

"Old girl?"

"My mother."

"What do you put in the sandwiches?"

"Cheese. And caviar, maybe."

"And cod-liver oil?"

"Not in butties."

"Butties?"

"Sandwiches."

"No, of course not. You take the cod-liver oil separately. From a spoon."

"I take it before I leave."

"It's also perfectly possible to take it in milk."

"Milk and cod-liver oil?"

"Is that your girlfriend?"

"Who?"

"The girl whose hand you're holding."

"That's my sis."

"Who?"

"My little sister."

Jesper lets go of Stine's hand, which she holds over her mouth to stifle her laughter. The pigeon takes off from the fountain. Its shadow flits in all directions.

"Well I never," Løkke repeats.

This time they are rid of him.

On the way home they drop into Samson's in Majorstua. Jesper has ordered a cake. There isn't enough room for forty candles on it, but he couldn't afford a bigger one. In fact, it is doubtful whether forty candles would have been a good idea anyway. By the time you were lighting the last one the first will have gone out. Jesper pays using the money he has in his other back pocket. This is the right amount, too. Then he carries the cake along Kirkeveien, on the left-hand side, while Stine keeps a lookout to make sure as few people as possible see them. Rumours travel fast in Fagerborg and this is meant to be a surprise. But is it possible to carry a cream sponge cake down Kirkeveien without attracting attention? And it isn't a very good idea to run while holding a cake. If you fall flat on your face, you will definitely be noticed, but if you do, basically it won't matter because the cake will be ruined anyway. The coast is clear. Seeing Stine ahead of him, Jesper has an odd thought: one day she will overtake him. She started at school six months early. He started a whole year late. Will she be looking after him in the end? That is a long way off, at least as many years as there are between them, but what seems distant soon comes round. Now the coast isn't clear. Dr Lund has appeared by the corner of Ole Vigs gate and there is no walking past him, either.

"Hello, stranger," Dr Lund says.

Jesper doesn't respond. Nor is he sure if this is a question. If it is, Dr Lund is equally strange. Dr Lund turns to Stine.

"And who's going to eat this wonderful cake?"

"Jesper."

"Is it his birthday?"

"Mamma's."

"Say hello from me and many happy returns."

"She doesn't want a birthday."

Dr Lund turns back to Jesper.

"A piece of that cake works out at two and a half laps of Frogner stadium. How far will you have to run if you eat two pieces?"

"Five laps."

"And five laps is two thousand metres. We may as well do two and a half more and that's three thousand. Will you join me?"

Jesper shrugs.

"I'm not hungry," he says.

"Well, you look a bit pale and off-colour to me."

Dr Lund places a hand on Jesper's forehead, putting in a bit of overtime, but he can't feel a temperature, only expectation and the pressure of time. Then finally they are rid of him, too. They walk the final stretch, past Marienlyst, and reach the safety of the back-yard. It is best to use the kitchen stairs when something has to be kept secret, even though no-one can keep a secret in Fagerborg, especially those who have one. Jesper planned this several weeks in advance. But now he changes his mind. Where is his mother

15

usually? In the kitchen. They can't just burst in. So they go through the cellar and take the main staircase. A new plan: Stine rings the bell while Jesper waits on the ground floor with the cake. The coast is clear again. Mamma isn't at home. Stine has the key around her neck and has to stand on tiptoe to open the door. Mamma? They shout her name to be on the safe side. She doesn't answer. They hurry into the kitchen and put the cake in the refrigerator. Then they sit and wait. She doesn't appear in the first half-hour. Nor in the second. They set the table in the dining room. This is where they find the note: *Hi. Had to go to a Red Cross meeting. Could be late. Warm up yesterday's leftovers. Ring 22 18 76 if there's a problem. Did you remember to buy the sheet music, Jesper? Love, Mamma.* At half past five the doorbell rings. Jesper opens the door. It is Jostein. He has cleaned himself up. At any rate, he doesn't reek of pigs. He stinks of Old Spice. What is more he has put on a black suit that is eight sizes too big. They go into the dining room and sit down. Jostein puts his present – a cylindrical cudgel wrapped in grey paper, probably a salami – on the table, casts a glance at Stine, immediately looks away and blushes. Actually, blushing suits Jostein. Then his spots aren't so obvious.

"Isn't your mother even at home?" he asks.

"She'll probably be here soon," Jesper says.

"Why's she having a party then?"

Stine holds a hand over her mouth, as is her wont, and tries to stifle her laughter, but she snorts between her fingers. Jostein blushes even more. Jesper sends his little sister a stern glare. There is only one person who can laugh at Jostein, and that is Jesper.

"Did you fall in the bristle remover or what?"

"One of the pigs escaped."

"Escaped?"

Jostein looks down:

"S'pose she didn't want to die."

"She?"

"Sow."

"Do they know they're going to die?"

"How should I know?"

"Did you find her?"

Jostein looks up.

"Aren't we having any cake either?"

At six Enzo Zanetti turns up as well. He arrives late for everything. He calls it his Italian half an hour. At least he has mown the lawn on his face and clipped the hedge. In several places on his mug he has stuck bits of paper he has torn from a newspaper, probably *Aftenposten*. You can almost read the headlines from the last three years on his jaw. He is a walking news agency. James Dean is dead. Thomas Mann is dead. Albert Einstein is also dead. Enzo's hands are shaking again. He is shaking so much he will soon be able to play a piano duet on his own. In a low voice he asks:

"Is your mother in the kitchen?"

"She'll be here soon."

Jesper accompanies Enzo into the sitting room. He puts a bottle on the table and lays a flower beside it. He has probably picked the flower on the way, perhaps in Valkyrien, where there are wild tulips growing. It is in fact the first time he has been here. He says hello to the rest of the company. Stine curtsies as if this were a dancing school. Jostein, who hasn't forgotten that he called Enzo Zanetti a drunk and pinched his lighter, neglects to bow and instead asks:

"Guess what the difference is between Jesper and me."

Enzo recoils. Not only does this boy stink to high heaven, he is brazen as well.

"Jesper plays the piano. You don't."

"What?"

"You don't play the piano. Jesper does."

Jostein tosses back his head and laughs.

"I earn money and Jesper doesn't!"

Enzo Zanetti sits down on the piano stool and strikes a key, a C, which oscillates through the room. Untrue. This is his way of saying it; a note is untrue, not false. Then he heaves a deep sigh and looks at Stine again.

"Would you be so kind as to fetch me a glass of water?"

Jostein makes another brazen remark:

"If he's allowed to drink, we can eat the cake."

The telephone rings. Jesper gets up and puts a finger to his lips. Then he goes into the sitting room and lifts the receiver.

"This is the Kristoffersen household, hello."

But it isn't his mother. It is Fru Hall, the former widow Fru Vik. She gasps at the other end, which is in Nordraaks gate.

"Jesper?"

"That's me."

"My goodness. Has your voice broken already?"

"I haven't been listening."

"I hardly recognised you."

"It's still me."

"Yes, now I can hear it is. Suddenly I thought it was . . . No, I'm going all doolally."

"Who did you think it was?"

"No, no, forget it. Tell me what you're doing, Jesper. It's been such a long time."

"Twiddling my thumbs."

"Sorry? Twiddling your thumbs? But you still play the piano, don't you?"

"I'm about to start on Satie now."

"Promise me you'll let me hear you play one day. Will you promise me that?"

"If it's worth listening to, yes."

"I'm sure it will be. Can I talk to the birthday girl?"

"She's not at home."

"Isn't she? On her birthday?"

"She's at a Red Cross meeting."

"Oh, my word."

"Yes."

"I thought there must've been something as I hadn't been invited."

"I don't think she's very keen to turn forty."

"You can console her with the thought that it gets worse with age."

"It must be terrible for you, then."

Fru Hall, the former Fru Vik, laughs, but her laugh sounds rusty and strained, it is altogether a harsh laugh. Then she lowers her voice.

"You're taking care of my flat, aren't you, Jesper?"

"Sort of."

"Could you just pop by? And make sure everything's alright. When you have the time. Maj has a key to the kitchen door."

"OK. Now I think I have to go."

The harsh laughter sounds different now and is more like tiny sobs, or perhaps she has something stuck in her throat.

"It was so nice to talk to you, Jesper. Give Stine my love. Is she well?"

"She started school in the autumn."

"Golly. At school already? I'm sure she's clever, isn't she?"

"Cleverer than me."

From the dining room comes the sound of a bottle being opened.

"Are you having a party anyway?" Fru Vik asks.

"We're just repairing."

Jesper hangs up and joins the others. Enzo Zanetti is drinking from the bottle. There isn't room in it for more than one swig at a time. The lifeless-looking spirit smells strong and reminds Jesper of rotten apples. The sun, sinking between the blocks of flats on the other side of Kirkeveien, gathers itself into a tight ball for a moment, and the last rays of light filter through the bottle and fill the dining room with a restless, green shadow.

"Wasn't that Mamma?" Stine asks.

Jesper shakes his head. Jostein, who appears peeved and sullen, presumably he has the cake on his mind, is about to say something, probably regarding this cake about which rumours are circulating. The telephone rings again. This time Stine goes to answer it, but Jesper won't let her. There has to be a pecking order. When Maj isn't at home, Jesper is next in line. Stine can answer the telephone if he is out, unavailable or has moved out for good. It is Maj. Jesper can hear that at once and he puts a finger to his lips. Stine does the same and turns to the room, where eventually there is silence.

"It's just me," Maj says.

"Oh, is anything wrong?"

"No, no. Why should there be?"

"I don't know."

"I just wanted to say I might be a bit late home."

"Late?"

"So you don't need to wait up for me."

"Right."

"That was all."

Jesper shifts the telephone into his other hand, and a back-to-front thought strikes him: he regrets looking forward to anything.

"That was all," Maj repeats.

Worried, she hangs up. She is worried because Jesper always seems worried, perhaps it is she who worries him. Then she turns to the other women waiting in the hallway. The meeting is over. She has been given a present by the board, a vase from Glasmagasinet. It is much too elegant. Anyway, she didn't want anything. The chairman, Fru Lund, officiated at the ceremony. And as if that wasn't enough, now they are going to the restaurant in the swish Hotel Continental. Maj doesn't feel like going. She doesn't like surprises. But she has no choice. The secretary, Else Larsen, has already booked a table. On their way down the steps they meet Dr Lund. He seems to be in a sombre mood, preferring to hug the wall in silence as he passes the ladies. However, the board of the Norwegian Red Cross, Oslo Division, Fagerborg department, is excited and does not let him slip by so easily. Fru Lund laughs.

"I can see my husband's run too fast today."

Dr Lund has to stop after all.

"That, I'm afraid to say, is what I haven't done."

The ladies behave like schoolgirls and want to comfort him.

"Did you lose?" the secretary, Else Larsen, wants to know.

Dr Lund takes two more steps and cannot quite make up his mind whether he is going to be in a better or an even worse mood.

"Losing is a term that men of my age refrain from using. But I was beaten."

"By whom, may I ask?"

This time it is the deputy chairman, Fru Vanda Aasland, who asks. Dr Lund doesn't take this well.

"By Putte Dedekam. The little shrimp. In our heyday he was seldom on the podium. And he's had two coronaries since then. What can you say?"

Fru Lund, his wife, sighs aloud, but the sigh hides laughter and condescension, the way you react with blithe resignation to a child.

"That now you're going to do more running than ever?"

The ladies hurry on, but Dr Lund puts out a hand and stops Maj.

"Happy birthday," he says.

"Thank you."

"Forty. A big day."

"I'd prefer not to be celebrating it."

"But apparently that's not what everyone else wants."

"No, they've already booked a table, so I can't exactly say no."

"I was thinking more about Jesper and Stine."

Maj looks up.

"What about them?"

"Didn't you know?"

"What? What don't I know?"

Dr Lund shrugs, but is aware it is in vain. The diagnosis is already out.

"They've bought you a birthday cake," he mumbles.

Maj Kristoffersen, Ewald Kristoffersen's widow, runs down the last steps and continues in the opposite direction while the ladies call after her from the bus stop in Ullevålsveien. She has to go home. She can't be with them. She has to go home. She is not only a bad mother. She is also a bad person. She doesn't even allow others to organise surprise parties for her. She is just sorry for herself. She has been for all these years. All these long years she has felt sorry for herself. What would Ewald have said? He would have said she was minoring. Now Jesper says it: she's minoring. Why can't she major a bit instead? Jesper has inherited Ewald's turns of phrase from the Bristol and she doesn't like it. It belongs, if anywhere at all, in the murky world of drinking. She rushes past Fagerborg School, where the gym lights are on. And what is that actually over by the old German barracks? Is it an animal? Maj stumbles, drops the packet and hears the vase break inside the paper as it hits the pavement. It *is* an animal. It gets up. It is a pig. There are no pigs in Fagerborg. There never have been. Now there are. The pig, pale and fat, scuttles down Lyder Sagens gate. Is Maj the only person to have seen it? She stands rooted to the spot and seems to be shaking off what she has witnessed, the way you shake rain from your shoulders. She leaves the broken vase where it is and runs down the last part of Gørbitz gate, into the entrance to the block, races up the stairs in long strides and when she stops on the first floor she can hear the piano. It is a beautiful, slow melody. Maj breathes out. Things are not so bad if Jesper can play like that. Quietly, she lets herself in, closes the door behind her and sees them in the dining room. Maj isn't just surprised. She is thunderstruck. Is she seeing things? It isn't Jesper playing the piano. It is Enzo Zanetti. What is he doing here? Has he come on his own initiative? Stine is sitting at the table with her eyes closed. There are bits of cake stuck to Jostein's top lip and down to the bottom of his tie. Jesper is standing beside Enzo and following closely. Then they change places and it is Jesper's turn to play. He plays faultlessly and even faster than his teacher, who still doesn't seem happy, rather the opposite. He shakes his head and drains his glass. Are they drinking as well? Now, that is the limit. Maj is about to make her presence known and give them what for, but she quickly straightens her hair first and hesitates as Enzo begins to speak in his jerky Norwegian. It is just as though the sentences, and sometimes the words, fall asunder in the middle and he has to build himself up in his next breath to glue the splintered language together.

"If you're trying to set a speed record, you'd be better off racing."

Maj goes in to join them. The dining room is a battlefield; there is cream on the floor, lemonade on the tablecloth, alcohol on the piano. It is only now that they notice her. Stine opens her eyes and smiles. Jostein wipes the cake from his mouth, blushes again, and his face resembles a map of the Balkans. Jesper rises from the piano stool, worried as usual, no, full of anxiety is what he is, and anxiety is worry plus a bad conscience, while Enzo Zanetti locates the flower, which is already withering, and passes it to her with a deep bow. She takes the tulip he picked in Valkyrien and is lost for words. Should she say they are not allowed to play the piano after nine o'clock? Should she say it is time for their guests to leave, the party's over, or that they could at least clear up after themselves?

"I hope I'm not too late," Maj Kristoffersen says.

28/8/1956. Committee meeting at Fru Skjelkvale's. Fru Lund, Fru Kristoffersen, Fru Sandaker, Frøken Smith, Frøken Jacobsen, Frøken Schanke and Fru Skjelkvale were present. We are still sewing and darning dolls. We have applied for a tombola stall, which we must have ready for the bazaar, but our poor little department has to fork up approx. 1,500 kroner for it. Hope it will be worth the trouble.

FEELING

Jesper is sitting in the middle row at the back of the class and when Ramm isn't looking, when he is standing with his back to them, for example, and struggling to pull down the map, he can lean against the wall, put both feet on the desk and close his eyes. In 1920, while on a study tour of Germany, Ramm had been inspired by the revolutionary teaching methodology that assumed pupils were also actually people and had a variety of personalities and therefore needed individual attention. Primarily these methods were applied in what were known as *Landerziehungsheime*, private institutions, but they were also used in state schools, such as those in the radical republic of Hamburg. Now Ramm is sixty-one years old, a teetotaller and a German teacher. He has one aim in life. He wants to show that Germany is more than militarism. Germany is Goethe, Rilke and Thomas Mann. Germany is Bach, Beethoven and Mozart. Germany is also everything that Nazism is not. Jesper is thinking about the pigs. Isn't it the same with humans too? We stay in our pens all our lives without any concerns, and we are not especially concerned about dying either, for that is the only thing that is sure. We grunt. We march. We smile at the executioner. But this isn't true. Jesper realises it is untrue the instant he thinks it. It is a false thought. There are untrue notes and false thoughts. Jesper knows he thinks about death every day and if he forgets he thinks about death at night instead. How come he is so different from everyone else? Perhaps it is the other way around – most people think about death and are concerned, while a few manage not to be? Which is better? He looks around. Is there anyone in the class thinking about death now? Is anyone concerned about it?

Axel, by the window, the boy with the precipitous profile and slick blond hair, who will inherit his father's cod-liver oil factory and regards school as merely a digression, does he think about death? Extremely unlikely. Elisabeth from Slemdal, the girl everyone has eyes for, even the oldest boys in the school, does she have time to think about death? Her father is in imports and exports. He is a big name in chocolate. Confectionery is his middle name. But does the best-looking girl in the class think about death? She probably has her hands full rejecting suitors. Or what about Jostein, down in the slaughterhouse, wading through intestines and bristles, what does he think about? Jesper cannot know. He will have to ask them and he can be fairly sure their answers will be a lie. In other words, thoughts of death engender a sense of loneliness. It is a vicious circle. At last Ramm has managed to pull down the map and turns to address the class. Jesper rocks forward, rather too quickly, the chair slides from under him and he tumbles to the floor. From where, on his back, he looks straight up at Trude Hagen and meets her eyes as she leans over towards him. To help him? Does Trude Hagen think about death? Her father is a journalist, a reporter on *Aftenposten*. She probably thinks death's name is Jesper and now death is trying to rise from among the dead, without success at his first attempt, and that is because she has lifted a leg and placed her foot on his stomach, just above his belt. An hourly lesson is not an hour but forty-five minutes. And when you are free in the break you are not free either. It is free time surrounded by a fence and if you leave school you receive a reprimand, two reprimands represent a warning and one more transgression means you have had it. By then you have a record. The class is in fact happy with this delay to the lesson. There is no doubt that Jesper Kristoffersen will need some individual attention. Also, Ramm may not be able to hold his German devotions, but will have to go straight into what he calls *the academic hole*, although why he calls it a hole it is impossible to know, probably because it affords his pupils an opportunity to find relief. Eventually Trude removes her foot. Under different circumstances Jesper would have liked her to stand on him with both feet for the rest of the day. Of course, it would have been best if she had stood on her hands. Then he could have stroked her hair and looked up her blouse. Jesper takes his seat again to a round of applause. Ramm steps down from the rostrum.

"And what lessons does one learn from one's mistakes, Jesper?"

Trude answers for him.

"I really believe Jesper learns them off by heart, sir."

Ramm is still pointing at Jesper.

"Would that be correct?"

"I really believe *Frøken* Hagen is right," he says.

Trude puts her hand up again.

"May I request that *Herr* Kristoffersen refrains from calling me *Frøken Hagen*?"

Ramm is in his element now and time is passing.

"You are well and truly in the dock here, Jesper. What do you have to say in your defence?"

"I promise never to go on a jolly again, sir."

The class hasn't a clue what Jesper is talking about, but he reaps another round of applause nevertheless; the clapping isn't malicious or embarrassing, it is more carefree and expectant, as it should be at this age, in the last lesson on a Wednesday at this particular stage of schooling, the bridge between compulsory and selective education. Jesper envies the others. It occurs to him that he is at the opposite end of the applause. It is a lonely place to be. It is in the shadows, not the light. Is that where he wants to be? Something even worse occurs to Jesper: he can't applaud. When he claps his hands there is no sound. Then he hears Europe being rolled up and disappearing around the pole above the blackboard. It is not long to the bell. They are in the academic hole. Ramm, the benign pedagogue, sits down on the rostrum and crosses his legs.

"Let's talk about pigs," he says.

It appears that a man called the police this morning and reported a pig lying in the middle of the Majorstua intersection. I beg your pardon, sir, but have you been drinking? It transpired that the caller was the very soul of reliability, working for the Gjensidige insurance company as he did. Apparently the pig was of this world and therefore trams heading in all directions were brought to a standstill. Most public employees were late for work, which in turn led to the national surplus falling by two percentage points and the value of the Norwegian krone sinking. It was below the Italian lira; soon a krone wouldn't be worth a handful of chocolate buttons in the sun. Halvor, Rune and Ulrik, all from Industrigata, insist that the currency of the pig is cutlets, while pork rind has only black-market value, at least if it is fried to a crisp. Incidentally, it took four police officers to catch this pig, which had escaped execution at Oslo Slaughterhouse the day before, and now the question is: should the pig be reprieved or face death like the others? In other words, the floor is open for discussion. It immediately becomes clear that, while the boys are in favour of death, the girls support a full acquittal, that is, a reprieve. Axel objects: Can a pig be reprieved? Aren't we anthropomorphising here? Isn't that basically un-Christian? Trude stands by her principles as firmly as she stood on Jesper a little while before. She asks: Do only humans feel pain? No, answers Elisabeth loudly, out of turn. Some of the boys are beginning to have doubts. They would like to be on the girls' side, especially Elisabeth's. Perhaps a conditional sentence might be a fair outcome? And what would that entail? Sending the pig to the farm it came from and not letting it leave its pen? At least they all agree that the break-out must not end in a collective punishment. The pigs that have controlled their instincts, so to speak, should be treated according to the UN's convention on the prevention of cruelty to animals. Ramm raises another issue: Is it not perhaps the case that we felt sympathy for the pig the moment it stood out as being different? Are we suddenly viewing the pig as an individual, and not a meal, having now looked it in the eye? The most obdurate of the boys protest, it is their way of winning the girls' hearts, because ultimately this is what it is all about, the girls' hearts: They haven't looked the pig in the eye. Protecting this sow is wasting food. Ramm turns to Jesper: Has he anything to add on this matter? Jesper shakes his head and says: "I'm afraid I'm a vegetarian." The great gong strikes. The bell rings. The classroom is empty at once, apart from Ramm who is wiping the blackboard because the class monitor has been remiss and one should leave a classroom the way one finds it: ready for new knowledge. Jesper wants to go home and play the piano. He can play until four o'clock. Between four and six there has to be silence in the block of flats. But there never is. There is a lot of noise. Running on the stairs. Saucepans banging in the kitchens. The rustle of newspapers. Snoring on sofas. Only playing the piano is forbidden. Then he can play from six to eight. After that there has to be silence as well. But the block isn't quiet after eight either. It isn't quiet until eleven. And even then there are sounds: raised voices, the drip of water, sleepless feet, and if anything falls, it falls on the floor. Jesper hears it. What if he moved the piano into the loft? There, he can open the skylight and keep to God's office hours, and they aren't very long, barely long enough for morning prayers. Someone stops him in his path. It is the caretaker. Jesper has to accompany him. For a moment the rest of the class watches Jesper cross the school yard with the caretaker. Some of the older pupils are practising penalties in front of the handball goal. The caretaker, Anders Bakke, had been in Grini concentration camp and escaped Buchenwald by the skin of his teeth. Peace came in the nick of time for Anders Bakke. Peace came in the nick of time for most people, if you are to believe what they say. Jesper is going to see the Headmaster in the other building. He is let in. The Headmaster is standing with his hands behind his back. A headmaster doesn't need a name. Headmaster is enough. The pictures on one wall show that all the headmasters, from the Silurian period up to the present day, resemble one another. There is something about the determined chin. Jesper doesn't put down his bag. This will be quick. He hasn't done anything wrong, at least not as far as he can remember.

"Put down the bag," the Headmaster says.

"I haven't—"

The Headmaster interrupts him.

"As you were absent, or to be more precise, as you skipped the last lesson yesterday, it's surely only right and proper that you do some overtime today?"

Jesper slips the bag from his shoulder and drops it onto the floor.

"It was my mother's fortieth birthday. I had to —"

Another interruption:

"But that's not why I've summoned you here. Come with me."

Jesper picks up his bag, follows the Headmaster and together with the caretaker, who is waiting for them in the corridor, they go down to the floor beneath, where the school's memorial board hangs. It is cast in bronze and intended to commemorate those who didn't make it to peacetime: *These pupils of Fagerborg School gave their lives for Norway during the 1940–45 war.*

"Read the names," the Headmaster says.

"Out loud?"

"That isn't necessary. To yourself."

Jesper looks up, thinking this, too, is a punishment. Heroes are a burden. The war isn't over. You can't move on from it. Has Jesper got what it takes to be a hero? Is he of the same stock as these youngsters? He is doubtful. In which case, a chance to prove it would have to offer itself, and he would prefer it if it didn't. It is exactly what this memorial board commemorates: his limitations. Jesper reads the names to himself. They have a resonance of their own. Perhaps it is the bronze that gives them that. The resonance is heavy and soft; it is staccato and yet still eternal. For that reason it is impossible: *Arne Kristian Myklebost – Isak Krupp – Kaare Hagen – Hallstein Bardi Valldal – Ernst Armin Fyrwald – Paul Bernstein – Martin Feinberg – Norman Morris Riung – Oscar Albert Lutken – Benjamin Garmi – Bjørn Lortsner – Kathe Rita Lasnick – Rolf Juul Henningsen – Esther Karpool – Knut Lindaas – Trygve Erik Svindland – Jan Eigil Løfsgaard – Herman Feinberg – Bernt Barge – Frantz Philip Hopstock*

– Mauritz Plesansky – Jan Erling Heide – Rachel Feinberg – Abraham Josef Arsch – Tor Greiner Stenersen – Per Lindaas – Gunnar Krogsbøl – Ola Christophersen – Peter Kristian Young – Kjell Dobkes – Fritz Jørg. O. Hvam – Peter Christian Ring – Aage Fritz Stubberød – Håkon Laksov – Per Jacobsen – Halvor Sverre Rødaas – Bjørn Hilt – Jaampa Krog – Jacob Friis. Then there is a silence, even though no-one has said anything. The Headmaster places a hand on Jesper's shoulder, an unexpected, barely credible gesture.

"Every May 17th the final-year students lay a wreath here," he says.

Jesper nods and wishes the Headmaster would move his hand. The caretaker takes out a rag, spits on it and rubs at a mark on the bronze. The Headmaster continues:

"And afterwards there's a celebration in the gymnasium. I expect you have heard about it?"

"Yes, I have."

"Students who have excelled read poems, sing or give speeches. This time we'd like you to play the piano."

Jesper doesn't get as far as being surprised. The Headmaster's hand on his shoulder is enough to deal with; it is binding, a voluntary command.

"Me? I don't know. I . . ."

"We've heard you're good enough."

"Have you heard me play?"

"People we trust have heard you."

"Who for example?"

"And we'd like you to play something Norwegian. Have we a deal? Will you play for us on May 17th?"

"Next year?"

The Headmaster laughs and at long last removes his hand, but the burden is no less heavy for that.

"Next year, yes. In eight months' time. Is that too early for you, do you think?"

Jesper thinks: It's too late. Having plenty of time is almost worse than having none. It would have been better if it had been tomorrow. The best would have been yesterday because by now it would have been over, but then it would be too late to change anything.

"Not really," he says.

The Headmaster's hand is back.

"So we have a deal, do we?"

And now Jesper realises why he was dragged here. In front of these names, face to face with this grim language beneath flowers and fire, there would not be a *no* on anyone's lips. Jesper hardly knows what he is saying *yes* to. He just knows he has to say it.

"Yes."

At last he is allowed to go.

On his way to the gate he sees a ball coming straight at him. It is a sizzler. It is a sizzling cannonball of leather and air. It is almost beautiful as it spins towards him, beautiful and dangerous. But Jesper doesn't duck; he just lifts a hand and catches the ball, which the very next moment is nestling between his fingers in a firm, tender grip. Then he throws it back to the upper secondary boys, who shout something after him, but Jesper ignores them. He walks home. Stine is sitting in the dining room doing her homework. How is he supposed to practise when there is somebody in the room? He can't if he cannot be alone. He is never alone. Perhaps it would be an idea to move the piano to the loft after all.

"Could you give me a hand?" Stine asks.

Jesper sits down beside her.

"I can't do an R."

"What do you mean?"

"R."

"R? Are you up to R already?"

"I can't say it."

"Soon you'll be helping me with my homework."

"I can't say R," Stine repeats.

"Let me hear you."

She makes a sound that is more like an L.

"Keep your tongue in your mouth," Jesper says.

She tries again. This time it is more like a whistle and doesn't sound like anything in the alphabet, it belongs to the animal kingdom, among the snakes. Jesper sighs.

"And don't bite your tongue."

Stine is close to tears.

"I'll never be able to do it."

"So? It's only a letter. There are loads of others."

"They laugh at me, Jesper."

"Who do?"

"The class. I'm frightened to read aloud."

Jesper sits in silence for a few moments. So? If he'd hit a false F on the piano, would he have said *So*? Would he have said you can easily get by with the other notes? He wouldn't. Not bloody likely. He has been unfair to his little sister. And if anyone laughs at her they will have him to deal with, possibly Jostein, possibly both of them.

"We can practise a bit every evening," Jesper says.

"Thank you."

"Where's Mamma, by the way?"

"At the hairdresser's."

Jesper thinks: Who goes there the day after they've turned forty? Don't you usually go a couple of days before?

"Why?"

Stine laughs and closes the same reader that Jesper used to have.

"So that her hair looks nice, of course."

Jesper hurries back to the hallway and opens the bureau drawer where his mother keeps memos to herself, shopping lists and money, mostly ten-øre coins, if a beggar should ring at the door or there is a poor soul by the entrance to the block singing their heart out. The keys to Fru Vik's, now Fru Hall's, flat are there too. He puts them in his pocket, takes the kitchen stairs up to the second floor and listens first before unlocking the door. He promised he would. He promised Fru Hall he would keep an eye on her flat. The door closes behind him. The crumbs in the bread bin have long turned to dust, which a slight draught swirls up, mingling it with the light. It strikes Jesper that there is no life in this flat. It has lost its feeling. He places his hands on the worktop and spreads his fingers. It doesn't help. He can sense only absence. There is no tension. It is like touching a key on a piano that has no resistance and is therefore also soundless. Then there is something after all. It is a little thud. Jesper raises his hands and listens again. No, it wasn't anything. There is always a draught in these flats, from air vents, cracks, windows and window frames. He walks through the pantry. The cabinet along the wall is empty. There is a mirror hanging in the bathroom. The glass is matt and equally empty. Perhaps the piano could be here instead? Then he wouldn't disturb anyone. And it was here he heard Satie for the first time, on the radio, when Fru Hall was Fru Vik, the widow. He could ask her. He is sure she will let him. He can play the piano and keep an eye on her flat at the same time. It is getting darker. The curtains in the sitting room are drawn. Did his mother do that? Jesper can't remember. He interrupts his own thoughts and turns to the chair, the wing chair, the only piece of furniture. There is a man sitting in it with his legs crossed. He is asleep. On the floor beside the chair there is a bag. The man is pale and his hair is thinning, he is almost bald, that is why he seems older than he is in reality. There are dark patches on his white shirt, especially under the arms, his tie is askew. He has removed his shoes. His socks are black. There are holes in one of them. Jesper retreats. The man isn't asleep. He looks up.

"Was the door open?"

Jesper stops.

"No. I—"

"You let yourself in with a key?"

"Yes."

"Let me have the key."

Jesper leans forward with the key. Not far enough. The man doesn't move. He is smiling. There is a smell of liquorice about him. Jesper has to take a step closer anyway. At length the man takes the key.

"Thank you."

Jesper bows, walks calmly back through the flat, but as soon as he is on the landing he runs down the stairs and charges into the kitchen. Stine is setting the table. His mother is standing by the stove, with her back to him, and stirring a pan. She is different, even from the back she is different. It is her hair. It is bigger than before. Her hair seems to have been inflated and dyed a darker colour. She turns, her face is flushed, as it sometimes is when you come in straight from the cold, but it isn't cold outside, it is September, the last remnants of the summer are being warmed. Perhaps it is because of the hotplates.

"Don't you like it?" she asks.

Jesper points breathlessly at the ceiling.

"There was someone in the flat."

"Have you been in Margrethe's flat?"

"Yes."

"What were you doing there? You have no—"

"I'm supposed to keep an eye on it."

"What nonsense."

"And someone was there."

It is only now that Maj clicks and she whispers:

"Was someone there? Who?"

"How should I know? He was just sitting in the chair."

"Was it Olaf?"

"Don't think so."

"And the keys? Have you got the keys?"

"I had to give them to him."

Maj removes her apron, places her hands carefully against either side of her hair, patting it into position, as it were, even though it is exactly how it should be. Then she goes up the kitchen stairs to the second floor where Halfdan Vik's name is still on the door, a faded, out-of-date sign. She rings the bell. No-one opens the door. She rings again. The same. No-one opens the door. Was Jesper seeing things? Has he been out of it again? But surely you don't give keys to a ghost? Maj bends down and peers through the keyhole. All of a sudden she has a feeling she is staring at another eye.

1/9/56. Committee meeting at Fru Lund's, where we drew up a rota for our shifts at the bazaar. Our prizes will be: 1 cuckoo clock, half a cord of sawn birchwood, 1 cookery book, 1 tea trolley and 1 basket of chocolates. We had actually been promised a flower table, but we were told it would have to be a tea trolley. Nothing we could do about that.

ZANETTI

Jesper is playing "Gymnopédie No. 1" by Erik Satie and so slowly that he is eight years older by the last bar, and after he has finally finished and can rest his hands in his lap, he is a plot-owner: as silent as the grave. He has no idea how long all this lasts. It is like falling. It is ages since Jesper last fell. The rain beating against the window pane tries to lift him again. A fire engine disappears down a dark street somewhere, the sirens seem lethargic, probably only flooding, not flames. All matchsticks are wet in Oslo in October. Or perhaps the call-out is for Jesper.

"Too fast," Enzo Zanetti says.

Jesper crawls out of the grave and plays the piece again, even more slowly. But this time it feels different. It hits him: a different temperament, *sudden and slow*. His fingers aren't glued to the keys. He doesn't die in the process. He doesn't need to order a headstone before the applause. On the contrary, he is able to listen, not that he enjoys it, not at all, but he has never actually heard himself play, at least not like this. Jesper leans forward and puts his heart and soul into every note. He shouldn't have done.

"What are you up to now?"

Jesper raises his fingers from the keys and turns to Enzo, who is sunk in the depths of a chair, smoking.

"Sorry?"

"Are you trying to impress me?"

"I was trying to play better."

"Well, it wasn't."

"Right."

"Your playing was heavy and untrue."

"I didn't make any mistakes."

"It's supposed to sound light and true."

"I didn't make any mistakes," Jesper repeats.

Enzo Zanetti stands up and lights a new cigarette from the previous one.

"You didn't make any mistakes? That's the very least you can do. That's the very least the audience can demand."

"Audience?"

"You were thinking too much, Jesper. That's when things usually go wrong."

"I was thinking about what I was playing."

"Once I accompanied a singer who was so moved by his own voice that he burst into tears."

Jesper is disheartened and looks down at his untrue fingers.

"I've been asked to play at school on May 17th."

"And you said yes?"

"Yes, but tomorrow I'm going to say no."

Enzo sits down again.

"Why?"

"Because I'm not good enough. You said so yourself."

"It was me who recommended you."

Jesper looks up as he allows this to sink in.

"Do you know the headmaster?"

"No. Only Bakke, the caretaker."

"How do you know him?"

"Automaten, Jesper. If you absolutely have to know."

"Automaten?"

"It's a bar with beer in the wall."

"What do you do there?"

"Drink beer from the wall. And sometimes I play."

"You play at Automaten as well?"

"All these questions, Jesper. I just tickle the ivories to earn a bit of cash. When your empty pockets gape at you, you'll play anywhere."

"Anyway, I'm saying no."

Enzo sighs in Italian and takes out some music, which he gives to Jesper.

"I thought you could play this on May 17th. The 'Ballad of Revolt' by Harald Sæverud. It's perfect for the occasion."

Jesper looks at the notes. They are clustered together. It is like jazz.

"Difficult," he says.

Enzo stands behind Jesper.

"Perhaps so. But not impossible."

It is Jesper's turn to sigh.

"I don't understand what you mean."

"You just have to keep a cool head when you're playing."

"Keep a cool head. Is that all I need to do?"

"And don't let emotions pickle your digits."

Now Jesper understands. Enzo Zanetti has finally become fluent in Norwegian, Bristol-style.

"You're not repairing today," he says.

Enzo stands by the shelf where the bottle is.

"First of all I have to break something."

Jesper puts Satie and Sæverud in his bag, arranges a time for the next lesson and goes down to the street between the church and the fire station. It isn't raining anymore. The tarmac is shiny and looks like black lakes or just a silent river in the reflection of the street lamps. The leaves are glued to the darkness like yellow stamps. A window opens on the second floor. Jesper peers up. It is Enzo Zanetti leaning over the ledge.

"I hope your mother wasn't fed up with me," he shouts.

"She went to the hairdresser's the day after."

"What? You're so far down."

"No, it's you. You're so far up."

"Send her my regards."

"She went to the hairdresser's the day after."

"The hairdresser's? Once again send her my best regards, and bye."

Enzo Zanetti closes the window.

Jesper regrets saying anything. He didn't need to tell him. He doesn't even know why he did. His answer was as stupid as Jostein. Why should Enzo know that Jesper's mother went to the hairdresser's? He says things he doesn't have to, he realises. He decides to talk less, as little as absolutely possible, it is best to keep your mouth shut. If he has to say anything next time it will have to be only what is necessary for survival. He decides to take the Industrigata route home. It is the right decision this evening. It is dark enough. There are tenement buildings in Oslo 3 too, not only in the Far East End. There is the mayonnaise factory and also Manfred's bakery. At Suhms gate Jesper turns right and continues up Pilestredet, which descends from the city centre, from the Rikshospital and, unlike Industrigata, changes character from corner to corner. Here, in the last part, there are large detached houses in timber and brick, with towers, oriels and deep windows. The gardens are well tended, but in this darkness they seem wild and unending. Dead apples hang from branches. This evening his bag is heavy anyway. There is too much music in it. There isn't a thing you can't worry about. Jesper stops and hears an animal moving in the wet grass behind the fences. It is probably a cat, but it might well be a badger. People have also seen foxes here. Even pigs have been spotted. It was, however, only a guest appearance. A couple in Lyder Sagens gate have a cockerel that crows every morning. And there are enough rats around the dustbins. This is Fagerborg's Zoological Garden. It is for this reason the Veterinary College is not far away. They only have to open a window and they immediately have a sample they can put to sleep and subject to research. Over in Stens Park the wind is blowing. It hits Jesper and brings with it the stench from the urinal, which it is best to avoid at this time of the day, but the next moment the same gust of wind wafts over a perfume. He sees her walking between the trees. She is carrying a rucksack. The hood on her yellow raincoat is up and looks like a halo. It is Trude. The rain starts again. It is too late. She is coming towards him.

"Are you really a vegetarian?" she asks.

Jesper shrugs.

"Why not?"

"Do you like nut roast?"

"So so."

"My mother's a vegetarian. You can have dinner with us one day."

"I'm pretty busy."

"I can imagine. You have to play on May 17th as well and it's already October now."

"How do you know?"

"The calendar says so."

"I mean, how do you know I'm playing?"

"Because I'm giving the speech."

"You?"

"Why not?"

They walk together for a while. Jesper has to go the same way, he says, although he will actually have to turn round and head in the opposite direction. No-one else is out apart from them. The rest have been washed away by the rain. Only a stooped queer slinks down to the urinal looking for sex. The darkness is still franked with yellow leaves.

"I might have to wear a zoot," Jesper says.

"Zoot? Do you mean a national costume?"

"A suit."

"No-one in the class understands what you say."

"Doesn't matter. So long as I do."

"What does *go on a jolly* mean?"

"It means to skive."

"Where did you learn that?"

"My father used to go to the Bris. I mean the Bristol. Sorry, I mean the Mauriske Hall. I drank it in with my mother's milk."

"I wasn't trying to get at you."

"No, it was sheer coincidence."

Trude laughs and stops by Suhms gate.

"Aren't you going the wrong way in fact?"

Jesper looks down. She is wearing rubber boots. They are two sizes too big. Or her feet are two sizes too small. Actually, she is pretty solidly put together.

"Where have you been?" he asks.

"Curious?"

"Just passing the time while we're standing here."

"The school garden. I was getting some food for my mother."

"In October?"

"She likes windfall fruit. And you?"

"I prefer leeks."

"I mean where have *you* been?"

"Training my keyboard technique."

Trude runs across the road, stops on the other side and turns to Jesper, who is standing in the rain. There is a river between them, it is a lake. They have just this evening.

"Do you promise then?" she shouts.

"Promise what?"

"You'll have dinner with us."

Jesper shouts back something, but Trude just turns and goes. Then he takes another detour home, this time around Blåsen Hill, past the barracks, across August Cappelens gate, down Kirkeveien and into the block of flats. He thinks he can hear a cock crowing. That must be malfunctioning too. It is not that late. He stops for a moment by the postboxes. Fru Vik's name has been removed. Now her box says *Bjørn Stranger*. Stine is waiting in the hallway.

"Mamma," she says.

Jesper doesn't have the time. It isn't late, but he doesn't have the time anyway. On reflection this isn't actually about time but space. He no longer has any more space. That is the issue. Jesper needs space. He pushes the foolish child away. But she grabs hold of his bag. Get off. Especially off this bag, because it is carrying his destiny, if she has any idea at all what that means.

"Mamma," she repeats.

Jesper's neck stiffens. What is this about Mamma? Has something happened? Has it? At last he comes to. He comes to his senses.

"What about her?"

Stine takes his hand and they go into the dining room. His mother is lying on the floor. She is wearing only her underwear and her legs are bare. It looks as if she is trying to cycle in the air or she has had a stroke and is vainly struggling to get up. At any rate, she is breathing hard and her face is shiny. Jesper is embarrassed.

"I believe that used to be called morning gymnastics," he says.

His mother cycles a bit further. She doesn't get far. Then she is finally able to stand up. She takes Jesper and Stine into the kitchen. First she drinks two glasses of water. Then she can speak.

"I don't have any time for morning gymnastics now. I've got a job, you see."

Stine looks up at her mother.

"With the Red Cross?"

"No, I'll carry on with them anyway, but that's not a job because we don't get paid. The Red Cross is a calling."

Jesper:

"What sort of work is it?"

"I'm going to start at Dek-Rek. As a secretary. So it'll be hectic in the mornings, won't it?"

Jesper doesn't like this. His father worked there. It isn't right that his mother should work there too. He isn't quite sure why. It just isn't right. She is getting involved in his father's business. She should leave him in peace.

"I can make my own packed lunch," Jesper says.

Stine immediately shoots up her hand.

"Me too."

Maj wraps her arms around them both.

There is a ring at the door. Maj steps back. She isn't sure which door. The bell rings again. It is the kitchen door. No doubt about it. She whispers and shouts at the same time:

"Don't open up until I've put some clothes on. Have you got that?"

She hurries into the bathroom. The bell rings for a third time. Jesper goes to the door. Stine tries to stop him. She whispers too, excited and anxious. Didn't he hear what Mamma said? They weren't to do anything. Jesper opens the kitchen door. On the narrow landing, leaning against the stair railings, stands the man who was sitting in the chair in the flat above them. His fair hair seems even thinner, perhaps because he hasn't combed it. You can almost look straight through his head without seeing anything. Otherwise, however, he is well turned out: tie, white shirt, green pullover, grey trousers and brown moccasins. In one hand he is holding a mug; the other is behind his back.

"You're the one who plays the piano, aren't you?"

Jesper nods without saying a word.

Bjørn Stranger smiles and takes a step closer.

"I didn't mean to be unpleasant last time we met. I'd travelled a long way. I hope you understand. And you burst in."

"Yes."

"You're not allowed to play the piano between three and six, is that right?"

"Four and six."

"I think it should be from three."

Jesper feels his mother's hands on his shoulder. They are firm. She pushes him towards Stine by the fridge and takes his place in the doorway so forcefully that Bjørn Stranger steps back.

"I came to ask if you had any sugar, Fru Kristoffersen," he says.

Maj takes his mug and leaves him standing by the stairs as she fills it, no more than two measuring cups, the minimum, opens the door again and passes him the mug. Bjørn Stranger receives it with a slight inclination of the head.

"Thank you. Of course I'll return the fa—"

He is interrupted:

"That won't be necessary. Just keep it. Thank you anyway."

Bjørn Stranger doesn't have a chance to say any more. Maj closes the door again, this time for good, or at least for today. He goes back to his flat. He laughs. His flat? Is there anywhere he can call his own? He puts the mug on the kitchen worktop. A thought strikes him: sugar, the sweetest condiment, has no smell. How much furniture do you need to call somewhere a home? He has a chair. It was already here. He needs a wardrobe. Bookshelves aren't necessary, nor are lamps. He can manage with daylight. You can sleep on the floor too, but a bed wouldn't go amiss, preferably a double bed. It isn't a home until you have a family. Bjørn Stranger changes his mind. It isn't a home until you have a job. He needs to get some work. He can't do anything. He could become a criminal. He essays a laugh, but this time he can't carry it off. A thread has come loose in his pullover. As he continues through the empty flat it amuses him to pull at it until he is standing in front of the bathroom mirror with a long thread between his fingers.

21/9/56. The bazaar opens in the presence of Princess Astrid. Fru Lund and Fru Andresen represent our department. We have inaugurated our new tombola stall, which cost us 1,500 kroner.

PROSPECTS

"Why didn't you say Bjørn had returned?"

"I didn't know you were interested."

"He's staying in my flat."

Olaf Hall raises his eyes from the newspaper.

"Yours?"

"Ours. Sorry."

"Would you like him to stay here? With us?"

"He could stay in Nesodden."

"He'd probably freeze to death in winter there."

Margrethe gazes into the garden. The lawn is disappearing under a heavy layer of shiny leaves. She had wanted to rake them into piles the previous Sunday, but Olav said they were best left. And they would turn to compost over the winter. It is a lovely morning. Everything is shining. She is standing with her back to him.

"It's up to you. Or Bjørn," she says.

"He can't make up his mind about anything. He's useless."

"I think you should give him a chance."

Olaf gets up even though he hasn't finished eating and places his serviette on the table.

"A chance? He's had nothing but chances. He gives up his studies. He clears off. You can't trust him."

"Now you're being much too harsh."

"But the worst is that he's sentimental. He's inherited that from his mother. All the drama."

"What about his room?"

"What about it?"

"Are you going to leave it like that?"

Olaf comes closer.

"Don't touch it."

Margrethe leans against the window frame and breathes in.

"Alright."

"There's nothing he can blame me for. Is that understood?"

"Yes, Olaf."

He kisses her neck. She closes her eyes thinking: Please no further.

He says:

"By the way I'm having lunch with a client today."

"So I don't need to make anything?"

"That's precisely what I'm saying. You don't need to make anything for me. I'm having lunch with a client."

"But you'll be home for dinner?"

"Naturally."

Margrethe feels Olaf let go. Soon he will be going down to the shop. She waits. Then she opens her eyes again, clears the table and throws away the half-eaten fried egg. After she has finished washing up she doesn't know what else to do but start on the stewed apples. Finally she has learned how to do it. It has taken her three seasons. They picked the apples in Nesodden in September. She peels them, cores them and puts them in boiling water with two decilitres of sugar and a cinnamon quill. When the apples are soft enough for her to push a matchstick through them, she adds potato flour. Then she has to keep stirring evenly to avoid lumps. That is all there is to it. She can boil the apple peel and use it for soups and jelly. Olaf likes everything with an apple base. There is enough for an apple cake as well. There are always enough apples. They never run out. In layers, she places five sliced apples, crushed bread crusts, two rye rusks, sugar and cinnamon in a greased baking tin. Then she adds butter and water and puts the cake in the oven. Why can't they just eat the apples raw? Margrethe takes an apple, sinks her teeth into it, feels the acidic juice squirt into her mouth and bites off a piece. But there is something hanging from her lip, something soft and different, with no taste. She spits it out and sees what it is: a pale maggot wriggling on the worktop. It moves in a desultory manner. It has been chewed almost to pieces. Margrethe falls to her knees and vomits. She prays Olaf won't come up now. She can't stop herself. In the end there is nothing but a throaty cough. She hears someone go through the gate, it has to be Olaf; she can hear him in the distance. She stays on her knees, holds her breath, releases it, exhales and breathes calmly. A sweet smell is coming from the oven. She is on the point of vomiting again. She stands up, dizzy and unsteady on her feet, switches off the stove, washes the floor and flushes the maggot down the toilet. Then she rings Dr Lund. Luck is with her. A patient has cancelled. She can see him at one o'clock. She gets herself ready, drinks a glass of water and walks to the top of Kirkeveien. She needs some fresh air. She is hungry and feels empty. This is not only unpleasant. It is like a kind of high, a lightness of being, everything is happening in jerks, gentle but sudden jerks: the wind is murmuring through the leafless trees by Vestkanttorget. The next moment she is hanging her coat on the stand in the surgery. It is a long time since she has been here, since the time, no, she would prefer to forget it. The jerks are inside her too, like leaps of time. However, the waiting room is unchanged. At two minutes past one the nurse beckons to her. Dr Lund proffers a hand.

"Fru Vik, it's—"

"Fru Hall."

"Yes, of course, Fru Hall, how can I help you?"

"I've eaten a maggot."

They sit down. Dr Lund flicks through some old papers. Margrethe looks around; no changes here either. The furniture hasn't moved; the small instruments are exactly the same. Perhaps it should be a comfort, but it isn't, on the contrary it is more like a burden, it is time in disguise. The lightness she had felt has gone; the quiet high has formed a residue inside her. She is becoming sentimental. Dr Lund looks up and smiles.

"A maggot?"

"Yes, it was in an apple."

"In an apple. I assume you spat it out. Or passed it?"

"Yes. And then I saw there was only half."

"Goodness."

Dr Lund doesn't say anything for a while. Margrethe Hall doesn't know what this means. He is smiling again, isn't he? Is he about to laugh? She feels embarrassed. She is not in the habit of visiting the doctor for no reason. To be honest, she has only been here once, a long time before the war, she remembers the date, it was the day she turned old at the age of thirty-seven and Dr Lund had finished his studies, done the house year and was an outstanding sportsman into the bargain.

"In fact, I feel better now," she says.

"A little maggot—"

"It wasn't so little, Dr Lund."

"A maggot is completely harmless, but it is unpleasant nevertheless. The body reacts naturally, or, I should say, the *brain* reacted at the sight because if you hadn't *seen* the maggot you wouldn't have noticed it. As you've been sick you should drink a lot of water and preferably eat something light this evening."

"I haven't got much appetite."

"No, a little —"

"It wasn't that little, Dr Lund."

"A little creature like that can upset the best of us. At any rate you should rest."

"As I said, I feel a lot better now."

Margrethe Hall rises to her feet, as does Dr Lund.

"But now that you've come all this way, I might just as well check you over, don't you think?"

"If it's necessary."

"It probably isn't."

"Then I think we should skip it."

"As you know, it's been a long time since you—"

Margrethe Hall interrupts him.

"I'm not in the habit of running to the doctor."

"No, that's true enough."

"Besides, I've always been healthy."

She can't find her bag. Dr Lund watches her. For a moment this poor woman has lost her composure, that is how it seems, she is on the verge of tears, because of the bag she can't find, where she keeps her keys, and her purse, where she keeps everything.

"It's in the waiting room, I would guess," Dr Lund says.

"Do you think so?"

"You didn't bring your bag in. It isn't here."

"Thank you."

"I don't think you came all this way just to talk about a maggot."

Margrethe Hall leans against the chair.

"What do you mean?"

"I think you should remove your jacket so that I can . . ."

She tosses her head, laughs, looking more like her old self, though not completely; there are still detectable signs of panic in her sudden changes of mood.

"I apologise for wasting your time, Dr Lund."

"Dear Margrethe, we're not that formal. We were on informal terms before the war. We can be informal with each other now, can't we?"

"Yes, of course we can. And I'm a silly old woman who worries too much."

Dr Lund walks to the door still undecided as to whether he should open it or ask her to stay. He is tending to the latter.

"What's worrying you, Fru Hall?"

"The little maggot."

"There's no need, as I said."

"And my bag."

Dr Lund opens the door anyway. The bag is hanging over an armrest.

"Now we don't need to worry, do we?"

Margrethe turns to him.

"Do you still run as much?"

"Oh, no. Not nearly as much. I've cut down, as they say."

"Halfdan was always so impressed."

Dr Lund laughs.

"I didn't think the veterinary doctor was interested in sport."

"He wasn't. Not at all. He always switched off the radio when sport came on. But you impressed him."

"Is everything else alright?"

"Yes, why wouldn't it be?"

"I meant in your new life."

"Well, it's not that new now. Sometimes I miss Fagerborg. But I suppose everyone does who moves from here."

"You're always welcome back."

"Yes, that's good to know."

Dr Lund proffers his hand again.

"You can pay next time," he says.

Margrethe Hall lets go of his hand and forgets what she'd had on her mind. Next time? Dr Lund closes the door and walks over to the window. He feels a deep dissatisfaction. It is like after a run when you haven't given everything you have, when you haven't done your best. He has let himself down. It is unforgiveable. He is certain of one thing. And it is the only thing he is sure of: there will be no next time. She won't come back. Why is she taking so long on the stairs? Should he ask the nurse to go down and check? Should he take the matter into his own hands and call her back in? Then at last he catches sight of Margrethe Hall. She is putting a hankie in her bag and tightening the kerchief under her chin as she squints into the wind. She looks wretched, like an old dear from quite a different part of Oslo to Fagerborg. Dr Lund thinks: This lady is in a bad way. And what is worse is that he didn't do anything to help. Few people value the peace of home life more highly than Dr Lund. No intruders are allowed there. And by intruders he means politicians, beggars, missionaries, sales reps, tax officers and journalists. However, for doctors it is different. A doctor must have access to a patient's private life. This is where most accidents take place. The bus pulls in at the bus stop outside. Margrethe Hall is about to run the last few metres, she can catch it, but she decides against it. She has already changed her mind. She knows all too well that Dr Lund is standing at the window and watching her. She knows he is thinking about her. She doesn't turn around. Instead she crosses Kirkeveien, to Gørbitz gate, raises her gaze to the windows where the Virginia creeper hangs loose, the last tinges of red fading more and more with every gust of wind swirling around the corner. Soon it starts to rain. She enters the block of flats. There is a piece of paper stuck on the postbox: *Bjørn Stranger*. It seems temporary. How long is that? How long is temporary? On the first floor she rings Maj's doorbell. No-one is at home. She goes up to the second floor, hesitates. Halfdan Vik's name has been removed here too, but there isn't a new nameplate in place yet. It is the same doormat. She recognises it. She is moved by the sight and feels stupid. It is the residue in her, the sentimentality. A doormat is all it takes. Then Margrethe rings the bell. She has to ring twice. Only then does Bjørn Stranger open up. He hasn't changed much over the years, you don't at this age, not until you hit thirty, but his hair is thinner, besides, he hasn't combed it, and in this sense one might well say that he has lost weight. Olaf would have said "gone to the dogs". Bjørn Stranger for his part doesn't recognise Margrethe immediately, or so it seems, or perhaps he is just taken by surprise, or embarrassed, and needs time to gather his wits. Margrethe wants to help him out and forestall the embarrassment.

"I'm not surprised you don't remember—"

Bjørn Stranger interrupts her.

"Of course I do, Margrethe Vik. You—"

It is her turn to interrupt.

"Hall. Margrethe Hall. I just wanted to thank you for your letter. Or should I say speech."

"No need."

"No, you're right. Because it isn't true."

"What isn't true?"

"What you wrote about Olaf."

"I'm glad to hear that."

"Do you think I look rotten? Like a rotten apple?"

"No, of course not. Yet you remember that. After all—"

Margrethe interrupts him.

"Didn't you dare say that to his face?"

Bjørn Stranger takes a step back.

"Won't you come in?"

Margrethe wipes her feet, with great assiduousness, before walking past him. The doors to all the rooms are open. There is hardly any furniture. She can see only Halfdan's chair in the dining room. That pains her. She feels her insides turn. On the floor there is an empty plate and a glass.

"It's nice to live somewhere without memories," Bjørn Stranger says.

She turns to this overgrown boy in the unravelling jumper. He leans closer.

"Don't you think so too, Margrethe?"

"I have many memories of this flat."

"Are they good?"

"Most of them."

"I was thinking more of Nordraaks gate. You haven't got any memories of that."

"No, it would seem we've swapped places."

Bjørn Stranger is silent for a moment. It occurs to Margrethe that he too is unfurnished. He is an unfurnished man.

"I'm afraid I can't offer you anything," he says.

That doesn't surprise her.

"You didn't know I was coming, did you?"

"Are you sure?"

"I beg your pardon?"

Bjørn stands by the window. There are no curtains either. Soon he will be receiving complaints from the caretaker. If that doesn't work, the residents' committee chairman will have to tell him to comply with normal rules and regulations. Margrethe considers this embarrassing. She feels a certain responsibility. Some people might also think that she is still living there, without curtains. Bjørn Stranger says:

"I knew you would come. But I don't know why."

"I've been to see the doctor."

"Are you ill?"

"His surgery is across the street."

Bjørn Stranger walks away from the window.

"Are you ill?" he repeats.

"And when I saw the bus I thought of you."

"I don't believe that."

Margrethe thinks: No-one believes me. There's no-one who believes me any longer. She experiences a loneliness she has never known before. It is total and unbearable.

"Maybe Dr Lund was one of your lecturers at university?" she says.

"I don't remember."

"Did you study in Copenhagen as well?"

Bjørn eyes her and smiles.

"Now I know. Olaf sent you."

"Sent me? What do you mean?"

"To *snoop*."

"Now I think you're being unfair."

This word, *unfair*, does something to Bjørn Stranger. For a moment he seems furious. His fury has engulfed him, as loneliness has engulfed Margrethe. These are entities that cannot be repressed – loneliness and fury – they are a torrent. There is hardly any room for anything else. Then he relaxes, or rather he exhales and looks down, ashamed, as though it is only now that he becomes aware of the hole in one sock. It doesn't last long.

"I attend the school of life," he says.

"Harrumph."

Bjørn Stranger looks up and his sombre self is back.

"Isn't the school of life good enough?"

"There are lots of bad teachers in it, Bjørn."

He laughs, the laughter is as sudden as his fury, and he moves closer.

"You're right. You're absolutely right."

"What about?"

"I didn't dare say it to his face."

"Because it's not true."

"No, because it *is* true. And I didn't want to ruin the wedding party for you."

"That was considerate of you."

"I don't think so. I let Olaf ruin you instead."

Margrethe raises her hand, poised to slap Bjørn Stranger's face. He tilts his head, waiting for the slap, and turns his cheek. She refrains. It was only an idea. It reached her arm, but not her hand. Instead she says:

"I think there's some furniture in the cellar. If no-one's taken it."

Bjørn Stranger slowly straightens up.

"Thank you. Thank you very much."

He accompanies Margrethe to the door. There he leans towards her, almost touching her shoulder with his forehead, she sees the thinning hair, withered, white, and she doesn't know why, but she puts a hand on his neck and holds it there for a while, holding him tight, he is a child, he is only a child.

"You smell of apples," Bjørn Stranger says.

9/10/56. Meeting at Fru Lund's. Fru Kristoffersen, the treasurer, presented the accounts. The bazaar brought in 2,204 kroner, gross, and the tombola 490 kroner, gross. Those in attendance were Fru Lund, Frøken Jacobsen, Frøken Smith, Fru Kristoffersen and Fru Endresen.

RUMOUR

It is Dr Lund who mentions it first, to his wife during dinner, while they are having dessert – rusks in hot milk – and the twins, Sigrid and Odd, are already sitting in front of empty dishes, their hands in their laps.

"I wonder if this Olaf Hall is being good to Margrethe."

Fru Lund puts down her spoon, dabs at her mouth with the serviette, slowly and precisely, then looks up at her husband, but it isn't him she speaks to.

"You can get down from the table."

Sigrid and Odd jump up, bow their heads and are gone in a flash.

Dr Lund is uneasy.

"What's the matter?"

"What's the matter? We don't talk about such matters in front of the children."

"It won't hurt them . . ."

"Besides, there's your oath of confidentiality, dear."

"You're quite right."

They finish the dessert without another word. But as Dr Lund thanks her for the dinner, his wife interrupts him.

"Why are you wondering?"

"About what?"

"You know what. About whether Olaf Hall is being good to her."

Dr Lund folds his serviette.

"She was in the surgery today. She said she'd eaten a maggot."

"A maggot?"

"In an apple. But I imagine there was something else she had on her mind."

"You don't usually imagine things, do you?"

"No, that's what I mean."

"What made you . . .?"

"She didn't want to take off her top clothing."

"That doesn't necessarily mean anything."

"No, of course not. It's probably only . . ."

"Something you're imagining."

Once again Dr Lund folds the serviette.

"I'll do the washing-up," he says.

When they are in bed and the lights are off, Dr Lund approaches his wife. It is sudden and soon over. The following morning he gets up early and runs eight kilometres before breakfast. The children, Sigrid and Odd, who are not children anymore, they are adolescents, go to school together, to Katta, which is the nickname for Oslo Cathedral School, where they started the first year this autumn, but not in the same class. She has chosen the languages line. He has gone for natural sciences. They will both be fine. Then Fru Lund is alone in the house. This is perhaps the best part of the day. She can enjoy some peace and quiet in the kitchen over a cup of tea. But this morning she is in a more restless frame of mind. She is thinking about Fru Hall. She decides to do her errands before getting down to cleaning the bathroom. It is drizzling. Everything is grey, one might say dirty, the air, the pavements, the sky, the buildings; even Broadcasting House is grey today. It is this October. It is as if the war isn't over. Outside the chemist in Suhms gate she meets Fru Dunker, concealed beneath a gentleman's umbrella. She has bought some B tonic, apparently it is better than the usual cod-liver oil, if you are to believe the advertisements.

"By the way, have you seen Fru Vik recently?" Fru Lund asks.

"Do you mean Hall?"

"Yes, Fru Hall. Margrethe."

"She should've kept her old name, I think."

"Do you mean Berntsen?"

"Berntsen?"

"That's her maiden name. Berntsen."

Fru Dunker laughs.

"No, she doesn't need to go that far back. Vik's fine. Did you say Berntsen? The Berntsen who had a wholesale business? Was that her father? I'd completely forgotten that. I've almost forgotten what my name was before I got married. Your husband says I lack C vitamins. Or was it B?"

Fru Lund laughs too.

"And now you've probably forgotten what I asked you about."

Fru Dunker lowers her voice and invites Fru Lund under her umbrella.

"I saw her in the cemetery last Sunday."

"Alone? Or with . . .?"

"Alone. She was standing by Halfdan's grave. And between you, me and the bedpost, she's gone downhill."

"In what way?"

"She looked shabby. And not very happy."

"Who does in a cemetery?"

"No wonder, though."

"What do you mean?"

"With a husband like him."

"Like him?"

"I'm just saying what I've heard."

"What have you heard?"

"Apparently he has some nasty habits."

The two women are silent, thinking their own thoughts. Perhaps they are the same: Who does look happy today, or will tomorrow for that matter? Is it obvious from their facial features, the colour of their eyes, the lines around their mouths and the shape of their hands what their husbands are like?

"Is there anything we can do?" Fru Lund asks.

Fru Dunker stretches out a hand from under the umbrella and can feel the rain has stopped.

"We don't know what we're dealing with, do we," she says.

"You're right."

"It's good we met by the way. It almost slipped my mind . . ."

Fru Lund laughs again.

"You obviously need a good dose of vitamin B tonic."

"The board meeting has been moved to today."

"Have the others been informed?"

"Maj hasn't. I rang her, but no-one answered."

"She's started a new job."

"Is that right? Where?"

"Dek-Rek. Her husband was employed there as well."

"And there's her on her own with two children."

"That's maybe why. I suppose she needs the money."

"Nevertheless. Could you try to get hold of her?"

Fru Dunker doesn't close her umbrella. It's not worth the effort in October. Fru Lund carries on walking to Majorstua. She has a similar feeling to the one her husband experienced the previous day: dissatisfaction. But how to tackle this problem? How do you intrude in someone's private life? Imagine you were wrong. She goes to the butcher's first and buys half a kilo of sausage meat, so that she can make two dinners at once. Melsom feeds the meat through the mincer and is in a good mood, perhaps because his son has found his feet: he is following in his father's footsteps; he is an apprentice at Oslo Slaughterhouse. He gives Fru Lund a recipe with her purchase: cut a cabbage into strips, don't use the grater – he makes a special point of this – then add the strips to a sauce made from two egg yolks, two tablespoons of vinegar, a knob of mustard, preferably French, butter and salt. Mix everything together and thicken in a bain-marie while stirring continuously. Once the sauce is smooth, take it off the heat and add sugar, and after it has cooled down dilute with thick cream. And, hey presto, you have the perfect accompaniment to any meat, not to mention rissoles. Fru Lund promises she will try it. Afterwards she gets a standard loaf from Samson's and at Smør-Petersen's she buys vegetables, milk, margarine and sandwich fillers. Then she walks home via Jacob Aalls gate, it is more pleasant than Kirkeveien on a day like today, it isn't quite as grey, the house fronts are lighter and in some window boxes there are still pelargoniums growing, on balconies there is some red heather. But the birds in Jessenløkken have collected around a dustbin full to overflowing and this reminds Fru Lund of the unhealthy conditions in backyards, they aren't only apparent on the other side of the Akerselva, or in the Far East, as some wags call East Oslo, there are unhealthy conditions here too. We have only ourselves to blame. It costs nothing to wash your hands. Keeping clean is free, or at least cheap. After she has hung her coat to dry in the bathroom, put her shopping in the refrigerator and pantry and massaged her feet, she looks for the Dek-Rek number and calls. Maj Kristoffersen answers. It is her job: to answer the telephone, nod and cradle the receiver.

"Dek-Rek. How may I help?"

"You've really got the hang of this, Maj."

It is Fru Lund.

When there is an unexpected phone call Maj's first thought is the children.

"Nothing's happened, has it?"

"No, no, no. I just wanted to tell you that the board meeting will be this evening. I hope you can make it?"

"Yes, I think so."

"If you need a babysitter, I'm sure Sigrid can help out. She's old enough."

"Jesper is too. Thank you anyway."

Maj notices Rudjord in the doorway and immediately rings off. You are not allowed to have private telephone conversations in working hours, even if you have been called. It will be deducted from your pay packet. He beckons with two fingers. It is a sign that she should come. She follows him into his office. He closes the door, lights a cigarette and stands leaning against the desk.

"I hope the boys out there aren't pushing you too hard."

"No, they're quite considerate."

Rudjord smiles.

"Do you remember the little conversation we had *en passant* at the Bristol? No, you probably don't. It's a long time ago. But you said that honesty was important."

Maj puts her hands behind her back and is suddenly afraid that she has done something wrong. Is this leading to a reprimand?

"I'm not complaining and I haven't received any complaints either," she says.

"No, no, I think you've misunderstood. I set great store by that conversation."

"And I really hope you didn't employ me out of kindness. If so, I'll stop."

Rudjord shakes his head and smiles.

"Everything has two sides, doesn't it? If we say Blenda washes whitest, of course that isn't untrue. It's just that we're not saying everything at once."

Maj doesn't quite understand, but she is relieved anyway.

"Honesty has only one side, surely? The right one."

"Then we're talking from a moral perspective. And that's all well and good. But advertising's about practical life."

"And dreams."

Rudjord casts around for an ashtray. It is on the bar cabinet. Maj quickly places it on the desk. He puts the cigarette down.

"Exactly. That's what I mean. Dreams. Something to strive for. It's our – what shall I call it? – our mission. To make people strive. And hopefully we can earn a little money along the way."

"But if what they are striving for is out of their reach, they give up. And they won't believe you anymore."

"Let's say we take Pep, a competitor, as a client. Don't you think we should say that Pep washes *even* whiter?"

"Then you should say that you were lying previously."

"Lie? That's a strong word. We don't use it in this establishment."

Maj puts her hands behind her back again.

"Sorry. I didn't mean it like that. That you're lying. I'm better with numbers. Numbers don't lie."

Rudjord laughs.

"You should just see how much numbers can lie."

"If the telephone out there rings . . ."

"Then we can take the call here. Is everything okay with the children?"

"Yes. Stine has started the first class. And Jesper goes to *realskole*."

"He plays the piano?"

"Yes, he's going to play on May 17th. When they commemorate the students who died in the war. He's the youngest to be asked."

"You must be proud."

"I didn't mean to show off."

"Why not? If you have something to flaunt, flaunt it."

Maj takes a step towards the door.

"Can I go now?"

"Not quite yet."

Rudjord stubs out his cigarette, takes a seat behind the desk and produces a sheet of paper with the company logo on.

"I'd like to have your advice in the future too, Fru Kristoffersen. You give me your honest opinion, while most try to guess the correct answer."

He looks up and beckons with two fingers. Maj goes over to him. He gives her a pen and turns the paper towards her. It is a contract. He laughs.

"It's not dangerous. It's the oath of confidentiality. Everyone working here has to sign one. It's the firm's policy."

Maj signs her name at the bottom.

"I haven't said anything anyway," she says.

Rudjord puts the document back in the drawer and takes out a little box, a sample of Pep, which he wants Maj to try out.

"See what you think and let me know."

"I can wash a sheet."

"That's your decision. So long as it's white. And one more thing. Go to Steen & Strøm and buy yourself a suitable dress."

Maj's shoulders slump. Is that actually why she was given an audience, to receive the message that she isn't suitably dressed? She blushes and for a moment has to breathe in deep, down to where anger and shame start.

"I'm sorry if I'm not . . ."

Rudjord waves away her apology.

"Dear Fru Kristoffersen, you mustn't take everything in the worst possible light. At Dek-Rek we try to take most things in the best possible way. It's also the firm's policy."

"Of course. There's no reason to do anything else."

"Exactly. I just want to do you a favour."

"Thank you. I didn't mean to be ungrateful."

"And in all modesty I believed you would be happy. Surely any woman would be happy to receive such an offer?"

Maj looks up.

"Could I go to Franck instead?"

Rudjord laughs.

"I appreciate your good taste, Fru Kristoffersen. But we have an agreement with Steen & Strøm. You'll find something nice there too."

Maj goes back to her place and notes down appointments and times, alone this week there are Nordstrøm & Due A/S, Sandnes Worsted Mill and Nørrona Watches & Jewellery, and the following week will be dedicated to the Pep campaign. She notices that the boys, as Rudjord calls them, even though some are older than he is, are scowling. Do they think she spent too long in the office or what? Now and then someone comes from the design room and says he has to go out, an important client is expecting him, but Maj knows they are only going to the Bristol to get Dutch courage because she organises all their appointments. Is this what Ewald did, told transparent lies, as though the whole performance was a charade? Probably. She has heard the boys say to one another: *Shall we go for an Ewald?* It means they are thirsty. She consoles herself with the fact that no-one here is better than anyone else and that means they are all equally good. That is the best interpretation Maj can muster. At half past four she locks the cabinet, puts the key and the box of Pep in her bag, clears her desk, says goodbye or see you tomorrow to Rudjord, who is always the last to leave, and catches the Metro to Majorstua. By the time she is home, Jesper has already boiled the potatoes and Stine has set the table. All she has to do is change her clothes and fry the fishcakes that she bought the other day. Then they sit at the table and it is ten minutes past five at the latest. Maj feels a profound happiness. Things are turning out alright. They have more money. Jesper isn't falling at night. The days are even slotting into place, despite everything, like neat calculations. Afterwards she helps Stine with her homework. She has had a dictation and has to correct the mistakes. There aren't many. *Per hadde et lite hvitt lam. Om sommeren gikk det ute og åt gras. En dag kom lammet bort for ham. Far fant det igjen ved en dam. Det hadde kommet sammen med noen andre lam. Alle lammene hadde lagt seg ned ved dammen. Det var ikke lett og se dem.* The last *og* should be an *å*. It is a common mistake, perhaps the most common, but no less serious for that reason. The common mistakes are the most serious because we continue to make them. That is why it is important to correct them. We have to learn from our mistakes. Stine writes *Det var ikke lett å se dem* eight times. It is a fine sentence. There is only one R in it and if she imitates Jesper's way of speaking she won't need to worry about it. *Det va'ikke lett å se dem.* But there is no problem writing an R. Jesper is sitting in the hallway, flicking through his music and waiting for six o'clock. But he can't play the piano until Stine has finished her homework. His fingers are itching to start. He is beginning to feel short of time. There are only seven months to May 17th. The "Ballad of Revolt" has so many notes that he has to learn at least two every day. And after that he has to decide how to play them. He is on the verge of falling. A wind is blowing through his head. At half past six Stine still has two sentences to write.

She writes so slowly. On the other hand, her writing is attractive, even the Rs. Jesper tries to imagine how it would be not to play one of the notes, for example, a G. He might as well give up. There isn't a piece of music in the world without a G. And you would have to think pretty hard if you were going to say a whole sentence without a single R. Maj shouts something, throws a coat over her shoulders, dashes down the kitchen stairs and crosses the yard to the entrance where Fru Endresen lives on the third floor, with a view of Jonas Reins gate. The others have already arrived. Once the formal requirements are fulfilled they get to grips with the practical side. Fru Sandaker and Fru Smith have, moreover, brought something to eat with them, a chocolate cake and an apple pie respectively, while Fru Lund places a bottle of liqueur on the table. In the midst of a busy autumn they have deserved it. Fru Endresen is not slow to fetch glasses. The atmosphere is very good, unrestrained even, until Frøken Smith asks, and Maj is unable to remember how this topic came up, perhaps they had been discussing it before she appeared:

"What do you think Ewald would say?"

There is a sudden silence; everyone looks away.

"About what?"

"You getting a job. And at the same place where he worked."

Maj counts the crumbs in her lap before raising her gaze and saying:

"Sadly my husband is no longer alive, so he can't say anything. But actually I think he'd be proud of me."

Frøken Smith takes another sip of the port.

"I don't understand how you can find the time to do everything."

Fru Endresen puts the cap back on the bottle before unpleasantness ensues.

Maj accompanies Fru Lund home, not through the block of flats, but up Jacob Aalls gate. She needs some air. She needs someone to complain to.

"The cheeky wench," she says.

Fru Lund puts her arm under Maj's and laughs it off.

"Don't take any notice of her."

"I'll call it a day if she carries on like that."

"Some people are stupid. Others are even more stupid."

"Is this how people talk about me? That I—"

Fru Lund interrupts.

"Don't listen to them. They're just jealous."

"Jealous? Of me?"

"Of how you can make time for everything."

"Can I? I wish I could. My impression is that I don't have enough time for anything."

"There's something I'd like to talk to you about."

They stop on the corner of Gørbitz gate. Fru Lund looks around, pulls Maj closer and lowers her voice.

"Have you met Margrethe recently?"

"No, it's a while ago now."

"I've heard she's going downhill."

"Is she? Who told you that?"

"Fru Dunker. Don't say I've told you. She was simply wondering whether this Olaf was being good to her."

"Why wouldn't he be?"

"As I said, she's going downhill. And isn't it strange that we no longer see much of her?"

"Yes, it is. I've been wondering the same myself."

"I didn't mean to unsettle you, Maj."

"Don't worry. I'm glad you told me."

"Perhaps we should ask her to join us?"

"Yes, let's do that. My God, isn't he being good to Margrethe?"

"You can never know, Maj. But just keep this between you and me."

"My lips are sealed."

"She could replace Frøken Smith, for example. What would you say to that?"

"I've asked Margrethe before and she thought she was too old."

Fru Lund shakes her head.

"Can't you ask her again?"

Maj hurries back home. She isn't wearing enough clothes and she is cold. The moon is shining over Fagerborg. It is dripping light. It is half past nine. On the staircase she stops and listens. There is silence. That is good. She lets herself in. Jesper is sitting at his little desk in the hall leafing through his music. He barely notices his mother. It is strange: he can hear the music by only looking at the notes, the way others imagine the protagonists of a book while reading. Stine is already asleep on the sofa at the back of the dining room. It is her room, the corner of the dining room. Soon Jesper will have nodded off too. But Maj can't get to sleep. The moon moves from window to window. Day doesn't break at any rate. There are worries. There is too much on her mind: Jesper, will he be able to teach himself the new piece of music before May 17th? And Stine, why does she never bring any friends home? And this Bjørn Stranger, will he never stop pacing up and down? And now she has Margrethe to worry about as well, on top of the dress from Steen & Strøm, the sheet she has to boil with Pep, and time, the time that is never enough. These are the thoughts that keep her awake. And they culminate in what Maj would most like not to think about: she hasn't been with a man since Ewald. Will she spend the rest of her life like this? She gets up, tiptoes over to Stine and opens her home-work book, which is still on the dining-room table. *En dag kom lammet bort fra ham.* Stine has corrected the mistakes. Maj signs: *Checked, Maj Kristoffersen.*

19/10/1956. It is like a party at Fru Endresen's. We are gradually starting to make prizes for a tombola again. We haven't any Red Cross dolls anymore and so we have begun to make small Bambis from the velvet samples we have been given, but the idea is to make giraffes and dogs as well. Fru Lund talked enthusiastically about hygiene and felt it should be a special area we should get involved in, not only with young people, but also with adults. You just have to take a look at dustbins in backyards. She reminded us that we have rats in our part of town too. We decided to return to this matter.

MEMORIAL

The worst of it all is that Maj hardly thinks about him. The very idea is almost unbearable. Weeks, sometimes months, can pass without her giving him a single thought. Is that how it is? Someone disappears out of your life, and afterwards out of your mind, and the memories commingle, like water with juice, at first the colour is strong and the taste pronounced, then the mixture becomes complete and transparent and bland. And it is a mere seven years since he died. She is ashamed. But whenever Maj begins to think about Ewald it is so overwhelming that the thoughts last until the next time. She gives the candle to Stine, who brushes away the leaves and puts it in the earth in front of the headstone. Jesper tries to light it. Whichever way he turns, it is windy. It takes four matches. Then he finally gets one to catch. The little flame is blown hither and thither on the wick. Jesper straightens up.

"It'll go out anyway."

Maj wraps an arm around his shoulders and Stine's.

"At least it'll burn while we're here."

"And most of the time we're somewhere else," Jesper says.

Maj cannot get these words out of her head as they walk back through Frogner Park: *Most of the time we're somewhere else*. It is true. But where is this somewhere else actually? Is it simply where life happens? Or is it where we turn away from life? Wherever it is, she wishes Jesper hadn't said it. Now he is grimacing at Vigeland's sculptures, which he calls stone-flesh. She can't be bothered to correct his language anymore. He has inherited Ewald's vocabulary and her anxieties. It is Saturday, the last in October. The air is no longer grey but clear. The dome on the Colosseum cinema is supporting the sky. Maj has the day off. She is free every other Saturday. They pass the bridge; Maj and Stine hand in hand, Jesper a few steps behind. The swans in the pond are still, their necks bent and white, like question marks. The red telephone box glows between the black bushes where the path forks. Maj stops.

"Can you two walk home on your own?" she asks.

Jesper catches up and groans.

"No, we'll probably get lost at the Majorstua crossing and end up behind Sinsen and never be seen again."

Maj laughs and takes out her purse, but then Stine starts crying. Jesper groans even more.

"If the stick insect keeps on blubbing I won't be able to practise."

"Now you be nice to your sister, Jesper."

Maj goes into the telephone box, looks up Olaf Hall in the directory, inserts two coins and dials his number. She gazes out while waiting for an answer. Jesper is holding Stine's hand. Stine waves, but still she seems unhappy, almost offended. However, Jesper is in his own world, where he usually is, there is a nonchalance about him that Maj is not sure she likes, it appears affected, it appears *untrue*. It is his age. He will grow out of it. Now, in fact, she knows where this somewhere else is. It is the world we all live in and which is closed to outsiders. Olaf Hall answers. Maj asks if she can speak to Margrethe. It takes him quite some time to fetch her. Can't he just shout? Surely their house isn't that big. Maj is already suspicious. The tiniest sign can be interpreted. When she looks out again, Jesper has set off. He is walking down the path by Frogner Lido, faster and faster. He doesn't turn around. The diving board towers over the empty pools. Stine is standing where she was, dejected and obedient. Margrethe is on the line. Why isn't her voice happier? Maj isn't the type to squander money, so she gets straight to the point.

"Would you like to come with us to Steen & Strøm?"

"I don't know . . ."

"Go on, I need your advice. And it's been such a long time."

"Us?"

"Yes, Stine and I."

They eventually agree to meet in Frogner Plass in half an hour, so they have time to catch the tram to town and reach the shops before they close. Maj rings off and waits; she might get a coin back. No, she has used up all her time, however little she said. Suddenly she remembers Ewald also called from this box once. For a second it seems to her that his voice is still here. He is closer to her now than at the cemetery. And something else strikes Maj: she is not going to make the same mistake with Olaf Hall that she made with Ewald, casting suspicion on him. She leaves the box and joins Stine.

"Did Jesper have to go home and practise?"

"He had to have a piss."

"Stine! The word is *wee*."

They stroll down to the bottom of Kirkeveien, where the tram turns east. Margrethe is already waiting there. But she isn't alone. Behind her is Olaf Hall. He takes a step forward and greets them first. Margrethe crouches down and gives Stine a hug. Is the old lady crying? No, she is only moved. She sees her own time disappearing in the time that has fallen to Stine. Soon she will be grown up. This is the plan: while the ladies, and by ladies Olaf Hall means Stine as well, of course, do their errands at Steen & Strøm, he will go to Halvorsen's Konditori and book a table. He will even pay for their tram fares. They don't say much during the journey. Maj casts a hasty glance at Margrethe. They are sitting opposite each other. Has she gone downhill? Impossible to say for certain. The coat must be new or maybe it belonged to Ragnhild Stranger? It is sumptuous at any rate. It suits her. She puts on more make-up than she used to, a little too much, Maj thinks. Then the ladies part company with Olaf Hall in Wessels Plass and walk down to the department store. In the doorway warm air streams over them. They step into a different season. The world is full of worlds. They have an hour to themselves. They take the escalator up to the second floor. Maj hopes no-one will recognise her. There is little chance of that happening. The shop assistants change like fashion. Maj and Margrethe think the same: Everything is suddenly more modern than before. Or perhaps it is just they who are out of touch. Maj can't see the blue dress she tried on last time she was here. Of course not. What had she been imagining? Nothing is as faithless as a department store. Basically it doesn't matter. It wouldn't have fitted her anyway. Her middle has filled out. Everything goes to her stomach. She has so many spare tyres she is afraid she might roll off the bed after she falls asleep. It is just age's law of gravity and the direction is down. What was it Ewald used to call the New Look? *Nytt lokk*. The new lid. That is what she needs. However, Stine is staring with saucer eyes at the clothes hanging on stands in alluring rows; she tiptoes closer and finally is lost among the colours, as though she is walking into an expensive autumn forest.

"The previous secretary always wore a grey outfit," Maj says.

Margrethe snorts.

"How boring."

"Grey can also be elegant."

"Colours suit you, Maj."

"I'd prefer not to be too provocative for the boys."

"The boys?"

"In the design room. They're cheeky, but nice. And they're not that young anymore, either."

Margrethe laughs and chooses two dresses.

"You haven't met anyone?"

"What do you mean?"

"Oh, don't give me that. A man, of course."

"Where on earth would I meet him? Not in the design room, that's for sure."

"I met Olaf in the cemetery. You can meet a man anywhere."

Maj looks around for Stine. She is coming towards them, from the shoe department, and her eyes are still big.

"See if you can find something you like," she says.

Margrethe tousles her hair.

"And I'll pay."

Stine runs away again and Maj turns to Margrethe.

"How's it going with you two by the way?"

Margrethe doesn't answer at once. Maj pulls her into one of the fitting rooms and starts to change.

"What about the piano teacher?" Margrethe says.

"What about him?"

"Couldn't he be an option?"

"Are you crazy? Don't make jokes."

"Isn't he Italian?"

"Yes. So what?"

"I'm only asking, Maj."

"And I asked first. How are things with you two?"

Maj puts on a grey tweed skirt and Margrethe helps her with the top.

"Now you look like a secretary," she says.

Maj looks at herself in the mirror, which is placed diagonally on the wall, probably to make one look slimmer. But the skirt is still too snug and Margrethe is right. She does look like a secretary. She sighs.

"Perhaps a new pair of shoes will add some sparkle."

"I doubt it."

"Nothing suits me."

"Don't be silly."

"Besides, I've put on too much weight."

"Can you expect anything else if you haven't got a man?"

"Do you think I'm too fat?"

"Your words, not mine, my dear."

"I just said that so you'd say I had the same figure as Janet Leigh."

"Who's that?"

"Forget it."

Margrethe laughs, but not for long.

"By the way, I hope Bjørn's not being a nuisance."

Maj sends her a glance.

"We don't see much of him."

"I'm pleased the flat isn't empty."

Maj tries on the next outfit. The skirt is brick-red and the top a deep yellow. She isn't used to such colours and in the diagonal mirror she looks like a different person. She likes it. This is who she wants to be: a different person.

"Tell me what you think."

"You know I always do, Maj."

"Go on then."

Margrethe lays a hand on Maj's shoulder and their eyes meet briefly in the beyond, as they stand looking at each other in the cramped fitting room of Steen & Strøm just before closing time on the last Saturday in October 1956.

"Olaf's the best thing that's happened to me," she says.

Maj changes back and they leave. She wants this outfit. The sales assistant flicks through a card file and finds Dek-Rek. Maj has to sign twice and closes her eyes when she sees the price. Where is Stine? She appears from the other side. Margrethe takes out her purse and can hardly wait.

"What have you chosen?" she asks.

Stine shows her: a pair of mittens, a pair of ordinary mittens.

Margrethe tries to conceal her disappointment, the disappointment of a generous benefactor.

"Was that really all you could find?"

Stine nods.

"Don't you want a scarf to go with them? Or a little shawl?"

Stine shakes her head.

Margrethe sighs.

"At least you can grow into them," she says.

Then all three of them take the escalator down and walk through the hot air that makes the season outside seem even colder. The heat is the department store laughing at them: Now you've spent all your money. The wind lifts the chimes from the City Hall towers and carries them past them. It is one o'clock and Maj has completely forgotten to think about Ewald. The tramlines along Tollbugata are glistening. At the back of Halvorsen's, Olaf Hall has secured a table for four.

"Well, are the ladies content with their shopping?"

Margrethe points to the bag in Maj's hands.

"She's bought herself a lovely outfit to wear for work."

"And Stine?"

Margrethe laughs.

"The finest mittens in the world."

They sit down and order coffee and the bakery's famous mille-feuilles. Stine has a Pepsi with a red straw. They don't say much. Olaf Hall shows them the correct way to eat millefeuilles. You press the top layer down with the little fork so that the cream oozes out at the sides. You start there and save the top till last.

"Isn't it easier to remove the top first?" Maj asks.

Olaf Hall turns his attention to her.

"You've started at Dek-Rek, have you?"

"Yes, a post became vacant and I was offered the job."

"I'm impressed."

"Why?"

"By how well you make use of your time."

A tram passes Wessels Plass and for a moment their cutlery rattles. Maj looks at Margrethe and asks, as though this is the first time she has thought of it:

"Why didn't you buy yourself something?"

Olaf Hall answers for her.

"Margrethe prefers to wear Ragnhild's wardrobe."

No-one says a word.

Margrethe pokes at the cream.

Maj asks again:

"By the way, do you fancy joining the Red Cross board? We need a new member after Christmas."

Olaf Hall speaks up again.

"Margrethe has more than enough—"

Maj interrupts him.

"I'm sure she can answer for herself."

Margrethe looks up, almost horrified.

"Olaf's right. I've got the house to see to. And the garden. Besides I'm too old."

Maj shakes her head.

"You said that last time too. Besides, everyone's got older."

"And I haven't got any younger since the last time."

"Well, at least I've asked you."

Olaf Hall waves to the waiter and insists that it is his treat. Maj doesn't like this. He is making a big deal out of this. They walk together to the National Theatre. They don't discuss meeting another time. On the Metro under the city Maj notices that Stine is uneasy and distant. She sits closer to her.

"What's the matter?"

Stine hesitates for a long time, almost all the way to Valkyrien, but in the end she looks up at her mother.

"What about us?" she asks.

"What about us? What do you mean?"

"What about Jesper and me?"

"Yes, what about you?"

"If you meet a man."

Maj is silent for a while, knowing that whatever she answers it will be wrong.

"It'll never happen," she says.

We met at Fru Sandaker's on 7/11/56. We are still working on the animals we started with for the tombola prizes.

THE PENALTY SAVE

In the last lesson on Friday – Norwegian, with Rolfsen – the gym teacher, Rilke, a former Resistance man, comes to collect Jesper. Rolfsen allows him to leave the class. He has no choice. No-one has a choice when Rilke asks for something. Jesper follows him to the changing room. Inside are the school's handball team, exclusively upper secondary students, most from the final class, sitting and waiting impatiently. The captain, Lorentz Bull, stands up.

"You're going to be our goalkeeper," he says.

Jesper can't believe his own ears.

"I'm not a goalkeeper."

"How do you know?"

"I've never stood in a goal."

"Then you can't know."

"I've never done any training either."

"I, or we, are of the opinion that you're a born keeper."

"How come?"

"Because we've seen you catch a ball. And we liked what we saw."

Jesper looks around and realises they are serious.

"But I can't," he says.

The captain takes a step closer.

"Can't?"

"No, I can't."

"Are you ill? Are you an invalid? Are you dead?"

"I don't have any gym stuff."

"Good try. But we've got some team kit for you."

Jesper tries again.

"Unfortunately I have made another arrangement."

"Another arrangement? What kind?"

Jesper looks down.

"With someone in the class."

The changing room is silent.

Rilke speaks up and his word tends to be the last.

"Aren't you playing the piano in honour of our fallen students on May 17th next year?"

Jesper gives a little nod.

"Yes."

"And yet you won't defend the school's honour when we need you most?"

Jesper lowers his gaze and basically doesn't know how to answer; he only knows he has to answer correctly.

"Of course I will," he says.

It transpires that the regular goalkeeper has Asian flu, the second-in-line is at home with a case of delayed mumps, the reserve was caught smoking in the lunch break and Fagerborg are playing outdoors, but on their home ground, against Hegdehaugen, who for this occasion have to change in the girls' changing room, which naturally enough is an insult. Jesper is not exactly the first choice. He is the last resort, at the very last minute, for the last game of the season, a so-called local derby, where the weather is the third team that both schools have to face: the snow in the air, the first sub-zero temperatures, the northerly wind that swirls around Ullevålsveien and Pilestredet, the eye of the storm in the school playground. Rilke doles out camphor, before leaving to sweep the pitch, this is exactly how Fagerborg will sweep Hegdehaugen off the pitch. Got that, have you, boys? Jesper is the only player to wear tights and a long-sleeved top. Over the tights he wears shorts. But before he puts them on, Lorentz Bull comes over to him with a previously unseen item of clothing, a grey pancake, which looks like some fur-lined bikini bottoms from the Salvation Army.

"Just to be on the safe side," he says.

It is an athletic protector, popularly known as a jock, or often a ball bag or a dick sling. Lorentz Bull explains, although Jesper doesn't need any explanation, that when the goalie does a star jump, in other words spreads his arms and legs as wide as he can, and the ball is travelling at sixty-five kilometres an hour, it is a good idea to wear a jock if you are planning on starting a family in the future. He doesn't need to worry at all about his face as no self-respecting player would aim at the face. But it is not his face or his crotch Jesper is worried about. It is his hands. And a handball player who is worried about his hands is not just up against it, he is heading for disaster.

Suddenly the whole team turns around as one. There is a girl in the boys' changing room. It is Elisabeth from Jesper's class, Elisabeth Vilder. She is wearing a short white skirt, a tennis skirt, and a sleeveless top. Her bra straps slip off her shoulders now and then and she pops them back with a toss of her head. Jesper doesn't know where to look. He watches the others. They seem hungry and shy. They blush at their own dreams. Lorentz Bull starts to clap, slowly at first, soon the whole team is clapping and the tempo increases. Jesper claps too. Elisabeth dances. She whirls around. She lifts her arms. The team stamp their feet. Jesper stamps too. The boys' changing room is a blur of motion. Nothing is still. Then Elisabeth runs out and just as quickly there is a silence, as though this hasn't happened, as though time has been rewound into a numbing smell of camphor: Elisabeth Vilder hasn't been here after all. Lorentz Bull sits down beside Jesper again.

"Actually, that's why we wear a jock," he says.

Then Lorentz Bull marches ahead of the team to the school playground. Jesper follows as number two. The goalkeeper is the next most important person. If the captain dies, Jesper will have to wear the armband. Pupils stand in a ring around the pitch. The away team's supporters have colonised the south-facing end. You can feel the atmosphere, especially when the home team hove into view. It reminds Jesper of something he has seen in a history book, about the Roman Empire: gladiators, lions, and not least capricious emperors who give a thumbs-up or thumbs-down, depending on their mood. He notices that the girls are more excited than the boys. They are the ones who shout loudest. A certain silence descends, however, when Jesper takes his place in goal and receives a couple of testing overarm shots. The ball feels like a punch. Where is Trude? She is standing with Elisabeth, who is wearing more clothes now, fortunately. But Trude is probably the one person who doesn't appear at all impressed. Perhaps she is only nervous on his behalf, or at least the school's? That is doubtful. She seems more indifferent. Then the referee, a neutral family man from Heming Sports Club, blows the whistle. The match immediately flows from end to end. There are steps, dribbles, passes, steps, dribble, dribble, shot. When Fagerborg score, Hegdehaugen draw level straight afterwards, and vice versa; when Hegdehaugen score, Fagerborg throw everything into attack and score again. Jesper can barely keep up. Before five minutes has gone the score is 11–11. They will soon need a cash register to keep track. It doesn't make any difference what jumps Jesper makes. The opponents shoot from the crease and are so close that Jesper can see the amalgam in their fillings. At the moment he has a save percentage of zero, unless you include the shots that go wide, and realists don't include them. But when Lorentz Bull is blown up for running with the ball, which the home crowd consider unreasonable, Hegdehaugen can turn the game and take a two-goal lead. Jesper hurls himself and gets his fingertips to the ball, plus four grazes, a stubbed big toe and wild applause. He can barely raise his arms in acknowledgement. Where is Trude? Trude has left. It is Trude Jesper has a date with. Didn't she see that? Didn't she see the save that meant Fagerborg could go into the break ahead on 21–20? A thought fixes itself in Jesper's brain: Do you need spectators for your contributions to have any meaning or value? And by spectators he is not thinking about a crowd, but a few people, maybe only one is enough. The team is together in the changing room again. Jesper gets some ice for his knees and pats on the back. He is doing well. Suddenly he is enjoying himself. This is camaraderie. It won't last all his life. It is just this unity in the changing room, the team's scaffolding: they are building a victory. In the second half it is end-to-end again. Now Jesper is enjoying himself less and less. He is glad Trude isn't there. The game is going too fast. He can't keep up. He can't see the beauty of the sport, if such a thing even exists. So he will have to find himself another sporting activity. What about football? At least it takes longer to get from one end of the pitch to the other. But is it any more beautiful for that? Or figure skating? In figure skating there are floodlights and broadly speaking you stand on the same spot and twirl around. Figure skating is for women and that is different. Is there a sport where the gentlest player wins? Is there a sport for Satie? Or is everything just the "Ballad of Revolt"? Javelin! That is an Olympic event. How slowly can Egil Danielsen throw a javelin and still cover the greatest distance? Then Jesper finally realises: the goal of sport is beauty and his goal is to get this over with. And a goalkeeper shouldn't think. The ball hits him in the face from close range. It could be termed a save, but also an accident, at worst a crime. Jesper is felled. Rilke feels his nose, wipes away the blood and pokes a wad of cotton wool up each nostril. Can Jesper carry on? Will they have to ring for an ambulance or find a nurse? It is 26–25 to Fagerborg. There are two minutes left. Jesper struggles to his feet. Jesper can carry on. Hegdehaugen have to play with a man short. Nevertheless, they draw level with a lob that scrapes the sky first. Fagerborg are fighting against the clock. Their goalie won't survive any extra time. His face has been rearranged. His nasal bone starts in his forehead. His mouth finishes by an ear. There should be jocks for the face as well. But his hands are fine. His hands are fine for the moment. Lorentz Bull exacts revenge. He scores with a curveball from the edge of the circle, a curveball that dips like the Big Dipper. It is twenty-eight seconds to victory being a reality. Then Hegdehaugen get a penalty. It is so dubious that even the away fans blush, but they cheer nonetheless. The most solidly built opponent takes up position on the seven-metre spot, winds himself up, contorts his body like a plumber from hell and juts forward, face screwed up in concentration, hairline down by his top lip, and shoots. There is total silence. Even the wind drops. Jesper changes tactics at the last moment. He stands still. He doesn't jump. He doesn't hurl himself. He stands on the same spot. The ball hits his hand, the right one, with such power that it is flung backwards in an unnaturally crooked curve, and even those furthest away, behind the other goal, can see that the whole of his forearm has swollen up like a tree trunk. The referee blows the final whistle and Jesper is carried shoulder-high around the schoolyard. His teammates hold him aloft. Things are going on beneath him that he cannot account for. His jock is itching. Jesper has saved the match, but the match hasn't saved him. When at length the injury is examined closely by Rilke and Rasmussen, the natural sciences teacher, who has experience of the Gjøvik field hospital, it is clear to them that Jesper has to go to A&E. They drive him down to the casualty department in Storgata and almost carry him into Acute Fractures on the ground floor. Jesper isn't alone. Asian flu is in front of him: a queue of women and children with runny noses, covered in germs. If you want to die, this is where to come. Rasmussen takes charge and instead they go up to the first floor, to Instant Admissions. They have to wait there too. Nothing in this world is instant anymore. Rasmussen complains that it was better during the war. There was no treatment then, but at least you got it instantly. They sit on the hard chairs in the corridor. Rilke is tormented. He doesn't stop talking: I'm sure you'll be fine for May 17th. It's most likely just a little sprain. If it were broken you would've felt it. You can't feel it, can you?

"I want to ring my mother," Jesper says.

"We can do that for you."

"I want to talk to her myself."

"Can you manage it?"

"It's probably just a little sprain."

Rilke hasn't any money on him, but Rasmussen finds three krone coins in his coat and gives them to Jesper. There is a telephone on the wall by the exit. He goes there, stands with his back to them and pretends to insert the coins into the machine. Instead he drops them into his pocket, waits a little and dials any number. Then he talks for a while to no-one and replaces the receiver. When Jesper returns, Rilke and Rasmussen are with a nurse, who leads him into an operation room where another nurse is waiting for him. She is older and wearing a hat that looks like a white paper boat. He has to lie down on a bench. There is a strong ceiling light. The walls are yellow. They start to cut up his sports jersey. Has he got any other injuries? He is a casualty. For a moment he enjoys the pain. Pain is a blessing for thoughts. They disappear of their own accord. The nurses study his swollen wrist.

"How did you manage to do this, then?" the older of the two nurses asks.

"I was carried shoulder-high."

"Yes, that can be scary. Did you fall?"

"My mother's coming to pick me up."

"That's nice. We may have to give you an injection. And then you may feel a little dizzy."

"You can tell the others to go. They don't have to wait."

"Fine."

The other nurse has started cutting his shorts to pieces. She doesn't need to. She does anyway. She loosens the protector as well. Then a flat packet falls out of the pocket. What was it? Goalies don't keep anything in their pockets, no matter how flat. The nurse picks up the packet and holds it between two fingers, as far away from her as possible, and she has long arms. Her mouth is like a dried date.

"Ugh!"

She tosses the packet into the bin.

The older nurse smiles.

"Your nose is crooked too," she says.

She takes his nasal bone between her finger and thumb, squeezes, counts and then presses it into place. Jesper hears a rockfall in his face. He wakes up in another room with his right arm in a sling. He tries to breathe, first through his mouth, then his nose. It works, not as well as before, but he won't die for the time being. His fingers are another matter. They are blue and hard to distinguish. He can just forget finger positions on the keyboard from now on. He will be all thumbs. The same nurse, the older one, comes in with his bag and his clothes in a carrier bag.

"When was your mother supposed to be here?" she asks.

"What's the time?"

"At least there's nothing wrong with your speaking. Ten minutes to four."

"Four."

"Really? Four on the dot?"

"Yes, more or less."

The nurse sits down on his bed and takes out something. It is the thin packet. She reads aloud what it says on the packet, apart from the word Durex: Have a good time. She looks at him.

"I should've left this in the waste-paper bin," she says.

"I didn't know it was there. Word of honour."

"I should also tell your mother. Or the gym teacher."

"Then it's better in the bin."

"But I'm not going to do that."

"What are you going to do? Keep them?"

The nurse leans closer and shakes her head.

"You don't have to act tough all the time."

"Sorry."

"Because I don't believe you're so tough when it comes to the crunch."

"I didn't mean to be."

"Incidentally, do you know how to use these condoms?"

Jesper stares at the ceiling. Fortunately it is not quite so bright in here.

"I have a vague idea, but I—"

She interrupts him.

"When your penis is stiff, you roll on the condom and you have to do it carefully. It's important that it doesn't come off in the middle of everything, as I'm sure you know."

"I have plenty of time."

"Yes, you do. Think about it, Jesper. You can keep them for another occasion."

"Perhaps."

"If you hurry, she'll probably be disappointed."

The older nurse drops the packet in the waste-paper basket and leaves Jesper alone.

She?

Jesper changes clothes, throws away the tights, the team jersey and the ruined shorts, keeps the jock, retrieves the rubbers and puts the packet in his pocket. Then he goes into the corridor. Trude is sitting on the chair furthest away with her hands in her lap. She gets up slowly and comes towards him, just as slowly, and stops twenty-two centimetres from Jesper, who doesn't move from the spot.

"My God, Jesper, how stupid can you be," she says.

"Stupid? I saved the school, didn't I?"

"And damaged your hand in the process."

"Lucky it was only my right hand."

"Lucky? Now you can't play on May 17th."

The thought swirls around in his thoughtlessness and returns in a new form, twofold and ambivalent: at first relief because now he won't disappoint anyone, he is free, and at the same time fear, because now he has nothing. Now he has nothing to show for himself. Jesper's mouth is dry. He needs an ocean at the very minimum.

"Of course I can."

"Furthermore, you look like a bulldog."

"My chops?"

"Chops?"

"Mug."

"Where else? Does it hurt?"

"Yes. How did you know that . . .?"

"Elisabeth rang me to say you were injured and had been sent here. Is your mother coming too?"

"Actually she isn't," Jesper says.

Trude takes his bag and they leave. A tramp with blood running from a cut to the forehead is being held by two police officers. It is the same tramp everywhere. He is a tail. He has come from the war with secret messages. Jesper has a sense that he is being tailed. Or perhaps it is Jesper who is the tail. He has a temperature. Do fish have eyelids? Yes, they can close their eyes. Darkness is beginning to fall. It falls differently. There are different smells. There are different sounds: the rhythm of the cobblestones, coke crunching in backyards. They hurry past. The Akerselva runs under their feet, a brown stream, with ducks on. You can become intoxicated just from the air around Schous brewery. It is stronger than around Frydenlund brewery. Perhaps people mostly drink Export here, while lager is brewed for wimps in Pilestredet. Jesper has some money in his pocket. It is not his. But so what? He can invite Trude to a snack bar. It is enough for a shared Coke and one straw. The Far East must be teeming with snack bars. He has a Durex too. How is he going to put it on with one hand? Will he have to ask for help? A sign flashes in front of a grey building: BLÅ KORS. The cross is blue, not red, on this side of the city. They catch a tram in Schous Plass and Jesper pays. Jesper is generous. Jesper pays for the tram home even if they are going different ways.

"Sport is just about the most stupid thing I know," Trude says.

Jesper looks through the window. There is so much scaffolding that it is impossible to know what is being demolished and what is being built. But when he dies he can at least buy a black suit at Storkofa in Storgata.

"Just about?"

"No. Definitely."

They don't say any more until Jesper stands up on the Holte bend and says:

"Come on."

They alight and are in Briskeby, an Oslo West street about half-way between Fagerborg and where Trude lives, Inkognito Terrasse, which is probably closer, furthermore it is downhill. It is the short-est route to Enzo Zanetti's. Trude goes with him. At the entrance Jesper has to breathe out. Wearing a sling is tiring. He kisses her. At least he tries. Her lips are dry and hard. And they should be big and soft. Her mouth is closed too. She isn't willing. Jesper quickly retreats with a sheepish smile. His nose aches. Her eyes meet his and she is on the point of laughing, but doesn't. She is almost afraid. He is serious.

"You can leave my bag here," Jesper says.

On every landing there are coloured windows, a bit like in a church. Jesper is reminded of a physics task: you have to place a ruler or a pencil, or anything else that can stand up on its own, on the desk when the sun is shining into the classroom. Then this object casts a distinct shadow, which isn't particularly surprising, but why does it do that? Because light goes in straight lines. How does darkness work? Does darkness stand still and wait to become light, wait for God, the electrician or spring? Isn't it like that with piano keys as well? They are silence waiting for a touch, for *pressure*. Isn't it like that with everything? Everything is waiting. Jesper rings the bell on the second floor. There is no immediate reaction. Then the door opens, fractionally at first, then wide. Enzo Zanetti is unshaven, but dressed, fortunately. It takes him a while to digest what he sees.

"What have you done to your hand?"

"Sprained it."

"But how did you do that?"

"I was in goal."

Enzo Zanetti holds his head and becomes more Italian than

ever, as though he has forgotten what it is really like and now he is trying to be himself. He is even tearing at his hair. It is opera. At length he lets Jesper in and Trude manages to slip through the door before it closes. Jesper has already sat down at the piano and is playing something with his left hand while this Zanetti stands behind him and barely notices her. She is suddenly superfluous and just stands in the hallway without taking off her shoes. She doesn't even know why she is here. And why did Jesper especially want to come here when she went to pick him up? Is he having a piano lesson now? Then she watches Zanetti crouch down by Jesper and hold his bad hand in both of his. They don't say anything. Trude knows, without really knowing, that this is something beyond her. Is this what Jesper wants to show her? Does he want to show her what is most important to him? Trude only knows that next time she will ask Jesper to go to her home. At that moment he comes towards her while Enzo Zanetti is still in a crouch position. Zanetti hears the door close behind them. Still he remains in the same position, crouching by the piano. Then he pours himself a drink, he has managed to get hold of more grappa at the harbour, and walks over to the window. He watches them cross the street. She is a good-looking girl. He saw that at once. She is carrying his bag. Jesper didn't say what her name was. Enzo Zanetti is unsure who will make whom unhappier. But he is sure that one of them will. Now she is stroking Jesper's fringe, lifting it and letting it fall over his eyes. Soon they are around the corner and gone. Yet Enzo Zanetti can hear it from right where he is standing: Jesper is in love. Jesper is so in love that he could cause Briskeby fire station to send vehicles out on a major incident, fire engines with ladders, pumps and smoke-divers. There won't be much piano practice in the near future. That is the way it is in all countries. Falling in love is like becoming mentally deranged. Enzo Zanetti sits in the chair furthest from the piano and refills his glass. It isn't the best grappa; you can only drink that in Italy. It will do, however, for the time being. He is gripped by homesickness, but it no longer has a destination. That is the nature of the wanderer: never to feel at home. Perhaps he should find himself a band he can travel round with and forget? Enzo Zanetti envies Jesper. What significance does a bad hand have when you are in love? He stays in the chair until he reaches the bottom of the glass. Then he searches for Maj Kristoffersen's telephone number, which he has jotted down somewhere, and rings her. She answers at once. Sadly, Enzo has to disappoint her. He isn't Jesper.

"Hasn't he turned up yet?"

Maj Kristoffersen speaks before Enzo has finished.

"Do you know where he is?"

"He was here."

"Has he got a lesson today?"

"He's hurt his hand."

"What did you say?"

"You don't need to worry."

"Of course I'm worried."

"He was accompanied by a girl."

"That's too much to take in at once, Enzo Zanetti."

"You can complain to the school."

"Why?"

"First they invite Jesper to play the piano, then they force him to play sport."

"Now you just tell me calmly and quietly what's happened. Otherwise I'll ring off."

"Jesper injured his hand in goal and has been to hospital. Relax."

"I will not relax."

"By the way, I'd like to thank you for the birthday party. I hope it was worth the effort. Besides I should've rung a long time ago."

"I'm beginning to lose patience."

"My Norwegian won't work today."

"Is Jesper on his way home or not?"

"He's with a girl."

"Now I'm going to ring off, Enzo Zanetti."

"Apropos. May I ask you out one evening so that we can discuss your son's future?"

Maj puts down the receiver. It isn't a second too soon. More like too late. Instead of thinking about Jesper, she has Enzo on her mind. Had he been drinking? She turns to the dining room where Stine is no longer sitting at the table practising her Rs, but standing in the doorway, her mouth quivering.

"What's the matter, Mamma?"

"What do you mean?"

"You're so strange. What's happened?"

"Jesper's hurt his hand. It's not serious."

"Can't he play the piano anymore?"

Maj goes over to Stine and lifts her up.

"He'll be here soon. And do you know what we're going to do in the meantime? You're going to help me to clean up."

They put on aprons and rubber gloves, take out brooms and cloths, fill the bucket with warm water and into it Maj pours the white powder from the Pep packet which says: *It's easier to clean – and dishes gleam.* Then she stirs the water and it turns grey. They start on the doors. Fingerprints and other marks disappear at the first wipe. Soon the handles are shining as never before. It is like magic. How can the dirty water wash so clean? Afterwards they tackle the floors. That is no problem either. Stine manages the whole of the dining room on her own. It smells good too. It is redolent of throat pastilles or toothpaste. Time passes. Yet everything takes only a minute. Why hasn't Jesper come? In the end they do the leftover dishes from lunch. Maj can use the same powder. Grease and milk tidemarks dissolve automatically. She barely has to raise her hands. Stine dries and puts everything back in the cupboard. Then they hear Jesper in the hallway. Maj tells Stine to wait and runs out to meet him.

"What happened?" she almost shouts.

Jesper barely looks at her.

"Relax."

"Relax? We were worried, Jesper."

"There's nothing to be worried about. I've only sprained my hand."

"What about playing the piano?"

"Yes, what about it?"

Jesper tries to go past Maj, but she holds him back.

"Have you been drinking?"

"Drinking? I certainly have not. Are you stupid? I've been in hospital."

"You've been at Zanetti's. He called us."

Jesper stops and looks down.

"Can't you take off your rubber gloves? Or stop touching me?"

"Zanetti said you were also with a girl."

"Also?"

"Why didn't you go and see Dr Lund?"

"Because I was taken to casualty."

"Skip school tomorrow and go to see Dr Lund. I want him to examine your hand. Do you understand?"

"Yes. Tomorrow I'm going to school first and then I might go and see Dr Lund if my hand's falling off."

Stine appears in the doorway to the pantry and looks at her big brother with red eyes.

"Did it hurt?"

Jesper smiles.

"Not at all, babs. Actually, it was quite good."

Maj doesn't recognise her son. Not only does he speak with a different voice, he speaks differently as well, not Ewald's language this time, but something that is bigger than the Bristol. It is the language of love. She can't get through to him. Instead she heats up some leftovers from lunch and tries to feed some sense into him, but it doesn't help much. He isn't hungry either. The telephone rings. Jesper is first on the spot. He defies the pecking order. There is a state of emergency in Fagerborg. To be on the safe side, he closes all the doors and the draught excluders before answering. It isn't Trude. It is Jostein. Actually, Jesper doesn't have any time for Jostein now, and time means space. Jostein is wasting his time. He is taking up space. Jostein starts chattering before Jesper can even say a word, so he stops listening.

"Is your hand broken or sprained? Did it hurt? Can you still play the piano or will you have to give up? Do you have to wear a sling? I would've liked to see the penalty save, but I was at the slaughterhouse and couldn't. Have you got a girlfriend?"

Finally there is a silence. For quite a long time. Jostein and the telephone are a bad combination. Jesper doesn't understand why Jostein didn't come to see him.

"Why are you calling?"

"What?"

"Why are you *calling*, Jostein?"

"I'm grounded. Isn't that unfair?"

"Depends what you did."

"Didn't realise you could be grounded if you were hard of hearing."

"You're not hard of hearing."

"Almost, anyway, I earn my own money. Can you be grounded if you earn your own money?"

"What did you do, Jostein?"

"When I've got enough money I'm going to leave home and then I won't be grounded ever again."

"But why were you grounded?"

"We can live together. Then you won't have to sleep in the hallway. I can pay your rent."

"Why were you grounded, Jostein? Tell me right now! Otherwise I'll hang up."

"Don't know."

"Course you know."

"Might tell you another time."

"You might? See you then."

"Is Trude your girlfriend?"

"You just gossip in your shop, do you?"

"What?"

Jesper shouts:

"Do you just gossip in your shop?"

Jesper can hear the butcher in the background. He doesn't sound as if he is in a good mood. Jostein is suddenly in a hurry.

"So it's true?"

"What is?"

"That you and Trude are going out?"

"Don't know," Jesper says.

Jostein's voice is also strange.

"Course you know."

Jesper lies on the sofa bed for the rest of the evening until he has to go to bed. He goes even before Stine. Maj is the last to go. She can't fall asleep. There is too much going on in her head. Thoughts crowd in on her and create an unease in her body she hasn't experienced for years. What is she thinking about? Jesper has an injury. Stine can't say R. Enzo Zanetti wants to talk to her about Jesper's future. The wiring in Maj is shorting. She gets up, goes into the kitchen and drinks a glass of water. Even in the frugal light she can see that the floor and doors have lost their shine. Nothing shines anymore. So that was how long it lasted. She tiptoes back. Stine is asleep, her mouth half-open, her eyelids two thin arcs, almost transparent. Jesper on the other hand is just pretending to sleep. Maj stands watching him. His injured hand is on top of the duvet. He is smiling. Did he grow up today? Did he grow up without her noticing? Again this worry and panic: will she miss most things from now on?

"Are you awake?" Maj whispers.

Jesper doesn't answer. He is busy with his own thoughts. He has more than enough to keep him awake. He doesn't want to miss anything at any rate, not even thinking about it, he doesn't get tired of thinking about it: the first time they got their front teeth in a tangle and that wasn't exactly great. But the second kiss, when they said goodbye in Vestkanttorget, that was better. It was a real kiss. It was as though they would never see each other again. He even got the tip of his tongue inside.

22/11/56. Committee meeting at Frøken Jacobsen's. Those present: Lund, Smith, Kristoffersen, Jacobsen, Schanke, Dunker and Endresen. Sent 12 Christmas parcels, two double-packs and ten single-packs.

DIAGNOSIS

Rudjord looks up, places his cigarette in the ashtray and lifts his glasses as Maj Kristoffersen comes in, closes the door behind her and curtsies.

"Well I never."

"Sorry?"

"The outfit. Fetching. Very fetching."

She straightens her skirt and curtsies again.

"Thank you. I hope it wasn't too expensive."

"If it was, it was worth it."

Maj walks over to Rudjord and gives him the invoice from Steen & Strøm, plus the finished meetings schedule for the next two weeks.

"I think you should move the Skiing Association and Bertel O. Steen to earlier in the day," she says.

"Why?"

"Because both are more important than Arts and Crafts and the Co-op. It's important to be rested."

"OK, please do that."

"It's already done. I took the liberty."

Rudjord gets up, takes the last drag of his cigarette and places his glasses on his nose.

"You took the liberty? And what does the secretary think about the new Pep?"

Maj senses a reprimand and looks down. She definitely won't curtsy again. Twice is enough, thank you very much. She will have to choose her words with care or keep quiet.

"I didn't mean to—"

Rudjord interrupts her.

"No apologies. As I said, what I appreciate is personal initiative."

Maj breathes out, but doesn't know why she suddenly feels ill at ease in her new outfit, however well it fits; perhaps it is too elegant, perhaps she should have chosen something plainer, a pleated skirt, a jumper? She says:

"The effect of the washing powder was striking."

Rudjord shakes his head.

"Striking? Was *striking* the first word that came to mind?"

"No, the first was *double*."

Rudjord walks around the desk and puts away his cigarettes for this morning.

"Double? That's interesting. Explain."

"I mean the powder's intended for washing up and cleaning. So the effect was double."

"Exactly. And so you were doubly . . . doubly happy?"

Maj laughs.

"Yes, something like that. But it didn't last long."

"What didn't?"

"The effect, Herr Rudjord. The following morning everything was as dull as before."

Rudjord counters:

"Perhaps you didn't use the powder properly?"

Maj bridles and speaks her mind.

"I know how to clean, Herr Rudjord."

"Yes, of course. I didn't mean to cast—"

"And the effect didn't last long."

"All you have to do then is clean again."

"Yes, but—"

"Listen. A detergent like this can't last for ever, can it now? Pep would've gone bankrupt long ago."

Maj knows she is right, even if she is never given her due.

"Yes, but it could have lasted longer," she says.

It is Rudjord's turn to laugh.

"So that's why you don't look doubly happy today? Surely we won't have to talk about the truth again? If so, I would say the truth lasts exactly one day."

"Not even that long."

"The truth lasts for twelve hours then, and that'll have to do for Norwegian housewives."

"You have to remember that Norwegian housewives are a conservative bunch. That's why they strongly dislike being tricked."

"There may be something in that, Fru Kristoffersen. But please don't use the word *trick*."

Maj heads for the door and knows now why she feels ill at ease in her clothes. It is the effect they have on her. She is ablaze with colour and wilting. That is how she feels. She blazes and wilts at the same time. She stops and turns.

"Could I go a little earlier today? I have to take Jesper to the doctor."

"Yes, of course. I hope there's nothing—"

"He hurt his hand when he was in goal."

"Now I understand better why you aren't doubly happy."

"Thank you."

Outside the office two designers, Kinck and Gullberg, are waiting. They are beginning to get impatient. Maj closes the door behind her, blocks the way and smiles at them.

"I'm afraid Rudjord's busy, boys."

Gullberg speaks up.

"You know we have an appointment."

"*Had* an appointment. But now Tuesday's Friday and Thursday's Monday. And from tomorrow onwards it's winter time as well."

"Come on, Maj."

"I'll see what I can do."

Maj doesn't budge. She is amused. These boys are not so tough when it comes down to it. But deep down they are good people, though not all the time; no-one is. They hover between their jargon and melancholy. Kinck chances his arm.

"Dressed up for the boss?"

"No, only for you two."

In a lower voice:

"Did he say anything?"

"What about?"

"Pep. About who's going to get Pep."

"We don't talk about things like that. I just answer the telephones and leave messages. But he—"

Maj stops. The boys move closer and say in unison:

"But he . . .?"

Maj lowers her voice as well.

"He wanted the truth."

Kinck and Gullberg exchange glances.

"What truth?"

In an even lower voice:

"The most truthful truth, boys. And *now* Rudjord's free."

Maj opens the door, lets the designers in and closes it quickly. She needs a cup of coffee. While drinking, she wonders whether she should start smoking. She likes the smell. It will have to wait for the time being. Anyway, cigarettes are expensive. It is cheaper to stand next to Rudjord or poke your head in the design room. She waters the flowers on the windowsill. The cars down in Rosenkrantz' gate move slowly or not at all. For a moment she is reminded of tortoises. She doesn't know where that thought has come from. Darkness has clung to the area between the Bristol and Bondeheimen hotels. If heaven exists, how far has Ewald reached? The cloakroom? Maj thinks about him. The toilet is never free. The boys are in and out all the time. If she stays here for more than a year she will make one demand: her own ladies' toilet. She dashes in before Hammer and after Randolf. The worst is that she has to clean up after them, not only the floor, but also the seat. She doesn't like sitting there. To Randolf and Hammer, Kinck and Gullberg or to whatever their names are she should have said: Clean the bowl with Pep before you write your slogans. At two o'clock she tidies her desk, takes the lift down and walks up Pilestredet, past Frydenlund brewery, where the beer lorries ply to and fro with huge barrels on the back, across Bislett, to the public urinal and Fagerborg church, and lastly alongside Sten Park. The leaves on the grass are covered with rime frost. The treetops are just a jumble of thin, black lines, which the wind keeps redrawing. There isn't a bird for miles around. The schoolyard is empty as well. She has twenty minutes until the bell rings. Maj stops and stares at the large building, which resembles every other school in the city. She finds what she considers must be the right window, on the first floor. She can make out a boy sitting with his head down, a fair-haired boy who suddenly meets her gaze. It is Axel. He doesn't move, his head is at first averted, dreamy, with weekends and the cinema on his mind, then he seems to alight on what he can see, to be precise, the old biddy standing by the school gates, there is something familiar about her, she is wearing a scarf, and where Axel comes from scarves are something mothers wear only in the summer holidays, at a pinch on Sunday mornings or when they are going to pick plums or burn garden rubbish. The teacher, Ramm, attracts his attention and he slowly turns to the board, waving his hand in the air and thinking it is time that Jesper was brought down a peg or two.

"The hero's mamma is here," Axel says.

"I beg your pardon."

"Fru Kristoffersen's outside waiting for her son."

Everyone looks at Jesper. Jesper shrinks a size. Ramm walks over to the window and waves.

"You can go, Jesper."

Jesper doesn't want to go. There are still twenty minutes left of the lesson.

"You can go now," Ramm repeats.

But Jesper still doesn't want to go. Why should he? The bell hasn't rung. He would like to learn more about German conditional tenses. Ramm goes right over to him and this time it sounds more like an order, because Ramm, who is a civilised man with the future on his side, doesn't know how much of a disservice a service can be.

"Don't keep your mother waiting," he says.

Jesper reluctantly stands up and Ramm even wants to help him pack his books and writing things into his bag. Enough is enough.

"I can manage on my own."

Jesper empties his desk with his left hand, for that matter he can empty the rest of the world with his left hand, glances at Trude, who just shakes her head, and once out in the corridor he leans against a wall with a lamp burning in his head and dazzling him from inside. He falls. Every clothes hook is a memorable gibbet. Then it is over. He walks to the stairs, fuming. He has been the class hero ever since this morning, not that he cares much for it, but he has been sort of the school hero as well, and then this tiresome mother of his comes and ruins everything in one fell swoop. It is not that he will have his name in bronze on the memorial plaque, which is reserved for those who have given their lives, and that requires a war, but nevertheless. He walks down the staircase thinking there are some things that have to be kept apart, or else they clash, and those things are girlfriends and best friends, music and sport, and, last but not least, school and home, in this particular case, mothers. If these elements clash there is a danger of chaos, betrayal and other mistrust. If he gets the chance he will write an essay on the topic, preferably in German. He strides across the schoolyard and his mother is so on edge that she goes to meet him and wants to take his bag. Jesper just walks straight past her and she hurries after him. He stops, hidden from view, around the corner in Pilestredet.

"What are you doing here?"

"Aren't we going to see Doctor Lund?"

"We?"

Jesper's mother looks at him and suddenly lowers her gaze.

"I thought you wanted company. I can—"

And Jesper can see at once his mother's awkwardness, almost

despair, he can see that she is at a loss, and he wants to make it up to her, but what has been done cannot be undone, nor what has been said, in an emergency it can be repaired, the way that Enzo Zanetti dulls headaches and melancholy with more of the same. At least he manages to interrupt her.

"But you stay in the waiting room, right? Is that a deal?"

His mother nods and they don't say any more until they reach Ullevålsveien.

"I'll come in with you for a little bit," she says.

Dr Lund has a new nurse, Frøken By. The previous one has married an engineer in the Wilhelmsen shipping company and returned to Arendal, where she waits for him every summer and winter. Frøken By asks them to take off their shoes and leave them on the newspapers by the door. They don't have an appointment and so have to wait. There is one patient before them, Hartvigsen from the mayonnaise factory in Industrigata, he has the Asian flu as well and his face is yellow, but that may be due to all the mayonnaise. He greets Jesper formally.

"I hear you hurled yourself several metres to save the penalty," Hartvigsen says.

If he had been forced to do that the ball would have gone out anyway, Jesper thinks. He feels like saying that actually he didn't move a muscle and that is the best thing a goalkeeper can do. If you stand still for long enough, sooner or later you will be standing on the right spot. It is like holding a musical note. Instead he shrugs.

"A couple of metres at least."

"And on the hard tarmac. Goodness me. I suppose you were wearing knee guards?"

"Just a jockstrap."

The door opens. Esther, the severe woman from the kiosk on the corner, comes out with a bandage around her little finger. Perhaps she cut her finger on the till. It is Hartvigsen's turn, but he says youth first, no, he insists, it is a long time since Fagerborg has had such a brave goalkeeper. Jesper and his mother go in to see Dr Lund, who closes the door, sits down and sighs.

"It's a joy to see you here with a sports injury, Jesper. There's nothing better than that. But the fact that you chose a *team* sport is disappointing."

Jesper doesn't have much to say.

"I was only standing in goal," he says.

"Yes, that is an extenuating circumstance. The keeper is the nearest you get to a genuine individualist in a team. But I assume you've learned now."

"Learned what?"

Dr Lund undoes the sling and begins to unwind the bandage.

"Next time choose running, javelin, the high jump, whatever, so long as it has nothing to do with a team."

"What about relay running?"

"Relays are four individualists linked by fate, Jesper, a baton, to be precise. Let me see now."

Dr Lund gently bends Jesper's wrist and pulls his fingers, one after the other. Jesper's mother moves closer.

"What can you see, Doctor?"

"I can see that this hand needs some long-term rest."

"But it will be fine by May 17th, won't it?"

"The seventeenth next year?"

"Jesper has to play the piano on the seventeenth. At school."

Dr Lund applies a new bandage and puts Jesper's arm back in the sling.

"The question is whether he will ever be able to play the piano again."

Maj stands up, almost knocking over her chair.

"I beg your pardon! Whether he'll ever—"

"Now, now. I mean whether he'll be able to play the piano at the same *level* again. Anyone can play, can't they?"

Jesper stands up too. It is strange: all of this is happening without him. He is the main person, but he is not taking part. He is only being talked about. Actually, that is pleasant rather than strange.

"Time heals all wounds," he says.

Dr Lund pats him on the shoulder and accompanies him to the door.

"Well said, Jesper. But completely untrue. By the way, have you fallen recently?"

Jesper's mother answers:

"He doesn't do that anymore."

Dr Lund stops and turns to her.

"I was asking Jesper. I'd like to hear it from him."

Both of them look at Jesper, who is thinking about all the ways you can fall, you can fall into a reverie, into step, from grace, but you can also fall headlong in love.

"Have you fallen recently?" Dr Lund repeats.

"I have risen," Jesper says.

Frøken By shows them out.

Walking down Kirkeveien, Maj is furious.

"We're going to change doctors," she says.

"Why?"

"Saying you won't be able to play again."

"He may be right."

"He isn't."

"Besides, he doesn't know how I play."

Maj stops and looks at Jesper, probing his eyes in an attempt to find him, but he is evasive, it is exactly as though he is trying to escape her attentions.

"Do you *want* your hand to heal?"

Jesper gives this some thought as an ambulance interrupts the whole of Fagerborg. Then there is silence again.

"Would you rather have a doctor who tells you lies?"

"I only want a doctor who keeps to the point."

"And then suddenly you die because you couldn't bear the truth."

"What *are* you talking about, Jesper? Don't speak like that."

"Just like Pappa."

Maj takes the bag from him.

"Pappa knew he was ill. And I did too. We should have told you . . ."

Now Jesper is an ambulance with the alarm wailing and interrupts his mother.

"He did tell me. When we were in the City Hall bell tower."

Maj pulls up smartly.

"Did Pappa tell you?"

"Yes. So what?"

"What did he say?"

"That he was ill. And was going to die."

"Did he tell you when you were in the bell tower?"

Maj feels like wrapping her arms around Jesper in the middle of Kirkeveien, but she is frightened of pressing against his injured hand. Then he says:

"I heard his heart burst as well."

"What did you say?"

"I heard it that night. When he died. His heart broke."

Jesper starts to walk, but now Maj holds him back.

"Have you fallen recently?" she asks.

He shrugs, hurting his right shoulder.

"Now you answer me, Jesper. Have you?"

Jesper still doesn't answer because he knows that he won't be able to lie and if he tells her the truth, there will just be more fuss and there is already enough. But not giving an answer isn't a reassurance either; on the contrary, in silence there is plenty of room for doubts, suspicions, accusations, worry and other crap. So he says:

"What are we having for dinner, Mamma?"

Maj has forgotten. How could she? She is ashamed of herself. She is a bad mother. Now it is out in the open. Soon they will all be going to the dogs. What good is earning money if you can't remember to spend it when it is needed? Jesper says he can do the shopping for her. However, she won't let him. How will he carry it? He should go home and rest. Buy something I can eat with one hand behind my back, he shouts from across Kirkeveien. Maj walks down to Melsom's and asks for something good, chops maybe, Fru Melsom suggests entrecôte, she pronounces it without the second "t" and it is probably quite expensive, but Maj says yes anyway. Today she can afford it.

"It's a long time since we've seen Jostein," she says.

"He works now, of course."

"I suppose he's free in the evenings, though, isn't he?"

Fru Melsom weighs the meat.

"We can't keep him under control."

"Jostein? What does he do then?"

"It's easier to ask what he doesn't do."

Maj thinks of the stamps that time; is Jostein really a crook?

"I'm sure he's not up to anything serious."

"We thought it would be better when he had a job."

"It'll sort itself out, you'll see. Jostein hasn't had it easy since the accident."

"No, he hasn't. But I'd hoped Jesper would be a good influence on him."

"He could be. Jostein should just come round."

Fru Melsom wraps up the meat and passes it across the counter.

"Don't you want something for the injured hero as well?"

Maj laughs and puts the packet in her bag.

"For Jesper? I think there's more than enough food here. And Stine doesn't eat so much."

"Hasn't Jesper become what they call a vegetarian now?"

"Oh, give over, will you?"

"Jostein told us."

"A vegetarian? What next?"

"He comes up with all sorts, our Jostein does, and you can't rely on half of it. Please excuse us."

"I'm sure it'll be fine. You'll see," Maj says.

Fru Melsom smiles wearily.

"I should have asked how things are with you. And how's the job?"

"There's enough to keep your eye on. There are four man-children who can't stir their own coffee."

The women laugh, much-needed laughter, a carefree breather between shopping, work and the rest of life.

"I have enough to do with my two. I only just keep my head above water," Fru Melsom says.

Maj makes for the door.

"But actually they're very nice."

"Mine too."

As the street lamps flicker into life on both sides of Kirkeveien, snow appears in the air, a fine, billowing mesh that soon covers the lawns in Marienlys, the district that was potato fields before the war, it is the country inside the city, it is the city inside the spruce forest, it has in fact been calculated that there are six hundred thousand spruce trees in Oslo, but then you have to remember that Oslo also includes all of Nordmarka; if you ski to Kobberhaugshytta lodge you are actually close to the centre. In the entrance to the flats, it is just as cold. Maj opens her postbox. There is a letter for her. Her name is written in big letters and there is something familiar about the writing. Did Jesper know the whole time that Ewald was ill? Did he know before her? She feels deceived. Sometimes showing consideration is the worst thing you can do. She feels angry with Ewald. It feels almost good finally to lose her temper with Ewald again. Someone is coming down the stairs. Maj hurriedly sticks the letter in her bag. It is Bjørn Stranger. He is wearing only a dressing gown and slippers. Either he hasn't got up yet or he is about to go to bed. Maj would prefer to walk straight past him, but that isn't possible. It is unpleasant. Bjørn Stranger stops on the lowest step and produces a bunch of keys.

"He'll have to put in a bit of extra practice now," he says.

"Sorry?"

"Jesper. Now he's damaged his hand."

"Yes, he will."

Bjørn Stranger takes a step closer.

"And that's perhaps not so easy when Stine has her homework to do and you, Maj, sorry, Fru Kristoffersen, are tired after work?"

Maj doesn't like what she hears, the confidential, almost importunate tone, she imagines him kneeling with his ear to the floor and listening, it is obnoxious.

"I think we're on first-name terms," Maj says.

Bjørn Stranger shakes his head.

"I just wanted to be on the safe side. It's not so easy being the newcomer."

"No, that's true enough."

"But everyone's been new once, haven't they?"

Maj is not sure she understands what he means and couldn't care less, either.

"You just have to stick to the house rules," she says.

At last Maj slips past. On the next landing she glances over her shoulder: Bjørn Stranger opens his postbox, empty, he slams it shut, the noise resounds around the whole block, the name card falls down and lands in the grey slush the residents have brought in from the street. He picks up the bit of paper, carefully wipes it clean and expends a lot of time and effort putting his name back: BJØRN STRANGER. Jesper is already in the doorway.

"What the hell was that?"

Maj shoves him back in and closes the door.

"Nothing. And don't swear."

"Nothing? Is that how nothing sounds? If so, we're up the creek."

Jesper wants to have another look, but Maj stops him.

"It was Bjørn Stranger. I don't want that oddball on my back again."

Stine shouts that the water is boiling. They join her in the kitchen, Jesper puts in the potatoes, which Stine also peeled, while Maj switches on the other hotplate, takes the frying pan, adds a tablespoonful of margarine, which is soon sizzling and running in all directions. Then she washes the entrecôtes under the tap, dries them with kitchen roll and bastes the red, marbled meat in butter. A thought strikes her: Jesper and Stine have to do housework twice instead of their homework. Instead of becoming cleverer they have to do what she should have done. This depresses her. It is always the same. She is overstretched. She extends herself as far as she can, but it isn't far enough. She falls short. She might have made ends meet if she hadn't gone to work. But then she would have had to save in other areas: holidays, clothes, food, hairdresser, tram fares. Is this the same for everyone? Surely not for those at the top, but at least Maj isn't alone in this. Is it because we demand too much or receive too little? She knows for certain that there is an imbalance somewhere in the great calculation where debit and credit have to meet in a zero. She fries the meat thoroughly. Jesper opens the window and lets out the smoke. They sit down at the table. Maj won't ask if he has become a vegetarian, nor if Ewald said any more in the bell tower. She will let it go. That is the best. As the dish is eventually placed before him, Jesper asks:

"Is this pig?"

Maj smiles as she says:

"Pig? No, it isn't."

"Sure?"

"It's entrecôte."

"And what animal does it come from?"

"Entrecôte? It doesn't come from pig."

"How do you know?"

"Because it was much more expensive than chops, Jesper."

"And so?"

"Have you seen anything of Jostein recently?"

"Why?"

"I was just wondering, Jesper. It's as if you've lost contact."

"We haven't lost anything."

"But you're very busy at the moment."

"What do you mean by that? Busy?"

Maj looks up and can't let it go after all.

"Zanetti said you were with a girl."

"So?"

Jesper helps himself with one hand and passes the plate on to Stine, who looks at him with those big eyes of hers.

"It's from cow," she says.

Jesper turns to her.

"And since when have you been a professor of meat?"

"We learned about it at school."

Jesper sighs.

"It's what I said. You're going to catch me up one day. Perhaps you can cut up this shoe sole for me as well?"

Maj, whose mind was elsewhere, puts a potato on his plate.

"You could at least tell us what her name is. Is she in your class?"

Jesper hasn't taken his eyes off Stine.

"And you might just as well eat it too. Since you're so smart and—"

Maj interrupts him.

"Jesper! You don't need to be rude even if you . . ."

"Even if you what?"

"Even if you've injured your hand. We're only trying to help you."

Stine starts to cut up his meat. Jesper looks down, wishing his whole arm was in plaster, or better, both arms.

"Her name's Trude and she's in my class. And we're not going out. Just for your information."

Maj feels a stab to the heart, or wherever it is in her body, and is at a loss to know what has caused it.

"I didn't ask," she says.

After they have eaten, without saying much more, Stine and Maj wash up while Jesper does his homework – history and German – and waits for six o'clock to come around. Then he sits at the piano and practises with his left hand, Harald Sæverud's bass, merely hearing it is like entering a piece of music through the kitchen door or up through a cellar hatchway in the floor. Stine has already done her homework and is lying on the divan in the corner, listening. Maj is sitting at the dining-room table surrounded by a pile of invoices, lists and numbers, doing the accounts for the Fagerborg department of the Norwegian Red Cross. Then someone stamps three times on the ceiling. It is Bjørn Stranger. Jesper stops playing. It is one minute past eight.

Then they put this day to bed as well.

There is something Norwegians call *klokkerkjærlighet*. It is when emotions, specific, yet unimaginable emotions, are in idle mode. They are ticking over and emit no heat. Not that her feelings for Ewald had always been gusts of passion, but they were ultimately directed at another person. Maj remembers the word as she stretches out a hand to switch off the bedside lamp. Then she thinks about the letter. She finds her handbag, perches on the edge of the bed in the yellow light and opens the envelope. She reads the few lines and quickly hides the sheet of paper in the bedside-table drawer because her first thought is as impossible as it is unavoidable: Ewald mustn't know anything about this.

Extraordinary board meeting, December 9th, at Fru Skjelbred's. Those attending were: Fru Lund, Fru Sandkaker, Frøken Jacobsen, Fru Kristoffersen and Fru Skjelbred. The meeting was held at the request of our treasurer, Fru Kristoffersen, who, after reviewing the accounts for 1956, said we could afford to hand out more Christmas parcels, a suggestion which everyone supported. However, we agreed to give three presents of 50 kroner instead as we had no more tobacco, fruit or stockings.

BUFFET

Enzo Zanetti must be in a strange mood. Not only has he shaved, he has also been to the hairdresser, gone is the long, thick hair with grey curls, back is a straight, dark hairstyle, like a helmet with a parting. What is more, he is wearing a suit, with a white shirt and slim tie protruding from under his jacket. Actually, Jesper prefers how he was before. He didn't look like anyone else then, only himself. Now he looks like a poofter. He isn't repairing either. But even stranger is the fact that he is surprised. Surprised when he sees Jesper, even though the piano lesson has started at half past five every Wednesday for more than three years. It is Wednesday, the last in Advent, and it is half past five now. Has Enzo been caught up in Christmas fever? Or was the idea that they would defer the lessons until his hand was better? Jesper can't remember any mention of that. Enzo Zanetti only lets him in grudgingly.

"Haven't you spoken to your mother?" he asks.

"Of course."

Jesper takes out an envelope and gives it to Enzo Zanetti, who glances quickly at the contents.

"That's too much."

"It's 750 kroner. She said she would pay for the next six months too."

Enzo Zanetti just shakes his head, hesitates, then puts the fee in his pocket.

"Sit down."

Jesper sits at the piano. Enzo Zanetti looks at his watch; in fact, he keeps looking at his watch.

"How's your hand?"

"Can't feel anything."

"No? That might be good. I didn't think you would have the lesson today."

"Why not?"

"So you haven't spoken to your mother?"

"She's doing overtime today and then she's got a Red Cross meeting."

Enzo Zanetti takes a long walk around the room and reappears with a little booklet that he puts on the keyboard stand in front of Jesper.

"I thought you could practise this in the meantime."

"Right."

Jesper looks closer. It is the interval signals for Canada, Denmark, Finland, Poland, Britain, Sweden, West Germany, Austria and the Soviet Union. Some nations have two signals, such as Poland with the "Polonaise" in A flat major and the "Revolutionary Étude", and Norway, which alternates between an interval signal and a signature tune, as well as Great Britain, which of course is an empire, a commonwealth, and for that reason has several radio channels and just as many signals. Enzo sits down beside Jesper on the stool. He must have been repairing with aftershave lotion.

"You can play them with one hand," he says.

"They're interval signals, Zanetti."

"I know."

"Am I supposed to play interval signals?"

"Of course. In the signals you find the soul of individual nations, Jesper."

"Souls?"

"The interval signal is the most genuine of all music, you see."

"Why isn't there one for Italy?"

"Because we don't have intervals."

Jesper starts with Canada. There are four notes in G major.

"I thought Canada was pretty big," he says.

Enzo Zanetti puts his arm gently around Jesper's shoulder.

"But not many people live there, Jesper."

He tries Finland, which is in B major and far more complicated – actually you need two hands for it – whereas Denmark is only a flat sequence of simple notes in C major and Sweden is like a sullen descent. Enzo gets up and looks at his watch.

"How's it going with the girl?"

Jesper continues with Poland, which is extended chords that require everything from the thumb to the little finger. Poland must have some quite big intervals.

"Well, I suppose," he shouts.

"Good. Unless I've misunderstood, your mother hasn't said anything?"

Jesper stops Poland and rests his hand on his lap.

"What's up with you actually?"

Enzo Zanetti lights a cigarette.

"I'm going out with your mother tonight, Jesper."

Jesper is silent. He thinks it strange she didn't ask more about what Pappa said in the bell tower. Wasn't she curious? But now he knows. She is going out with Enzo Zanetti. Jesper can't think straight.

"Out with her? What does that mean?"

Enzo stops smoking.

"That I've asked your mother out, Jesper."

"Out?"

"Exactly. Of course, we'll be in, but I've asked her out."

"Where to?"

"Frognerseteren, Jesper."

"Are you going skiing?"

"No. To the buffet."

They don't speak for a while. Why does an interval need a signal? You can hear when there is an interval. Why does silence need to have a signature tune? Isn't silence a signature in itself? Jesper is about to say something, but Enzo speaks first.

"You can come with us."

"Brilliant."

"There's room for everyone at the buffet."

"I have to see to Stine."

Jesper puts the interval signals in his bag, goes to the hallway and fetches his jacket. Enzo hurries after him.

"Another time then? When you can both come."

Jesper turns to him.

"Another time?"

Enzo looks down.

"Tell me if you don't like this, Jesper."

"Like what?"

"My asking your mother out to the buffet."

"Does it make any difference? Whether I like it or not?"

"I'll ring her then to call it off."

Jesper thinks again about everything you should avoid mixing, especially mothers and piano teachers.

"Mamma will decide," he says.

At that moment the telephone rings. Enzo Zanetti hesitates, perhaps he is waiting for Jesper to go first, but he doesn't, Jesper is staying. In the end Enzo answers, grunts, listens, nods, mumbles *ja ja*, looks at Jesper, holds his hand over the receiver and says:

"Your mother would like to talk to you."

Jesper shakes his head.

Enzo says on the telephone:

"Just a moment and he'll be with you."

He passes the receiver to Jesper, who turns his back. His mother seems stressed.

"Are you at Zanetti's?"

"Where else?"

"I didn't think you would have a lesson today."

"Why wouldn't I?"

"Because you've hurt your hand."

"Only one of them. Besides, you put the money out."

"Yes, I did. But—"

"It doesn't matter."

"What doesn't, Jesper?"

"That you're going out with Zanetti."

Now Jesper understands the function of the interval signal. It is a cover. It is meant to cover embarrassing silences. Whenever you feel uneasy you need an interval signal. Mamma is quiet for so long the birds on the telephone wires in Kirkeveien are dying. At length she says:

"We're just going out, Jesper."

"Yes, have a good time."

"I intended to tell you. Just so that you know."

"Now I know."

"Are you coming straight home then? Stine's on her own."

Jesper puts down the telephone and turns to the piano teacher, who is standing with his arms folded and an equally folded smile.

"As you know, she invited me to her birthday," he says.

"So?"

"So? Fair's fair."

Jesper walks home, but not straight home.

On the corner of Suhms gate Jostein is waiting for him. At any rate, he is standing there. He is larger than before. It is hard to say whether it is muscles or fat. Perhaps it is just the clothes? He is wearing a reefer jacket at least eight sizes too big and smells of exhaust fumes.

"Aren't you grounded?" Jesper asks.

Jostein just shrugs and Jesper isn't sure whether he heard or he couldn't be bothered to answer.

"Guess who's the richest fifteen-year-old in Fagerborg?"

"Has to be you."

"You should start working too."

"I play the piano."

"You won't earn anything doing that."

"No, it's a calling."

"A what?"

"Everything you don't earn from is a calling."

Jostein just laughs and points to the intersection.

"That's where I was knocked down," he says.

"I know, Jostein."

"It didn't hurt."

"Because you were unconscious."

"I was awake the whole time."

"Awake? Do you remember everything, then?"

"I saw Jesus."

Jesper wants to laugh, but doesn't dare risk it.

"You didn't," he says.

"I did. Close up."

"What did he look like?"

"Thin, fair hair and quite pale."

"That was Bjørn Stranger. He pulled out your tongue."

"It was not."

"He lives in our block. Feel like saying hello to him?"

"I earn eight kroner a day. Apart from on Sundays."

"What did you actually do to be grounded?"

Jostein crosses over into Marienlyst without looking. Jesper follows him. They sit down on the last bench.

"What did you actually do?" Jesper repeats.

Jostein doesn't hear or pretends he doesn't. This is beginning to be wearing.

"Let's think up something to do."

"What?"

Both laugh and say in unison:

"That's what we have to think up, isn't it?"

They stop laughing. The laughter is actually wonderful; it binds them in ways that only they understand.

"We can throw snowballs through open windows," Jostein suggests.

"The snow isn't sticky enough."

"Doesn't matter. We can just gob in them."

"There aren't any open now anyway."

"We can use stones."

Jesper has a sudden, clear perception that he has left Jostein behind after all, they have grown apart. There is a moment of melancholy, perhaps his first experience of this feeling, or a tingle, which is like sorrow with goose pimples. He gets up.

"I have to look after Stine."

Jostein stands up too.

"I can lend you some money."

"Why?"

"Because I've got money, haven't I?"

"I don't need it."

"Everyone needs money."

Jostein stuffs a hand in his pocket and produces a fistful of coins – krone pieces, fifty-øre pieces and coppers. He is pretty flush, almost rolling in it. Jesper can't be bothered anymore.

"I've got to go. Stine's on her own."

Jostein selects a five-krone coin and holds it up in front of Jesper.

"Do you earn any money babysitting?"

"See you."

Jesper starts walking towards Kirkeveien. Jostein follows him. He hasn't given up.

"We can buy some chocolate for Stine."

That is perhaps not the most stupid thing Jostein has said today. They head for Esther's kiosk on the corner by Wilhelm Færdens gate. Esther always wears a blue coat. She is strict but fair. Anyone who pinches anything is reported to the police, regardless of whether they are the priest's son or the caretaker's daughter. If she is in a good mood, you get your hands chopped off. Esther is rarely in a good mood. You can rely on her. She doesn't beat around the bush.

"I'm closing soon."

"Not quite yet," Jostein says.

He scatters all his money on the counter. Esther's eyes light up immediately at the sight of this fortune, but are extinguished just as quickly. Now she looks fearsome.

"Where is this from?" she demands.

Jesper ventures forward a step.

"Jostein's got a job. This is his wages."

"Just for your information," Jostein says.

Esther lets this sink in slowly and livens up, as far as she is able.

"Now you boys had better make up your minds smartish," she says.

Jesper wants to select, preferably from the top shelf. But Jostein wants everything. As it is Jostein's money, it is everything, as far as it can go: milk chocolate, Firkløver, Japp, Non Stop, Texas, Troika, Daim, Sfinx, Eggecognac, but Esther draws the line there. You have to be over eighteen to buy chocolate liqueurs in Esther's kiosk, furthermore Jostein shouldn't spend all his money on sweets. What would his parents say? Jostein repeats that it is his money, it was in his pocket and the pocket is his too. Just for her information. That is not helpful. Esther starts to make a selection. In the end there are only bars of Firkløver and Japp and a packet of Non Stop left on the counter. Jostein pays with fifty-øre coins and takes the rest back. Esther turns to Jesper and releases a smile that hasn't been aired for quite some time.

"And you deserve this," she says.

Esther gives him a box of Sfinx chocolates. Jesper doesn't want it. He takes it anyway.

"Why?"

The smile is put back in the drawer.

"Because you're a good boy and you've hurt yourself. You should be grateful when you receive a present, young man."

They leave the kiosk. Jesper doesn't want to be a good boy or grateful. Jostein is grumpy and jealous.

"Shall we swap?" he asks.

"Swap what?"

"Whatever you want."

Jesper doesn't want to swap. He wants to go home.

"Stine likes chocolate," he says.

Jostein seems lost for a moment.

"Can you say they're from me?"

"They are, aren't they?"

"You won't give them to Trude, will you?"

"Are you stupid?"

Jostein places a hand on Jesper's shoulder and at this moment there are only two people in Fagerborg.

"Are you getting anything?" he whispers.

In an even lower voice – and if Jostein can hear he is definitely not hard of hearing – Jesper says:

"That's got nothing to do with you."

Jostein just laughs and finally Jesper can escape and go straight home. Stine is sitting in the dining room. He stands in the hallway listening for a moment. Then he hides the Sfinx chocolates behind his bag and joins her.

"There's some food for you in the kitchen," she says.

"Has Mamma been home?"

"No. I heated up some leftovers."

"Have you switched off the cooker?"

Stine nods. Jesper sits down and places the sweets between them.

"For you," he says.

"Who are they from?"

"Jostein. And me."

Stine seems surprised rather than happy. She doesn't touch the box.

"We'll save them until Mamma comes," she says.

"That might be a long time."

"Why?"

"We might've gone to bed."

"Isn't she at the Red Cross meeting?"

Jesper walks over to the window. Beneath the darkness lies

the light: the snow. It shines up. Stars are hanging in the windows across Kirkeveien. A forest of lonely Christmas trees is standing on balconies waiting to be decorated. If the moon was a magnifying glass Jesper might have been able to see the buffet in the Frognerseter restaurant where the guests were filling their plates to overflowing with sausages, ribs, goat's cheese, cream, cloudberries and halibut. The buffet has so much to offer that everyone wants everything. Now Jesper can see only the top of the ski jump. It looks like a black nail. He has to pull himself together.

"Mamma isn't at a Red Cross meeting," he says.

"I know. She's out."

"Then you know who she's out with, don't you?"

Stine is on the verge of tears.

"She said I shouldn't tell you."

"You didn't."

"She wanted to tell you herself."

"Is there anything else you know? That I don't? Or do you know everything?"

Stine is silent for a while, for maybe minutes. Then she says:

"Please play something for me."

Jesper sits on the stool and plays the interval signal for Austria with one finger. There aren't many Alps in the signal, or any Viennese waltzes, it is a stunted song in short pants. He continues with Great Britain's "Oranges and Lemons", which is both lively and dull, then he tackles the West German one, a challenging interval signal that cannot however be compared with that of the Soviet Union, which is sentimental and dogged. When he turns round, for a break, Stine has fallen asleep. Her head is beside the box of chocolates, her hand is under her cheek, her blonde hair on the blue tablecloth, and darkness is falling between the street lamps. Jesper won't forget this. He doesn't want to wake her, but strikes a chord with his left hand anyway, Stine's chord, and bang on time, as usual, Bjørn Stranger knocks on the ceiling, which is his floor, it is eight o'clock, or 20.00 as it says in the house rules, and Stine wakes up.

Jesper sits down with her again. They start the wait in earnest. On the chocolate box it says: *Whichever one you take – they are all great when you choose Sfinx.*

"Our pappa wrote that," Jesper says.

Stine looks up.

"What?"

"Whichever one you take – they are all great when you choose Sfinx."

"Did he?"

Jesper nods.

"Do you remember Pappa?"

Stine looks down again, unhappy:

"No."

"Nothing?"

Stine is welling up.

"No."

Jesper puts his good hand on hers.

"Not surprising. You were only a pudding when he died."

Stine has hardly any voice.

"What was he like?"

"He wore braces and told jokes about Cirkus Sjumann."

"What was Cirkus Sjumann?"

Jesper laughs.

"Pappa was an advertising man. Where Mamma's working now."

There is a short silence until Stine says:

"I wish I remembered a bit about him."

"It doesn't matter."

"Why not?"

Jesper pulls his hand away.

"Because he remembers you, doesn't he?"

There is another silence. No-one is going to disturb them. Stine turns the chocolate box and reads slowly:

"Whichever one you take—"

Jesper finishes it off:

"They are all great when you choose Sfinx."

Stine opens the lid. The chocolates, twenty-four in all, lie in small moulded cavities, each one with a Greek letter engraved in the coating, both light and dark, but what defines them is the filling: pineapple, mint, coffee, nougat and toffee. Who should start? They choose one. Stine goes for coffee; Jesper for mint. They aren't content with one. Once you have started, it is hard to stop. Jesper plumps for coffee; Stine nougat. They continue like this, competing with each other. The flavours, every one distinctive and distinct, merge in their mouths into an immutable sweet impression, which seems temporarily stimulating, but soon makes both of them feel tired and lethargic. At last, they finish all the chocolates. The Sfinx box is empty. They don't hear their mother come in.

13/12/56. The final board meeting of the year was held at Fru Skjelkvale's. Those present were: Fru Lund, Frøken Jacobsen, Frøken Smith, Frøken Schanke, Fru Kristoffersen and the hostess herself. We made keyrings and scissor cases from leftover bits of plastic. Frøken Smith informed us that she didn't want to be re-elected as she was getting engaged and didn't think she would be able to attend meetings. We all congratulated her and wished her well. Then we sat around eating some Christmas biscuits, without over-indulging.

DOUBLY HAPPY

The following morning, after Jesper and Stine have gone to school, Maj calls Margrethe. No-one answers. She tries again, perhaps she dialled the wrong number, but she doesn't pick up this time either. Maybe it is too early. It is only eight o'clock. She bangs down the receiver, shivers, hurries into the hallway and writes a note for Jesper: he has to fetch some wood from the cellar. Why hasn't he already done it? She doesn't write that. Instead she throws away the note. Jesper can't carry wood with one hand, nor with two. He has to take care of his hands. It is sixteen degrees below zero in Blindern. She can definitely put his thin windcheater away. She will have to do that later. Not even that has she got round to doing. And soon it will be Christmas. All the seasons are still hanging from the clothes hooks, even Stine's yellow raincoat. She is furious with herself, not only that, she is furious with the world. She is being squeezed into a corner; that is how it feels. Those things that should be good hurt her. She should at least put Jesper's jacket away, if he can't be bothered. It is in the way. She is furious with Jesper's jacket as well and almost rips it from the hook. A cardboard pack falls out of a pocket and lands at her feet. Maj lifts a hand to her face and strokes some strands of hair from her forehead. It is a packet of condoms. Her first thought is: Jesper has brought the wrong jacket home. It doesn't belong to him. The next is: The packet is unopened. Finally she thinks: He is already old enough to have secrets. On the packet it says: *Have a good time.* That would be like Jostein. Jesper has got the condoms from Jostein. That is how it is. Jostein is a bad influence. Even his mother said that. Maj puts the condoms back in the pocket and hangs the jacket on the hook, the way it was before.

Then she changes her mind, takes the jacket into the bedroom and hangs it in the wardrobe. If she hurries now she can catch the Metro leaving at twenty minutes past eight.

Bjørn Stranger is standing on the staircase with his hands behind him.

"Off to work in the cold?" he says.

Maj wants to slip past him as quickly as possible.

"Yes, that's how it is."

"And Jesper and Stine have already left for school. Busy time for you."

Maj stops. Is he keeping an eye on them? She is right about her suspicions. Bjørn Stranger is snooping on them.

"Don't you work?" she asks.

Bjørn Stranger laughs.

"Me? I work all the time, Fru Kristoffersen."

He follows Maj to the postboxes and opens the door for her.

The temperature has risen to only minus fifteen, but it is bitingly cold in Kirkeveien and luckily the tram is delayed due to frozen rails at Steinerud, which is seventy-one metres above sea level. So Maj will be able to blame this if she isn't on time for work. She arrives ten minutes late. It doesn't matter. Everyone is in departure mode anyway. What can't be done now will have to wait until 1957. The boys have bought a Christmas tree and decorated it with crayons and old champagne corks. Kinck is standing on a chair and attaching a red bow tie to the top. Maj laughs at them, she can't do anything else, and freshens up in the cloakroom that Rudjord has had fitted out for her behind the conference room. Then she is back at her post. On her desk is a copy of *Norsk Dameblad*, open at the middle pages. There are pictures of two happy women, one carrying a tray of gleaming dinner plates, the other holding a scrubbing brush over an equally gleaming floor, and they are beaming fit to bust. If you look closely it is the same woman. She is just a double. *She is doubly happy – with Pep for dishwashing and cleaning.* Kinck falls off the chair and pulls the whole tree down with him.

The boys laugh and pull him to his feet. It wouldn't surprise Maj if they have had a few already. But December is an exception to the rule. December is a different time. There aren't many appointments either, only this one: Rudjord has invited them to a Christmas lunch at the Bristol at one o'clock. Maj doesn't feel like going. She is still full from the buffet. Just the thought of the long table with all kinds of dishes makes her stomach ache. She puts the *Norsk Dameblad* to one side and tidies up the papers and pens, to do something, for appearance's sake. December is for appearance's sake. There are only a few pages left on the calendar while the receding year, which is about to be out of date, is a thick, uneven pile, of no use anymore, removed, but not discarded. Maj, who ought to feel some pleasure, if not a double portion, then at least a single one, more she does not require, is depressed. This is not like her. Suddenly Rudjord is standing in front of her desk. He must have been there for a while. No-one can be suddenly there. She smiles.

"A krone for your thoughts, Fru Kristoffersen."

She collects herself.

"There's so much to do before Christmas."

"Shall we cross the street and be a little thought-less for a while?"

Rudjord is already holding her coat.

They take the lift down and in Rosenkrantz' gate he slips his arm under hers as they walk into the cold, heads bowed.

"Would you mind if I don't?" Maj asks.

"Don't what?"

"Don't go to the Bristol."

"Why?"

"As I said, there's so much to do and . . ."

Rudjord holds her even tighter and laughs.

"No, Maj, I'm not going to let you go. But you don't have to return to the office afterwards."

The heat inside the Bristol causes their faces to redden. Everyone's face flushes at the Bristol in December. Pocket Venus Jenny takes their coats and they walk, still arm in arm, through the restaurant, where the guests turn slowly and intently after them, eyeball to eyeball, as they pass the abandoned grand piano and continue up to the little plateau by the stairs, where the boys have been waiting patiently for their boss to come so that they can order. They look like a temperance conference. But now he is here, with the secretary in tow. They can start. First of all they need something to wet the whistle. Then the meal can be organised. Ravn would like a Green Linctus, Strøm asks for a shot of aquavit, Johnsen could do with a Balu, Kinck asks politely for a Gimpson, and it is beers all round. It is like an act of alcoholic devotion. Maj sits at the head of the table, beside Rudjord, who has a Martini while Maj is happy with fizzy water and can't stop thinking about the wives who will be waiting in vain for their boys at night, even if two of them are bachelors and one got divorced a long time ago. She can remember how she used to, and a strange thought strikes her: she is still waiting for Ewald, who is lying incognito somewhere she cannot access. She hates the Bristol even more. Maj doesn't have to fetch anything. Whatever she needs is brought to her. She doesn't need much, just pork ribs, which she barely touches. She waits for an opportunity to take her leave, preferably without anyone noticing. Rudjord taps his glass before the boys start talking about the cold war and politics. Immediately there is polite silence on the landing. Everyone knows what this will be about: the Christmas bonus. And as is only right for a man who makes his living from slogans, Rudjord is brief and to the point: *1956 has been a good year.* Then he walks around the table and leaves an envelope by each place. The boys cast glances that can judge the width of a banana fly in a bale of cotton. Has anyone got a thicker envelope than the rest? All eyes are on stalks. Rudjord stops behind Maj and is concise again:

"And a vote of thanks to our secretary, Fru Kristoffersen, or perhaps simply Maj, who secured the Pep contract for us."

Rudjord places the last envelope in front of her. It is obviously thicker than the others. This doesn't escape notice. She slides it into the bag on her lap and looks nowhere in particular. The waiter arrives with more booze and the atmosphere dissolves into fragmented sentences and tobacco. Maj espies half an opportunity and goes downstairs to the ladies. There she leans against the sink and looks slowly up. What a sight. She takes out her lipstick and powder puff and remembers one of Ewald's many comments: *the over-made-up generation*. She used to laugh a lot at that one. She doesn't anymore. Now she is that generation. She is in the repair shop. She takes a deep breath, steps towards the door and decides she will be cheerful. Why shouldn't she be? She has been given a bonus. She has been given credit for her work. Kinck is in the foyer where all the shadows are dressed in burgundy and smoking cigars. He sees Maj and stands in her way.

"Congratulations," he says.

"Thank you. Rudjord—"

Kinck interrupts.

"I should've known you were insured by Norwegian Ass-ets."

Maj is not familiar with all the Bristol lingo, particularly the toilet dialect. However, she immediately grasps the gist of the message. Nevertheless she says:

"What do you mean?"

Kinck leans over towards her.

"I can smell bedclothes."

Maj feels a strong urge to slap him. She even has a hand at the ready. The plump man deserves nothing better. Preferably in front of everyone. But at that moment she hears the restaurant piano. Someone is playing "Für Elise". She lowers her arm. Kinck straightens up.

"Our macaroni musico is back," he says.

Kinck hurries into the gentlemen's. Maj lingers to collect herself. She is no longer angry, only ashamed. She would never have believed it. Is this how they view her? She would rather be angry. But shame is closer to sadness than anger. Enzo is playing. He is sitting at the piano, in the dark suit that is too big for him, and his hair is unruly again, black and grey cowlicks everywhere. He glances over his shoulder and sees her, smiles and during this smile there is a pause, not only in the music, but in life, and Maj Kristoffersen is sure the whole of the Bristol knows she is having an affair with the lounge pianist, and arriving arm in arm with Rudjord, a company director, her *programme du bal* is oversubscribed: she is a flirt in a skirt. It is too far to walk to the table. She would rather make a dash to the cloakroom, pick up her coat and disappear for good. She walks through the restaurant, Enzo Zanetti is playing more slowly as she passes behind him, and she also slows down, until she is in a hurry again and takes her seat at the landing table. Rudjord points to Enzo, who has started Chopin's "Berceuse", shameless as he is in his choice of repertoire.

"I asked the hotel manager to bring him back. Christmas at the Bristol wouldn't be the same without—"

Maj cuts him short.

"Without the macaroni musician."

Rudjord laughs.

"Ewald raved about him."

"Yes, I can imagine."

Maj looks away. Rudjord lights a cigarette, blows blue smoke across the tablecloth and fidgets nervously with the ashtray.

"I'm sorry if I said something wrong."

"You didn't."

"Shall I order you a dessert?"

"That would be lovely."

While Rudjord and the boys are browsing at the cake counter, Maj uses the opportunity to melt away. What a great expression. To melt away. Just to melt away. It is only when she is waiting in the cloakroom that she hears the silence. The piano stool is unoccupied. All she hears in the noise of laughter, shouting, bottles, glasses, ice cubes and pounding hearts is that the music has stopped. Pocket Venus Jenny leans across the counter holding Maj's coat.

"He's outside," she whispers.

"Sorry?"

"Enzo. He's waiting by the entrance."

Maj takes her coat, pulls it on and leaves, from heat to cold this time, but her cheeks are equally flushed. How embarrassing. Does everyone know? At the Bristol everyone knows everything, whether it is true or not. It makes no difference. So long as you know. He is in the cramped entrance around the corner. Maj stops.

"You mustn't get cold," she says.

Enzo drops a cigarette into the snow and burns a hole into the winter.

"I'm not. I have my hands in my pockets."

"I didn't know you were going to play here."

"Just a few days. Until Christmas."

"Poor you."

"I do it for the money."

"I didn't mean it like that."

Enzo laughs.

"Yes, it's sad about me."

Maj remembers something.

"Hasn't Jesper paid?"

"More than enough. But living's expensive. I mean surviving."

"You didn't have to pay for me."

"What do you mean?"

"On Holmenkollen. I can pay."

Maj opens her bag and takes the envelope.

"Now you're offending me," Enzo Zanetti says.

"Besides I ate too much."

"The more you eat, the cheaper it is."

"I hope you didn't see, but I ate brown cheese with salmon. I was so confused that—"

"Stop."

Maj closes her bag with a click and looks up. His face is half in shadow, but the light from the street lamp, which is lit twenty-four hours a day now, falls on his threadbare suit.

"But it was very nice," she says.

Enzo nods and takes out a cigarette without lighting it.

"I ate sauerkraut with cream, but you probably saw?"

Maj giggles.

"There was too much to choose from."

"Yes, one dish is best. And then a dessert."

"I'd better hurry."

"Me too. Otherwise the customers will be put out."

They remain standing there anyway. The wind gusts snow along the walls. In a street not so far away, maybe Grensen, they can hear a tractor scraping a snowplough over the cobblestones. Maj turns up her collar.

"Have a good Christmas then," she says.

Enzo holds her back.

"How's Jesper?"

"He's better."

"What would he like for Christmas? And Stine?"

"Don't buy any presents. Please."

"No, it wasn't a very good idea."

Maj releases herself from his hand. Then she hurries on. Enzo Zanetti watches her until she disappears among people in the darkness of Pilestredet. He lights the cigarette and takes a few quick drags, then throws this one into the snow as well and goes back in. Jenny is standing by the door and waiting for her relief to come.

"Are you already engaged?" she asks.

Enzo stops for a moment.

"No, God forbid."

"Thank goodness. Otherwise there wouldn't have been a dry eye among the ladies."

"Why do you ask?"

"You've been gone for so long Ulfsen almost reported you missing."

Jenny laughs and nudges Enzo in the direction of the piano. At length he takes his place and warms his hands between his thighs. Then he goes back to the beginning – that is the fate of the salon musician, to start at the beginning, to continue from the beginning and to finish from the beginning. A bit of Grieg never hurt anyone, time for a Christmas carol now, a few guests join in from the corner, soon they are all humming along, not easy to escape an old classic either, such as "We'll Meet Again", which, in the best possible way, takes account of and cultivates the era's cheery sentimentality with easy chords and good memories of the war years. Most important of all, the pianist must not introduce bad news. He should bring good vibes. But he won't play Satie. He has left Satie to Jesper. Enzo hears applause. It takes him by surprise. He hasn't earned it. There is nothing to clap for. He is mediocre this evening. He is mediocre every evening. He can't find any harmony between his heart and his hands. He doesn't know if he is on the threshold of happiness or disaster, freedom or prison. Enzo Zanetti gives this some thought. He has weighty matters on his mind. He is crossing bridges before he comes to them. Should he renounce his old life? Should he? He is a rolling stone, a drifter, not a husband and father. He is exaggerating. He is lying. He even lies to himself. He has lied to himself for so long. The lies form a queue inside him. He tries to think clearly. This is just a flirtation. She is just good company. She is just the mother of his pupil. Nevertheless Enzo's attention is diverted. His mind is elsewhere. Elsewhere is with her. Maj unlocks her front door and can already hear Jesper's voice:

"Have you seen my jacket?"

She removes her shoes and hangs her coat on the hook. Jesper is in the hallway and he is impatient. He has combed his hair as well as he is able and is wearing the new, blue shirt he actually should have waited until Christmas to put on. But he has buttoned it up wrongly and Maj has to help.

"What jacket?" she asks.

"My windcheater, of course."

"I put it away."

"Why?"

"It's winter, Jesper. Have you both eaten?"

Stine comes in from the pantry wearing an apron. It looks like a long dress.

"There's some kangaroo poo for you as well," she says.

Maj raises a finger and takes a step towards Jesper.

"Don't teach her your language. Do you hear me now?"

Stine laughs behind him.

"It only means fishcakes."

Jesper isn't laughing. He is just getting even more impatient; in fact, he seems to be on the edge of a minor breakdown.

"Can you please find my jacket for me?"

Maj scrutinises him.

"Why are you so dressed up?"

Stine answers first.

"He's going to meet his girlfriend."

Jesper is fighting on two fronts.

"Now you shut up! And you tell me where my jacket is!"

"Don't talk to your sister like that."

"Sorry. Please tell me . . ."

"Your girlfriend?"

Stine's turn again.

"Her name's Trude and she's in his class."

Jesper blushes, the heat rises in his cheeks and spreads to his ears. He looks away. What he sees is hard to discern, perhaps he sees a deserted island in front of him; perhaps he just sees what is there: photographs of the javelin thrower, Egil Danielsen, and the composer, Erik Satie, hanging above the little desk.

"I've been invited to dinner."

Maj tries to button his shirt at the neck.

"Maybe you should wear a tie?"

Jesper pushes her hands away.

"It's only dinner."

"You can wear the anorak instead."

Jesper's eyes widen.

"The anorak. Should I wear an anorak? I'm not going skiing."

"It's snowing, Jesper."

"And that's exactly why I want my windcheater."

"You could at least put on a jumper."

"Alright, I'll put on a jumper. Two even. If you can knit me another one."

"And don't forget to invite Trude here."

Jesper is fraying at the edges.

"Where would we go? I can't close the door as it is."

"You two can have the sitting room. We won't disturb you. Will we, Stine?"

Stine shakes her head for a long time.

Maj strokes Jesper's cheek. He tosses his head to one side. Then she goes into the bedroom and fetches his windcheater. For a moment she stands still, wondering what to do. Should she confiscate the packet or leave it? He is too young. They are too young. No, he only has it to show off. He doesn't need to show off. She puts the packet in the bedside drawer and goes back. Stine helps Jesper to put his injured arm through the sleeve. Maj tells him to lift his feet so that she can check if there are any holes in his socks. He refuses, but does it anyway, so that he can get away. No holes. She lets him take the windcheater.

"Have you seen anything of Jostein recently, by the way?" she says.

"Why?"

"I was just wondering, Jesper. You look good in the jumper. Don't forget your scarf."

"I met him when we were getting the sweets."

"You didn't get anything else, did you?"

"What do you mean?" Jesper asks.

"You know very well what."

He doesn't want any help from anyone with putting on his windcheater.

"Have you gone crazy or what?"

Jesper eventually gets out of the flat with some of his brain intact, but not much. Crossing Bogstadveien, he knows what he wants to imagine: the evening as a piece of music, already written note for note. Who is the composer? In what key? What sort of tempo? These questions emerge at Vestkanttorget. By Solli Plass he still doesn't have an answer. He is freezing like a dog. It doesn't matter. What does matter is that the jacket is cool. And he would rather lose his ears than wear a stupid hat. The English quarter casts white shadows, unlike the university library which looks like an enormous bunker. A solitary student with a copy of *Norges Lover* (*Norwegian Law*) under his arm comes to a halt on the steps and lights a cigarette. Observatorie Terrasse is a narrow side road to the park where the old observatory is. Once you used to be able to see stars close-up there. Now it is Jesper's turn to see them. At any rate he finds the right number and hurries in. Trude lives on the first floor. He stops on the ground floor, takes out his comb, sees his reflection in a copper sign on a door and tidies his hair with one hand. His fringe keeps flopping down. As he puts his comb back and straightens up, he remembers: the condoms. He searches all his pockets. There are only two. He searches them again anyway. The packet isn't there. Have a good time. He panics. His mother! Not that he will need the condoms now. He will have to wait until his hand is better. Then he hears someone shout:

"Jesper. Where have you been?"

It is Trude. She is leaning over the banister. Her hair falls down on both sides of her head. Jesper hurries up the last stairs. His steps, which should be light, are heavy. He has to shake off the heaviness. He has to rid himself of worries and arrive unburdened and carefree. What does it matter if Mamma has found the Durex packet? She shouldn't be rummaging through his pockets. He is the one who has something on her. No, he hasn't. The packet might have fallen out. When he reaches the first floor the door is closed and Trude isn't there. Is he so slow? Couldn't she be bothered to wait? Both names are on the sign: ALFRED AND GUNN HAGEN. Jesper rings the bell. If Trude doesn't open the door he will be in a fix. He will have to remember to bow. It isn't Trude. It is a lady in a white apron and flat shoes. It must be Gunn Hagen, the mother. Jesper proffers the wrong hand and almost loses his sling in the process. He manages to sort out his arms, but Trude's mother is apparently not interested in shaking hands, she just nods and lets him into the hallway, where she helps him off with his jacket and hangs it on a coat stand while Jesper is thanking his lucky stars that his mother took the condoms after all – imagine if the packet had fallen out here! – and that she checked his socks because of course he will have to remove his shoes, but as if that weren't enough, Gunn Hagen, Trude's mother, gives him a pair of guest slippers, two enormous floating docks, and helps him on with them. Jesper can't bear helpful people. They are presumptuous. But he had better like Trude's mother. Where is Trude? Did she just close the door and go through the rear entrance? This hallway isn't a room, it is a national gallery. There are paintings all over the walls, landscapes, portraits and colours that don't represent anything, just themselves, like music. In the lounge, to the right, which is dark and long, he catches sight of a piano. He is glad his hand is injured, so he won't be asked to play. Finally Trude appears, from another door. She stops and looks at him.

"You look nice in that jumper," she says.

Jesper nods without moving from the spot. This is the moment he should say something to her too. All he can muster is:

"I shook hands . . . I mean, I don't think I shook hands properly with your mother."

He feels stupid. He is stupid. Trude laughs.

"Relax. That was our house help, Judith."

"Have you got a house help?"

"Yes, because Mamma works in the evenings."

"We should too. Have a house help, I mean. My mother works too. But not in the evening. Although she does have to work in the evening sometimes."

Trude watches him.

"Does your hand hurt?"

"Not much."

"Pappa would like to say hello."

"I thought he worked in the evening."

Jesper follows Trude into the apartment. She stops in front of the last door and turns.

"He won't bite. Just for your information."

Then she knocks, grabs his hand and they walk in. It is a kind of library, or office, with shelves up to the ceiling, a globe in the corner, piles of old newspapers on the floor, a drinks cabinet, a vase full of fountain pens instead of flowers and a typewriter with a sheet of paper in. Trude's father is sitting in a worn, broad, leather chair leafing through a foreign magazine, probably *Time*. He is wearing a brown suit, a bow tie, horn glasses and patent-leather shoes. His almost white hair hangs down over his collar like dry hay on a rack. And his chin sticks out like the prow of a submarine. But above all else he is old. He could have been Trude's grandfather, even great-grandfather for that matter. He is a journalist at *Aftenposten*, not your regular journo but a *cultural correspondent*, and has interviewed Crown Prince Olav, Trygve Lie, Hauk Aabel, Danny Kaye, Tancred Ibsen, Louis Armstrong and Charlie Chaplin.

"This is Jesper from my class, Pappa."

The man in the leather chair, who *is* actually Trude's father, raises his gaze and removes his square rhino horn-rims.

"What's with your hand?"

Jesper tries to release his hand, but Trude has a firm hold. Her father shakes his head.

"I mean the one you've hurt."

"A handball match."

"Right. I assumed it didn't happen while you were playing."

"No, I was in goal."

"I mean while you were playing the piano, Jesper. Trude says you play."

"Yes, a little."

"Do you know how much Wilhelm Kempff insured his hands for?"

"No. Has he?"

"Twenty thousand German marks. And one mark is worth three kroner."

"That's a lot," Jesper says.

Trude's father puts his glasses back on and looks at his daughter.

"You can let go of the boy now. Before both of his hands are damaged."

Trude laughs and sits down on the armrest of his chair. Jesper notices that there are no more chairs in the room. He has no intention of sitting on the other arm and remains standing. How long is this going to last? What he needs now is interval music.

"Tell us a bit about what's happening in the world," Trude says.

Her father closes *Time* magazine and sighs.

"First of all, there's Hungary. More than a hundred thousand refugees are on their way to Austria. And how many is Norway taking? A thousand. Do you think that's too few or too many, Jesper?"

"It depends."

"Exactly. But *what* does it depend on?"

"Who they are," Jesper says.

Trude's father pauses to reflect.

"Not bad. On who they are. So we should take those we need? But who do we need?"

It is Jesper's turn to reflect. It would have been easier to say who we didn't need, such as nosy parkers, people with no musical taste, headmasters, accordion players and poofs. He knows the answer is wrong before he says it.

"House helps."

"Look around Oslo, Jesper. Or Norway for that matter. And what's the first thing you see? Yes, cranes. We're building the country. So we need more builders, electricians, engineers, welders, fitters and bricklayers. We'd really like to have them here. In addition, architects to design the whole shenanigans. Can we agree to call this *practical humanism*?"

Jesper realises that actually he quite likes being in Alfred Hagen's company. He doesn't understand much, but at least he has a sense that he is being taken seriously and that is not always the case, except at Enzo's, when he isn't repairing, mind you, and definitely before he started taking Mamma out.

"Agreed," Jesper says.

Trude doesn't shift her gaze from him. He is being put to the test, it seems.

"Agreed," he repeats.

Herr Hagen laughs.

"You can only agree once, Jesper. But what is it that the Hungarians are fleeing?"

"Communism," Trude answers.

"Communism is an *idea*. They aren't fleeing an idea, but the consequences of this idea. And that is suppression. They're fleeing from the absence of liberty. The communists are *taking* liberties and that is the absolute opposite of liberty. What's freedom for you, Jesper?"

His first thought is of course *school holidays*, but that is quite different, that much he does know. Free time is impossible too. Doing what you want is no good as an answer in this company. Having the right to vote, taking your driving licence and buying alcohol are out of the question as well. He has to come up with something better. And then it flashes into his mind: You just have to be honest.

"Playing the piano," Jesper says.

Herr Hagen raises his glasses, nods and lets them fall back.

"Then you'll have to liberate your right hand as soon as possible," he says.

Trude jumps down from the armrest and pushes Jesper towards the door. However, her father has more issues on his mind.

"And then you two shouldn't forget the Suez Canal. It's a short cut, just like the North-West Passage was in its day. One goes through ice, the other through the desert, but with precisely the same objective: to take a short cut to wealth. More often than not short cuts don't come cheap. Now I'd like a bit of peace and quiet."

Trude is about to close the door behind them, but the journalist has more to say. He has even stood up.

"And one thing while you're still here, Jesper. I don't mean to cram your head with information, but sometimes it's necessary. Because surely you wouldn't want the devil's piano rattling over us again, would you?"

Jesper looks down at the unfamiliar slippers on his feet. He recognises the words Trude's father uses, but doesn't understand a bloody thing. The devil's piano? He daren't ask. He just raises his eyes and shakes his head. Finally Trude can close the door and take his free hand.

"Pappa likes you," she whispers.

Then Jesper follows Trude back the same way, through the pantry, past the bathroom, the maid's room, the kitchen, the dining room, the hallway, another room with a veranda that has been converted into a conservatory and is like a jungle full of blue, glowing light bulbs. The house help isn't to be seen anywhere. She is probably a ghost, employed only to answer the door. In the end they reach a door with a sign on: DISTURB. Trude turns the sign round. Now it says: DO NOT DISTURB. Then she opens the door and lets Jesper in. This is Trude's room. It is strange: Trude's room is on the ground floor while the rest of the apartment is on the first floor. Then Jesper grasps the connection: the lawn outside is higher than the street at the front. And within a second he has seen everything, he assimilates the room in one sweep, and it is the first time this has happened to him, that his surroundings, everything within sight, is a chord he can comprehend at once: the yellow sofa bed, the pictures of ski-racer Stein Eriksen, Albert Schweitzer and James Dean on the wall, the reading lamp on the desk by the window, where her school books are, the shelves of Nancy Drew mysteries, Ibsen's collected works and a row of small trophies, eight in all, the mirror, the gramophone, which is a Radionette Combi, the standard lamp in the corner with the dark-yellow shade, a wardrobe that is closed but is sure to have a mirror inside, a mirror that has seen most of life, and last but not least the unusual rugs with multi-coloured geometrical patterns and fringes, and all the cushions strewn around, there are twelve of them. Trude sits down among them. Are there no chairs in this house? However, Jesper doesn't mind. He does the same. He doesn't know quite who he should be envious of, James Dean, Stein Eriksen or Albert Schweitzer. Probably James Dean. Jesper decides he is going to buy a white T-shirt, comb his hair back and start smoking. If his right hand hadn't been injured he could have put his arm around Trude now.

"Where did you get them?" he asks.

"From the Shah of Persia."

"The cups?"

Trude laughs.

"No, the cushions and rugs. Dad interviewed him. And he was given some presents."

"But how did you win the cups?"

"I lost. Slalom. That's why the cups are so small."

"Do you really do slalom?"

"Not anymore. They didn't have any smaller cups."

"Has your father really spoken to the Shah of Persia?"

"Really, really. Cross my heart."

"Not many people have done that. Talked to the Shah, I mean. Of Persia."

If Jesper wriggles across to the other side, to the orange cushion, he can run his good hand, the left hand, which is by far the better one, along her neck and perhaps, if it is in the right position, let it wander in a gentle caress across other hills and dales. There is a knock at the door. It is Judith, the house help. Unfortunately she is not a ghost. Ghosts don't appear with supper. She places a tray on the floor and withdraws without saying a word. There is one slice of bread with just cucumber, two halves with liver paste and soft white cheese and a glass of milk for each of them. Jesper prefers Trude to start.

"Do you drink milk?" she asks.

"Milk? Yes, of course."

"Mamma doesn't."

"Really? Your mother doesn't drink milk?"

"She thinks it's bad for the cows."

"Ah, the cows."

Jesper suddenly remembers he is also a vegetarian. He catches himself at the last moment. A bluff has to be second nature. He takes the rye and cucumber. The thin, green slices are almost transparent and resemble the goggles that divers wear.

"I'll have this one."

Trude takes one of the half-slices. She eats quickly. Jesper can't keep up. Afterwards she washes it down with milk and wipes away the white moustache with the back of her hand. Just watching her, without touching, makes Jesper's skin tingle. He takes a drink of milk too and wipes away the moustache with his sling. Probably that doesn't have the same impact on her.

"Who should start, do you think?" he asks.

Trude smiles.

"Start what, Jesper?"

Jesper would have liked to answer: kissing, holding each other, lying down and carrying on from where they had started.

"Your talk or my piano."

"Do you think you'll recover in time?"

"There are still four months. And twenty-three days. Besides, I can play with one hand."

"Play what, though?"

"Anything. I can play with one finger as well."

"Chopsticks?"

"No. I can play a C that would make you cry."

Trude stares at him. He can feel her eyes on him, even if he looks down. He blushes fire-engine red. He has bitten off more than he can chew. A C that would make her cry. He should have kissed her. That would have been an easier promise to keep. He is about to make a smart comment, but she speaks up first.

"Was the cucumber good?"

"It really was."

"You say *really* quite a lot."

"Do I really?"

"I think the senior teacher starts, then I do my talk, then there's the laying of the wreath, after which you play and at the end we all sing. Standing."

"Something like that."

Jesper repeats the phrase, deep inside where he has never been before, *something like that, something like that,* and he leans closer, but at that moment Trude gets up and goes over to the portable record player, which they can take with them to the Huk or Hverven beaches when it is spring, if the seasons ever get that far, and Jesper still exists and Trude wants to go with him.

"Do you like Elvis?" she asks.

Jesper shrugs, the way you should if you are sophisticated and pretty blasé.

"He's O.K."

"He's *O.K.*?"

"I like his voice."

"The record hasn't actually come out yet. Pappa was given a sample."

"Does your father like Elvis?"

"Why do you think he gave it to me?"

"Perhaps because he's too old to dance."

Trude blows on the stylus. For a moment the room is filled with the sound of her blowing and Jesper is sitting in the middle of it. This is where he wants to be. He holds his breath and then inhales deeply. They are as one. She is inside him. In fact, it is not Elvis. Some mould has crept into the stack of 45s. It is the Norwegian "Tango for Two". It is schmalz. All that is missing is cowhides, a

Hammond organ and yee-haw boots. The best thing about it is that it doesn't last long.

"Did you like it?" Trude asks.

"Loads."

"You liked it loads or you really liked it?"

"Especially the accompaniment."

"Actually you're a bit of a *blupper*, aren't you, Jesper?"

Blupper? Jesper doesn't know the word. He has no idea what it means. And there's him knowing all the words in the underground vocabulary. But this is a new item in the alphabet. *Blupper*. Shit, is it a term of respect? He doubts it. The word *blupper* doesn't bode well. Is he a blupper who plays the devil's piano? When Trude sits down again, she is closer than before. At least there is no doubt about that. Jesper takes a risk, or rather grasps the opportunity, and presses his lips against hers, but they are dry, even the milk has gone. He remembers the previous kiss, the first one, that was a different matter, but then they were kissing outdoors, in Stens Park, perhaps kissing outdoors is better, the air is clearer, the sky is higher and you aren't held back by thin walls, doors and keyholes. There are no ghosts outdoors. Trude might also have decided that one kiss is more than enough, or that he wasn't up to it, he is a retard, he is behind in the kissing syllabus, in other words he is a blupper. That is what he is. At any rate she twists her body so that she is resting her forehead on his shoulder.

"Shall we say hello to Mamma?" she whispers.

That is the last thing Jesper would like at this precise moment. Perhaps she has a word he has never heard of as well. He isn't playing on his home ground. But he meekly follows Trude to the kitchen. Gunn Hagen is standing by the window eating an apple. She is wearing checked slacks and a man's white shirt that is at least three sizes too big. Her hair is short. She could easily be her daughter's elder sister or vice versa. This family is basically a one-off.

"This is Jesper," Trude says.

Her mother puts the apple down on a napkin and smiles.

"Hi, Jesper. Apparently we're in the same team."

She is a prompter at Oslo Nye Teater and is used to whispering. Nevertheless it is not difficult to hear her. Jesper is slow on the uptake, however, and doesn't understand.

"Which one?"

"Trude said you were a vegan. Or is that just something you say?"

Perhaps that is what a blupper is, a bluffer? Will he have to eat swede for the rest of his life to prove he is telling the truth? A vegan?

"No, I'm also a vegetarian."

"So you're not a vegan?"

"No, for the time being I'm just a vegetarian."

"You eat fish even though they are living creatures tortured to death?"

"Not much. Maybe the odd haddock now and then."

"Do you eat eggs as well, Jesper?"

"Sometimes. On Sundays."

"You have a long way to go, Jesper. Eggs are foetuses. An egg is a *latency* and you choose to eat it. Tell me, why did you become a vegetarian?"

"I visited a friend of mine at Oslo Slaughterhouse and saw how the pigs . . ."

Trude's mother turns away in disgust and puts her hands over her ears.

"I don't want to hear. I don't want to hear."

There is a pause in the performance. Jesper can envisage this lasting quite a while, but he would prefer it to be somewhere else. Trude, however, doesn't seem to be much for moving. She doesn't say anything either. In the end, it is Jesper who speaks.

"Do you know the actress Ragnhild Stranger?"

Trude's mother lowers her hands and turns.

"Ragnhild Stranger, yes. Things went downhill with her. She remembered fewer and fewer lines. There were probably too many sherbets in between. She played Nora Helmer and even forgot to leave the family. Dearie me. Why do you ask, by the way?"

"Her son lives above us."

Jesper doesn't know why he is telling her this. It has nothing to do with the matter in hand. Nothing has anything to do with it apart from Trude. She is the matter in hand. He regrets having said what he did. He has said too much. And everything he says is irrelevant. Trude's mother seems both shy and animated.

"Bjørn, yes. He idolised the poor wreck. Apart from that, he's a good-for-nothing, I've heard. If I were you, Jesper, I'd . . ."

Trude's mother doesn't finish what she was saying and washes her hands under the tap.

"What would you do?" Trude asks.

"Keep well away from him."

"Why?"

Now it is Jesper who doesn't want to hear any more. He simply can't bear it. He doesn't want to know all about people. He wants to escape. Fortunately they are interrupted by Trude's father, who stands in the doorway wearing a long coat with a fur collar and carrying a stick. Jesper would never have believed he would be happy to see him. He wants to go back to Trude's room, "Tango for Two" or no.

"I have to pop down for a paper," Herr Hagen says.

Trude's mother goes to her old husband and kisses him on the cheek while drying her hands on her shirt.

"Anything serious?"

"You'd better read the paper tomorrow, darling."

Trude's mother laughs.

"And as usual there'll be nothing."

Herr Hagen pushes her away in a friendly but firm way and turns to Jesper.

"You live in Fagerborg, don't you?"

"Yes, in Gørbitz gate. Actually it's Kirkeveien, but the entrance is in Gørbitz gate."

"Well, then we can walk together up to Solli Plass," Herr Hagen says.

And that is what happens. That is all there is. That is all there is for Jesper. In fact, he is relieved. Trude helps him on with his windcheater and for the second time this evening he is relieved he doesn't have the condoms in his pocket. Ah, there is a little something for Jesper after all. She plants a fleeting kiss on his neck. It isn't a little something. It is a lot. It will keep him going for a while, and some more. Then he hurries after the father. On the slippery pavement his stick sounds like a metronome. They walk side by side to Observatoriegata and around the corner, which is the university library. Jesper doesn't know why, but the dark walls remind him of the war, even though he has no memories of it, apart from a smell that he recognises on the nights when he still falls. It is a mixture of coke and herring. Snow hangs from beneath the street lamps. Trude's father stops by the roundabout in Solli Plass.

"Do you know who the friendliest person is I've ever interviewed?" he asks.

"Ludvig Armsterk."

"Who?"

"Louis Armstrong."

Afred Hagen laughs.

"He was in a good mood, but he wasn't necessarily the friendliest. Great artists rarely are."

"James Dean?"

"No, I haven't interviewed him. But he seems too sullen and introverted. As most young men are nowadays. Don't you think?"

Jesper realises that James Dean is the one he should be envious of. It doesn't help in the slightest that he is already dead.

"What about the Shah of Persia?" he asks.

"He was merely cultured. And that's not always enough either. No, we don't need to go all the way to Persia."

"Stein Eriksen, the skier?"

Alfred Hagen raises his head and is clearly amused. Jesper would rather ask him what a devil's piano is, but doesn't get that far.

"Crown Prince Olav, Jesper. I'm happy to say that the royal family is in good hands. By the way, have you noticed his voice?"

"Not really."

"It's a bit nasal, if you know what I mean, and many people believe that's because his father was Danish. Not at all. Or that he's superior. That's not the reason either."

"What is it then?"

"The salty sea air. Fridtjof Nansen's voice was similar. All the great seafarers talk like that."

Herr Hagen takes out his wallet and gives Jesper two coins. What is he supposed to do with them?

"Money for the tram," he says.

He pats Jesper on the shoulder and walks down Drammensveien. After a few moments he stops and shouts:

"Don't forget the devil's piano!"

Jesper saves the money and walks home. It is good to put a little by for a rainy day. On top of that, he has time to think of everything he is going to say to his mother and they are not trivialities, for example, she should keep her hands out of his bloody pockets. For her part, Maj is trying not to think about everything she is going to say to Jesper. She is sitting in the kitchen doing her bookkeeping. It requires all her concentration and some more. The board is already thinking about next year's bazaar. Next year is soon. There is also talk of giving money to the Hungarian refugees. She looks at the figures. They are big ones. And in red. The Red Cross' figures are red. Being in the red is Maj's nightmare. There isn't enough money. There isn't enough for everything however you spread it. It was easier to bring in money before. It is strange. When you could afford less, you gave more. When you have enough money, you tend to be mean and selfish. She hears Jesper arrive. He is taking a long time. Maybe that is not so surprising. His injured hand is holding him up. She wants to go into the hallway and help him. She closes her ledger and is about to stand up. She doesn't. She waits. Then at last he is standing in the doorway, leaning against the frame, watching her and saying nothing.

"Was it nice?" Maj asks.

Jesper nods.

"You didn't get cold, did you?"

Jesper shakes his head.

"What did you do then?"

"Talked about the Suez Canal."

"The Suez Canal?"

"Yes, the Suez Canal."

"Is it her father who writes in the paper?"

"Yes."

"Are you and Trude—"

Jesper interrupts.

"Jostein didn't give me the packet, if that's what you think, just for your information."

"You bought it yourself then?"

"I was given it by the captain of the handball team."

"Right. Are you hungry? I can—"

"No, thank you."

They both go quiet. The block is silent. Stine has gone to bed. Then there is a terrible racket above their heads. It is as if the ceiling is falling in. Bjørn Stranger must at the very least be pushing a strongbox through the flat. It is quiet again.

"What's a blupper?" Jesper asks.

"A what?"

"A blupper. B-L-U-P-P-E-R."

"No idea. Did Trude call you a blupper?"

"Forget it."

"Don't forget to invite her here one evening. It's your turn."

Jesper is about to ask her what a devil's piano is, but instead he says:

"Should we keep inviting each other for the rest of our lives because it's our turn?"

Maj watches Jesper withdraw, as though he wasn't already with-drawn enough. She leaves him in peace. She can hear him getting on with his own business, quietly so that Stine doesn't wake up. There is no danger of that. Stine can sleep for Norway. Maj opens her ledger again, but can't concentrate on what the numbers are telling her. She is thinking about Jesper falling in love, for he is in love, it isn't hard to see. He walks in a different way; he speaks with a different voice; he looks with different eyes. It is the first time he has fallen in love. He will probably be disappointed, hurt and abandoned, or perhaps he is the one who will disappoint, hurt and abandon, but still his love is refulgent, fragile and untested, light and heavy at the same time, a wind and a passion. On the other hand, Maj's love is spent. It won't shine. It is matt and insensi-tive. She closes her eyes and sees the smoke-filled restaurant at the Bristol. She is no visionary. Only those in love can share the same gaze. She sees him in her mind's eye. Enzo Zanetti, unfortu-nately, cannot avoid noticing the man zigzagging towards him, from the landing where the mortal remains of Dek-Rek's Christmas dinner lie alongside empty envelopes and full ashtrays. It is Didrik Kinck. He is sobering up again, to his horror, and has obvious plans to get as stewed as a prune at least once more this evening. He has set a course for the bar in the distance. The counter is a ship. Ulfsen is standing on the bridge mixing a Balu. There is a long time to go before the last round. There is still time for a Gimpson. The next round is a drop of the hard stuff as a nightcap: the last rites. But on the way there Kinck stops by the piano and places his hand on the shoulder of the lounge pianist, the unpredictable Italian who thinks he is moving gold bars in Fort Knox and not ice cubes and drinks at the Bris.

"You don't by any chance know a brand-new Norwegian tune called 'Tango for Two', do you? Or are you only into opera tonight?"

*

For the bazaar we decided to buy: one lamp in the shape of a globe, one flower table, one set of bathroom scales with a Terylene towel, one cookery book and one cuckoo clock. From the remains of the material we sewed pairs of small dolls we called "tinker kids".

The following morning Jesper jumps up to get the *Aftenposten* before it lands on the mat. He sits on the sofa bed and flicks through it. He finds only articles about the general strike in Hungary, skiing conditions and Christmas shopping, sports results, interviews with Audun Boysen, Emil Zatopek and Egil Danielsen, reviews of Christmas films, the radio programme and readers' letters, but no reports written by Alfred Hagen. There is also an article about civil defence in wartime. The C.D. director says we can rely on our bomb shelters. You just have to know where they are. Otherwise it is mostly obituaries. Most people die in December. If Jesper was about to die, he would do it in October, before the snows arrive, so the gravediggers don't have to shovel snow. He isn't going to die though. He just has to learn to play the piano first. There is nothing about the devil's piano. Maj hurries past, with barely any time to speak, and goes to the bathroom. Soon Stine wakes up and waits for her turn. She is standing in the pantry with the duvet wrapped around her and shaking. It is only now that Jesper notices how cold it is in the flat. He goes into the sitting room and puts two logs on the fire, finds the matches and finally gets them alight. He likes to see the flames through the little window. Soon the heat spreads through the flat. By the time the Kristoffersens have breakfast no-one is cold any longer. Maj has something she is keen to get off her chest. She says it quickly and bluntly, as though asking for another slice of bread.

"Do you mind if I invite Enzo Zanetti over on Christmas Eve?"

Jesper gets up.

"Here? Why?"

"Because he'd be all on his own otherwise."

Jesper sits down. Stine looks at him and seems unhappy.

"Is Trude coming too?" she asks.

"Button it."

Maj smacks the table, but not very hard because at this moment she is on the defensive.

"Don't speak to your sister like that."

Jesper sips his tea.

"Sorry. May I ask my little sister not to poke her nose into my private life?"

They fall quiet. The sound of cutlery is like a symphony. Maj puts down the butter knife again.

"I won't invite him if you two don't want. Just so that is clear."

Jesper looks at his mother as he asks:

"What do you think he would like as a present?"

Then, as usual, they are in a rush. There is a queue for the bathroom again, a traffic jam in the hallway, and space is as tight as in a department-store fitting room. Eventually Jesper sets off for school – it is only around the corner – while Maj and Stine walk together to Majorstua, where they part company. Maj watches her daughter. Why doesn't she meet some girls she can walk the last part with? There are other girls around, the same age, but Stine just walks through them, not with them. Maj catches the tram to the city centre and doesn't know whether to be worried or not. Is there something she should discuss with her? She decides to wait and see. At Dek-Rek there are worries enough anyway. It is nothing less than a funeral march. The boys move around in silence, heads pounding and eyes sunk in concrete. Some have had an Oslo break-fast already. Or else it is bicarbonate of soda, aspirin and a white stick. Rudjord doesn't leave his office. A wise move. If he had, he would have declared himself bankrupt or sold the whole firm to his worst rival. In the break Maj rings Margrethe again. This time she answers and Maj gets straight to the point: Frøken Smith has resigned from the committee of the Fagerborg department of the Oslo Red Cross because she is about to become Fru Smith and for that reason has no time for charity work. No time. Have you ever heard the like? She will hardly be missed. But would Margrethe like to take up the vacant post? She hesitates. She hesitates for so long that Maj becomes impatient.

"Please," she says.

"Surely there are other people you can ask?"

"It might do you good, Margrethe."

The other end of the line is quiet. Maj sees Kinck approaching. He is walking on eggshells, with his hands behind his back. At length Margrethe is there again.

"Do me good? What do you mean?"

"I just mean it would do you good to get out a bit."

"I do get out. I have a garden."

"I mean out out."

"I'll give it some thought."

"Don't think too much."

She has already rung off. Maj wonders what she said wrong. It surprises her. Shouldn't Margrethe be happy to hear this news? Anyway, she has told her. When she looks up, she sees Kinck standing in front of her, still with his hands behind his back and his head bowed. He is extremely ill at ease. He is a tormented man, crucified by remorse and a hangover. His voice is trembling into the bargain.

"May I offer abject apologies for my behaviour yesterday?"

As Maj says nothing, Didrik Kinck is obliged to continue.

"I was boorish, thoughtless and coarse."

"Yes, you were."

Didrik Kinck looks up, grateful that Maj Kristoffersen has deigned to speak to him.

"The worst, however, is that I was unfair."

"No, the worst was your vulgarity."

"Let's agree on that then."

"You can retract stupidities, Kinck, but not stupidity."

He lowers his gaze again.

"Can you not find it in your heart to forgive me?"

"What have you got behind your back?"

"A mere trifle."

Didrik puts a poinsettia on the desk.

Maj eyes him. He is also a sorry sight.

"Do you think you can bribe me?" she asks.

"Pardon? What . . .?"

"Do you think you can say I smell of bed sheets and then come with a plant and pretend that everything is fine afterwards?"

Kinck's eyes wander off.

"If you don't want it, then . . ."

"You haven't answered me, Kinck. Do you really think you can bribe me?"

"No, no, of course not. It . . ."

"Then you're wrong. The plant is beautiful. And I'm gullible."

Maj gets up and pats Kinck on the cheek. He blushes and utters a chuckle, almost a sigh, a sigh of relief.

"So this will remain between us?"

"It'll remain at the Bristol," Maj says.

Didrik Kinck returns unburdened to the design room and continues to study the empty sheet on his drawing board while mixing bicarb with water. At half past one Rudjord appears in the doorway, claps his hands and sends everyone home. They are doing more harm than good here. Best to go home where most accidents occur. That is an order. And by home he means home, not the Bris, not Skalken and definitely not Cordial. Tomorrow is another day. It isn't Christmas until Jesus takes an active part. Maj manages to do some shopping on the way home and she finds a pleated skirt for Stine at Franck's. On the corner of Jacob Aalls and Jonas Reins gate she stops and quickly scans the area as she goes into a telephone box, inserts two krone pieces and calls Enzo Zanetti. She hears the first coin drop as he answers: "Pronto."

"How are you?"

"Hello? Maj? Are you in another town?"

"In a telephone box."

"Is something wrong?"

"I was just wondering if you'd like to spend Christmas Eve with us?"

The other end goes silent. Finally Maj has to ask before the money runs out:

"Are you there?"

He coughs and has apparently lit a cigarette in the meantime.

"Can I sleep on it?"

"Don't oversleep then."

Maj puts down the receiver and hurries homewards. Two thoughts strike her in Gørbitz gate: first, she hopes that no-one in the school playground saw her. After all who would use a public call box if they had a telephone at home? It smacks of something shady. That is what it smacks of. She daren't think about it. And second, perhaps Enzo thought it was someone else ringing, another woman, he probably has lots. She doesn't want to think about that either. Nothing has happened. Yet she feels she is being secretive, furtive. She can still hear Didrik Kinck's words cutting through the perfume and cigar smoke outside the men's toilet at the Bris. *She was covered by Norwegian Ass-ets.* Maj knows what assets he was referring to, but she is no swinger. She doesn't want any presents and throws the poinsettia in the litter bin on the corner. She doesn't want to put Didrik Kinck's guilty conscience on the windowsill. She almost sprints up the stairs and lets herself in. She just catches a glimpse of Jesper and a girl jumping up from the sofa bed in the hall. They are flustered. The girl stands with a smile on her face while Jesper straightens his shirt, seeming to forget his right hand is still badly injured.

"Are you home already?" he asks.

"Apparently so."

"Us too. There was no German lesson. You did say I had to invite—"

"Can't you introduce us?"

Jesper steps aside and points to the girl, as if there was ever any doubt.

"This is Trude. Trude Hagen. We're in the same class."

"Obviously that's not all you have in common. And I'm Maj, Jesper's mother."

Trude passes her hand and curtsies. Still wearing the same smile. There is a self-possession about her, although she looks decent enough otherwise, apart from her hair, which is a mess.

"I'd just like to say that nothing happened," she says.

Maj eyes this girl who seems dishevelled and far too blunt and decides to like her.

"Perhaps you could help me with some baking?"

In the background, Jesper rolls his eyes – which is his place in this context, the background – hoping for the right answer. Unfortunately, it is wrong.

"Of course," Trude says.

Maj hangs up her outdoor clothes, puts Stine's skirt in her bedroom and moves towards the bedside-table drawer to check if the packet is still there. But she doesn't. She takes Trude with her to the kitchen, gives her an apron and they get started. Jesper stands in the pantry watching. This could go on. Yeast is a slow business. In addition, there are: wheat flour, margarine, sugar, cardamom, milk, raisins, currants, salt, candied peel and mustard gas. Then, after a year, you have the famous Hurdal Christmas cake. He should find a refuge shelter as soon as possible. Nevertheless Jesper cannot help but enjoy the sight of Trude and his mother working together over the kitchen worktop. He would never have believed it, but it strikes a chord inside him, a piano key he knew nothing about, maybe it is the C that is supposed to make people cry. Now he knows what chord it was in Trude's room: B minor. It is very strange. Both of them turn to him at once and smile.

"If you're only going to stand around, you can take the rubbish down," Maj says.

Jesper takes the bin, puts on his galoshes and runs down the kitchen stairs. In the yard he meets Bjørn Stranger, who is carrying a plant wrapped up in old newspaper. So this is where the interviews with the Shah of Persia, Olympic champions, Nobel Prize winners and actors end up. Where obituaries also end up, around withered plants and finally in the rubbish bin. That is perhaps handy to know. Soon Jesper won't know what to do with all he knows. Bjørn Stranger stops.

"You can come up and use my telephone," he says.

Jesper shrugs and is cold.

"No need. We've got a phone."

"Does it work?"

"Of course."

Bjørn Stranger runs a hand through his thinning, fair hair.

"That's strange, then."

"Strange? What's strange about it?"

"I saw your mother in a telephone box. I was curious, that's all. Sorry."

Bjørn Stranger goes on his way to the laundry cellar. Jesper considers what Trude's mother said: Keep away from him. But it was Bjørn who saved Jostein's life. Isn't that enough to make him a hero, or at any rate a good person? Should you keep away from a good person even if he has bad sides? Couldn't his name hang on the wall in bronze too? Jesper gives this some thought, or he uses his senses, because his thoughts aren't clear, they are merely the first steps to wonderment: We know no more about one another than what we can see and hear. The rest is in shadow. And the rest is most. We are vaults that cannot be opened. It is actually dispiriting. The dustbin lid is frozen shut. Jesper has to fight to open it and when he does eventually, with one hand, a rat jumps out from the stench, its tail tense and sharp as it brushes against his cheek, before disappearing into a hole in the yellow snow under the verandas. When he returns with the empty bin, Stine is standing by the worktop as well and has flour all over both hands, they are almost luminous. She tosses the fringe from her forehead and hopes it will stay, while he tries to look sullen, introspective and tough, well, tough and sullen is good enough. Trude spins round and sends him a smile, then continues to roll the dough. Jesper is surplus to requirements anyway. He goes into the sitting room, lifts the receiver and hears the dialling tone. He calls Jostein. He doesn't know what to say. It is scary. He doesn't know what to say to his pal, perhaps the only one he has, because Trude is not a pal, nor is Enzo Zanetti, Stine is only his little sister and his mother is his mother. Happy Christmas? The telephone works. Jostein's father picks up. Jostein isn't at home. He is working overtime. Didn't Jesper know they work round the clock at the slaughterhouse before Christmas? Is Jesper working overtime as well, because they don't see a lot of him? Jesper asks him to say hello to Jostein and wish him a happy Christmas. He rings off and stands listening to the laughter in the kitchen. It comes closer. His mother appears in the doorway. She has red cheeks. Bits of dough hang from between her fingers.

"Couldn't you play something for us?" she asks.

"You mean with one hand?"

"That doesn't matter."

"Matter? No, but it'll be bloody difficult."

"Trude asked, by the way."

"How long are you going to keep at it?"

Maj goes over to Jesper and leans towards his ear.

"I like her anyway," she says.

"Anyway?"

"And now you play a bit of piano. It's not four o'clock yet."

Maj has to go back to the kitchen. Jesper opens the sliding doors and sits down at the piano in the dining room. He should be happy. He has everything after all, except a father, but his father hasn't abandoned him for ever, he has only taken a step to the side. However, it was a definitive step, a stride so great that it is still resounding. Perhaps that is why Jesper plays the note with tears in his eyes.

*

We finished sewing the rest of the Red Cross dolls. We had also bought cotton yarn and crocheted all the oven cloths – really nice. Fru Lund taught us a pattern for them. At the last board meeting she told us she had been invited to take part in the annual conference in Stavanger. It is something of an honour for our chairman to be chosen and we are overjoyed.

BLUPPER

It is Christmas Eve. Jostein is in the family shop looking out. Light snow is falling. Soon silence will descend over Oslo and later it will be filled with the peeling of church bells. He is thinking about what he would most like for Christmas. He doesn't want anything. As long he is earning money he doesn't need anything. He takes a decision. He will never make a Christmas wish list. Then Jesper walks past with a present he is trying to hide in his pocket. When he was walking the opposite way, towards Majorstua, and it is beginning to be a while ago now, he had no present. Jostein rushes out and stops him.

"What have you been given?"

"What makes you think I've been given something?"

"Haven't you?"

"I might be giving someone something."

"Is it for me?"

Jesper looks down at the heavy pitch-seamed boots he is wearing today.

"No."

"I don't want anything."

"That's good."

Jostein laughs and stares at Jesper. There is something different about him or is it because they have drifted so far apart that he can't see clearly? It could also be the snow.

"You're not giving a present to someone."

"How come?"

"You wouldn't have stuffed it in your pocket like that."

Jesper shrugs.

"I haven't opened it yet."

"Who's it from?"

"Trude."

"Probably a sweater she's knitted."

"A sweater? Toddler size or what?"

"Or a scarf. Or gloves."

"Or mittens. I'll tell you when I've opened it."

Now Jostein knows what it is about Jesper.

"What are you up to actually?" he asks.

Jesper wants to walk on by, but there isn't enough room. Jostein is everywhere.

"Up to? Nothing. What do you mean?"

"However hard you try, it won't work."

"I'm not trying to do anything, am I?"

"Combing your hair and looking cool. You're a blupper."

Jesper stops in his tracks.

"What did you say, Melsom?"

Jostein, a little gentler:

"Blupper."

"Talk Norwegian, will you? Or did you learn that up at the deaf school?"

Jostein bursts into loud laughter.

"Don't you know what a blupper is?"

Jesper chances his arm.

"A vegetarian."

"A mummy's boy."

"Piss off."

Jesper feels like pulling his hair down over his forehead or punching someone, such as Jostein. But Jesper is no fighter, and on top of that he is injured, or at least he was. He just pushes Jostein away and lopes up Kirkeveien, upset. Jostein follows him.

"I didn't mean it, Jesper."

"Piss off."

"I didn't mean it," Jostein repeats.

Jesper has no choice but to stop to get rid of him.

"Have you recovered all your hearing or what?"

"A blupper is a well-dressed West End kid."

"Well dressed?"

"Grey trousers with a crease and an ironed shirt."

If this is correct, Jesper can live with it, not very comfortably, but he will survive.

"Am I wearing grey trousers with a crease and an ironed shirt?"

"Compared with the petrolheads who live in Oslo East, wear leather jackets and ride mopeds with their hair greased back, yes."

"How do you know?" Jesper asks.

Jostein blows out his cheeks and produces two packets. One is small and flat; the other small and square.

"I know stuff too. You're not the only one."

Jostein gives the presents to Jesper, who hardly dares meet his eyes now.

"I haven't got anything for you," he says.

Jostein laughs and prods him.

"It doesn't matter. You haven't got a job anyway. It's the least I could do."

They shuffle around without saying anything. Jesper wonders for a moment whether he should ask him what a devil's piano is, as Jostein appears to be omniscient on Christmas Eve, but refrains.

Then they shake hands and say Happy Christmas instead, like two old Fagerborg gentlemen.

When Jesper arrives home, Stine has set the table in the dining room while Maj is busy in the kitchen cooking. Stine has set four places. She has also laid a red plaid rug over her bed to make it look like a sofa. Jesper places Jostein's presents under the tree, which is in the other room with eight electric candles dotted around the lonesome forest. Afterwards he goes into the bathroom where he changes into a white shirt, grey trousers and a jacket. He regards himself in the mirror. Yes, he is a blupper, he is a real blupper. Jostein was right. Trude was right too. There is no doubt about it.

Jesper is not only a blupper, he is a poof, a mummy's pet. He might just as well take a comb and part his hair at the side in one straight white line, once and for all. He doesn't have a hope. Or a moped. He pulls off the bandage, then the sling, he can't be bothered with it anymore. His hand flops down, heavy and pale. Then he opens Trude's present. It is a scarf, a black scarf she knitted herself. He can wear it as a sling or hang himself with it. He throws it around his neck and ventures a glance in the mirror. It helps a little. It gives him something, what he doesn't know, but something. Jesper has to decide what it is that the scarf gives him. It gives him *something else*. He can wear it when he plays the piano if he can ever play again. After all he has to play on May 17th. His name is already on the programme: *Jesper Kristoffersen: Sæverud's "Ballad of Revolt". Piano solo*. He'll wear the black scarf on May 17th. He raises his lifeless hand. It is as though the fingers aren't his anymore. There is a ring at the door. Has Enzo Zanetti come so early? Is he running on Italian time today? Jesper forgets to remove the scarf and goes into the hall, where his mother has already opened the door with Stine waiting behind her. It isn't Enzo Zanetti. It is Bjørn Stranger.

"I have something I'd like to show you," he says.

Maj takes a step back and keeps the door open in such a way that he can't pass.

"What's that?"

"I'd particularly like to show it to Jesper."

"We're busy. It's Christmas Eve."

"Of course. It won't take a second. But you have to come up to my flat."

Maj reacts in the same way that Jesper did a moment ago. You have to acquiesce in order to liberate yourself. It is wearing, but necessary. Stine holds her hand. Jesper brings up the rear. They follow Bjørn Stranger. He is wearing a dark suit that is much too tight. The flat on the floor above is still as bare and empty. On the walls there are the light patches where Halfdan and Margrethe Vik had pictures hanging. But when Bjørn Stranger shows them the sitting room they understand what he means. In the middle there is a piano, and not just any piano, it is a Steinway. Maj and Stine turn to Jesper who has stopped in the doorway. They haven't noticed the scarf until now, or that the sling has gone. He looks like someone else. That is the point. They say nothing. It is Bjørn Stranger who speaks.

"Wouldn't you like to try, Jesper?"

Jesper hesitates for so long that his mother answers.

"Of course he would."

Jesper walks over to the piano and sits down. He rests his left hand gently on the keys, without pressing, then the right. He can barely lift it, so swollen are the fingers, and white. They are hard to move. He tries a bass note. The sound is clean and full. He imagines that no-one has played this piano before, not even the tuner. Jesper is the first. He is inaugurating the piano. He plays the Polish interval signal, which is a bar from Chopin's C minor "Revolutionary Étude" and uses his left hand for the melody and the right for chords. Sometimes he crosses hands and plays back to front. He adds and subtracts. He has never done this before. A sound that hasn't existed before emerges. When he has finished, Bjørn Stranger is standing by the window and crying. Jesper feels ashamed and jumps up. Everyone is ill at ease. There is little that is as intimate as tears, regardless of whether they are occasioned by sorrow or happiness. But what Maj notices is that the damaged plant on the windowsill behind Bjørn Stranger is a poinsettia.

"You can practise here any time you like," he says.

Jesper goes over to his mother and Stine. Silence reigns, which unnerves them all, as the crying did. Then Bjørn Stranger blows his nose good and hard.

"Sorry. I'm so easily moved."

He gives another snort and there is silence again.

"Are you going to Olaf and Margrethe's tonight?" Maj asks.

Bjørn Stranger just looks at her as he folds his handkerchief into a compact square. Then he shifts his gaze to Jesper.

"Well, what do you say?"

"We've got a piano," he says.

"Not as good as this one, though. I think I've heard a few bum notes downstairs recently."

Jesper shrugs with only one shoulder; the one on the right is weighed down by the heavy hand. He looks as if he is about to keel over.

"I've got a bad hand."

"But it's better now, isn't it?"

"A little."

"You can have a key and come and go as you wish."

Maj takes Stine's hand. It is her plant in the window. Didrik Kinck's appeasement is in Bjørn Stranger's flat. She doesn't want to be here any longer.

"That's very kind of you, but—"

Bjørn Stranger suddenly directs his gaze at her.

"Why did you ask?"

"About what?"

"If I was going *there*?"

"You're dressed up."

"I'm going to work."

"On Christmas Eve?"

"Someone has to."

"Then we won't disturb you any further."

Maj pushes Stine and Jesper ahead of her and doesn't let them out of her sight until they are safely downstairs. What sort of work does Bjørn Stranger have, and on Christmas Eve? Enzo Zanetti arrives at exactly five o'clock, Norwegian time. He says he is happy to see that Jesper has removed the sling and the bandage. He also says the food is delicious, he can't remember ever tasting anything as good, especially the sauerkraut. Stine has to look away to hide her giggles. Otherwise Enzo Zanetti is reticent and careful. Only on one occasion does he become heated and talk without a break. That is when Jesper, against Maj's wishes, tells Enzo about the piano in

Bjørn Stranger's flat, it was like playing on velvet, almost automatic. Then Enzo Zanetti talks about *resistance*. An instrument has to offer resistance so that there is a struggle between the piano and the pianist. The pianist must never believe it is easy. Wilhelm Kempff, the great Beethoven interpreter, who plays on the finest grand pianos in the world, reverts twice a year to his childhood piano, a wretched Blüthner, so as not to forget resistance. Whatever comes easily, goes easily. It just comes and goes. That's why Jesper has to turn his injured hand to his advantage. Soon the most beautiful music will flow from those acoustic fingers of his. Enzo Zanetti is drinking wine with his food.

"Let me see them," he says at last.

Jesper lays the pale hand on the tablecloth and tries to spread his fingers. Enzo strokes them gently again and again until you can see the blood pumping beneath the skin.

After eating they open the presents: a bar of perfumed soap, a pencil case, a metronome, a pleated skirt, a tie, a globe, a pair of pyjamas, a tie clip and a suspender belt set. Stine has a jewellery box from Jostein, with nothing inside. Now she is on the verge of tears. But Jesper gets a wallet and it is just as empty. He tries to explain that Jostein thinks they have to earn the money and the jewels themselves. That is how it is, at least according to Jostein. Enzo Zanetti leaves early. He has a job with Herberth's travelling circus show, accompanying Karin Hox. They are heading north the very next day, all the way to Bodø, and will be entertaining audiences from there down to Oslo. So he will put all three of them down as guests for the show. What about Jesper? What is he going to do in the meantime? He should read the music so carefully that he dreams about the "Ballad of Revolt" every single night. Then they can practise it in February, put the finishing touches to it in March and elevate it to new heights in April. Maj stands by the window as Enzo Zanetti leaves. Is she the one who's is making him feel ill at ease, restless, and sending him off on a tour with Karin Hox? She has seen pictures of her in *Norsk Dameblad*. She is young and dark-haired and has big earrings. They will be staying at the same boarding houses. Maj knows what will happen. Enzo Zanetti is a silver fox who can charm even the smallest birds down from the trees. She is ashamed. She forgot to devote a thought to Ewald this evening. She forgot to open a present for him. She is so deeply ashamed. She doesn't know what has got into her. And this on Christmas Eve. Yes, she does. It is the scar that has opened up again. The matt surface is cracking and glistening. The wound is more attractive than the scar. For a moment she thinks Enzo has changed his mind and turned back. Then at length he emerges from the entrance. He isn't alone. He is with Bjørn Stranger, who is carrying a small, black bag. They have a brief conversation in Gørbitz gate, look up at the window where Maj is standing, doff their hats and leave in separate directions, Enzo Zanetti around the corner to Kirkeveien, Bjørn Stranger towards Jacob Aalls gate. When Bjørn turns there is no longer a soul to be seen anywhere. Light and sound are also shut up inside flats, which contain the life whence the city derives its power. It is only half past eight. It has stopped snowing everywhere in the world. He continues through Stens Park, past the church and the public urinal and down to Bislet. The Olympic rings still hang above the entrance. If you listen carefully you can hear the applause rising slowly from the empty stands around the shining ice-bound track. Bjørn Stranger walks between the tramlines with his eyes closed. Nothing is gone for ever. Everything lasts, even if it is just fragments and shadows: applause, cheering, clapping and laughing. Then he bears right by Oscars gate and eventually reaches Grønnegata 19. This is his destination. He hangs his winter clothes in the porch, tidies the slippers so that they are in pairs, chooses one, puts down his bag and carries on into the lounge. There are twelve men sitting there. Holding cups of coffee in both hands. They look very similar to one another. They are wearing their best clothes. As mentioned before, it is Christmas Eve. Red Cross parcels are under the tree. They didn't want to open them until Bjørn was there.

"Where's Walter?" he asks.

Hilmar points to the ceiling. The others nod.

"Has he been drinking?"

Hilmar shakes his head.

Bjørn Stranger fetches his bag, goes up the stairs to the first floor and along the corridor, where the doors are ajar, in some cases wide open. In one room two women are sitting with their hands in their laps. They seem to be praying. Bjørn Stranger stops. They raise their gaze and shake their heads, then look down again. They are not praying. They are cursing. One shouts: *Come and see to us too, Doctor.* Bjørn Stranger continues. At the end the door is closed. He knocks. To no avail. He enters the room. It is narrow with a bed against each wall, two bedside tables, two lamps and a desk in front of the window where the curtains are drawn. No personal effects are visible, only a shirt and suit jacket, which have been thrown on the floor, like an accident, Bjørn thinks, and these items of clothing aren't personal either, they are from flea markets. The only personal effects here are memories and there are fewer and fewer of those. Walter is lying in the bed on the right, with his back to Bjørn, in black trousers, braces and a singlet, huddled up like a child. Bjørn Stranger sits on the edge of the bed.

"Have you been dreaming again?" he asks.

Eventually the answer is forthcoming.

"You dream. I don't."

"What happened?"

"You can't see them, boy. You can't see them. They rush through the water. And they all climb towards the prow. And they all die."

"But you're alive, Walter."

Walter starts crying. Bjørn rolls him over gently so that he is on his back. He is emaciated. The stench of sweat fills his nostrils. His eyelids are blue and swollen. His face is chapped. His voice is barely audible from between cracked lips.

"Alive? Is this a life?"

Bjørn Stranger opens the little bag, takes out a stethoscope and listens to Walter. His heart is beating softly and irregularly. It is not going to give out just yet. His lungs are not providing a lot of air, but they will still last for a while. Bjørn Stranger tightens the rubber cuff around Walter's thin upper arm that starts with a tattoo on his shoulder: an anchor. His blood pressure is too high. It is the only thing about him that is. Walter was born in 1922 and was eighteen when war broke out. He is only six years older than Bjørn Stranger, yet they stand on opposite sides of nightmares and it is impossible for one to understand the other's pain. Then Bjørn Stranger taps parts of Walter's body, mostly for show. He knows what he will find. When he reaches the liver and stomach a twitch goes through Walter. Bjørn Stranger removes his hand and Walter calms down.

"It is indeed," Bjørn Stranger says.

"What?"

"A kind of life, despite everything. Don't you think?"

Walter starts to laugh. It turns into a cough.

"You're not a proper doctor, you aren't."

"Oh, why do you think that?"

"You don't wash your hands first."

Bjørn Stranger packs up his things and closes the bag.

"Shall we go downstairs?"

"You go, Doctor."

"I think you should come with me. They're waiting."

"I'll just ruin the atmosphere."

"You don't need to worry about that."

"It can't be that bad."

Bjørn Stranger picks up the clothes and gives them to Walter.

"Anyway, you're needed," he says.

"Needed?"

"If you don't come we won't be able to make a circle around the tree."

"Surely it's not that difficult, is it?"

"We need two hands, to be precise."

"I'm shaking. Can't you see?"

Walter shows him his hands. They are not good. He has nerves under his nails. If he cuts his nails he is a dead man. Bjørn Stranger mixes a pill in the glass of water on the bedside table. The water clouds up as though white sand is swirling up from the base. Walter drinks it, closes his eyes and breathes out. Bjørn Stranger waits for a few moments. Then he gets Walter to sit up, helps him on with his shirt and jacket, and parts his hair with a shiny comb. They walk down together to the lounge. No-one looks up. The coffee has gone cold. They open the presents. There is one for each of them. The Red Cross parcel contains sugar, butter, prunes, spiced sausage, biscuits and a twist of tobacco. They have to dance around the Christmas tree. It takes time for the men to stand up properly. Bjørn Stranger is between Walter and Finnen. First he holds Finnen's hand and then he closes his fingers around Walter's hand and sends him a smile. Isn't this what he said? If you don't come, we won't make it around the tree. The circle is finally closed. The men, the homeless, sing "Fair Is Creation" as they begin to move in a circle, like the children they once were.

The board had its first meeting at Marie Endresen's. Fru Lund, the chairman, presented the applications of two women, both of whom live in Grønnegata 19, strangely enough. One, Fru Solveig Jensen, is in Aker Hospital at this time. The other, Fanny Hammer, uses strangely high-handed language and sets out conditions for the clothes, colours etc she would like and states that she doesn't want any home visits either. Nevertheless Fru Lund and Fru Endresen will go to see her to form a better picture of her. She may be somewhat off her chump.

We have provisionally decided to make the following small items for the autumn tombola: dolls' aprons, plastic cuff protectors, clothes hangers for children and adults, oven cloths, paper candle holders, possibly plastic bags to keep underwear in, balloons, and we filled rag dolls with all the cotton we had to hand.

Finished off with a cup of coffee.

THE FALLEN

Jesper has been sent an appointment for the last Friday in January, at 1.15 p.m., in the neurology department of the Rikshospital. Maj doesn't understand why. She has to reread the letter to be sure. After all, his hand has almost healed. He can play the piano with it, as well as before, at any rate she can't hear any difference and he hasn't complained at all. On top of everything else, they will both have to ask for time off to attend the inconvenient appointment. She calls Dr Lund to ask what it might be about. At first Dr Lund seems evasive, which is not at all like him, and says that it is a purely routine examination, nothing else. Maj is petrified and has to sit down, but can't keep still. This isn't something hereditary from Ewald, is it? That awful cancer? Dr Lund can assure her that it is not. What is it then? It is a long time since Jesper wet himself. He has been grown up for a long time. Now let's take things one at a time, Dr Lund says. One thing at a time is even more frightening. It means that we can't bear the things if they all come at once. Maj hangs up and immediately she knows what it is: this has something to do with Jesper's falling incidents. But that is a long time ago too. Jesper definitely hasn't said anything. She can't remember the last time he talked about it. She writes a note to the school saying that Jesper has to leave at 12.30 the following Friday because of a hospital appointment and gives it to him straight after dinner, while he is doing his German homework, or pretending to at least, because actually what he is swotting up on in the windowless hallway is the music for the "Ballad of Revolt".

"Friday? Not for a week, more or less," Jesper says.

Maj nods.

"It's best if we give them advance notice."

Jesper reads the note again and looks up at his mother.

"We?"

"Yes. Of course I'll—"

"Don't you think I can find my own way there? Eh?"

"Please, Jesper, don't say 'eh'."

"Don't you think I can find my own way there?"

"I'm sure you can. But I'd like to be with you anyway."

"And what if I say you can't?"

"Then I'd say it's not up to you. And that's final."

Strangely enough, Jesper doesn't have any more complaints. Perhaps he simply wants someone with him. Maj feels such tenderness for her son, not that she hasn't before, but at this moment it is almost too much. He says:

"Then let's meet at Bislet. Not outside the school. Alright?"

"Come home first and drop off your satchel."

"I haven't got a satchel. I've got a bag. Get that into your head."

"Drop your bag off and we can go together to the hospital."

That night Jesper lies awake. It may be the first time he has thought about death in this way, as a frightening fact: he is ephemeral, he is transient, he, too, will die and have his own plot of land, like his father. He will be divisible by zero. Zero is the worst of all. It might happen as soon as tomorrow. It might happen on Friday. It might happen in sixty years or a hundred. But it will happen. It is certain. What good is a plot of land if you can't enjoy it? Others will have to tend it. Perhaps they won't be bothered. Jesper isn't scared. He is merely filled with a sorrow so great that soon there will be no more room for it. He will leave Fagerborg. He will leave Trude too. Death means breaking up for good. They can die at the same time. That is probably the best. But does she love Jesper enough for that? This is like a novel, or a film. Jesper takes stock of himself. Is he falling now? Is he falling backwards into the darkness and landing in the wet marsh? He isn't falling. He is standing. He is lying. He sits up and listens: only the normal sounds of the building – the water, the electricity, the plaster crumbling somewhere in the stairwell. Now he knows the stage name he will use if he ever gets that far: Alf Iversen. Anyone who is anyone has a nickname: Duke, Count, Satchmo, Empress, Hjallis the speed skater and Sputnik. Jesper will be known as Alf Iversen. It will be on the poster. Then he falls asleep. It is like this every night. In the meantime, the days pass. Jesper merely follows. He says nothing of the impending hospital visit to Trude. He will shoulder this alone. It is a sort of pleasure to burn inside with this, with the agony. He becomes bad-tempered and unapproachable. He becomes sullen and hard. He becomes almost overbearing. He is gripped by a haughty indifference. On Friday morning Maj wakes him up early so that he won't forget that he mustn't have any breakfast. The hospital letter said he should fast, in other words, that he should have an empty stomach. This is serious. Stine wants to come along as well. Jesper puts his foot down. Is the whole of the Kristoffersen family going to turn up at the neurology department? Who is actually ill in this house? Out of the question. The person who is sick decides. It's bad enough with Mamma.

"You're not sick," Maj says.

"Why am I going to hospital then?"

"Off you go, you two, so you won't be late."

Jesper slings the bag over his shoulder and Stine follows him. Maj stands at the window and sees him give his little sister a hug. She doesn't seem to want to let go, then he sets off, but changes his mind at the last moment as though he is stumbling at the starting blocks, of course you can't run with a bag, you can with a satchel on your back, but not a bag. He walks slowly, with long, somehow reluctant, strides, that is the point about the bag, you mustn't run, you have to stroll, with the bag over your shoulder, and he has all the time in the world up to the corner by Jacob Aalls gate, where Trude is waiting for him, while Stine walks down towards Majorstua, alone on her side of Kirkeveien. Maj waves to both of them, even when neither of them can see her anymore. Then the telephone rings. She nearly tears the receiver from the cradle. Is it Rudjord to say she has to go in anyway? Dek-Rek can't manage without Maj Kristoffersen. Or is it from the hospital? Does Jesper have to prepare for admission and take a toothbrush and his homework? Is it Enzo ringing from some godforsaken town to say he will never return? The telephone guards its secret until someone grasps the receiver and opens the signals' bouquet. It is only Fru Lund.

"I thought you'd be at home."

"Ah, it's you. How did you know?"

"You have to take Jesper to hospital, don't you?"

"Yes, I do. Ugh."

"You'll be fine. Listen, Fru Endresen can't go with me to Grønnegata today. She's in bed with gastric flu, the poor thing, so could you come to mine instead?"

"I don't know. Jesper—"

"I'd prefer not to walk alone to that place, Maj. And we can make it easily before one."

And that is what they do. Actually Maj is happy not to walk on her own with her mind running riot. She is generally on edge. Not only about Jesper, but about Stine too. She is also worried about herself. This isn't like her. She no longer knows what is like her. They meet an hour later outside the chemist in Majorstua and walk together down Bogstadveien. There is a sale on at Franck's and they have enough time to stop for a moment to wonder at the prices, but they both agree that sales can leave you out of pocket. The conductor on the Disen tram gets off at the bend and switches the points so that passengers don't end up in Holtet instead of Oslo East station. A fine mess that would be. He doffs his peaked cap and warmly greets the ladies. Fru Lund links arms with Maj and they laugh like young girls. Was it really them he was flirting with, the cheeky chappie? If so, he has made their day, and maybe the following one too. They hurry past the Homansbyen gardens and down to dismal Grønnegata, which lies diagonally between the evenly grey facades of the blocks where remnants of Christmas still hang in the windows, the last faded star that refuses to fall. It is as though time has stood still in this cramped zone behind the shops and bakeries and can't quite struggle free. But Grønnegata finishes with a brilliant flourish, number 19, which is an old timber construction, a country residence, the so-called Lassonhuset, where the Krogh family lived, all artists, the father and the daughters, who also painted, played the lute, drank, smoked cigarettes and swore. Now they don't live there anymore, they are dead, they have their plot of land elsewhere and the homeless have moved into the shadows of bohemian living. These people have a title that no-one says aloud, but everyone thinks, *the fallen*, because most know that the occupants of Grønnegata 19 will never rise again, however much the Red Cross believe they will, and it is a good belief to have, they live well off it. Fru Lund and Maj remove their winter clothing in the porch. There is a stale smell emanating from the clothes hanging there: coats, scarves, reefer jackets and Icelandic sweaters. No-one welcomes them although they are expected. It is ten o'clock. They are punctual too. They enter the lounge. The men are sitting at small tables playing cards. They don't let the women disturb their concentration. From a distance they can see that charity is arriving. They would like the presents, but otherwise they would prefer to have nothing to do with charity. Fru Lund coughs and smiles. Maj stays in the background. Walter gets up and goes over to them. His hands aren't shaking today. He is a gentleman. Fanny Hammer is in her room on the first floor, number 11. Solveig Jensen has been to Ullevål Hospital and may return during the course of the day. Should he accompany the ladies? It isn't necessary. Walter turns.

"We should say thank you for the Christmas presents, shouldn't we?" he says.

The men raise their gazes from the cards, nod and mumble something, then continue playing. They have tobacco and chocolate in the kitty. Maj follows Fru Lund up the stairs. She suddenly feels unsafe. She has never felt anything like it. She is afraid. What she is afraid of she doesn't know. Is she afraid that the men, the poor men, will attack her? She is ashamed, but still keeps a firm hold on her handbag. Fru Lund knocks on the door of number 11 and opens it before she hears a response. A woman is sitting in an armchair by the window. She is wearing only a brown dressing gown. Her hair is lank, unwashed and uncombed. Everything about her could do with some care and attention. She appears to be asleep, with her chin resting on her chest. There is a strong smell of sleep in the whole room, not unlike that of the clothes in the porch. Sleep is the night's overcoat. Fru Lund shudders and keeps her gloves on.

"Frøken Hammer?"

Frøken Hammer sleeps like a cat, with only one eye closed.

"And you are?"

"We come from the Fagerborg department of the Oslo Red—"

Frøken Hammer interrupts with a more hospitable tone this time.

"Have you brought what you promised?"

"That's precisely what we'd like to talk to you about."

Frøken Hammer is immediately testy again.

"There's nothing to talk about."

"Yes, there is. Firstly, we haven't promised anything. We've received your application and it's—"

"Just give me the money and I'll get what I need myself."

Fru Lund shakes her head and smiles.

"And secondly, I'm afraid that's not how we work, Frøken Hammer."

"No, you want me to grovel on my knees, so grateful that I'm crying my eyes out with pure happiness."

"Not at all. We don't ask for gratitude or any other sacrifices from your side."

"And how come only the men get tobacco for Christmas? Don't you think that we women also need a drag now and then?"

"We'd only like to see if your needs are appropriate," Fru Lund says.

Frøken Hammer bursts into laughter, her chest gurgles and the laughter soon mutates into a deep, tight cough. She doubles up in the armchair, but when Maj goes to help her she is shoved away. No-one is allowed to get close to Frøken Hammer, and definitely not the Fagerborg department of the Oslo Red Cross. She looks up, her face aflame, then the fire goes out.

"If your needs are appropriate! I ask you."

Fru Lund takes out a handkerchief, which she holds over her mouth.

"All I'm trying to say is that we have to know who we're supporting, Frøken Hammer."

"Take a good look at me and assess my needs!"

Frøken Hammer places one leg over the chair arm in such a way that her dressing gown opens to reveal pale, stained thighs and a stomach with rolls of fat that hang down to her crotch. Fru Lund steps back and almost trips. She drops her handkerchief, but doesn't bother to pick it up. Maj has to grab her. At that moment the door opens. It is Bjørn Stranger, accompanied by Solveig Jensen, the other woman in the house. They bring with them a waft of tobacco and cold air. Frøken Hammer puts down her leg and wraps her dressing gown around her.

"It's good you've come, Doctor. We have unwanted visitors here."

Frøken Jensen slips into bed while Bjørn Stranger runs his fingers through his hair, his gaze flitting from one to the other and resting on Maj, who gives an imperceptible nod. He is about to speak. Fru Lund grasps the door before anyone has a chance to close it and says:

"We have what we need to know."

Frøken Hammer goes to stand up, but cannot manage it.

"You two haven't got anything you need to know," she almost shouts.

Fru Lund smiles.

"Oh, yes, we do. Thank you."

She lets Maj pass and they walk very slowly down the stairs so that no-one can say they couldn't wait to get out. They find their coats where they left them. Walter comes over and wants to make a good impression again, but by then they are already in Grønnegata and don't stop until they are in the safety of Hegdehaugsveien. They enter Sim. Solberg's cake shop and occupy a table in the corner, but first both have to go to the toilet and wash their hands. You never know what you might have touched, even wearing gloves. Finally they sit down, order coffee and breathe a sigh of relief.

"You weren't exactly much help, my friend," Fru Lund says.

"I didn't know what to—"

"It was good to have you there anyway. My God, what people."

The waiter comes with the coffee and fills their cups. He has also brought some gingerbread biscuits. They are on the house. In this part of town clearly there is no end to Christmas. Maj isn't hungry.

"How do you end up like that?" she says.

"Well, I'll tell you."

Fru Lund takes a few sheets of paper from her handbag, lays them on the table and reads aloud.

"Fanny Hammer, born in 1921—"

A gasp escapes Maj.

"Isn't she older?"

Fru Lund laughs.

"Younger than us, Maj. Perhaps it's that we are unusually well preserved?"

"Perhaps."

Maj sips her coffee, which is lukewarm and thin, but after the war all coffee tastes better. She doesn't like the tone of Fru Lund, who continues to read.

"Born in 1921 in Kristiansand, moved to Oslo in 1936 and went into service in the house of wholesaler Alm in Skillebekk, got a job as a cook on board a ship in 1947, came ashore, it says here, in 1951, had various posts as a house help, also worked for a time in the canteen at Aker Mekaniske Verksted, but was homeless from 1953, until she was given a room in Grønnegata 19. She has also contracted certain diseases. I won't say any more."

Fru Lund puts the sheets back into her handbag and glances around quickly, but mostly for appearance's sake.

"And this of course is highly confidential."

Maj nods, holding her coffee cup with both hands.

"Where does it actually go wrong for such a person?" she asks.

Fru Lund looks up.

"Where? Do you think it's one single step out of line? Do you think everything's the result of bad luck and fate?"

"I don't know. It might not be only her fault."

"It's nice to have such faith in humanity, Maj."

"What do you think?"

"I think she went to too many parties. I think she took too many steps out of line. I think she's a bad person."

"But she did at least try."

"Try what?"

"To get some order in her life."

Fru Lund puts down her cup and stares at Maj.

"Then I'll leave it to you to make the decision."

"Which one?"

"Whether to provide Frøken Fanny Hammer with blankets, shoes and bed linen."

Maj summons up her courage and says:

"Yes, I think we should."

"So you're willing to take the risk?"

"Risk? We don't have anything to lose, do we?"

"We don't, no. Apart from the Red Cross' reputation and trust in it. But others who are suffering real deprivation and are maybe slightly more grateful have something to lose, namely blankets, shoes and bed linen. We don't have enough for everyone. Accordingly, we have to make a choice."

Maj raises her cup and sets it down again.

"I don't think we should demand too much gratitude from those who are already down."

Fru Lund smiles and appears amused.

"Besides she might sell the goods we give her on the black market and buy tobacco and alcohol with the money, or waste it."

Maj sticks to her guns.

"That's the risk we have to take."

"Then I'll write in the report that it was your decision."

Maj feels like banging the table.

"There's a limit to how far we can scrutinise those suffering hardship," she says.

Fru Lund smiles again.

"You've clearly learned the odd thing or two working at Dek-Rek."

Maj looks down and feels an urge to stand up and leave. She has other things on her mind.

"I don't know. I just think it's a shame . . ."

Fru Lund takes her hand and squeezes it.

"You're quite right, Maj. It's not our job to judge. The higher authorities will have to take care of that. Naturally I'll write the decision is unanimous."

"I'm happy to hear that."

"And it's true that Fanny Hammer is not right in the head."

"I also agree with that."

Fru Lund lets go of her hand.

"And now let's enjoy ourselves. We've earned it."

They sit for a while without speaking. Neither of them is at ease. A horse trots past the window towards Hegdehaugsveien, it is one of the last, a nag, head lowered, making for Sankthanshaugen to die there. The snow is turning to slush before it lands and streams down the tramlines in thin, dirty rivulets. Fru Lund takes out the green, lined journal for the Fagerborg department of the Norwegian Red Cross in Oslo, in which all the reports, from and including 1947, are kept. She has brought along a pencil as well. She likes to have everything in order. Maj lets Fru Lund work in peace, until she breaks off and asks:

"By the way, isn't this where Margrethe Vik got married?"

"Yes, it is. They had the reception here."

"In a cake shop. But I suppose that's how it is when you re-marry. You don't make a big thing of it."

Maj studies her hand and suddenly catches sight of a flat, black insect crawling between her fingers. She tries to shake it off.

"They'd both lost their partners," she says.

"Yes, yes. I'm sure it was all very proper."

The insect won't let go. She has to use her serviette.

"Yes, it was."

"Incidentally, that boy, or rather that man, isn't he the son who lives above you?"

"Yes, he is. Bjørn Stranger."

"Is he really a doctor?"

"He studied medicine at any rate. And he saved Jostein's life when he was knocked down by a bus."

"But he didn't finish his studies, did he?"

"He might have finished them while he was abroad."

"Did you know he was working in Grønnegata?"

"No, I know hardly anything about him. He keeps himself to himself. But do you know what? He's bought himself a grand piano and he says Jesper can practise on it."

"Surely you don't want him to, do you?"

Maj puts down the serviette and cannot refrain from asking:

"Has Per Fredrik said anything about Jesper?"

Fru Lund looks up in surprise.

"My dear, you know he can't do that. He's taken the Hippocratic Oath. He could lose his licence. He could be arrested."

Maj shakes her head.

"I didn't mean that. I just . . ."

Fru Lund leans across the table.

"But I can certainly tell you that he's said Jesper is very sensitive."

"Does he have to go to hospital because of that?"

"Per Fredrik always does what's best for the patients, Maj."

"I don't doubt that."

Fru Lund laughs.

"Except when he tells them to run ten thousand metres at Frogner stadium. And now I'll have to finish the report, so we can put this tart behind us."

Yours truly and Maj Kristoffersen paid a call on Grønnegata 19 today to hear Fanny Hammer's side of the matter regarding her application for support. The board is, as we know, not wild about her peremptory tone. We can confirm that she didn't show herself from a better side, rather the contrary. The meeting with her was not a pleasant experience, not to put too fine a point on it. Nevertheless, we saw a person in great need, physically and mentally. Fanny Hammer is one of those poor souls we like to call "the fallen". Our support might perhaps put firm ground beneath her feet, at least temporarily. We therefore recommend that the board grants her application.

Jesper is allowed to leave school at lunchtime, or he can wait until the next break, which would easily give him enough time as well. But it is a question of finding the right moment. He has understood that. He would like to attract a certain amount of attention, not too much, just enough. The right moment is now. Jesper packs his bag, throws it over his shoulder, nonchalantly, that is his motto, *play it cool*, hands his mother's note to Ramm and makes for the door. Herr Ramm turns to him.

"And what do we say?"

"What?"

"When you leave in the middle of a German lesson?"

Jesper bows.

"Alf Iversen," he says.

Jesper hears the class laughing as he closes the door and stands in the empty corridor where the clothes hooks now remind him of Oslo Slaughterhouse. The coats resemble abandoned carcasses with the intestines removed and while he is searching for his windcheater the hooks start moving, faster and faster. They glide, as though on a rusty conveyor belt towards the bristle remover and the boiling vats: not death, but life. The door opens again and Trude comes out with the dry sponge in her hand.

"Jesper?"

Everything stops at that moment and he has to lean against the wall.

"What's the matter, Jesper?"

"I have to go to the Retch, Spit and Ail."

"Where?"

"To the Rikshospital."

Trude goes closer, but she isn't laughing.

"Are you ill?"

"Not that I know of. But perhaps the doctor knows something I don't."

"Is that why you've been so down in the mouth recently?"

Down in the mouth? Jesper doesn't want to be down in the mouth. He wants to be hard and sullen and have a rich internal life. But how can you know if you have a rich internal life? How was that supposed to manifest itself? At any rate he doesn't want to be down in the mouth. That is the last thing he wants to be. Who wants to be down in the mouth? Down in the mouth is for dunces, deadbeats and milkmen. Down in the mouth is for the National Theatre and the Hansen bakery. Out of habit, he lifts one shoulder, straightens his windcheater and retreats.

"I'm nowhere, nowhere near down in the mouth."

Trude follows him and seems disappointed, almost angry. That is always something.

"I thought we were going to share everything," she says.

Share everything? The thought is quite simply mind-boggling. Now at least Jesper is beginning to get some circulation in his internal life; however, he can't come up with a better answer than:

"Maybe next time?"

"Next time?"

Jesper is on shaky ground.

"Yes, next time."

"Next time you're ill?"

"No, next time I'm well, sort of."

Trude stops and pretends that she has to shade her eyes to see him at all.

"Who's Alf Iversen?" she asks.

"That's my stage name."

She bursts into laughter.

"Alf Iversen? That's the worst stage name I've ever heard."

Nothing is more wearing than explaining a good joke.

"Alf Iversen's a Norwegian version of *auf Wiedersehen*," Jesper says.

He has to explain further and so the joke is ruined for ever.

"So when I introduce myself as Alf Iversen I'm really saying goodbye."

Trude goes closer again.

"You're weird. And quite funny."

"Oh, I don't know about that."

"Is it your hand you . . .?"

"Don't think so."

"It's nothing serious, is it?"

"If it was I would've been dead a long time ago."

"Don't talk like that, Jesper."

"I hereby retract what I said."

Trude leans forward and kisses him on the forehead. At that moment Ramm pokes his German head out of the classroom and asks what has happened to the sponge. The blackboard is covered in writing. He catches sight of Jesper as well.

"Are you still here?"

"Not anymore."

Jesper does an about-turn and runs towards the staircase. He hears Trude turn on the tap, and afterwards she shouts:

"Ring me tonight, Iversen."

Jesper swivels round and walks the last part backwards. Trude raises the sponge and the water runs down her arm. She laughs. Jesper laughs. The corridor isn't a slaughterhouse. It is more like a church and they are standing at opposite ends of the aisle. When he arrives home his mother is in the bathroom. She is taking a shower. Usually she does this only on Sundays. He knocks on the door. She probably can't hear. The shower is beating down. Pounding. Steam is seeping through the keyhole. He takes a seat in the kitchen and waits. At least it won't be his fault if they are late. Eventually his mother appears looking parboiled.

"Hurry up. I've called a taxi," she says.

The taxi is a black Mercedes. There is a similarity to the hearse that sometimes drives down Kirkeveien on its way to the crematorium in Vestre cemetery. The only difference is that they can pay and get out. That helps. They pay and get out in Langes gate. Maj has been here before. It doesn't bring back happy memories. To her amazement they aren't bad either. Ewald is fading away. Ewald has stepped to the side, but his place still isn't free. The area is enclosed by a high wall, as though someone is frightened that the patients will escape or they want to protect the healthy folk from them. In the same way that Vestre cemetery is a town within a city, a town for the dead, the Rikshospital is the capital of the ill.

"There's nothing to worry about," Maj says.

Jesper starts worrying for the first time.

They track down the neurology department in Building 4, second floor. This corridor is neither the central aisle in a church nor a slaughterhouse. It is a narrow, unending waiting room. There is linoleum on the floor. Two roses are withering in a vase. A woman in a white dressing gown can't stand still. A man is trying to grip one of her hands. He can't. He needs a repair. Jesper is reminded of Enzo Zanetti, who is still touring with the Herberth Circus. By the time he returns Jesper will have learned the "Ballad of Revolt" by heart. Perhaps none of that will happen. Perhaps all roads terminate here, where everyone has a crooked face, as though they have been divided down the middle. A nurse collects Jesper and guides him to a room at the end of the corridor. There he has to bare his chest and lie on a bench facing the wall. The nurse asks him to close his eyes. Jesper catches sight of the needle – it is the size of a knitting needle – and then she plunges it into his back, between the second and third discs, takes a sample of spinal fluid and fills him with an emptiness only more pain can relieve. When he comes to again he is sitting in another room. It resembles a laboratory. Another nurse is attaching electrodes to his head. Eighteen of them. There are just as many leads coming from these electrodes, half of them green, the rest blue and red. They are tied in a bundle and feed into a square machine with three different flashing lights, a bit like traffic lights at a crossing where everything is allowed. Then the nurse disappears and reappears behind a window with a doctor. Both are nodding and Jesper hears a buzzing that comes closer and closer. Then he realises it isn't coming closer. The buzzing is inside him. He is electric. It is he who is illuminating the town. He can hear his nerves, an irregular waterfall or rather a slow fire. It all goes quiet again. Jesper wishes he had never heard this sound. No, it wasn't like either a waterfall or a fire. It was reminiscent of a wind in a forest where dry branches keep breaking. The nurse returns, removes the electrodes and says she will inform Dr Lund. Jesper gets dressed and goes into the corridor. His mother jumps up as soon as she sees him and raises her hand to her mouth as she essays a smile. He darts into the nearest toilet and looks at the mirror. He doesn't even look like a pig in the slaughterhouse. His hair has been hacked at. There are eighteen marks scattered across his skull: eighteen holes in the head. If he can get hold of a military coat he would look like a tramp with scabies. It will take at least a year and a day for his hair to grow back evenly. There is a knock at the door. It is his mother.

"Jesper. It doesn't matter."

"What doesn't matter?"

"You can take tomorrow off school."

"Why?"

"It'll soon grow out."

"Very funny."

Now he knows what the noise reminded him of.

Jesper opens the door. They walk home. Stine is sitting in the dining room doing her homework. She never does anything else. She drops what she is holding when she sees her brother. He is beginning to be seriously fed up. Perhaps he should stay at home after all. Then he can practise all day, or not, and listen to his hair growing.

"It's very contagious," he says.

Jesper doesn't call Trude. He is not bloody ringing anyone with his hair like this. He lies on the sofa bed and plans the rest of his life. It doesn't take long. In fact, the noise reminded him of cables in the wall, the point where all the voices meet, the voices of buses, bus stops, cemeteries, shops, lawns, gateways and tenement entrances. Is this what a rich internal life is? Hearing the world go about its business in the distance? He goes into the sitting room and rings anyway. After all, she won't be able to see him. That is kind of the whole point of a telephone, to blather, not to see. Unfortunately her father answers.

"This is a late call, Kristoffersen."

Jesper takes a risk.

"But hopefully a pleasant surprise?"

"That depends. Let me ask you something first. What's the difference between a cold and a hot war?"

"A hot war?"

"A war on the battlefield, Jesper, in the air and at sea."

"The number of dead maybe?"

"A hot war makes people courageous, whereas a cold war makes people nervous. What was it you wanted?"

"To talk to Trude."

"She's in bed. You should be too, Jesper."

"Could you say hi from me?"

"Gladly. Tomorrow morning."

"And say it all went—"

Jesper spots something moving by the skirting board. It is an insect, a flat insect with a hard shell and antennae and lots of legs. It stops under the telephone socket. Jesper hangs up, takes off one slipper and is poised to kill the insect. But as he is about to strike, it scuttles into a crevice in the wall that only insects can see.

The bazaar meeting at Frøken Jacobsen's. We have started buying the previously mentioned items: a globe, bathroom scales with a towel, a cuckoo clock, a cookery book, and Fru Lund will donate a flowering hibiscus. The board has received an application from Margrethe Hall, formerly Fru Vik, saying that she is available as she has been told there is a vacancy after Frøken Smith's departure. The board is positively disposed to her application even though Margrethe Hall, formerly Fru Vik, now lives outside the Fagerborg District. The chairman will write a letter welcoming her to the next board meeting.

THE CLASS PARTY

"It is with a heavy heart that I have to say you won't be able to play anymore."

Dr Lund rises from his chair and walks over to the window. He puts his hands behind his back. It is Saturday, the first in March, the light is white and damp, outside all is quiet. Jesper remains seated. He is nervous enough from before.

"I can't play anymore?"

"But this may release energy and time for you to start running, initially short intervals."

"Instead of playing the piano?"

Dr Lund turns and laughs.

"No, no, no, you can plonk away as much as you like. I was thinking about handball. I'm afraid you'll have to shelve that."

Jesper thinks: I can live without handball.

"What's actually wrong with me?" he asks.

Dr Lund takes the weight off his feet and looks Jesper straight in the eye.

"Avoid putting yourself in very stressful situations."

How do you measure stress? Is Sæverud more stressful than Satie? Is Jostein a stress? What about Trude? She is obviously a stress, but one Jesper would not be without. He has no idea why he says this, but he does anyway.

"I have a class party this evening."

Dr Lund nods.

"Of course, you're too young to partake of alcohol, but keep away from it anyway. Alcohol's no good for anyone."

They are silent for a few moments. Jesper thinks about the greatest stress of all, but can't bring himself to ask.

"It may be important to sleep well," he says.

"You've hit the nail on the head there, Jesper. A good night's sleep is the best medicine of all. You should sleep eight and a half hours every night, but what counts most is not how long. It's how deep."

"How do you mean?"

"Never go to bed at odds with the world. Go to sleep with a smile on your face."

They are silent again.

Who knows if you smile when you are asleep?

Dr Lund shuffles his papers.

"You have a steady girlfriend," he says.

How does the doctor know? It is not hard to guess. He knows from the Fagerborg department of the Norwegian Red Cross. It is a charitable centre for gossip, rumours and innuendo.

"Not sure about how steady," Jesper says.

"Alfred Hagen's a good writer. Shame he never writes about athletics."

"He's interviewed the Shah of Persia."

Dr Lund looks up.

"Let me give you a piece of good advice, Jesper. If in doubt, don't do it."

Jesper has to think long and hard about this.

Dr Lund examines his right hand. It will soon be as good as new.

But on the way down to Majorstua to buy Wellaform hair gel at Estelle's Perfumery in Bogstadveien, Jesper changes his mind. If in doubt, do do it. Otherwise you will never experience anything new. He asks for a comb while he is at it. When he gets home he goes to the bathroom, washes his hair, which is still uneven, dries it, squeezes the cream out of the tube and rubs it into his scalp. Then he takes the comb and runs it through his hair backwards. It is like lifting seaweed. Jesper has never lifted seaweed in his life.

He looks in the mirror. He doesn't want to look like a petrolhead after all, combs down his fringe and parts it to the side. He doesn't want to look like a blupper either. Who *does* he want to look like? He doesn't want to look like anyone. He wishes he didn't have to decide. That would be the simplest. Then he would be saved. But perhaps he would be bored to death.

"A parting suits you."

Jesper turns to the door. It is Stine.

"And who let you in?"

Stine doesn't answer. She just stands staring at him. Jesper moves the parting to the other side, but it isn't straight there and he moves it back. He remembers something his father used to say: The mirror and I are not good friends. But at least the ragged patches will soon be gone.

"Is Trude going?"

"Yes. The whole class is."

"She's pretty."

"Why don't you have any friends?"

"You know nothing about that."

"I never see them here anyway."

There is a silence by the door and when Jesper turns to his sister again her mouth is quivering. She can hardly articulate the words.

"They don't like me."

Jesper stuffs his comb in his back pocket.

"Don't like you? Of course they do."

"No, they don't."

He crouches down and places a hand, still clammy with Wellaform, on her cheek.

"Have you done something silly?"

Stine shakes her head and Jesper doesn't quite know whether that is an answer or if she wants him to move his hand.

"Sure?"

"Yes," she says.

"But how is it possible not to like you?"

At that moment they hear a scream. It comes from the sitting room. They run there. It is their mother. She is standing in the middle of the floor and pointing to the telephone.

"It was there! It was huge!"

Stine hides behind her mother. Jesper buttons up his white shirt and sighs.

"What was there, Mamma?"

"An animal."

"What kind of animal? A badger?"

"An insect. He must've brought it in."

Maj is pointing to the ceiling.

Jesper sighs again.

"I've seen an insect there too. It wasn't that big."

"Oh, my God. We have to get rid of them. I can't sleep here if they . . ."

Maj falters and holds her hand over her mouth.

"Kill them," she whispers.

Jesper kneels down and peers under the sofa, only to keep his mother happy. Insects don't hang around waiting. There is a ring at the door. He bangs his ear on the table and knocks over a vase. Only now does he realise that the telephone is off the hook and someone is speaking in it. Is it Trude? Is it Trude ringing? He takes the receiver and groans. It is Fru Vik, now Fru Hall.

"We're going to see a lot more of each other now, Jesper. I've joined the board of the Fagerborg department of the Oslo branch of—"

"The Norwegian Red Cross. Congratulations."

"Thank you. How are you?"

"I'm a bit busy right now."

Jesper hangs up, runs into Maj's bedroom and rummages through the bedside-table drawer, but the packet isn't there. However much he rummages, it isn't there. He runs out again. Of course it isn't Trude. They have arranged to meet in Majorstua. It is Jostein, the blue-eyed rascal. Mamma and Stine have let him into the hall, no further, fortunately. That is inconvenient. If Jesper can't chase away the insects for good, he can at least get rid of them for a while. Jostein is a harder case. It is too much to take on board. Then he is alone with his pal.

"Have you put margarine in your hair?" Jostein asks.

"Wellaform."

"Are you going to a party?"

"Yes."

"Can I come?"

"No."

"Why not?"

"Because it's a class party."

"So? Surely there'll be room for me? Axel has got a big house, hasn't he?"

Jesper sighs.

"It's only for the class, Jostein."

"But I know you."

"I'm afraid that's no good."

"I can be your bodyguard."

"A bodyguard? I don't need one."

"I suppose not."

Jesper opens the door slowly and hesitatingly.

"I have to get ready."

"Stine's becoming quite attractive," Jostein says.

Jesper turns to him equally slowly.

"What did you say?"

"Are you deaf or what? Your sister's pretty."

Jesper pushes Jostein onto the landing and doesn't let go of him.

"My sister's seven, you retard."

"So what? She can still be pretty."

"You keep your sausage fingers off her."

Jostein just laughs.

"I'm going to be the first deaf millionaire in Fagerborg. And then I'll invite Stine to a restaurant."

Jesper gives up. There is no doubt. Jostein is a stress.

"First things first, you're not deaf."

"What did you say?"

"Second, you'll never ask her out."

Jostein shrugs.

"I can't hear what you're saying. Shall I get the post for you?"

"Yes. And take the rubbish down while you're at it."

Jostein straddles the banister and slides down a floor. There he jumps off and shouts:

"At least you'll be able to borrow money from me when I'm a millionaire."

He breaks into a run and Jesper waits until he hears the front door slam. When he returns his mother is in the hallway.

"What were you doing in my bedroom?"

"Looking for a tie."

"A tie, you say? You think you'll find a tie in my bedside table, do you?"

Jesper takes a step closer. He knows he has the upper hand.

"I went to see Lund today," he says.

Maj raises a hand to stroke Jesper's cheek, but holds her other hand instead.

"Today? I thought it was next—"

"Are you as deaf as Jostein or what?"

"Don't talk like that, Jesper."

"It was today at two o'clock."

"What did he say?"

"That everyone should take care of me."

"Speak properly. Or I'll ring him right now."

"I think you'd be better off ringing Pest Control."

"Take care of you? Don't we do that? We do take care of you, Jesper, don't we?"

"Anyway, Dr Lund has taken the oath of confidentiality. Unlike the Fagerborg department of the Oslo Gossips in the Norwegian Red Cross Rumour Mill."

"What do you mean by that?"

"You can tell the board that Dr Lund said I can't take stress."

"Otherwise there was nothing wrong?"

"What would there be?"

Maj finally places a hand on Jesper's cheek.

"I'll find you a tie."

She goes into her bedroom. Jesper wonders if there is anything he has forgotten. Should he take a Coke with him? They weren't asked to. Stine is sitting in the dining room reading about nutrition in the cookery book for primary and secondary schools. The introduction says: *If we starve we get thin. If we eat more than we need, we get fat.* But Jesper can see that Stine isn't reading. She is just turning the pages. She is somewhere else in the syllabus. It is a different weighing scale she has in mind now. She looks up.

"Why does Jostein speak so loudly?" she asks.

Jesper is forced to give this some thought.

"So that he can hear what he is saying," Jesper answers.

"Hmm."

Stine leafs through the book, but her fingers are distant and slapdash.

Jesper steps closer.

"Did you hear what he said?"

Maj returns from her bedroom with two ties. One belonged to Ewald and is brown, about three metres wide with yellow dots on. Hasn't she thrown his clothes away yet? Is she collecting them? Or is the idea that Jesper will inherit them? If so, he will have to put on at least eighty kilos and rearrange his height and centre of gravity. He will have to look like his father. He is on the point of saying something, then refrains. It will have to be another time. The tie smells of stale leaves and tobacco. The second tie is a present from Margrethe Hall, the former Fru Vik. It is light blue, four and a half metres long and already has a knot.

"Think I'll give the tie a miss," Jesper says.

Maj sighs and hands him ten kroner.

"In case the two of you have to take a taxi home."

"And if we walk?"

"Then you can buy her something nice."

"Thanks."

"And no later than twelve. Do you promise me?"

"Yeah, yeah."

"I'll stay up waiting for you. Just so you know."

"You don't need to."

"Come on. Off you go."

Maj gives Jesper a quick peck on the cheek and lets him go. That is what she is doing. She is letting him go. He shrugs on his windcheater and soon he is running down Kirkeveien. He catches a glimpse of Jostein in the butcher's shop. He is sitting under the lamp studying a colour illustration of pork cuts and what the various parts are called: chop, leg, shoulder, neck and knuckle. Fortunately Jostein doesn't notice Jesper as he dashes past, even though he doesn't like running, but Trude is already waiting on the steps in Majorstua and Jesper has no time for anything except being punctual. She is wearing a coat and a yellow scarf wound amply around her neck, at least four times, and is carrying a handbag. He stops in front of her, out of breath and in pocket and at once remembers what he has forgotten: yes, Trude is a stress as well. Fagerborg is a stress. Life is a stress. They reach the Holmenkollen line and sit at the back. In the smoking compartment a cigarette is doing the rounds between Halvor, Rune and Ulrik. Everyone in Industrigata takes the Metro from Valkyrien station. They wave, their expressions glazed. There is a smell of pre-drinks. Rune's father is a manager at the mayonnaise factory. Halvor's father is a rep for David Andersen and both Ulrik's parents work at Hagen Shoes.

"I've forgotten to bring some slippers," Jesper says.

"You can borrow some from Axel."

"I don't want to wear his."

"Then you'll have to walk in stockinged feet."

"I might have holes in my socks."

Trude leans over to him.

"Are we going to the party or not?"

"We're going to the party."

"Is your hand better now?"

"It's absolutely so-so. It works. How about you?"

Trude laughs.

"I'm absolutely so-so too."

Jesper would like to know Trude's opinion about doubt. If in doubt, should you do it or not? But in Slemdal Elisabeth gets on and joins them. She has on a thick layer of lipstick and heavily pencilled eyebrows, razor-thin. Her hair was done at the Continental. And then of course Halvor, Rune and Ulrik come over like moths around a candle. But they are afraid of getting burned. They stay at arm's length from Elisabeth. Yes, they do have pre-drinks on board. The only question is who will throw up first.

"Axel's mother has invited Ramm," Elisabeth says.

That puts a damper on the atmosphere.

Halvor:

"Shit, then we'll have to drink cod-liver oil all evening."

Elisabeth turns and dignifies him with a gaze.

"And what are you drinking now?"

"Gin," Halvor whispers.

"Stay on your feet then because I haven't got the strength to carry you."

The boys from Industrigata exchange glances and laugh nervously. No-one feels secure around Elisabeth. She is like Cleopatra, or an Egyptian queen, but fortunately the back of her head isn't that long. Even Jesper has to tell himself not to stare. Trude rolls her eyes and gazes out of the carriage. The Metro stops at Midtstuen and a couple with a setter alight from the train. Then at last it is Gulleråsen. It is still 181.5 metres above sea level. Axel lives right by the station, in a timber house with muntin windows, blue shutters and fencing around. In the snow there are lines of lit torches. In the shadows beyond, hip flasks glisten. Trude lags behind the others. Jesper waits for her.

"Do you think she's good-looking?" she asks.

"Who?"

"Don't pretend. Elisabeth. You almost stared her into the dust."

"Good-looking? Well, she's no better looking than—"

"Don't lie, Jesper."

"Lie? I'm not—"

"Besides, I don't care."

"What about?"

"About whether you think she's good-looking or not."

Jesper leans closer.

"I think she's boring."

"You know her that well, do you?"

"Know? Well, I suppose I don't know her, but she *seems* boring."

"So she's boring and good-looking?"

"Something like that."

"And I'm amusing and ugly."

Trude moves away.

"You are not. You're . . ."

"What am I, Jesper?"

"I was at the doc's today."

Trude stops between the torches.

"What did he say?"

"My hair's grown back."

"Not completely."

"He said I can't play anymore."

Trude's expression changes.

"The piano?"

"Handball."

Her expression changes again – how many has she got? – and she shoves him.

"Don't make jokes about this. Ever."

"In addition, I can't take stress."

"What kind?"

Jesper thinks: Why does this have to be so difficult? Why can't it be easy? Wouldn't everything be so much simpler then?

"Air raid alarms, oral exams, German jazz, Jehovah's witnesses, pigs and arguments."

"We don't do arguments."

"What do we do then?"

"Let's go in."

They walk faster up to the house, where Axel's mother lets them in. There are antlers on all the walls. There are slippers to spare. The father, the cod-liver-oil king himself, is sitting in a deep chair in the hallway busily at work with a shoe horn. He comes from a direct line of Hansa League merchants, rolls his Rs and has a factory in the Oslo fjord, where he boils the oil. He can make liver paste as well. There is mineral water and cake in the kitchen, there are small, open sandwiches in the sitting room, and peanuts and savoury sticks in the library. Smoking is not allowed. In the cellar there is a guest toilet and a washbasin. The first floor is strictly out of bounds. In emergencies, girls can use the bathroom there, but only if it is an emergency. At 19.04 Axel's parents are picked up by a taxi and taken to the Continental, where they have reserved a table. After they have eaten they are going to see "The Mountain" with Spencer Tracy at the Scala. The film finishes at 22.54. There are three hours and eighteen minutes of the party left. But when Axel has collected the hip flasks and is about to mix a tub of the very special cocktail 85.71, so named after Eigil Danielsen's world record javelin throw in Melbourne, and which according to reliable sources is supposed to have the same lofty trajectory, the doorbell rings. All the flasks are hidden under cushions, behind books and in inside pockets. It is Ramm. He hangs up his coat in the hall and enters the sitting room on stockinged feet. Everyone stands up. He raises his arms and tells everyone to sit down. His glasses steam up and he has to clean them with his handkerchief. He puts them back and stares at his pupils, who are dressed for the occasion, not in an exaggerated but in a seemly fashion. The boys wear white shirts and tweed jackets or a blazer, apart from Jesper, who has only a shirt. Some wear ties too, with shiny pins attached at an angle. The girls wear skirts or slim dresses, most of them green, and their hair is especially neat. They are hardly recognisable, his students, they are almost adults, peering over the edge to the rest of their lives, in party mode. A few words from Goethe occur to him: *All theory is grey.* Ramm starts to speak:

"I've arrived late and I'll go early. For where the young gather, old men should not disturb."

There is a ripple of clapping in Industrigata, but it soon dies down. Ramm continues:

"But I so wanted to see you all in different surroundings from the classroom and the schoolyard. I so wanted, if only for a moment, to see you as happy, broad-minded people."

Embarrassed silence.

Everyone looks at one another or somewhere else. Has Ramm also had a drop or two before coming?

His glasses steam up again. He lets them and curses himself. He is becoming sentimental. That is the last thing he wants. It is utterly obnoxious. It was dutiful sentimentality that sent Germany into the darkness. Ramm raises his hand as though in an admonitory gesture to the enemy that lurks within and is blind.

"And for Monday you—"

He is interrupted by the host.

"There's no homework for Monday, sir."

"Is that written in the Norwegian Constitution, Axel? That there shall be no homework for Monday?"

"No, only in the Ten Commandments."

Ramm cleans his glasses again after all.

"Then I'll shift to Tuesday. I wouldn't like to get into trouble with God. But by Tuesday I'll expect you to have learned Goethe's 'Über allen Gipfeln' from 'The Wanderer's Nightsong', and to have considered how this beautiful poem could be translated into Norwegian.

And so, my dear friends, not my dear students this evening, I shall be off, and don't do anything you might regret after I've left."

Now there is a storm of clapping. And stamping too. Ramm knows all too well that this is mostly because he will soon be leaving and giving them the green light. He doesn't begrudge them that. Everyone needs the green light once in a while. But as the applause subsides and he is on the point of departing, Axel comes with a glass of Coke in his hand, wanting to propose a toast for Ramm, who drinks the vile concoction to show his goodwill. Once again he becomes sentimental. Axel refills his glass and says:

"And before Lektor Ramm leaves us, Jesper Kristoffersen, former handball goalkeeper, will play for us."

Everyone turns to Jesper, who gazes at his hands. The right one is paler and thinner than the other. It looks like it will have to be a left-hand job.

"Have you got a piano?" he asks.

There is always an extra room in Gulleråsen and in it is a piano with candelabra on top. As so often, it is rarely used, but the lid is a fine place to put family photos. It is an instrument of torture that for appearance's sake is tuned every autumn equinox.

"What do you think?" Axel asks.

Everyone follows him to the room, or the conservatory, behind the library. In Gulleråsen there is no way out. Jesper sits down on the stool and rolls up his sleeves. Afterwards he is known as Jesper "Have-you-got-a-piano" Kristoffersen. He plays two bars of Symphony No. 2 in B flat major, to be more precise, *allegro non troppo*. It takes no time at all; he knows it by heart and plays it twice. When he rests his hands in his lap, Ramm's eyes are misty, he has been moved to tears, yes, indeed, he is sentimental this evening.

"Dear, dear Brahms," he whispers.

Ramm has to take recourse to his handkerchief again. It is not just his glasses that are steaming up, but his whole body.

"There you heard the profundity of genuine European culture."

Jesper doesn't dare say that it was only the West German interval signal.

Then the girls accompany Ramm out. Those who can be bothered can watch him disappear between the burning torches in the snow, but the flames continue to glow in the arched sky over Oslo and finish on the edge of Ekeberg with a touch of early Munch. What they see is the back of a happy temperance man. He floats like Egil Danielsen's javelin in Melbourne. And the class party can finally get underway, at the same tempo as all such parties, it is this class first, but it is a faithful copy: some of them play cards, others stand in a corner exchanging secrets, Halvor and Rune argue and make up again, three girls go to the first floor, one in tears, some find each other and switch off a lamp, soon there will be no 85.71 left, Ulrik considers himself drunk and Axel, who is the Kapellmeister for the occasion, puts on "Rock Around the Clock". Fortunately Ramm's fears were groundless. They aren't adults. They are children in their parents' clothes. The gramophone changes records like a jukebox, Harry Belafonte sings "Jamaica Farewell", however calypso isn't yet on the Norwegian dance school syllabus, but at the bottom of the pile Frank Sinatra sings "Songs for Swinging Lovers" in high fidelity and muted lighting. Elisabeth sits by the wall tightly holding on to her beauty. She doesn't know what to do with it. Suddenly she gets up and goes over to Jesper, who is standing next to Axel, brushing the dust off Reidar Bøe and Kurt Foss' slow smoochie "De Nære Ting", and there is a silence.

"Shall we dance?" she asks.

Jesper looks for Trude. He has seldom looked for her so intensely. She is standing by the library door eating peanuts and appearing otherwise unaffected, and of little or no use.

"I'm afraid I'm not wearing the requisite patent leather shoes this evening," Jesper says.

Elisabeth smiles through her make-up, her lips suddenly reminiscent of liquorice.

"What?"

Jesper bows and points to his slippers. Axel pushes him aside.

"I am, though."

With that, Axel drags her onto the floor and is the first in the class to try his luck with her. He is going for a black belt in leg clinches. It won't be long before he is glued to her. The host is always right. There is another ring at the door. A long, long ring. Axel lets go of Elisabeth and switches off the music. It could be Ramm who has got lost or a hostile visit from Holmendammen below. He takes all Industrigata and a poker with him into the hall and opens the door. The class waits in silence. Elisabeth stands beside Trude, who puts her arm around her and sends Jesper stern glares. He is confused. Didn't he behave correctly? Didn't he do what was right? He said no. He refused a dance. He sat it out. Axel returns alone, puts the poker back in the fireplace and turns to Jesper.

"You've got a visitor."

Jesper doesn't understand this either.

"Visitor? You're the one who lives here, Axel."

Axel closes the door and climbs onto a chair.

"Listen everyone. Jesper 'Have-you-got-a-piano' Kristoffersen's bodyguard would like to join us. First, though, what does Jesper 'Have-you-got-a-piano' say to this?"

Everyone laughs, apart from Trude and Elisabeth, who are no longer there. They are crying on the first floor. Jesper looks down and curses the day he was born and had to interact with the world, where nothing is discrete and independent.

"You're the one who lives here," he repeats.

"Exactly. In fact we're talking about Jostein Melsom, the deaf pig-slaughterer from the shady side of Kirkeveien, who at the moment is being scrutinised by Industrigata. However, as we're civilised North Germanic types, happy and broad-minded, I think we should weigh up the pros and cons of whether to send him packing or let him in. The floor is yours."

There is silence. Then Bente from the functionalist street in Vinderen puts up her hand and asks:

"Does he smell of pig?"

The girls shudder.

Axel laughs.

"Luckily I haven't been that intimate with him, Bente. So I'll pass the question on to someone who knows him better."

Why doesn't Trude come back down? What is she doing with Elisabeth? Is this anything to cry about?

"Jostein's very hygienic after work," Jesper says.

Bengt-Ove from Gaustadalléen opines that they should think along mathematical lines:

"There are already more boys than girls."

Some of the girls laugh.

"So what?"

Bengt-Ove blushes and withdraws from the discussion, flourishing a drinking straw.

Reidar, who is the proud owner of a moped and therefore worth listening to, tackles the principle head-on:

"Jostein Melsom isn't in our class."

"What if Jostein had been a Hungarian refugee?"

That is Trude's question. She is standing halfway up the stairs with Elisabeth, who has been struck by acute Black Death. Her eyebrows are running down her face. Reidar for his part has been afflicted by acute mental confusion and looks around him for some first aid.

"I've got a moped," he says.

Trude laughs.

"But you're not allowed to ride it yet."

Axel claps his hands.

"We need to ask Trude to expatiate on her comment, as butcher's boy Jostein is self-evidently not a refugee, nor Hungarian, but born and bred in Majorstua in a partially furnished flat."

Trude leans over the banister.

"I assume that everyone's read Stefan Zweig's *The World of Yesterday*. I'd like to reiterate his main point about the status of a refugee. He writes that one refugee is a friend, ten are hospitality and a hundred are politics. In other words, Jostein has come alone and is a friend we should let in."

Axel groans.

"But we've already established that we are *not* dealing with a refugee here, so Stefan Zweig's argument is irrelevant."

Trude will not yield.

"I'm not talking about refugees in a legal but a metaphorical sense. Jostein—"

Bengt-Ove has plucked up courage in the meantime and interrupts.

"Metaphorical sense? In other words, Trude doesn't mean what she says."

"I mean only that Jostein has walked all the way up here alone—"

"He might've caught the Metro."

The boys laugh. Trude points to Bengt-Ove.

"O.K., he took the Metro, you hair-splitter. Perhaps he dodged paying the fare as well. The point is that he's alone and we should treat him as a friend."

Bengt-Ove has tasted blood now and obviously thinks he is on a winner.

"Ultimately the point is that Jostein doesn't belong here."

There is some booing now, but it is hard to distinguish between those who are for and those against. It is probably a gender divide: the girls are in favour of letting Jostein in and the boys are not. Class 1Ef is about to be split on two fronts, possibly three. There may be irreparable damage. Class unity is threatened. The class' humanistic capital may disintegrate into petty point-scoring and misunderstandings, small change in other words. Justice is a tricky business when there is a class party. Axel claps his hands again and asks for moderation and calm, after all he is the host. He has not only Jostein to consider, but also the contents of the house and personal property.

"It appears that we aren't going to reach a swift agreement. Therefore Jesper 'Have-you-got-a-piano' Kristoffersen will have to take the decision. It's his friend who has come knocking. Shall we open the door for Deaf Porky Jostein or not?"

Everyone turns to Jesper, apart from Trude, who has to look after Elisabeth, but he definitely knows what he *isn't* going to say. Before he has a chance to speak the door opens and there is Jostein, in a yellow shirt and blue pullover looking like a stray Swede. Rune shakes his head, as do Halvor and Ulrik, and indeed everyone in actual fact.

"He needs a piss," Rune says.

They take Jostein down to the cellar.

Trude comes over to Jesper. She is wearing a coat. Is she going already? He is so confused and wants to apologise even though he has no idea what he has done wrong, perhaps it is just him there is something wrong with and so there is little he can do, except apologise for the fact that he even exists or disappear for ever. Trude quickly places a finger on his lips and won't let him speak at first.

"I'm taking Elisabeth home," she says.

"Why? It's not—"

"That's the way it is, Jesper."

"What is?"

"Don't you stand up for your friends too?"

"Of course."

Trude leans closer.

"Meet you in Slemdal at eleven, OK?"

Jesper nods and she hurries towards the hall. Not long afterwards he can see them through the window. Trude and Elisabeth walking arm in arm through the darkened garden, one slender and unsteady on flimsy high-heeled shoes, the other well shod, are they old pitch-seam boots or perhaps overshoes? Jesper didn't notice her footwear on the way here. Her eyes were enough to deal with. He will have to start noticing more, not just the obvious. But he is aware of Trude's neck. When he holds it in his hand and feels all her movements, even the very slightest. Why won't she turn around? Has she forgotten him already?

"Bloody hell. I'm going to live in a house like this too. What do you reckon, eh?"

Jostein is suddenly at Jesper's side eating peanuts with both hands and talking with food in his mouth. Yes, Jesper thinks, and before Jostein moves into Gulleråsen he will have appeared on stage in Carnegie Hall playing the "Moonlight Sonata", with Liszt's "Hungarian Rhapsody" as an encore, accompanied by the New York Symphony Orchestra conducted by Herbert von Karajan, assisted by Wilhelm Kempff turning the pages and Glenn Gould polishing his shoes. He also wonders whether Jostein suffers from diminished intelligence and should have gone to a special school, but says nothing, he supports his pal, of course, but without taking his eyes off Trude, who closes the gate and finally looks up at the window where the two boys are standing side by side, one quite thin and serious, the other broader and happier, or so it seems. She raises an arm and waves to them before joining Elisabeth, walking arm in arm, down towards the town below them, a bowl of mist, dots of light and silence. They don't speak for some time. One hill is steeper than the next, in some places it is slippery, Trude has to hold Elisabeth even tighter, so that both of them don't fall, they should perhaps have taken the Metro after all, but it is good to have fresh air coursing through your nostrils after all that aftershave.

"Are you going out with Jesper?" Elisabeth asks.

Trude hesitates before answering.

"I think so."

Elisabeth chuckles.

"You think so? You don't know?"

"I suppose we are."

"Is he nice?"

"He's great."

"Only great?"

"I don't know him that well yet."

"Haven't you done it?"

Trude lets go of her arm.

"Do you fancy him?"

"I don't fancy anyone."

"Not even Axel?"

"No, yuk. I'd prefer Jostein."

It is Trude's turn to laugh.

"Jostein?"

"He's quite cool. But a little slow too."

Elisabeth looks down at her hopeless shoes. Then she kicks them off and wants to walk the rest of the way in her stockings. She doesn't even want to carry them. She just leaves them where they are on the last hill between Midtstuen and Slemdal. They don't say another word until they are outside the house behind the school, in the narrow cul-de-sac.

"No, we haven't," Trude says.

Elisabeth shrugs.

"There's no rush, is there?"

Trude is cold for an instant and shivers.

"No, there isn't."

"Do you want to come in for a bit?"

"Don't think I will."

"Are you meeting Jesper?"

"Yes."

"Alright."

"Are you OK?"

Elisabeth walks towards the house where only one window is lit. She is hobbling. She turns and smiles.

"I'm a lot better now."

Trude takes a step closer because a shadow falls over Elisabeth's face, it is the light from the window, the curtains that are only half drawn.

"Sure?"

"You're nice to me. It was a lovely party, by the way."

"Are you all on your own?"

Elisabeth nods and is both excited and tired at the same time.

"I can have a nightcap."

"Isn't it a bit late?"

"Isn't that the point of a nightcap? That it's late?"

"I have to get home anyway."

"Weren't you meeting Jesper?"

"Yes, I am. We're going to walk home together."

"Say hi."

Trude is about to go, but hesitates for a moment as Elisabeth turns again and unlocks the door.

"You could ring Axel and ask if they want to come for a nightcap," she says.

Elisabeth doesn't answer. The door glides shut behind her. She puts the keys on the chest of drawers and hangs her coat in the wardrobe. She doesn't switch on the light. She knows the way. She goes up to the bathroom on the first floor and drinks a glass of water. In the mirror she can see her face, it is tilted to one side between her bony shoulders, it could have been the face of a stranger, someone standing on the other side and secretly staring at her. But Elisabeth has seen her. She runs her fingers through her hair and destroys the style. Her right foot hurts. She switches on the light after all and catches just a glimpse of the stranger, who immediately disappears from the mirror with a grin. She sits on the edge of the bath and rips the stocking that is already full of holes. There is a black dot in the skin by her heel, a little stone, a tiny piece of gravel. She finds a pair of tweezers in her mother's toilet bag and tries to pull it out. She can't move it. She starts crying. The tiny stone grows into a mountain under her foot. She leaves it where it is. It doesn't matter. It will grow into her skin and disappear in the end, become part of her, her mountain range. She limps to her room and lies down on the bed. She feels like playing a record, but can't be bothered to get up. Instead she hums the tune she would have liked to hear, the one the disabled beggar, Porgy, sings: "I Got Plenty o' Nuttin'". She translates the title into Norwegian and starts laughing. Then she gets up anyway, combs her hair and goes down to the sitting room. On the bookshelves she finds Gyldendal's Encyclopaedia and leafs through in the darkness until she finds Goethe. The poem is in German first and she reads the opening lines: *Über allen Gipfeln / Ist Ruh / In allen Wipfeln / Spürest du.* Afterwards there are two examples of Swedish translations. The first was made by Anders Wåhlin in 1892: *Öfver Jord och Himmel / tystnad rår / Allt lifets vrimmel / Natten når.* Carl Snolinsky is the translator of the second: *Ingen Trädtopp röres / i skog / Knappt en suck kan höres / Vinden drog.* She wants to attempt a translation herself and goes into her father's study. She sits behind the broad, heavy desk made from dark, fiery wood, switches on the green reading lamp and places a sheet of letter paper on the felt protector pad. In the top corner is her father's name and profession in blue letters: *Henry Vilder Jr, Import/Export.* She unscrews the top of the fountain pen, closes her eyes and visualises the trees, the forest, profiled against the sky. She opens her eyes and writes: *Above all the treetops / it is still / there is a pair of high heels / on the last hill.* Again she laughs and at that moment a pool of black ink from her pen spreads across the whole sheet of paper. Elisabeth Vilder leaves it and goes back to the sitting room. It is twenty minutes past ten. She calls Axel. Jostein is the only person who hears the telephone ring. Beneath him the music is so loud the floor tiles are unsticking and the toilet seats are chattering like false teeth. He is in the first-floor toilet having a piss. They have two bathrooms. The one downstairs was occupied. He has never pissed in a bathroom with a telephone before. What is the point? Are you supposed to chat while having a crap? That is worse than talking with your mouth full. The telephone is white and mounted on the wall. It is still ringing. When he has his own house there will be a telephone in every room, not only in the bathroom. He buttons up his fly and washes his hands. He sees himself in the mirror and wishes he could get rid of the spots on his forehead. If he combs his hair forward he can hide them, but then he looks like a Soviet girl and he doesn't want that either. A spotty forehead would be better. Everyone in Oslo Slaughterhouse has spots, even those who have worked there from before the war and will soon be eighty. He envies the people dancing downstairs. He has received the message. He is an intruder, a *gatecrasher*. He knows what they are saying: he's an oik. One day they will earn more money than he does when they become lawyers, directors, heirs and shipowners. But he does have a head start. He is already earning money. Louis Armstrong is singing "Mack the Knife". Deaf Jostein Melsom is the only person in Gulleråsen who can hear the telephone ringing. Should he answer it? Perhaps it is the father calling to ask if his house is still standing in the same place? He definitely shouldn't pick it up, if so. Then he understands. Someone is taking the mickey. Probably Industrigata. Someone is calling from downstairs to tell him the first floor is out of bounds and to wipe the seat clean. Didn't they say he could go to the toilet in the basement or use the urinal by Fagerborg church? Has he forgotten he had a leak in the basement first and he should go there afterwards as well? Has he forgotten his place, on the bottom rung? Does he really imagine Herr and Fru Werner would want to sit on the same toilet seat as a slaughterhouse apprentice? Anyway, what is the number of Axel's toilet? Is it in the telephone directory? Jostein grabs the receiver. At first he can't hear anything, just a buzzing noise and some music, which is no longer "Mack the Knife" but "Arrivederci Roma".

"Who's there?" he shouts.

Still there is noise and silence on all sides, then he hears a reedy voice, it is a girl saying the same as he did:

"Who's there?"

Jostein hesitates. Perhaps it is a trap? Perhaps they are standing around the telephones downstairs waiting for him to fall into it?

"And who are you?" he asks.

He has to wait, but not for long.

"Where have I come through to?"

Jostein is unsure whether to answer. Are they playing a prank on him? Has someone rung the wrong number?

"The first-floor toilet at Axel Werner's," he says.

"The *toilet* at . . .?"

There is laughter in the receiver, which grows into a dissonant motley chorus in Jostein's head, and he forgets he is deaf.

"Fuck all of you!" he shouts.

"It's—"

"The one in the basement was occupied. And I needed a leak. I couldn't hold it any longer."

"Is that Jostein?"

"Yes, who else?"

"This is Elisabeth."

"Who?"

"Elisabeth from Jesper's class. Elisabeth Vilder."

It could still be a trap, an even more cunning one than the first.

"Didn't you go home?"

"Yes, I did. I went with Trude."

"Where are you ringing from?"

"Home, of course. The cul-de-sac behind the school."

"Which school?"

"Slemdal."

"Ah, that one."

"I'm here on my own."

"Are you?"

"Would you like to come here?"

Jostein didn't hear. Or he heard wrong. It could also have been a slip of the tongue. To be on the safe side, he should say no. That was the first thing he learned at deaf school. If in doubt, say no.

"Yes," Jostein says.

"What would you most like to do?"

"Do?"

"Yes, what would you most like to do?"

Jostein doesn't hear himself say:

"Go to yours."

"You said that."

"Did I?"

"Do you feel like a swim?"

Jostein knows that he will soon have to start saying no. He should have done ages ago. This is and will be a trap. It could also be a dream. Perhaps he is drunk and hearing things. But he hasn't been drinking. No-one has spoken to him like this before. That is for certain.

"Yes," Jostein says. "Yes."

"We can have a swim together."

"Isn't it cold this time of the year?"

"Not in the bathtub. We've got hot water."

"I'm on my way."

Jostein doesn't hear what she says at the end. He just hangs up, washes his hands again and tiptoes towards the stairs. He doesn't know what he can expect, probably the worst: everyone in the sitting room laughing at him, Elisabeth didn't leave after all and now she will be laughing the loudest. He believed me! Jostein thought she wanted to be with him! In the bathtub! His heart was pounding like a pig's before they use the bolt gun. But as he holds the banister, taking one step at a time, no-one notices him. They are busy doing their own thing. They are busy with each other. They are dancing close together in the semi-darkness to the Werners' latest record – "Love Is a Many-Splendored Thing" – apart from Jesper, who is standing by the hall door in his eternal windcheater waiting with a desperate expression on his face. He is about to say something, but Jostein strides straight past him, finds his coat in the pile on the floor and almost runs into the cold, moonlit night. In the end it is Jesper who has to hurry after Jostein. He has to take him down a peg. Not only did he gatecrash the party, he also used the first-floor toilet. Bloody Jostein still isn't house-trained.

But what is worse is that he will have to get rid of him. He doesn't particularly want all three of them walking home together. They catch the Metro at the last minute, pay the conductor and sit in the last carriage. Jostein is mulling the same problem: how to get rid of Jesper. He doesn't want to tell him anything. He won't tell him until it is a reality. The second lesson he learned at the deaf school was how to keep secrets. He sneaks a look at his pal, who looks back and gives an involuntary shudder. Jostein's forehead is covered with spots. He will have to use a berry picker at the very least. He is a loser. He feels sorry for him. Jesper is ashamed of himself.

"Of course," Jesper says.

"Of course what?"

"Of course you'll live in a house like that."

"Do you think so?"

"Why not?"

"I feel like doing a ski jump."

"What did you just say?"

"Did you know that you can eat a pig's heart too?"

"Not me."

"No, you're a vegetablist. But people can. Eat a pig's heart. You can eat everything from a pig, not just the liver and the teats."

"Vegetarian."

"What?"

If we were standing on the moon tonight, preferably sheltered, and were watching the slow-moving, blue earth, we would see the Holmenkollen train winding its way down from the ridge like a millipede with headlamps. Many have described this sight. It is not only a sight for the gods but for humanity too. Humans should see themselves. They should travel as far away as possible and watch. Then they would see two adolescent boys, so different that they almost resemble each other, sitting in the last carriage, face to face, waiting until the last moment to stand up and get off at Slemdal, both hoping that the other will stay on board. Instead it is they who are standing on this earth and watching the moon, which is only borrowing the light it is shining in and is uninhabited and empty for the present, not abandoned, but empty.

"Why did you get off here?" Jesper asks.

Jostein is nervous and happy and wants to tell Jesper.

"I'm allowed to get off here as well, aren't I?" he says.

Jesper sees Trude coming past the school carrying a bag.

"I just wondered why."

"Because I want to walk home and sober up on the way."

"First, you're not drunk."

"And second?"

"Forget it."

Jostein shrugs and strolls away from the platform, as though he has no fixed destination. If he is walking home, he is going in the wrong direction. He is setting a course for the moon. Jesper shouts, but Jostein doesn't hear. Jostein is deaf. Jostein is listening. No-one listens more than the deaf. He hears everything else, heartbeats, the wind, running water. Trude stops in front of Jesper and gives him a quick kiss.

"Was that Jostein?"

"Apparently."

"Didn't he want to walk with us?"

"I asked him several times and in the end I went down on my knees and begged him. But he didn't want to."

Trude laughs.

"I'm glad you came."

Jesper takes her bag and they walk hand in hand down towards Vinderen. The moon glides behind a cloud and reappears on the other side, right above Ris church tower, making the houses shine like white ships, moored at the ends of the gardens.

"How many pairs of shoes have you got with you actually?" Jesper asks.

"I've got Elisabeth's too."

"Are you going to borrow her stilts?"

Trude lets go of his hand.

"You did notice them then?"

"It wasn't hard. She could've keeled over at any moment."

"She thinks Jostein is cool."

Jesper has to stop.

"Elisabeth Vilder thinks Jostein Melsom is cool?"

"Yes. So what?"

"Did she *say* that?"

"Yes. Does that matter?"

"No, I don't suppose it does. Why should it? Did she really say that Jostein was *cool*?"

Trude lowers her voice, but there is no-one nearby.

"And a little slow."

"Jostein isn't stupid. He's just a bit hard of hearing."

"Don't say I said so."

"I thought Elisabeth said so. Bitch."

They walk hand in hand again. The sky is thickening. Music is belting out from a window, a bottle is smashed, another party, some people arguing behind a fence, others laughing. They hurry past.

"She's not in a good place," Trude says.

"No, she can't be if she thinks Jostein is cool."

"Stop that. I mean it."

"In what way?"

"She seemed so lonely. So frightened."

"Perhaps she's just haughty."

"That wasn't nice. Why would she be haughty?"

Jesper is about to say because she is so beautiful. And that is why she is lonely too. Instead he suggests:

"We can go back and give her the shoes."

"Do you think so?"

Jesper squeezes her hand.

"Or go to Jeppe before they close. My treat."

They decide on Jeppe's bar. Who needs high heels when you are asleep? There is a free table near the door. They sit down and don't say a word until the waiter comes. Trude orders an Earl Grey. Jesper says casually, naturally, as if by the by:

"And a half-litre of draught, please."

They don't say another word until the waiter returns. He brings the tea and places a cup in front of Trude. Jesper sighs urbanely.

"And the beer? I think you must've forgotten it."

"Not at all. Won't be long."

The waiter goes away again and this time it seems as if it is for good.

"Do you miss your father?" Trude asks.

Jesper is looking in a different direction. At the other tables men with beards and slim ties are smoking pipes, while the women flick filter cigarettes from long packets: Ascot, Pall Mall, Craven A. The mist hangs low in Jeppe's bar.

"The devil's piano," he says.

Trude is silent and just stares at him. Couldn't she tell him what it meant either?

"Don't you want to talk about it?"

"It's fine by me."

"Then you don't have to."

Jesper hastens to add:

"Actually I don't remember much. Only that he was quite funny, came home late and smelt of overtime at the Bristol."

"Did you learn all those words from him?"

"Which ones?"

"Zoot. Map of the Balkans. Poof."

"Maybe."

"And now Enzo's teaching you to play the piano?"

Jesper doesn't quite know where she is heading with this, but he doesn't want to go there.

"Something like that," he says.

"He could almost be your father."

"Why do you say that?"

Trude sips at her tea, which is going cold. She doesn't take sugar.

"I don't know. He just looked like a father. As he was tending to your hand. You're not angry with me, are you?"

Jesper shakes his head and raises his hand. The waiter eventually catches sight of him and approaches their table with glue under the soles of his shoes.

"The beer?" Jesper says.

"Ah, the beer. It's coming."

"And how long will I have to wait?"

"Until you're eighteen. Anything else in the meantime?"

Jesper remembers that he can't tolerate stress and this is stressful. Humiliation is the biggest stress of them all. How many age limits are there in the world? There is an age limit for tobacco, cars, booze, a pension and bonking. Shouldn't there be an age limit for the "Ballad of Revolt" as well? Should there be an age limit for snotty waiters? Jesper doesn't even have time to break open a ten-krone note because Trude already has her money out and pays with coins. She looks up and smiles.

"Shall we go, Alf Iversen?"

They hurry out. It has started snowing. It is winter's last gasp. A horse is running in circles behind the Hippodrome. Its back and muzzle are steaming and this makes the snow that falls on the horse shine with a dark, restless glow. It is like instant circus. All that is missing is the blare of trumpets. There is no noise. Jesper puts his arm around Trude.

"Let's take a taxi," he says.

"We can walk."

"I've got money."

"Doesn't mean you have to waste it."

"Do you think taxis are a waste of money?"

"Especially when you can walk."

"Besides I have to be home . . ."

Jesper shuts his mouth and can hardly understand how he almost said it.

"She's lovely," Trude says.

"Who is?"

"The horse."

"How do you know it's a mare?"

"I've got to be home by half past eleven as well."

But they have to walk down to Majorstua anyway to find a free taxi. They climb onto the rear seat and are driven the rest of the way, past Vestkanttorget, through Briskeby, along Skovveien, across Solli Plass, into Inkognitogata and they pull in there. The driver is either considerate or just dying for a fag. He leaves them alone for the time it takes to finish a cigarette. Jesper kisses Trude again. Then she dashes into her house. Jesper wonders if he should walk home, but he doesn't have the energy. He is too happy. He will have to be careful. Happiness is stressful too. Happiness takes it out of you. He will catch taxis for the rest of his life. But he forgets to check the taxi meter. Happiness is not only stressful. It also costs. In Fagerborg the driver charges him twelve and a half kroner. Jesper is short of two and a half. It was the last kiss that did it. He was kissing on the slate.

"I've only got ten," Jesper says.

The driver sighs.

"You'll have to wake your dad then and tell him to pay the rest."

"He's asleep."

"That's why you have to wake him."

"He's dead."

"Can't be helped."

Jesper runs up and finds his mother in the kitchen. She is sitting by an empty cup of coffee and seems equally empty herself. Only the ashtray is full.

"I need two and a half kroner for the taxi," he says.

Strangely enough, she doesn't ask why, despite being so precise with her accounts. She just fetches three kroner from the surplus housekeeping money in an old cake tin in the larder and gives it to Jesper, who doesn't have the time to ask if something is wrong, but races back down to the driver to settle the fare. Maj stands watching. Stine hasn't woken up. She wonders if something has happened. Stine was suddenly different this evening, after Jesper had left, quiet in a reflective, almost gentle way. There isn't a sound to be heard from above, either. She empties the ashtray in the bin and washes it. Then Jesper returns, more slowly this time, takes off his shoes and windcheater. He looks nice in the white shirt. He puts the fifty-øre coin on the worktop and turns to his mother.

"Something the matter?"

"No, why should there be?"

"I said you didn't have to wait up."

"Did you two have a good time?"

"Jostein came."

"Was he invited too?"

"He gatecrashed. It was a class party."

"You let him in, though?"

Jesper looks around.

"Is Enzo back from touring?"

"Hm?"

"Or have you started smoking Teddy fags?"

"Come with me. And be quiet."

They tiptoe into the dining room. There is a new piece of furniture by the piano, an old stool with a round seat you can wind up and down, according to the height you want. Enzo Zanetti bought it in a second-hand shop in Eidsvoll. Stine is asleep in the corner. She is sleeping on her back and her hair is spread across the pillow. They tiptoe back to the kitchen. Maj takes a glass of water. She stands at the sink and downs it in one go. It is a wonder she doesn't break her neck. Jesper can tell there is still something wrong, there is more she wants to say. You don't need to be particularly sensitive to feel this; even an alligator would have felt it. Jesper doesn't quite know how to broach the subject.

"How far can you wind it down?"

"What?"

"The piano stool. What else?"

"Erm, he didn't say. You can adjust it to your height. And when you're bigger you'll have to lower it—"

Jesper interrupts her.

"Until I'm sitting on the floor. What is actually the matter with you?"

Maj turns to Jesper.

"Have you said something to Stine today?"

"How come?"

"Well, I don't know. She's just so – what shall I say? – changed after you left."

Jesper bursts into laughter. Now he understands. It all fits. So this is what was on his mother's mind all this time.

"I haven't said a word, but that idiot Jostein did."

"Don't call him that, please. Jostein is Jostein. What did he say?"

Jesper lowers his voice.

"He thinks Stine is *pretty*. And he said it so loud that the whole of Oslo heard it."

Maj laughs and sits down.

"It's true, of course. Stine is pretty. She always has been."

"In contrast to me, you mean?"

"Don't be silly. You're handsome, Jesper. Not pretty."

"And now she knows, she's become uppity and conceited and probably unbearable. Like Elisabeth."

"Elisabeth?"

"The best-looking girl in the class."

"Jesper. Isn't Trude the best-looking?"

Jesper remembers he is hungry. He opens the bread bin, spreads liver paste over a thick chunk of bread, forgetting that he is a vegetarian, and eats in silence.

"Ye-ah, she is, but that's not the point."

"Sit down, Jesper."

He does as she says. Here we go, now we'll hear what the matter is, and it must be something serious. He has been wrong all along. It doesn't all fit. It's all come apart at the seams. Is it something he has done? He can't remember having done anything, not something wrong anyway. This thought again: it's him there's a problem with. Was that why he had to go to hospital and have his noggin connected to the national grid? Have they received a letter saying there will soon be a nuclear war and everyone has to go to the nearest bunker armed with aspirin and a parasol? Maj takes a deep breath and braces herself.

"What would you say if I left you two on your own for a week?"

"Super duper."

"I mean it."

"Me too. You can go for a fortnight if you like."

Maj leans across the table and almost snarls:

"Can't you take something seriously for once?"

Now, finally, Jesper knows what is wrong with him. His mother told him. And so it must be true.

"You mean I'm just like my father?"

Maj holds his hand between hers, unhappy and ashamed. Her eyes are welling up.

"Forgive me, Jesper. I don't know any longer . . ."

"Where do you want to go?"

She looks away.

"Enzo Zanetti has invited me to Rome."

"Has he?"

"And I haven't said yes. Just so that you know."

"Why not?"

Maj lets go of his hand, rises to her feet and stands by the window, irresolute. She speaks quickly in a low voice.

"I've been thinking, Jesper. You could come with us. I'm sure they'd let you go if I tell them you're going to Italy with your music teacher."

It hasn't stopped snowing.

"But what about sis?"

"Margrethe can look after Stine."

"Out of the question," Jesper says.

"Or Fru Lund."

"I'd rather stay at home."

Maj sits down again, relieved and calm, though hiding her face in her hands.

"Then it's decided. Thank you, Jesper."

"What is? That madam, Fru Lund—"

"Shh! I'm not going. My God. Forget I ever told you. Do you promise me, Jesper? Do you promise?"

"I can look after Stine," he says.

Everyone is crocheting oven cloths.

RECORD

Jostein wakes up thinking he has been dreaming. He certainly wishes he had been. Then he could just have forgotten the whole business because dreams don't exist, they are merely films no-one else can see that disappear as soon as the lights are switched on. Imagine being able to say: Life is based on a misunderstanding. But what about daydreams? Do they disappear in the same way when darkness falls? Will he never become rich and live in an even bigger house than Axel's? In other words, Jostein is confused, and not only that, he has also been rejected. Confused and rejected means he was taken in hook, line and sinker, and that would make anyone angry. But that is not Jostein's way. He doesn't lose his temper easily. Unhappy is a closer approximation. He is in bed and unhappy. The bitch couldn't even be bothered to open the door when he rang. She must have been lying in the bath sniggering at him all evening. And when she goes to school on Monday morning she will still be convulsed and in the end the whole of Fagerborg will be laughing at him. Jostein the spotty apprentice thought he had a chance with Elisabeth Vilder! What a joke. He never wants to get out of bed again. However, in the long run being unhappy is pretty boring. So he gets up, draws the curtains and has to close his eyes for a minute or two. The backyard is white and virgin. There is even snow on the clothesline. Now Jostein knows better: living in a grand house and becoming rich isn't a daydream. There are such things as plans. And that is something else. He has to make plans; he mustn't dream. The first plan is to do a ski jump. It is the last chance this winter. He doesn't hear the church bells, but he sees the clothesline vibrate and shake off the snow, which falls like powder between heaven and earth. That is all. Sunday is the day for the deaf. He goes into the bathroom and gets ready. The pustules on his forehead are still there. Except that there are more of them. Perhaps that is why Elisabeth didn't open the door? Who would want to share a bath with such a zit-pudding? Who would want to exchange fluids with a pimple? Not Elisabeth Vilder Jr, that is for sure. When Jostein examines himself in the mirror again he can, to a certain degree, understand her. She is not a bitch. It is him. He is a shrimp. He puts on the appropriate gear: boots, long socks, breeches, anorak with pockets and zip, and on top of his head the bobble cap he was given for Christmas. Pulling it right down over his forehead, enough so that he can still see, he feels it prickle and itch. That, however, is better than revealing the entire redcurrant patch. There is breakfast for him in the kitchen – a glass of milk, porridge and salami on rye. Jostein isn't hungry. He is pensive. He puts the sandwich in his anorak. His mother comes in and sits down, a black hymn book sticking up from her handbag. She has been to church again. It is a bad habit she has got into.

"Where were you yesterday?" she asks.

"Around and about."

"Alone?"

"With Jesper."

Jostein eats the porridge so that at least he doesn't have to speak with food in his mouth.

"You didn't get up to any tricks?"

"What did you say?"

"You heard what I said."

"What sort of tricks?"

"You know that best yourself."

"I don't get up to any tricks. Because there are no bloody tricks to get up to. I'm eating."

"Jostein! And take that hat off!"

Jostein's mother bangs the table with her hand. His glass of milk topples, but he catches it.

"Has Pappa been to church too?"

"As if. By the way, you should go down and help him."

Jostein keeps his hat on.

"I'm free on Sundays. That's in my contract."

His mother smiles and sighs at the same time.

"If you get up to any more tricks, you'll lose your apprenticeship. Are you aware of that?"

"It wasn't my fault."

"Besides, Pappa let you sleep in. He's a nice man. Much too nice."

"I'm going to do a ski jump. Can't you see that?"

"With Jesper?"

"I expect he'll just watch. He hasn't got the guts."

Jostein's mother puts another sandwich in his anorak pocket. Jostein is beginning to look like a blue kangaroo. He fetches the skis and poles from the cellar and pops by the shop on his way out. His father doesn't keep the Sabbath holy. He isn't merely a butcher. Melsom is also his own man, as far as that is at all possible. That is why he is stocktaking. He is checking the stock he hasn't sold. Sometimes there is more stock left than customers have bought. It is a sad toll. It is the trade surplus. The good times have a cost. And the state takes the rest. It isn't fair. Melsom isn't a burden to anyone. He is never ill, he never claims welfare benefits, he never cheats and usually he is honest in almost every respect. It is true that Jostein had to go to a special school, but now he has finished and is doing an apprenticeship. Unfortunately his wife has Seen the Light and goes to church every Sunday. However, that shouldn't cost 9,756 kroner. Melsom, the butcher and shopkeeper, moves a leg of ham along the rail, notes down another minus and turns to Jostein, who is in the process of wrecking the whole shop with his skis. That is all he needs. He feels a sudden urge to give his son a real thrashing. Why, he doesn't know. He can feel his hands itching to slap him.

"That's good," he says.

"What's good?"

"That you're going to get some fresh air. Not much of that in a slaughterhouse, is there?"

"I can help you when I get back."

"You don't have to. Thank you anyway."

"Why?"

Melsom closes the ledger, he is beginning to get sick of all these questions. It is like primary school: "wh-" questions all day long.

"Because you need a head for this," he says.

Jostein switches the skis to his other shoulder.

"And don't I have one?"

"I didn't say that. Tell me what your mother said."

"Haven't I got a head?" Jostein repeats.

"Take off that girl's hat and I'll tell you."

Melsom laughs and tries to snatch it from his head, but Jostein puts up a fight, scrambles through the doorway with the skis and poles all at sixes and sevens and disappears up Kirkeveien. Melsom watches him and already has pangs of conscience. Words come out wrong so easily when they are together. It is as if they can't talk to each other anymore. There are only misunderstandings and squabbles. If only Jostein would turn and wave to show a notional white flag on this Sunday morning that will soon be midday. But Jostein is definitely not going to turn. Not bloody likely. He hasn't got a head, so what is the point of turning? Instead he pulls his woollen hat further down over his non-head, hurries on and crosses Suhms gate, where there should be a memorial plaque: *Jostein Melsom fell here in front of the number 20 bus*. By Jonas Reins gate he spots Jesper, who is hanging out of the window for a breath of fresh air, which according to trade union rules is forbidden on Sundays. Jesper also spots Jostein, who waves his ski poles, and it is too late to back away quietly. Actually, he'd had other plans for the day, among them to practise the piano, go for a walk with Trude, along Frogner bay perhaps, or the other way, past Banana-Matthiessen's and over to Akers Mek, where the black ships are in dry dock waiting to slip into the equally sombre waters that immediately begin to rise. They can also admire Samson, the crane that lifts only fifty tons of nothing on Sundays and public holidays. But now stress is beckoning for Jesper and he can't reject his pal twice in a row. That is simply the way it is, stress or no stress. A remarkable idea strikes him, it is much too large for him, yet he does think it: he could die for Jostein. He closes the window and shouts through the flat:

"Watch out! Monster on the loose!"

Then he goes to the hall, opens the door and has the skis thrust into his face.

"We're going ski-jumping," Jostein says.

"You're going ski-jumping."

"That's exactly what I said."

"What happened to you yesterday?"

"Nothing to do with you."

"Why's it nothing to do with me?"

"Because it's not your place to ask."

"Right. But you could've joined us."

"Joined?"

"We took a taxi."

"Have you gone all posh as well now? Just like Axel."

Maj calls from the kitchen: "Have a bite to eat before you go." That's all we need. Jostein parks his equipment. Jesper pulls him closer.

"Don't you say a bloody word to Stine."

"Such as what?"

"Such as how pretty she is, you idiot. She's seven years old."

"I didn't say it to her. I said it to you."

"But she heard. And she's been walking around with her nose in the air ever since."

"I could say she's ugly. Even though that's not true."

"Don't say anything at all."

"My father said I haven't got a head."

"Did he?"

"Is that what you think as well? That I haven't got a head?"

"Well, you've definitely got a hat on it. Are you coming?"

Jostein stomps after Jesper to the kitchen, where Maj has set the table for them. Stine is sitting in her place and staring at Jostein in such a way that Jesper feels like moving her, plus the chair, into the loft. Jostein is hungry again and helps himself with both hands. With his mouth full, he turns to Stine.

"Your brother doesn't dare jump. He's a wimp."

"He is not. The doctor said he's not allowed to."

There is a silence. Jostein looks at Jesper.

"You're not allowed to jump?"

"I could damage my hands. But you probably wouldn't hear the difference if I played with my toes."

Stine laughs. Maj tops up their glasses of milk.

"You should take care anyway. And take your hat off when you're indoors, Jostein. Even if it is very nice."

"I can't."

"Oh? Why's that, Jostein?"

"I haven't got a head underneath."

"Time will tell. But take it off for now."

Jostein hesitates, but does as Maj says, pulling off the woollen hat as if he were unveiling a failed statue and dropping it onto his lap. Stine stares at him with big eyes that get smaller and smaller until she ventures to ask:

"Why have you got so many spots on your forehead?"

"Because I work in the slaughterhouse."

"Do you get spots there?"

Jostein drinks up his milk and wipes his moustache with the whole of his anorak.

"You can squeeze them for me."

Stine grimaces.

"Yuk. You're disgusting."

For a moment Jostein seems unhappy and lost for words.

"It's not my fault. The air's bad. Everyone has spots."

Maj puts the bottle of milk in the refrigerator and rests her hands on his shoulders.

"There are creams you can use."

"Where?"

"At the perfumery."

"I don't go to perfumeries."

Maj laughs.

"And at the chemist."

"Think I could jump twelve metres today."

Jostein puts his hat back on and is in a hurry. He doesn't want to be late for the winter's last ski run. But he insists they don't go via Kirkeveien, which is the quickest route, he demands that they go round Frøen and Tørtbergjordet and approach Majorstua station from the west. Fine, if that is what he wants. It is all the same to Jesper. He isn't going to jump. He is graciously given permission to carry the bamboo poles. The Sunday is ruined anyway. He knows that detours are sometimes quickest. Probably Jostein's father wanted him to work, even though the shop is closed. They race past the police college, along the railway platform and through the waiting room, but Jesper stops there and holds Jostein back. Standing on the big weighing machine in the corner, which costs 25 øre per person to use, and gives you a prediction at the same time, is the priest. The one from Majorstua church, mind you, not Fagerborg. He is checking how much he weighs and then takes the card and quickly reads what the near future will bring him. He is thin, as most men of his age in this district are, so it can't be the kilos he is worried about. But doesn't the future rest in God's hands and not in those of the weighing machine at Majorstua station? The priest drops the card and rushes out. Jesper picks it up and reads aloud: *You will go far.* Jostein asks Jesper to put the card in his anorak pocket. It is an omen. Jostein suddenly becomes profound and carefree: *You will go far.* It is Jostein's future. He will go far. Then at last they take the quickest route, past Frogner stadium and the blue diving boards in the lido, which during this month is no more than empty scaffolding above equally empty pools, of no use to anyone except the homeless and left-behind migratory birds. The sun makes an appearance. This is disappointing. The snow crumples, and rises as steam and light. Jostein quickens his pace before it has all gone. Then they are there, by the waterfall that lands between the rocks at the end of Frogner Park and runs into the fjord, taking ice floes and swans with it. The in-run consists mostly of snow crust. The out-run is mostly stones and mud. And the ski jump itself is made of chipboard, roofing felt, orange boxes and the remains of a crooked picket fence. Jostein straps on his skis and twists his bobble hat round until the Norwegian colours are facing the right direction.

"Do you think this is wise?" Jesper asks.

"Poles," Jostein says.

"You're not going to jump with poles, are you?"

"Why do you think I brought them?"

"So that I had something to carry."

"It's the latest trend. Jumping with ski poles."

"You could stab yourself in the eye."

"Not me. I'm going to go far."

Jesper gives the poles to Jostein, who winds the straps around his wrists and climbs sideways to the top. Jesper stands at the very bottom. He is going to measure the distance and count the number of severed body parts. A crowd is slowly gathering on the bridge. The noise of the waterfall sounds like applause. Applause sounds like the noise of a waterfall swans fall into. That is how sounds interconnect. They merge into one another and mingle. To play music is to keep them apart. To play music is to tidy up the noise. Jesper raises a hand and waves, but regrets this instantly. It could make him an accessory to homicide. Jostein sets off. He digs the poles in hard over the first strides to achieve maximum speed, then he crouches down with the poles tucked under his arms and as he hits the rickety edge of the jump he sticks his bum in the air as he leans forward elegantly and stretches out his arms to steer with the poles. Jesper has to shield his eyes. The flight seems to last for ever. In the meantime the rest of the snow melts, the ice disappears, the swans return, the waterfall acquires a new sound, more like the rustle of sweet papers and whispering, and the crowd goes elsewhere, probably to the lido, which has just opened, or the outdoor restaurants, where there are no free tables. Jostein beats all the records. He set off in winter and landed in spring. But it would not be right to call it a Telemark landing. A Telemark pile would be closer. Jesper picks him up.

"No worse than the number 20 bus," Jostein says.

At that moment they hear a dreadful racket coming from inside the ski jump: cursing, shouting, banging and other commotion that you don't associate with the insides of a ski jump and which even Jesper has trouble explaining. Immediately afterwards, directly below the top edge, a hatch opens and the most overgrown cabbagehead in Vigeland Park appears. Jostein undoes his skis and the two boys move closer. It is the tramp Jesper can't seem to get away from. Now he is here too. It is the merchant seaman who lives in an out-of-season ski jump.

"Isn't it possible for a poor man to have some peace and quiet?"

They approach him. The face inside the hair and beard is as furrowed as dry arable land and the eyes look inwards while the mouth is a black pit. However, this is not what primarily attracts Jesper's attention. He notices that the tramp is quite young, at any rate younger than his mother. Nevertheless, he soon has a nickname: Old Shark.

"We won't bother you anymore," Jesper says.

"Thank you."

It is as though Old Shark has fallen asleep where he is sitting and has entered a state of hibernation unrecognisable to anyone else – escape, fear, thirst. Jostein pokes him with his ski pole.

"Why do you live here?" he asks.

"Because the Bristol is fully booked."

Old Shark bursts into song. His voice comes from the depths of a nightmare and is therefore quiet and beautiful. Perhaps it is a song he has learned from other Oslo originals: Lousy-Frants or Astrid, the Queen of Homansbyen. He might also have picked it up at the Herberth Circus. But most likely it was sung by the crew of M/T *Varanger*, loaded with twelve thousand tons of fuel oil, when it was hit by three torpedoes off the east coast of America in January 1942. Jesper can't get the song out of his head.

We are still crocheting oven cloths.

STOWAWAYS

On Monday morning Elisabeth's desk is unoccupied. She doesn't appear for the second lesson either. Actually this is nothing to make a fuss about. She is often late on Mondays and brings a note from home. Her mother will write whatever is necessary, except the truth. Sometimes Elisabeth writes the notes herself. She has mastered her mother's signature and hasn't been caught yet. She never will be. In the break, Trude puts the high-heeled shoes by her chair. The mood is generally quite sleepy and charged at the same time. Some of the class overstepped the mark, are embarrassed and blush at the slightest provocation, while others swagger and make cheeky comments, apparently of the opinion they put in a real performance on the dance floor or in adjacent rooms. Most, however, are quiet and expectant. It is a strange atmosphere on the whole, more like remorse than joy. But no-one has done anything wrong. That is what is so strange. In the third lesson Ramm just has time to remind them about Goethe's poem "Über allen Gipfeln" before he is summoned to the headmaster's study. The class sits in silence waiting for him to return. Time passes. Soon the bell will ring. Nothing like this has ever happened before. Something is wrong. The pupils exchange glances. Does anyone know what is going on? No-one does. But they sense that some heartache is in the offing, a great, incomprehensible woe. It is the unoccupied desk that casts the shadow. It fills the room. Yet what is to come is impossible to predict. It is beyond their imagination and experience. Ramm opens the door, steps inside, slowly closes it with both hands, as though he is shutting a bank vault, and stands in front of his desk, head bowed, almost incapable of raising his gaze and looking his pupils in the eyes. When at last he does, the mild-mannered man's hair has gone white.

"This is hard for us all," he says.

Ramm hides his face in his hands. He was at the class party himself. He was there. And for the rest of his life he will have to wrestle with this question: should he have seen something? He drops his arms and stands defenceless in front of the blackboard.

"Elisabeth Vilder is dead."

At first the silence is even quieter. Then some of the girls start crying. Jesper turns to Trude. She is slumped across her desk. Her back is heaving. Axel puts his hand up and is not as jaunty as before.

"How did she die?"

Ramm doesn't answer. Perhaps he doesn't want to. Perhaps he doesn't know. Perhaps he didn't hear the question. He doesn't appear to be with us. It is a stranger standing there. Then he explodes. They have never seen him so angry before. But it is a different kind of anger. Its source is elsewhere, who knows where? His hand shaking, he points.

"Who put those shoes there?"

Trude slowly rises to her feet.

"I did."

"Move them. Now!"

"Where shall I put them?"

"Wherever you like. Just not there. Do you understand?"

Trude takes the shoes, which she had even cleaned, puts them in her net bag and sits down. There is a long silence. Everyone is looking down. Ramm coughs and his shoulders slump. His voice is low and thin.

"Those of you who wish to go home can go."

No-one moves.

In the lunch break rumours are rife. Some purport to know how Elisabeth died. She fell down the stairs and lay at the bottom bleeding to death. She was ill, say the girls who didn't know her.

Everyone could see how thin she was. The older boys have foolish grins on their faces. No, she hanged herself in her room. She used a knife from the kitchen drawer. The bell rings. It is hard to say whose idea it was, but initially everyone thought it was a good idea, even Ramm agreed. Everyone should write one word, only one, on a scrap of paper, to describe Elisabeth, then the scraps would be collected and read aloud. In the last lesson Trude and Axel have the task of presenting these anonymous, pithy obituaries of Elisabeth Vilder. They stand in front of the blackboard and take turns to read out the unsigned notes: *pretty, pretty, sporty, lovely, golden, sharp, thoughtful, clever, nice, pretty, sparrow.* Ramm is on the point of stopping them, but doesn't. They can carry on. It is Trude's turn: *stylish, squirrel, pretty, party animal, goose, pulchritudinous, cheerleader.* Ramm's hand shoots into the air.

"Let's stop there. Who wrote *goose?*"

No-one reacts.

"And *pulchritudinous?*"

"I did."

It is Axel who answers. Ramm turns to him, weary rather than angry.

"You should be above that, Werner."

"I just wanted to vary the language."

Ramm takes the rest of the notes and puts them in the desk drawer, which he locks. He composes himself and then talks again.

"We should remember the dead with respect and reverence. Don't forget that. When a young person dies, he or she hasn't yet had the time to leave their mark. Youth is a mould in the making, unfinished and full of hope."

Here Ramm is forced to pause. It is as though the whole world pauses. He tries again:

"A young person is a mould in the making, unfinished and full of hope. That perhaps is the greatest joy. Being unfinished and full of hope. We will probably wonder if there was anything we could have done. But life is unpredictable. Please, I beg of you, do not feel any pangs of conscience. If anyone should, it's me. Concentrate on the happy memories. There's no homework for tomorrow."

The bell rings.

Not even now does the class want to go. Pangs of conscience? That was a truthful gaffe. A connection begins to dawn on them. They reluctantly leave the classroom, hesitantly, some with their arms around each other. Ramm asks Trude to stay behind. He waits until they are alone.

"I apologise. Do you accept my apology?"

Trude nods and lets him continue.

"Nevertheless, it was unseemly of me to talk to you like that. If you wish to make a complaint, you're fully within your rights. I can go with you to the office and ask for a leave of absence."

Trude looks up and shakes her head.

"Let's leave it there."

"I can take her shoes so that her parents have them along with the rest of her belongings. There's so much. Her gym togs, pencils, exercise book, grade book, even a jacket she left in the autumn."

"I'd like to return her shoes personally."

"Fine. And on May 17th you should hold your talk with the same enthusiasm. Can you do that?"

"Did Elisabeth take her own life?"

"Pretty? Cheerleader? Is that how most will remember her? Wasn't she so much more than that?"

"I'm not sure anyone knew her really well."

"What did you write? No, you don't have to answer."

"Lonely," Trude says.

Ramm gives her the shoes, sits down and doesn't move.

"Elisabeth's parents found her in the bath on Sunday night."

Jesper is waiting at the gates. They walk in silence to Stens Park and find a free bench. The last snow is melting behind the church. The sun has warmth now. The light fills the trees.

"I can't play the 'Ballad of Revolt' now," Jesper says.

"Yes, you can."

"It will have to be Satie instead."

"Or Brahms."

Jesper laughs, but quickly realises that is inappropriate.

"The interval signal from the radio. That would be good."

"What did you write?"

Jesper hesitates.

"Bombshell."

"No, you didn't."

"Didn't I?"

"Don't be silly. I recognised your writing and that wasn't what you wrote."

"I was thinking of writing *bombshell*. We were supposed to be honest, weren't we?"

"You wrote *failed*. Do you think *that*'s any better?"

"I can explain."

"You don't need to."

Trude gets up and walks down to Bislett with her bag over one shoulder and the net containing the shoes in her other hand. Her back bristles with defiance and Jesper doesn't dare follow her.

"You don't understand," he shouts.

Trude stops and turns round.

"The failure committed suicide, Jesper. In the bath."

She walks down Suhms gate and is gone.

Jesper stays on the bench until he starts to freeze. Then he stays a bit longer. He thinks about Stine and his head aches. Is she going to be as pretty and lonely as Elisabeth? He will have to make sure that doesn't happen. And then he will play Old Shark's song on May 17th, with one finger, and Old Shark can come out of the ski jump and sing all the verses. Who else should sing for those students who were killed in the war? The bench is sinking into the soft earth beneath Jesper. Everything is drenched. Suicide? Are there no other options? Wouldn't it be better to commit a crime or run away to sea, if it is change you want, and isn't that a change? The headache is here to stay. His mind is in a tailspin. Then Jesper walks home.

In Kirkeveien he meets Jostein. He is sporting a real shiner after the ski jump, and a plaster on one cheek. He needs a bandage for his forehead as well.

"I'm taking time off in lieu," he says.

"You're doing what?"

"Ah, don't you understand? Do I know an expression Jesper Kristoffersen Himself doesn't understand?"

"Why are you taking time off in lieu?"

"Because I worked extra shifts last week."

"Have you heard?"

"Have you heard what? I can't hear, can I?"

"About what happened to Elisabeth? The girl with the shoes . . .?"

"I know who Elisabeth Vilder is. I'm not blind. What about her?"

Jesper scrutinises his battered and bruised pal. At least he is wearing his best jacket, the tweed one, maybe only because the sun is warming again. After all it was he who brought in spring with his jump.

"She's dead."

Jostein closes his eyes and opens them with a start.

"When did she die?"

"Saturday evening. After Trude accompanied her home."

Jostein is struggling to digest the information, but all of a sudden he smiles as though everything has just fallen into place.

"So that was why she didn't open the door."

Now it is Jesper's turn to struggle to digest information. What is his pal talking about? He goes over to Jostein, who wipes the grin off his face as fast as it came.

"What do you mean?"

Jostein retreats.

"I let the pig escape," he says.

"What *are* you talking about?"

"The pig in Fagerborg. It was me who let it go. I took such a shine to it, Jesper. There was something in its eyes. I couldn't . . ."

Jostein falls quiet, wipes half an arm across his face and comes out on the other side with misty eyes. Neither of them says anything for a few moments. Then Jesper asks again:

"What do you mean?"

"Eh? I only tried to save one pig. Perhaps I'll go vegerarian too. I'm happy to be grounded if I can save one."

"What did you mean she didn't open the door?"

"It's the gospel truth."

"Did you go to Elisabeth's house?"

"Yes, of course I did."

"Why on earth did you do that?"

"She invited me. For your information."

"Elisabeth invited you? Did she hell!"

"I'm telling the truth."

"When?"

At deaf school Jostein learned to keep his mouth shut or to talk non-stop if he was in doubt.

"I answered the telephone when I was having a piss. It was her."

"You were pissing and answering the telephone?"

"It was the telephone they've got in the bog. On the wall beside the sink. And she asked me if I wanted to go to hers. And I said yes. Shouldn't I have done? Should I have said no? What would you have said if she'd invited you, eh?"

Jesper puts down his bag and believes him because today everything is possible, no matter what.

"Is that why you were grounded six months ago?"

"Yes. Actually, I don't think I'm suited to being a butcher. I'm too sensitive. What do you think?"

Jesper struggles to compose his thoughts.

"And so you just went to Elisabeth's and rang the bell?"

Jostein nods and remains quiet. The black eye quivers. The other one will soon be equally black. At any rate both are quite misty.

"Was she dead then?" he asks.

Jesper nods.

"She took her own life."

Jostein slowly crosses Kirkeveien, between the cars, as though he wants to be knocked down again and doesn't give a damn. He is heading for Therese's kiosk. He is in there for quite a while. That is why he has so many spots. He eats too many sweets. He stuffs himself by the bucketload. Eventually he returns and the cars honk their horns at the demented pedestrian with the black eyes. Jesper can choose between liquorice sticks, sugar candy, a Cuba nougat bar and Firkløver chocolate. Jesper isn't hungry. He doesn't feel like any of it. He'd rather throw up. He takes some sugar candy, puts it on his tongue and can feel the sweet, almost caustic taste spreading, as though a transparent, dark-yellow flower was blossoming in his mouth.

"How did she do it?" Jostein asks.

Jesper can barely talk; he is thinking more about Trude than Elisabeth.

"In the bath."

Jostein freezes.

"In the bath," Jesper repeats.

Jostein has already heard. He heard it so clearly. *In the bath*. He has never heard better. For a moment he is a statue in Fagerborg. Jostein is a stone sculpture. He is flesh turned stone in a tweed jacket. Then he comes back to life, puts the sweets in his pockets and walks off. Jostein Melsom, the butcher's son, just walks off. Jesper watches. Aren't there more than two types of people: those who ask *why* and those who want to know *how*? Today Jesper studies everyone and wonders whether he will ever be like them. When he arrives home there is a white van in Gørbitz gate with Oslo Pest Control, Birger Samuelsen Jr written on the side in black letters. Up in the flat a man wearing a boiler suit and gas mask, probably Birger Samuelsen Jr, is busily spraying the rooms. There is a smell of chlorine and pepper. Then he tackles the crack in the wall with a large suction cup. Jesper retreats to the kitchen where Maj and Stine have already barricaded themselves in. It is a fitting conclusion to this day, which still isn't over. Birger Samuelsen Jr comes out to them, removes his gas mask and reports back: the stowaways, as he likes to call them, have been temporarily destroyed. But the rooms mustn't be used for forty-eight hours at the earliest and the windows should be left open in the meantime. The bill will be sent by post during the week; payment terms are a month from the invoice date. Following which, interest is applied; any default will result in debt recovery or legal action. Maj promises to pay and would like to know what stowaways he found. Birger Samuelsen Jr counts on his fingers. Cockroaches, house longhorn beetles, larder beetles and flour beetles. But where do they come from? You only need one and soon you have a whole flock of them, says Birger Samuelsen, and they accompany him to the door. But that one beetle must come from somewhere, Jesper thinks. Bjørn Stranger is on the landing. He is worked up. His face is contorted. His fist is clenched.

"You're not going to have me exterminated while you're at it, are you?" he shouts.

It strikes Maj that that could be an idea. Birger Samuelsen Jr could use the suction cup on Bjørn Stranger and get rid of him. She assumes it is the noise the sensitive man was objecting to.

"Surely it wasn't that bad," she says.

Bjørn Stranger steps closer and is menacing. He is serious. Birger Samuelsen Jr puts down his equipment ready to intervene. But Jesper beats him to it. He stands between his mother and Bjørn Stranger, who is barely capable of speaking without spluttering. Saliva is running from the corners of his mouth.

"You had me removed from Grønnegata, so why not finish the job off? Eh?"

Maj doesn't understand and pushes Jesper aside. She isn't afraid of this poor devil; she feels sorry for him.

"What do you mean, Bjørn?"

"I'm no longer allowed to look after the residents there. And for that I can thank Dr Lund and the Red Cross. I don't have permission. I don't even have permission to check a pulse. Your friend snitched on me. And now I've got the medical council on my back."

Bjørn leans against the balustrade and the anger in him subsides, leaving behind great sadness.

"I loved being there," he says quietly.

Maj tries to pat his arm, but he flinches. The last thing he says is more like a desperate sigh:

"I have nothing else."

Bjørn Stranger walks slowly up the stairs. Birger Samuelsen Jr walks down. He carries the dead stowaways in a dust bag. The Kristoffersen family go back inside. There is a draught. Maj closes all the doors. That night Stine sleeps with her. Jesper hopes Trude will ring. Even in the middle of the night he hopes she will ring and say that everything is alright, nothing has changed. But all he can hear is the song he can't get out of his head, Old Shark's song, it is stuck, like a rusty merry-go-round in an amusement park:

> See the angel of peace sway
> From its lair it steals
> In the winter it moves by sleigh
> While in the spring it rolls on wheels

At the meeting on April 28th Herr Holm from HQ said that now they were making good progress with recovering membership fees, but the lists of members in the various departments were highly inaccurate and contained names of many who had died or moved to unspecified addresses years ago. He suggested departments should pay for help to update the lists and wanted to know whether they would be able to take on this expense.

Fagerborg department was asked to give 50 kroner to help a homeless mother and daughter living in a tent. We also planned to give 50 kroner, or possibly a larger amount, to mentally ill patients detained by police patrols and admitted to Ullevål Hospital.

THE CAMPAIGN

Maj closes the door after her and waits for Rudjord to finish his telephone conversation. Then she takes a step forward.

"I've been thinking a bit about the Valcrema campaign," she says.

"Mm."

Rudjord signs some papers, which he passes to her.

"And I think I may have an idea."

"I'm all ears."

Rudjord motions for Maj to sit down. She prefers to stand.

"A friend of Jesper's . . . that's my son . . ."

"How is he?"

"Jesper? He's fine. He's as well as you can be at that age."

"And how well is that?"

Maj laughs.

"Suspicious, introverted, short fuse, reflective, in love."

Rudjord interrupts her with a chortle:

"In short, like most men."

"Oh, I'm not sure about that."

Maj sits down after all. They both think about Ewald, or at least she does. He wasn't like that. He might have been reflective, but that was towards the very end, and he was probably in love only at the very beginning.

Rudjord lights a cigarette and rests it on a little ledge in the turquoise ashtray that wasn't there before.

"Signed by Lars Backer himself," he says.

"Lars Backer?"

"Norway's leading architect. Imagine, Maj. An architect who

works on the biggest projects – high-rise blocks, power stations, malls, skyscrapers and hotels – also designs an *ashtray*. The smallest of all household furnishings. That's modern times, the modern style. Nothing is too small. And this friend of yours?"

"Jostein. He works at Oslo Slaughterhouse and has a lot of spots on his forehead. It struck me we could photograph him before and after he uses Valcrema."

"I think most of us had imagined a girl. Girls and women are our target clientele."

"How come? Boys are just as bothered by spots. Perhaps even more so. Besides, women have sons they'd like to help. And I can promise you, young boys won't go to the chemist or a perfumery to buy Valcrema."

Rudjord lets his cigarette go out in the architect-designed ashtray.

"May I ask if we're dealing here with a good-looking boy?"

Maj laughs again.

"Jostein's not exactly good-looking, compared with film stars, but he's a good lad and easy to like."

"I'll give it some thought."

"But it depends on whether the cream works."

Rudjord lights another cigarette and blows blue rings towards the ceiling.

"Maj, Maj, you're too good for this world. We can't wait for six months to see if *perhaps* the spots go. We touch up photos."

Maj stands up, goes over to the door, pushes it half-open and pauses. Some of the men in the design room glance up and then carry on with their work. She is overcome by a depressing thought: nothing is true any longer. But this thought is also liberating. She can do what she wants. It doesn't make any difference. Nothing is true. Maj hears Rudjord's voice; he is talking on the telephone or to her. She closes the door after her and fiddle-faddles for the rest of the day. The designers taught her to do that. Fiddle-faddling is just pretending you are often deep in thought. When she gets home Stine is setting the table. They make dinner together: fried fishcakes, carrots and potatoes. Flatbread is good with it as well.

"Where's Jesper?" Maj asks.

Stine looks up and Maj notices only now that she is wearing lipstick.

"Don't you know?"

"Know what?"

"Someone in his class died."

"No. Oh, my God. Who?"

"Elisabeth. The prettiest."

Maj moistens a piece of kitchen roll, places a hand at the back of Stine's neck and wipes her mouth. She tries to wriggle free, but Maj doesn't let her. She just holds her tighter.

"If you want to borrow my lipstick, you ask me first, right? What's more, you won't be starting all that stuff for quite a while yet."

They sit down at the table. Stine is on the verge of tears and refuses to eat. Her eyes are strangely hard and intransigent. They don't seem to match the rest of her face. Maj is sure Stine can see right through her, to where everything is revealed. She knows that it is her daughter who should apologise, yet she says:

"Sorry."

"I just wanted to look nice."

"You *do* look nice, Stine. You don't need to use cosmetics."

"Lots of girls at school do."

"That's because they're not as pretty as you. So they have to cheat instead."

"She took her own life."

"What's that? Elisabeth? Took her own life?"

"On Saturday."

"Did Jesper tell you?"

"Everyone knows. In the bathtub."

"Oh, no. In the bath?"

Stine nods and at last her eyes brim over. Maj takes her hand and doesn't know what to say.

"Come with me to the meeting tonight," she says.

Stine shakes her head and pulls her hand back. For a moment Maj has a feeling she has lost her, incomprehensibly, and she has to catch her again.

"We're just going to chat. And I'm sure Fru Lund has baked a cake. Perhaps there'll be some pop as well."

Whatever Maj promises, it doesn't help. Stine doesn't want to go with her. She just carries on crying. In the end, Maj loses patience.

"It's dreadful, but after all is said and done, you didn't know her."

Both of them sit up straight when they hear Jesper in the hall. He takes his time. Then he comes into the kitchen, goes straight to the refrigerator, opens it, finds the milk and stands with his back to them as he drinks from the bottle.

"Why didn't you tell me?" Maj says.

"Tell you what?"

"About Elisabeth."

"If you already know, it makes no difference now."

"Have you been at school until now?"

"I went to thank Enzo Zanetti for the piano stool."

"That was nice of you. Don't you want anything to eat?"

"When can we close those bloody windows?"

"They have to be open for a couple more days."

Jesper puts the bottle back, swings the door shut and turns round.

"Do you know what Enzo Zanetti said, Mamma?"

She gives a start.

"No, what?"

"That I played well today."

Maj breathes out and looks at Jesper, who is standing there as closed as ever, as dissatisfied as ever.

"But isn't that nice?"

"Why did he think I played well today of all days?"

"Because you did, I suppose."

"And why would I play better than a week ago when I haven't even practised?"

"I have no idea."

"No, of course you don't."

"What do you mean?"

"Nothing."

"Alright. Now I have to go to my meeting."

"What do you actually do at these meetings?"

"What we do? We plan bazaars and trips and lotteries. We . . ."

Jesper can't be bothered to listen to any more and turns to Stine.

"What's up with you then? Have you been crying?"

Maj starts to clear the table, but leaves the plate of fishcakes.

"Stine's also sad about what happened to Elisabeth."

Jesper is about to say something, but holds back and places a hand on Stine's shoulder, and she leans her cheek, which is hot and damp, against it.

"We can wash up," he says.

Maj dashes into her bedroom and changes into something lighter.

Jesper sits down, squeezes a fishcake between two flatbreads and eats with his fingers. Stine waits for him to say something. She doesn't have to wait long.

"Elisabeth's silly."

Stine lets out a sigh.

"She's pretty."

"*Was* pretty. Sorry. She was silly and pretty."

"You're a naughty boy."

"Elisabeth was the one who was naughty. This is the worst thing you can do. To take your own life. Bloody hell, this is as bad as it's possible to be."

Jesper doesn't say any more for now because Maj is standing in the doorway and ready to leave.

"I won't be long. And I'll bring you some cake. If Jesper stops swearing."

Jesper is licking his fingers.

"And don't forget to ask Fru Lund what the heck she's done to Bjørn Stranger."

"That's none of our business," Maj says.

THE MINUTES

"We have fifteen takers for our old people's tour on the seventh of June. Fourteen women and only one man, Herr Ulltveidt from Vibesgate, I'm afraid to say. This should be a wake-up call. For a cosier atmosphere it's important to have a better gender split. It turns out, however, that men, especially the single ones, are harder to communicate with. As we have plenty of time and there are still free seats I think we should do our utmost to encourage these men to join in. With regard to the September bazaar we've never been so well prepared in advance. It's also a pleasure to announce at this meeting that Princess Astrid will be in attendance on the opening day. Any questions so far?"

Fru Lund closes the minute book and looks around. Fru Endresen, Fru Schanke, Frøken Berge and Frøken Jacobsen are sitting quietly with their hands in their laps. Fru Kristoffersen hasn't arrived yet. She could be late because she is accompanying Margrethe Hall, formerly Fru Vik. The chocolate cake in the middle of the table between the coffee cups and the plates is untouched. Frøken Berge puts her hand up.

"Has your husband said anything about what happened to Herr Vilder's daughter?"

Fru Lund glares at her.

"How could you imagine such a thing?"

Frøken Berge looks down.

"I was just wondering. It's such a horrible thing to have happened."

"Yes, it really is. And it shows we have to be alert. We have to keep an eye on our daughters."

"Our sons too," Fru Endresen adds.

Everyone nods and observes the silence.

"Apparently she was up to a bit of all sorts," Frøken Jacobsen says.

Fru Lund smacks the table and makes the crockery jump.

"Ladies, we are not gossiping fishwives! We're the Red Cross."

There is a ring at the door. She goes out and opens up. It is Maj.

"Sorry I'm—"

Fru Lund helps her off with her coat.

"You've arrived in the nick of time, my dear. Haven't you got Margrethe with you?"

Maj turns, surprised and happy.

"Is she coming?"

"She said she would at any rate. Maj?"

"Yes?"

Fru Lund pulls Maj closer and lowers her voice.

"This poor Elisabeth was in Jesper's class, wasn't she?"

"Yes, she was."

"Did he say what . . .?"

"Apparently they found her in the bath."

"Oh, my goodness, how could she do that?"

"I said the same."

They join the others in the lounge. Maj takes her place on the sofa between Frøken Jacobsen and Frøken Berge. Fru Lund stays on her feet.

"I would remind you that Herr Vilder was a notable sponsor, not only of the Red Cross, centrally, but also the Lions Club and Heming sports club. Maj Kristoffersen and I suggest we send a modest wreath to her funeral."

The rest of the committee agree, even though they are not all present, but two-thirds is more than enough. Fru Lund doesn't have time to sit down before the bell rings again. The ladies wait before they touch the cake, until she returns with Margrethe Hall, the former Fru Vik, who is barely recognisable.

Her hair is darker – has she dyed it? And the clothes she is wearing aren't hers. That is easy to spot. It is Ragnhild Stranger's clothes, the woman who was a well-known actress at the National Theatre and ended up doing cabaret. Maj looks down. Everyone looks down. This is not on. Wearing someone else's clothes. Especially not clothes belonging to the deceased wife of one's husband. Fru Lund claps her hands.

"I'd like to wish our new committee member a very warm welcome."

Margrethe Hall turns to her.

"I won't be stopping."

"But we've only just started."

"Why did you ruin things for Bjørn Stranger?"

Fru Lund takes a step forward.

"I beg your pardon?"

"You know very well what I mean. You removed him from Grønnegata 19."

"I don't think we should be discussing that here."

"But I do, Fru Lund. Bjørn was good to the people there and they liked him a lot."

"That has nothing to do with the matter."

"Has it anything to do with the matter that he was doing good work? Or that he has a good heart?"

"That's all very fine, but Bjørn Stranger has to comply with the law. Besides—"

Margrethe Hall interrupts.

"Isn't that what the Red Cross is about? Having a good heart? Do you have a good heart?"

Fru Lund raises a hand. She is pale and agitated.

"Having a good heart doesn't help if you don't have the requisite qualifications. Bjørn Stranger is a semi-trained quack. In addition, I will not put up with being upbraided in my own home!"

Margrethe looks away. It is as though Fru Lund has been a vessel for all her indignation and she is left standing there empty and perplexed. Her voice is weary and what she says next sounds like an apology.

"At least I've said what I came to say. And I have no wish to return."

She finds her own way out.

The ladies make a dash for the window. Olaf Hall is waiting for her in Kirkeveien, no, he isn't waiting; he is keeping watch. That is what he is doing. He is wearing a thin, light-brown suit and similarly light-coloured shoes. He seems to think it is summer already. Margrethe appears and together they walk down to Majorstua, him in the lead, her hard on his heels.

"Well, that was a new experience," Fru Lund says.

They eat cake and drink coffee in silence. The members of the Fagerborg department of the Oslo Red Cross are shaken. The last item on the agenda is to choose volunteers to accompany the old folks on the trip to Ingierstrand, which is this year's destination. Fru Endresen and Fru Schalke immediately put up their hands. Then Fru Lund reminds everyone to keep an eye open for men in the district to keep the widows company in June. It is never too late. The ladies allow themselves a titter, despite everything. As they are leaving, they pull Maj aside and whisper:

"Don't put this in the minutes."

Maj forgets to take a slice of the cake for Jesper and Stine. As she is crossing Gørbitz gate she spots Trude standing outside the entrance to the flats with a net bag in her hand. She turns and walks towards Maj.

"Do you know where Jesper is?"

"Isn't he at home?"

"No."

"Didn't Stine know?"

"She wasn't at home, either."

Maj thinks to herself: Jesper won't open the door for anyone. She takes Trude by the hand and they walk up the freshly washed stairs.

"It was terrible what happened," Maj says.

Trude stops on the first landing and beneath her sleepless eyes there are black bags that make her face appear strained and unhealthy.

"I walked Elisabeth home from the party."

"That was kind of you."

"I was the last person to see her."

No-one deserves this, Maj thinks. She hugs Trude quickly and sees that there is a pair of high heels in her bag.

"Don't blame yourself. Will you promise me that?"

"I could've gone in with her."

"But you couldn't have stayed with her for the rest of her life, Trude."

At that moment they hear the sound of a piano. However, it isn't coming from their flat but from the floor above, where Bjørn Stranger lives. Maj lets Trude go first and they carry on up. The door is ajar. Maj knocks. No-one opens the door. They walk in. Maj tells Trude to wait in the hall. She tiptoes closer to the music, she doesn't recognise the tune, it is new to her, and this makes her even more uneasy. The grand piano fills almost the whole room. Stine is sitting on the floor and drinking pop from a bottle through a red straw. Bjørn Stranger, in a white shirt, checked waistcoat and light-grey trousers with a neat crease, looking like a dandy, is leaning against the window frame. Jesper is totally concentrated on the next note. No-one notices Maj, who stops and captures the whole of this apparent idyll in a single gaze, the way that animals sense all danger through vision and smell, as they assess every option for fight or flight. Jesper raises his hands and the silence displaces the harmony in the room. Stine stands up. Bjørn Stranger takes a step forward.

"Who would ever believe that the Polish interval signal could sound so beautiful?" he says.

Stine walks over to Maj, who takes the bottle from her, sets it down on a small table and looks at Jesper.

"Come on," she says.

Bjørn Stranger stands between them. He is in the way. Maj notices his slippers; they are black and made of leather.

"I must have forgotten to lock the door."

"Come on," Maj repeats.

"Please stay. I can make some coffee."

"Trude's waiting for you, Jesper."

Jesper gets up, reluctantly, as though the echo from the large, polished instrument still has him in thrall. Then he finally tears himself away and heads for the hallway. Maj and Stine follow. Jesper and Trude are already on their way down the stairs, past their floor. Maj lets them go, hurries into their flat and locks the door. The first thing she does is to close the windows in the sitting room. The smell is still strong inside, reminiscent of manure, pigsty, ammoniac, in short it reminds her of her childhood and she doesn't want to be reminded in this way. Stine looks up.

"Why are you so angry, Mamma?"

"I'm not. But you mustn't visit people without telling me."

As Maj is about to close the last window she sees Jesper and Trude crossing Kirkeveien. They are walking apart, perhaps because of the tragedy that has entered their lives, perhaps because Jesper knows Maj is at the window watching them. He turns and shouts:

"We're just returning Elisabeth's shoes."

Jesper gives a start as Trude shushes him. The words are unholy. They are untrue. Elisabeth will never get her shoes back. They aren't even hers anymore. They don't belong to anyone. Or do parents inherit their children's possessions? They walk on in silence, still with the same distance between them, past Vestre Aker church, the rectory, Blindern, where the university will soon be finished, cross the Sognsvann railway and reach Vinderen Psychiatric Clinic, which resembles a palace, or a manor, and in the middle of the lawn there is a patient playing badminton on his own. His strokes are slow and ponderous. The shuttlecock takes time to fall. This makes Jesper think of the horse outside the Hippodrome riding centre, quite why, he doesn't know. He wants to say this, but can't bring himself to do so. It is still light, a fragile, yellow light, which soon gathers in the first coltsfoot plants growing by the fences. They continue along a street called Risbekken, the name of a stream, which will soon flood its banks, so to speak, with all the snow melting around Lake Sognsvann, and they emerge in Slemdalsveien, where the Gaustad fields start, fine, gentle slopes around a red farm, there is a different smell, it is a different world, it is a different time, which is still close at hand, almost closer than Trude is right now. Then at last they are in the cul-de-sac behind Slemdal School and turn into the house shrouded in the garden's sudden darkness. They stop at the front door. Trude takes the bag containing Elisabeth's shoes with one hand, inhales and rings the bell.

"You misunderstood," Jesper says.

"Misunderstood what?"

"Failed. She was a girl who had been failed. We could only write one word."

They wait. Silence. Trude rings the bell again.

"Do you think anything can be as it was?" she asks.

Jesper realises he has never been asked a more important question and so the answer is even more important.

"Yes," he says.

They hear someone coming. Trude takes his hand.

Party in Pilestredet 75, 3/5/1957

The room was very attractive. It was overflowing with the cakes all the committee members had baked. The coffee that was served by our own Red Cross ladies was particularly good. The tables were decorated with Red Cross flags. One marzipan ring cake was raffled.

Herr and Fru Vyrmore on violin and piano were responsible for the music, and later Frøken Berg-Vang sang. Afterwards there was a talk by Fru Sønne about the maternity services offered by the Red Cross.

Fru Øksenvad, the chairman of the Majorstua department, thanked us for organising this meeting (there were 40 of us) and looked forward to further co-operation. The meeting was opened and closed by our chairman Fru Lund in a very dignified and pleasant manner.

This was balm to troubled minds after the last committee meeting.

MOTHERS

Maj and Stine have sat down at the very back of the gymnasium, which has been decorated with fresh birch twigs, the school banner and the Norwegian flag. The school-leavers sit in a group on the left, weary and formal. Perhaps this is these young people's happiest hour, balancing at this moment between the solemnity of the occasion and happiness, finely attuned amid all their chaos. Maj envies them. She envies them the honesty of their youth, because they have nothing to hide, they are open, yet still inscrutable. Maj, however, is like a cat on hot bricks. She can see Jesper and Trude in the front row. They look so elegant, her in a white dress, him in a blazer, both sitting erect. Maj's eyes fill. She has to take out her handkerchief. One of the other mothers in the row in front turns and smiles at her. Now Maj can see who it is, it is Trude's mother, she is unmistakeable, wearing a loose outfit that makes the other mothers look like last year's remnants. Nevertheless they have the right to feel proud. Everyone has that right today. The headmaster is standing on the dais, directly in front of the piano. He talks about the future, which begins with that which has gone but is not forgotten. He repeats: *but is not forgotten.* It is already twelve years since the war ended in victory. Maj doesn't take in a single word. She isn't listening anyway. She has other matters on her mind. Now that she should concentrate, be present in every way, she thinks about other things. She is thinking that soon she will let down everyone she loves. She knows. She is going to let down Jesper. She is going to let down Stine. She is going to let down the Red Cross. She is even going to let down Ewald. It is unbearable. And yet she will do it. She glances at her watch as the headmaster hands over to Ramm, who

255

everyone can see has lost weight, several kilos, and his hair has thinned, the dark mane is like the fluff you blow off dandelions. But his voice is still firm. He asks the assembly to stand for a minute's silence after he has read the names of the fallen Fagerborg students, and concludes with Elisabeth Vilder, as though the headmaster had made an error, the war has lasted until now, and Elisabeth Vilder is the last hero in the cavalcade of the dead. Stine has to nudge her mother, who completely forgets to stand up, who is oblivious of everything around her, how embarrassing it is to have a mother like this, what is getting into Maj Kristoffersen? She suddenly thinks about Jostein and his spots: please don't let them disappear before she has asked him if he wants to be in the advertisement, but if you can remove spots from a photograph, surely you can make them reappear as well, if his forehead has cleared in the meantime? It is good to muse on all these things that aren't important. Ramm hands over to Trude Hagen, who mounts the dais and flicks through some papers before looking up. Everyone's attention is focused on her. She has to find a face she can rest her eyes on and trust, and she definitely does not choose one of the boys wearing the red school-leaving cap, with shiny, red-rimmed eyes and crooked, impish smiles, as from now on everything is permitted, it is open season, everything is fair game from here down to Pernille open-air restaurant and back to exams. A bad conscience about Elisabeth's suicide is forgotten. And it strikes Trude that she has forgotten too, at any rate she doesn't think about Elisabeth twenty-four hours a day. Does that make her a bad person? It definitely makes her sad. It isn't right that this should be over so quickly. But there isn't always room for it. There has to be room for other things than a guilty conscience and horror. She sees her mother, in that awful get-up, a tunic that looks more like a suffocating potato sack, and she is always so energetic and encouraging that you can lose heart with anything less. Her father isn't there, disappointingly, surely he could have taken time off today of all days, but firstly he had to go all the way to Vinger to interview Norway's first female priest, who unfortunately is Danish, and then he was unable to return home because he had to go on to Copenhagen where Crown Prince Olav was laying the foundation stone for King Haakon's Church, and not only that, the British have detonated their first H-bomb in the south Pacific, but he has promised he will read her speech later. She can just make out Stine, and Maj seems distant and distracted, she is probably only nervous on Jesper's behalf, so no help there either. Fru Vilder, Elisabeth's mother, is sitting next to Ramm. She is lean and dressed in sombre colours, she seems to be wearing black mourning crepe, but it is only make-up. She takes Ramm by the hand, he seems both anguished and embarrassed at this contact; grief is an intimate state of emergency. Henry Vilder is at home drinking the house dry, according to rumours. The newspaper boy saw him through a window one morning. Why isn't Enzo Zanetti here? Why isn't he here to listen to his best pupil play the "Ballad of Revolt"? He is probably indisposed or perhaps he wasn't allowed in, after all this is a school arrangement. It will have to be Jesper. He is dreading this, Trude knows that, even though he doesn't show it, but if she can rest her gaze on his eyes, he can do the same with hers. They can find composure in each other, at the same time and in turn. She meets his eyes and he smiles. That is enough. Trude starts reading Goethe's "Wanderers Nachtlied" and she has chosen Hartvig Kiran's translation into Nynorsk because she was unable to do it herself, nor could anyone else in the class, and why not choose the best if it already exists? "Vandringsmannens Nattvise":

> Over alle tindar
> Er ro.

Trude gets no further. Fru Vilder, Elisabeth's mother, stands up and almost shouts the next lines:

> And there is a pair of high heels
> on the last hill!

Then Fru Vilder bows her head and raises her arms. The auditorium goes silent. Sobs are heard. They are so deep inside her and undefined that they seem inhuman, like growling. Ramm guides her out. Trude waits. She doesn't know how long to wait. She would rather take her seat again. The poem is ruined anyway, her talk too. The plan had been to continue with a word she had found in one of her father's articles, about the new youth culture, rock'n'roll, from America, the word he used was *adiaphora*, or matters of indifference. Trude wanted to change the sense. She wanted to talk about the indifference that threatens us. This time it isn't an enemy attacking, as in 1940, this time the attack comes from within, from within ourselves. It is our own indifference we have to fight and win over. But now she cannot find a connection between Goethe and indifference. "The Wanderer's Nightsong" is about peace of mind and that isn't at all the same as indifference; peace of mind is active interplay between reason and emotions while indifference is merely empty and idle. It doesn't care. Trude is desperate. This had been exactly her point, to show that a committed person has to have peace of mind, peace of mind at a stressful time, and if one can find it, peace of mind, in nature, in oneself or in God, one will have space for others too. How much time has passed? She has lost track. Trude looks up from her papers, carefully, as though she fears the auditorium might be empty, and once again Jesper meets her gaze. Something happens between them. It is like an accord, made in total secrecy before the eyes of everyone in the gymnasium at Fagerborg School, on May 17th, 1957. Jesper sees Trude swallow, she swallows again, takes a deep breath and then she finishes reading the poem:

> Og alle vindar
> høyrast no
> Knapt som eit sóg
> Små fuglen blundar så varleg
> Vente no!

Snarleg
Kvilar du óg

Afterwards Jesper can't take in any more because he is thinking about the "Ballad of Revolt", the sequence of the notes, the fingering and the syncopated beats with his left hand that have to be performed with as much firmness and precision as if he is killing a wasp. Why can't he play the Danish interval signal instead? He is only glad that Enzo won't be here. He had to go to Italy. As he put it: *I have to go to Roma.* So at least there is one person fewer to disappoint. There is basically only one person Jesper does not want to disappoint, and that is Trude. And Stine. No, there are more. He doesn't want to disappoint his mother, or his teacher, Ramm. He would prefer not to disappoint anyone. That is his nature. It is his predisposition. Actually, Ramm hasn't returned to his seat yet. Outside, a siren can be heard, a brief, ominous spin of the alarm rotor causing everyone to turn. Then it is gone. Jesper suddenly experiences a huge sense of freedom. He can play what he likes. If he wants he can play the Danish interval signal. No-one will ever tell him what to play. Is it the devil's piano? A sentence from Trude's talk catches his attention in passing: *In peace of mind there is space for everyone.* The headmaster thanks her and says, so that the whole world can hear, in a voice even louder than Jostein's: *And now Jesper Kristoffersen will play Harald Sæverud's "Ballad of Revolt".* Jesper rises to his feet and Trude touches his hand as they pass. No, it is Jesper who touches Trude. It is another secret encounter before the very eyes of an unwitting audience. Jesper takes his seat at the piano. He wriggles until he is comfortable. He waits until there is silence. He lifts his hands. He has cut and cleaned his fingernails. His skin is smooth and light. They are not working hands. They are the tools of another trade. His fingers are ready. No, this can't be the devil's piano. Jesper plays exactly what he wants. The piece starts with a few simple notes and ends with booms and bangs. The simple notes are the hardest. It feels good to have them out of the way. As he is approaching the middle of the piece he is safe. He can hide in technique. He can exaggerate and pretend. Then he can fall. Four months pass between the final chord and the applause. Then he hears it, the waterfall running through the public, down their arms, finally to plummet from their hands in sudden streams that soon merge into one. Is the heart the source of this strange waterfall? Jesper is reminded of the applause that met Elisabeth the time she danced for the handball team in the dressing room. Where did that spring from, from shame? He stands up and bows. The audience stands up too, they are stamping as well, it is overwhelming, he doesn't really deserve it, he knows, he has just impressed them, but he is still happy. He feels exhausted and light, almost weightless. Afterwards he is back in the boys' dressing room with Trude. Now everyone is allowed in. And everyone wants to congratulate him. Fancy being able to play the whole piece *off by heart*! He didn't play a single wrong note. At least not that they could hear. Jesper remembers something Trude said once: Jesper Kristoffersen learns his mistakes by heart. But everyone is in a hurry. They have to see the King, if he is well enough to appear, that is. Perhaps it will be the last time. Trude's mother gives them both a hug and they almost lose themselves in her tunic.

"Pappa would be *so* proud," she says.

Trude frees herself with a smile.

"Not you though?"

"Goodness me, of course I am. How can you say such a thing? You were fabulous. You too, Jesper. I have no words for it. You can both go on tour."

"Mamma, that's enough."

"And now I have to hurry. See you on the hill in front of the Royal Palace? I'm sure we will. And don't eat ice cream, Trude. Remember it contains cream. And don't you, either, Jesper."

Trude's mother leaves backwards as Lorentz Bull makes his way through the crowd with a school-leaver's cane adorned with a red bow. As a former handball captain – happily that time is now over – he would like, on behalf of the school team, to praise Jesper "Have-you-got-a-piano?" Kristoffersen for his solo attacking play from the piano stool. Then he turns his attention to Trude.

"And what does *sóg* mean then, my dear?"

"Remorse," she says.

Lorentz Bull is taken aback.

"In Nynorsk? So Goethe's German night winds sound like remorse?"

In a friendly but firm manner, Ramm pushes Lorentz Bull aside and has a lot he wants to say, but Trude asks first:

"What happened to Elisabeth's mother?"

"She was taken to hospital. She's ill."

"She shouldn't have come."

Ramm looks at her and does his very best to smile.

"That was a wonderful talk, Trude."

"Thank you."

"No, we in the school thank you. As for you, Jesper, Sæverud would be proud of you."

Jesper looks to the side.

"I hammered away to the best of my ability."

"Then I have to say you hit the nail on the head. What should I say? Life's contrasts, we've seen them all today, in abundance. Let's learn the lessons we can. And Trude in particular mastered the conflicting emotions that came to the surface. Don't you think, Jesper?"

But Jesper has caught sight of Stine in the doorway. He beckons her over, but she doesn't want to come. Instead he goes over to her.

"Where's Mamma?" he asks.

Stine just shakes her head.

Jesper bends down.

"You don't know where she is? Has she gone?"

Stine gives her brother an envelope. He recognises his mother's handwriting. He heads for the toilets, into a cubicle and closes the door. Then he opens the envelope. First of all he finds some money, four fifty-krone notes. But between the notes there is a brief letter, written on lined paper with the Dek-Rek stamp at the top. Jesper reads it twice. Fastened to the paper with clips is a travel plan from Metrotravel A/S. He puts everything back into the envelope, stuffs it into his inside pocket and closes his eyes. As he does so he glimpses some letters carved into the wall with a penknife or a compass point: *Elisabeth is willing*. He hasn't noticed it before. Perhaps someone wrote it after she died. Perhaps the someone didn't know she was dead and still fancied her. Death makes everyone willing. No, death makes everyone accessible. When Jesper returns to the dressing room, Stine is with Trude and holding her hand.

"Mamma's on a business trip," he says.

Stine just looks up, her lower lip quivering. Jesper sighs.

"And she'll be away for a week. That's all. Don't cry now."

Trude bursts into laughter.

"A business trip? On May 17th?"

Jesper turns to her.

"It's not the bloody seventeenth of May abroad, is it?"

Trude looks down, upset.

"Sorry."

There is silence. Soon they can hear the marching bands and the church bells. The sounds fill the light with a kaleidoscope of colour. Jesper takes Trude's free hand and is equally upset.

"Let's go and buy ourselves loads of ice cream," he says.

21/5/57

The board has a meeting at Fru Schanke's. All the members are present, except for the treasurer, Fru Kristoffersen, who gave us no advance warning. The chairman will ask her for an explanation. It was also decided that we won't have a child's cot at the bazaar because we now have a doll that needs to be dressed. We would prefer to buy a doll's bed and a bathinette. We have been given an attractive tea trolley by Fru Skjelkvale and we are going to put tea cups, maybe a sugar and cream set, and a nice cloth on top. Incidentally, at this year's bazaar all departments have to provide their own aprons and we have ordered two pocket flaps with Fagerborg Dept embroidered on them.

At the League of Red Cross Societies' board meeting for trustees, held in Oslo from May 4th to 8th, our secretary, Fru Endresen, was the attaché for the Spanish-speaking delegates.

BEFORE

At a stroke Jostein is a changed person. It is almost scary. It happened from one moment to the next. It was the instant he found out that Elisabeth Vilder died in the bath and was herself responsible. Not everyone approves of this change, especially not his father, who doesn't like it at all, and if there is change, it has to be for the better, and that is very rare. Jesper, in fact, has very little belief in Jostein's sudden transition. There is an expression that has stuck with him: *putting on an act*. Is this what Jostein is doing? Is he just pretending? Or is it genuine? At any rate, Jostein stops working at Oslo Slaughterhouse. He can no longer stand the sight of the skinned pigs. He had been on the point of letting them all escape. This says something positive about Jostein. His action is his signature. It is confirmation. His father prefers to think it says something negative. Has his son become sensitive or, even worse, up himself? Is he starting to take after Jesper? Animal slaughter is a blessing: pain-free and unexpected. What is brutal and painful is a natural death, especially for pigs: a slow, humiliating disintegration in foul-smelling, pokey stalls, death by neglect. And as for humanity? Does he think a natural death is anything to aspire to? According to the rumours, Ewald Kristoffersen staggered around his flat for hours gasping for breath. And, of all things, Jostein wants to go back to school. He wants to compensate for what he missed. He wants to apply for the two-year business course in Stenersgata, which will involve thirty-three lessons a week and, what is more, it is free. Fru Melsom shushes her husband, who doesn't hold back once he has got going. Slowly but surely he winds himself up: killing pigs is compatible with Jostein's abilities. If he wants to work in the shop, his father will teach him whatever is necessary; it is simple arithmetic and knowing the difference between kilos and grams. They can start today. What is more, handing in your notice is not a million miles from being given your cards. Jostein is in danger of being regarded as unreliable. He might be given bad references. Does Jostein think apprenticeships grow on trees? And what is Jostein going to do with more schooling? He is stupid enough already. Jostein runs a hand across his bumpy forehead, suggests that he might have gone vegetarian and storms to his room. His mother rolls her eyes as she hears his door slam.

"You could've saved yourself the trouble," she says.

Melsom looks down and wrings his hands.

"I suppose I could. Shit."

"And now you go to him and apologise."

"Me? Can't you?"

"I don't have anything to apologise for."

Melsom the butcher, the big man, looks up warily.

"You could come with me, couldn't you?"

"No, this is between you and Jostein."

"I'm sure it's easier for you now you've Seen the Light."

"My goodness, surely you can talk to your own son."

"That's the point. I don't know if I can any longer."

"You can at least say you're proud of him. Can't you manage that?"

The butcher gets up and ambles out of the kitchen. Fru Melsom remains beside her empty coffee cup. Her husband comes to a halt outside his son's room, hesitates, hand raised, then finally plucks up the courage and knocks. Jostein takes his time before he opens the door, and when he does, it is only a few centimetres. They glare at each other. This is hard. At length Jostein lets him in. The door closes. Fru Melsom closes her eyes. It is Saturday. In twenty minutes she will have to go down to the shop. There may be a queue already. No, not the last Saturday in May. Usually the shop is quiet then. The sun passes over the rooftops and lands on the floor in front of the stove. She decides to make something extra-special for lunch. Afterwards they can listen to the radio together or play Monopoly. In the *Arbeiderbladet* she reads that there has been a fire at the Grand Hotel and sixty-four Norwegian scientists demand a ban on H-bomb tests. She puts aside the newspaper and listens, but she can't hear anything coming from Jostein's room. Surely they are not sitting there in silence? Although that would not be beyond them. She hears the postman, who is early today. So he must have little or nothing with him. She can see that there is something, however. She brushes her hair, looks for the keys and hurries down to the postboxes. There is a letter. It is addressed to Jostein Melsom. Jostein never gets letters. Now she thinks about it, this is the first. And at once she wonders: Has he done something wrong? If so, it must be serious. Her heart sinks into her boots, such desperate straits one Saturday morning at the end of May, she doesn't know how she is going to get through the day. She is about to open the envelope. Then she sees it isn't from the police or any authority, but from Dek-Rek, which is where Jesper's mother is employed as a secretary in reception. Fru Melsom breathes a sigh of relief. Then it can't be so bad. It is probably an invitation. When is Jesper's birthday? She can't remember. Or perhaps he is going to give a concert? Everyone says he played so beautifully on May 17th, even though most talk about Elisabeth's mother. She stole the show, some claim. Now Fru Melsom doesn't need to read the letter anyway. She goes back upstairs and pauses outside Jostein's door. There is still total silence in there. They have had enough time. She knocks on the door and immediately hears the voice of her husband, who seems relieved: *Come in.* She opens the door. Jostein is sitting at his desk, facing the wall. Her husband is standing in the middle of the room and turns to her.

"OK, we've finished here. Haven't we, Jostein?"

Jostein doesn't reply and remains seated, stiff-backed, even more difficult and dismissive than usual, a sullen sleepwalker.

"There's some post for you," she says.

Jostein wakes up. He tears the letter from her hand and immediately turns his back on her again. Apparently he isn't going to open it right away. His mother nods to her husband. Reluctantly, they retreat and slowly close the door. They wait there. Perhaps Jostein will come out and tell them what it is. They sigh, each in their own way. Jostein's mother sighs because he doesn't come out. His father, however, sighs with relief that he has got away and, all things considered, it could have been worse, at least there hadn't been any abusive language. Then they go down to the shop and put on their white coats and clogs with the flat soles. And while she is in the backroom adjusting her hairnet, he turns round the sign in the window: WELCOME. NECK CUTLETS ON OFFER. The first customer is Herr Abrahamsen from Fauchwaldsgate, widower and skinflint, he asks for some bones for his dog, but Herr Melsom can't see any dog. Is it at home waiting? Is it too hungry to come with him? He will probably make a soup for himself. But Fru Melsom is happy to wrap up two juicy bones and passes them to Herr Abrahamsen, who has no intention of paying. Herr Melsom opens the door for him and performs a deep bow.

"Do you have a cat as well?"

Herr Abrahamsen is confused, a situation which skinflints do not much like.

"Cat?"

"In which case you can probably get some nice fish bones down at Schultz's in Bogstadveien."

Herr Abrahamsen just shakes his head and hurries on. Melsom turns to his wife, about to say something, but she doesn't give him the opportunity.

"What did you say?" she asks.

"What I said? I asked the old scrounger if he had a cat. We're not some soup kitchen serving free food for the poor. And nor are we the Sally Army. And we're definitely not the Red Cross. And incidentally, Abrahamsen isn't poor. He just scrimps and saves while I pay tax."

Fru Melsom lifts the counter flap and stands in the middle of the floor with her hands on her hips.

"Have you finished?"

"Finished? Yes, I suppose I have."

"I meant Jostein. What did you say to him?"

"Well, what did I say? A bit of this and that."

"Did you say you were proud of him?"

"Erm, I suppose I said that too, yes. What was the letter—"

He isn't allowed to finish the sentence.

"What did Jostein say to that?"

"To what?"

"To you saying you were proud of him."

"Well, what did he say now? He didn't say much. You know Jostein. He nodded anyway."

"He nodded?"

Herr Melsom takes a step forward.

"How long are you going to keep asking me questions?"

"How long?"

"Yes, just so that I know. So I can go for a walk in the meantime."

They hear someone in the back room and both turn. Jostein is standing in the doorway with the letter in his hand. He is open-mouthed in a happy kind of way.

"I'm going to be in an advert," he says.

His mother takes a step closer.

"What for?"

"Spots."

Jostein brushes his parents aside, goes into Kirkeveien and takes a deep breath. Life is a good place to be today. He is going to be famous. Then it will be easier to become rich. One thing follows the other. You don't cut up a pig until it is dead. And when the leaves on the trees that Fridtjof Nansen's mother planted here are also greener than yesterday, life can hardly be better. Leaves grow on trees! Even the number 20 bus is in a good mood and the exhaust fumes over the tarmac smell of liquorice. Jostein is on cloud nine. For a moment he has forgotten Elisabeth Vilder. It was so easy. It is so easy. It doesn't matter if it doesn't last. This moment is good enough. He decides to go and see Jesper, who barely opens the door and whose face looks tired.

"Didn't think you were at home," Jostein says.

"Why did you come then?"

"Because this is important."

"What is?"

"Let me in."

Jesper, who would prefer not to have any visitors this week, does what his pal tells him anyway. They go into the kitchen, where Stine is. Isn't it unusually messy? Jesper at any rate starts tidying up. And there are dirty dishes in the sink. Jostein lifts his fringe with both hands and shows his forehead in all its glory to Stine.

"But for these spots no-one would know who I was," he says.

Jesper laughs.

"P'raps that would be for the best."

But Jostein can't be bothered with Jesper today. Jesper is yesterday's news. Jostein is front page. He lets his fringe fall into place, takes out the letter and reads it aloud:

Dear Jostein,

Our colleague, Maj Kristoffersen, has told us about you and we would like to ask whether you would be willing to take part in an advertisement for Valcrema, an ointment approved by the Chemists' Association, for removing spots. There would be two photographs of you, one before and one after. These will appear in a variety of weekly magazines and help boys and girls to regain their confidence. As you are not yet eighteen years old, we will also need permission from your parents, or at least one of them. I am hoping for a positive response. Drop by our offices in Rosenkrantz' gate as soon as you are able.

Best regards,

Rudjord

MD, Dek-Rek.

The kitchen in Kirkeveien 127 has gone quiet. Jostein is looking at Stine, who turns towards her brother.

"Where's your mother?" Jostein asks.

Jesper stands between them.

"She's on a business trip."

"So that's why you're skulking."

"We're not skulking. It's a valid absence."

Jostein laughs and folds up the letter.

"But why's she on a business trip, eh?"

"What's it got to do with you?"

"Perhaps I can ring her and ask for some advice? After all she's—"

Jesper interrupts him.

"You can't."

"Why not?"

"What is this with all the bloody questions? She hasn't got a telephone where she is. Alright?"

"What kind of business is it? If it hasn't got a telephone?"

Jesper is beginning to get annoyed.

"Feel like washing some dishes? I can dry and Stine will put them away."

Jostein gently shakes his head.

"No, thank you. I have to take care of my spots."

"I think they'll manage fine without your help."

Stine laughs. She laughs at everything Jesper says. Jostein doesn't think he is very amusing anymore. On the contrary, he considers Jesper childish and *immature*. And playing the piano and having a girlfriend don't make any difference. Jesper is so far behind. He almost feels sorry for him. Jostein is the leader now. He is going to be in magazines. He is blasé and world-weary. He just shrugs as though nothing can touch him anymore.

"Can I use your mirror?" he asks.

Jesper opens the window. The sun will soon fill the whole of the yard.

"Which mirror?"

"In the bathroom. The light's better there than at ours."

Jesper scrutinises his pal, he is on the point of bursting into laughter again, is he supposed to admire his spots or what, but suddenly realises this is serious, this is Jostein's moment, and you mustn't mess with a pal's moment, he should be able to enjoy it in peace for as long as it lasts. And it is as though Stine also senses precisely the same, at any rate she sits perfectly still and lets him have his moment.

"Of course," Jesper says.

Jostein goes to the bathroom, stands in front of the mirror and brushes his fringe back. Perhaps he should cut it? They are bound to have their own hairdresser at Dek-Rek. He resists the temptation to squeeze a fat pimple full of eggnog. He will have to save his spots for Monday. Instead he wets his comb and gives himself a waiter's centre parting. That is the best view of his forehead. He turns to the bathtub and thinks about Elisabeth, but can't bear the thought. He has other things on his mind. However, there is one thought he can't rid himself of, it is crazy and certain: now Elisabeth is his girl for ever. He has to lean back against the wall. Jesper's blazer is hanging on the line between the air vent and the hot water cylinder. There is a big stain on the lapel. Jostein should have a blazer like that too. He has to look good when he is being photographed, at least in the "after" picture, when he doesn't have any more spots. Perhaps he could borrow the blazer if it isn't too small? His mother can probably remove the stain. Jostein unpegs the dark-blue jacket from the line, but can barely get his arm in the first sleeve. What a weed Jesper is. Something falls from the pocket and lands in the bath. He picks it up. It is a copy of a travel plan:

17.5 Oslo 15.00
18.5 Arr. Copenhagen 08.00
18.5 Dep. Copenhagen 10.00
18.5 Arr. Hamburg 19.08 (change train)

18.5 Dep. Hamburg 19.44
19.5 Arr. Munich 07.34 (change carriage)
19.5 Arr. Rome 23.55

In Rome Maj Kristoffersen is staying at Pensione Astrid. But why has she got a double room? At the top she has written: *You played so beautifully, Jesper. I'm so proud. I'm going to tell Enzo.* The return journey is:

24.5 Dep. Rome 06.40
24.5 Arr. Munich 22.49 (change carriage)
24.5 Dep. Munich 23.11
25.5 Arr. Hannover 08.07
25.5 Dep. Hannover 10.18
25.5 Arr. Copenhagen 20.45
26.5 Dep. Copenhagen 15.30
27.5 Arr. Oslo 07.30

Jostein carefully puts the timetable back in the pocket and hangs up the blazer exactly as he found it. He has his own ideas on this. He won't gossip. He goes back to the kitchen. Jesper and Stine are washing up. They will have to wash up before their mother returns and so it is best to start now.

"I'll dry and you can put away," Jostein suggests.

Stine gives him the cloth and glances at his centre parting, but also refrains from making a comment. Jesper is wearing yellow rubber gloves to protect his hands. He is as careful with his hands as a vain woman. Stine puts the dishes away. Jostein stands between them and dries. The grey water froths over the edge.

"Doubly happy," Jesper says.

"Why?"

"Because we can also wash the floor with Pep. Mamma came up with that one."

"Double room," Jostein says.

Jesper turns to him.

"What did you say?"

"I didn't hear."

"What did you say?"

"Doubly happy."

They don't say another word until they have finished the washing-up and they don't say anything then either. Stine goes into the sitting room to tidy up there, Jesper peels off the gloves and rubs his fingers, which are white and unrecognisable, a corpse's fingers. Jostein hangs up the cloth to dry in the window.

"Do you think the photographs will be colour?"

"If the spots have to be seen, I suppose so."

"Do you think I'll be paid?"

"If it's free it isn't a job."

"Then I'll ask Stine out."

Jesper looks up and smiles. For a brief moment Jostein is his old self.

"You can borrow my blazer."

"Too tight."

"You can diet, fatso."

"Besides, it's stained."

"Ice cream on May 17th."

"Did you play well?"

"Stains can be removed."

The dishwater runs down the plughole as the sun moves across the rooftops along Jonas Reins gate.

"What's it like being at home alone?"

"Just like being at home. Only alone."

Jostein shakes out his centre parting.

"Why do you never answer my questions?"

Jesper is standing with his back to him watching the colour coming back into his fingers. He can feel it too. It is like electricity, little shocks. Suddenly he remembers his answer to Trude after she asked if things could go back to how they were. He answered yes.

Wasn't that an answer either? Or was it just something he said because it was easier? Was it just an answer he *gave* to her? It was nothing more than that, a gift. Could he have said no? The thought is shocking: that yes and no are equally true. If so, everything loses meaning and you might just as well give up or go to the dogs. The thought launches itself over a high-jump bar, catches it at the last moment and lands in music. In music there is no yes and no. In music there is everything that exists between yes and no. That is what Satie does. He fills the space. He composes music for our void, which we had long thought mute.

"Because I don't want to talk about it," Jesper says.

Jostein nods quietly.

"Nor me."

Jesper isn't sure that they are talking about the same thing, but actually it doesn't matter.

"We won't talk about it anymore, then."

Jostein brings the cloth in again as shadow covers the window frame and passes it to Jesper, who puts it in the drawer under the cutlery. The yardarm is a clock from 1923, a latter-day sundial. Whatever *it* is, they don't talk about it anymore: bathtub, train times, double room and death. The kitchen stairs are the quickest exit. Jesper closes the door after Jostein has gone and when he turns Stine is there.

"He can ask me out," she says.

"Yes, in fifteen years."

"Ugh, he'll be too old then."

Stine runs back into the sitting room. Jesper walks over to the window and sees Jostein come out of the entrance. He crosses the playground and looks in every direction as though he were already famous and wants to makes sure he is recognised. This is also a way to achieve fame: through spots. Jesper wishes him well. Then a drain opens inside him, bigger than the one in the sink, bigger than the one in the yard and even more shaded: fifteen years. That is as long as he has been alive. *In fifteen years.* It is mind-boggling. That will be in 1972. Where will they be then? No, *who* will they be then? Will they have become steel magnates and concert pianists or will they be just button-pressers and street vendors? Will they still recognise one other? Jesper can barely remember what he did the previous day, except that he played the piano. How is he supposed to visualise a future that will hold more than everything he has experienced so far? He is on the point of falling, falling further than ever, down into what has not yet happened. There is a knock at the door. Jesper opens it. Jostein leans in again.

"You haven't split up with Trude, have you?"

"No. Split up? Course I haven't."

"She hasn't split up with you?"

"Trude? What are you wittering on about? Do you know something I don't?"

"Not that I know of."

"Why are you asking then?"

"Just wondering, Jesper. What was it now I wanted to say?"

"I think you've already said it. Or didn't you hear it?"

"I didn't mean what I said about Stine."

"Didn't mean what?"

"That I'd ask her out. Not even in fifteen years."

Jostein goes back down the steep kitchen stairs holding the banister. He is thinking about Elisabeth. If she weren't dead they could be together, at least after his picture is in the magazines. If she were alive, they could be together. Then there would be the four of them: Jostein and Elisabeth, Jesper and Trude. When he gets home, his mother is waiting for him in the kitchen. She hasn't taken off her white coat and the silly hairnet looks like something she could catch fish in.

"Not much going on?" Jostein asks.

"No less than usual, but . . ."

"We should advertise more."

"That's exactly what I want . . ."

"We can hang some posters in Majorstua. And put ads in the paper. Perhaps in the parish magazine too."

"It all costs money, Jostein."

"Getting rich isn't free, either."

His mother gets up quickly.

"Are you sure you want this?"

"Want what?"

"To be in the ad."

Jostein simply doesn't understand how she can ask.

"Of course I do. Why wouldn't I?"

"I'm just frightened you could become a figure of fun."

She shouldn't have said that.

"I'll show you who laughs last," Jostein says.

He goes to his room. His mother follows. He can't get rid of her.

"If you've decided, we'll support you to the hilt. You know we will. Alright?"

"Yes, thank you."

"We're proud of you. You should know that too."

Jostein turns to his mother who suddenly seems so small under the high ceiling in the narrow pantry.

"What did you say?"

"That we're proud of you. You're not having hearing difficulties again, are you?"

"Why do you two say that all the time?"

"Say what, Jostein?"

"That you're proud of me."

"Because we are. Proud that you're going back to school. And that you—"

"Don't say it more than once a week then, alright?"

Jostein would like to be alone for a while and collect his thoughts, but his mother has him in a tight grip.

"By the way, did you get to talk to Fru Kristoffersen? After all she's the one who—"

"She wasn't at home."

"But I suppose she will come home?"

"Not for a while."

"Is she ill?"

"Not that I know of. Let go of me."

"Is she on holiday?"

"On a business trip."

"How do you know she's on a business trip?"

His mother lets go of him and sighs.

"Yes, she's gone all posh, she has."

"You don't have to be posh to go on a business trip, do you? Why doesn't Pappa go on trips? He has his own business."

"Because it's not necessary. We've got what we need."

"Perhaps there's better meat abroad."

His mother laughs and grips her son's arm again.

"Better than in Norway? How can you say that, Jostein?"

"Or cheaper. So that we can earn more."

"Is Fru Kristoffersen on a business trip abroad?"

"Don't know. Let go of me."

"How do you know she's on a business trip then?"

"Rome."

"In Rome?"

Jostein wants to be rid of his mother.

"Let go of me," he repeats.

His mother lets go of him for the second time and straightens his shirt.

"You should put your tweed jacket on if you're going to be in a photograph," she says.

Jostein rushes into his room and closes the door. He tries to read a maths book. But none of the numbers finds any resonance in him. He tries to read a list of English words, but he has more than enough to cope with reading the Norwegian alphabet. He lies on his bed and reads the letter from the Dek-Rek MD again instead. This is the kind of required reading he enjoys. He can happily learn it off by heart. Jostein, the only son of Melsom the butcher and his wife, is certain he is happy. He had been on the cusp of thinking something else. Now he has no doubts. He is happy. He doesn't quite know what that means. But no-one does. There is a knock at the door and before he can say "Come in", his mother is already there holding his tweed jacket.

"What have you done to this?"

Jostein sits up.

"What do you mean?"

"It's ruined. You had chocolate in the pockets. And it melted. What were you doing with so much?"

Now Jostein can see the huge stains around both pockets and it is as though they are growing as he stares. He sees it: the world is full of stains. The world is dirty.

"Won't they go away?"

His mother sighs as only mothers can.

"I'll do my best. Shall I tell you how much this jacket cost when Pappa bought it at Øye's in Bogstadveien?"

"132 kroner."

"Plus they had to take down the sleeves."

"I'd like to be alone."

His mother looks at him, for a moment worried rather than resigned, and then eventually closes the door. Jostein lies down again and stares at the ceiling until it disappears and he can see straight up into the bottom of everything. After all, he is only another spotty, blue-eyed loser. He starts crying and holds his hands over his mouth so that no-one can hear. Now at least he knows what happiness isn't.

An application for help to the Red Cross office has been received from Dagny Lyder, of Theresesgate 29, and passed on to the Fagerborg department. Fru Lund has promised to ask Oslo Charity if they can help.

Two children from Fagerborg parish will be sent to the country this summer.

PS After the usual checks had been done and it was established that Frøken Lyder was a genuinely needy case, the board decided to give her 100 kroner.

AFTER

Early in the morning, at the end of May, at seven-thirty to be precise, because the night train is on time, Oslo East station can give the impression of a cathedral, Protestant in its colourless form, Catholic in its content. There are throngs of people, hurrying in different directions with purposeful step, work is calling, it is the allure of the city centre. Light falls through the arched glass roof and lands on the almost black platform where Maj Kristoffersen is finally standing alone beside her suitcase and waiting. She has tied a scarf around her neck. Her hair is dishevelled after the night. There is no-one to meet her. Jesper and Stine are at school. Who else would come? There are not many people who know where she has been. It is a normal day. From now on there will only be normal days. It is over. Thank God, it is over. She is herself again. She has come to her senses. Two people travelled and one has come home alone. For a moment she buries her face in her hands. She isn't alone after all. The railwayman walking between the tracks and measuring air quality turns and doffs his cap. His machine is like an enormous hourglass sucking in air. Maj Kristoffersen can't breathe. She takes her suitcase and hurries across the concourse. A pigeon, as grey as the dust and her arrival, flies in desperate circles beneath the roof. The wings sound like electric fans. She has never felt so visible, so importunate. She fills the whole of the station with her remorse and unease. She stops. A man opens a luggage locker and places a newspaper inside, how odd. A lady in high heels throws black mourning crepe to the side and lights a cigarette, even odder. A young man in blue overalls stands still as he sweeps the floor, for a moment Maj thinks he is cleaning his shoes, he will never finish the job. There is an invisible synaesthesia surrounding her. She rushes into the toilets, pays the attendant a krone and is allocated a cubicle. The stench is intolerable. She tolerates it. She can tolerate most things now, if only life goes back to how it was. She removes her scarf, brushes her hair and takes out her face powder and vanity mirror. Colour returns. She is pale. She wants to look how she usually does. There is nothing she wants more than that. Then she rushes out again, to the concourse, to the grey light, through the heavy doors, and the city streams towards her with all its noise, shadow and movement, yet seems small by contrast, by contrast with the city she has visited. She has to take a deep breath. Will everything from now on be in relation to Rome? She hails a taxi in the square. The driver stows her suitcase in the boot. She sits at the rear and wants only to sleep, to take a shower and sleep. Then she wants to forget. She tells the driver the address. The driver looks in the mirror. Can he see it in her face? The streets pass beneath Maj. Everything she knew from before is pushed aside and unfamiliar neighbourhoods unfold before her eyes. Has everything changed since she left? The taxi stops at the corner of Kirkeveien and Gørbitz. The taximeter shows seven kroner and forty øre. She pays. The driver doesn't even have to count. He just weighs the sum in his hand and laughs.

"These blighters probably have a value where you've been, but not here in Fagerborg."

Maj is given the coins back, she can feel them now, they are light, almost weightless, Italian lire have their own sound. She gives the driver Norwegian money and lets him keep the change. He carries her suitcase to the door. Fortunately she doesn't meet anyone on the stairs. She lets herself in, listens, she is alone. She puts down the suitcase in her bedroom and undresses. She doesn't want to wear these clothes anymore. She wants to throw them away. Or preferably burn them, stuff them in the stove and light a match. She doesn't want any reminders. She goes into the bathroom, takes a shower and lets the water run until it is cold. Then she takes out clean clothes. It feels good. For an instant she relaxes. It feels like happiness, a shot of happiness, stronger and more defined than ever she can remember. It disappears just as quickly. She feels heavy and lethargic. She walks through the rooms and sees that everything is tidy and in its place. There is not so much as a stain anywhere. She opens the fridge. On the shelves she finds goat's cheese, liver paste and caviar. In the bread bin there is half a whole-meal loaf. There isn't a single crumb on the kitchen worktop. Maj is tearful again. They coped. From now on they can cope. They don't need her. She is superfluous. It would have been better if the flat had looked like a pigsty. Couldn't it at least be a bit messy? She can't think straight. She hears someone. It is Jesper. She can hear that from the way he closes the door, quietly, carefully, as though he is saving the sound for another occasion. She doesn't go to meet him, even though that is what she would most like to do. Why is he taking such a long time? Is he skipping school? Is he not alone? She waits until he comes into the kitchen.

"Aren't you at school?" she says.

"It's lunch break. I forgot my fountain pen."

"You've both done a great job."

"Stine did a great job."

Maj nods.

"I've got some presents for you. You can have them this evening."

Jesper takes a banknote from his back pocket.

"We didn't spend it all."

"You can keep it."

"Fifty kroner?"

"Share it with Stine."

Jesper puts the note back, reluctantly, without any pleasure. The telephone rings. He looks at his mother, who is standing with her arms hanging down at her side, lost and remote.

"Aren't you going to answer it?"

Maj pulls herself together and goes into the sitting room, hesi-tates, please God it isn't him, please God he isn't ringing from

Rome, lifts the receiver and at that moment Jesper appears in the hallway, stops and stares at her. It is Rudjord ringing from the atelier at Dek-Rek.

"Maj? Thank God! How was it back on home soil? Is there still snow up there in where-was-it-again?"

"Hurdal."

"In Hurdal, yes."

She has become a skilled liar.

"No. Luckily there was none."

"We need you, Maj. Can you come in?"

"Now? I've just—"

"The photographer's struggling with this Jostein you recommended, you see."

"I'm on my way."

By the time Maj rings off, Jesper has left. She can hear the bell ringing in Fagerborg School. For an instant she feels like wearing the shoes she bought by the Spanish Steps, but immediately rejects the idea. She will never put them on. She will throw them away as well. She dabs on some make-up to hide her tan. You don't get a tan in Hurdal. You go pale in Hurdal. Then she walks down to Majorstua, catches a tram to the National Theatre and almost runs the last part to Rosenkrantz' gate. What has Jostein been up to now? However, it is good to have something else to think about. From now on she must always have something to think about. Outside the atelier on the fifth floor she meets Rudjord.

"The boy has some really great spots, Maj, but he's expensive."

"Expensive?"

"He wants a fee. Kids used to queue for this. They would pay to be involved."

"We can give him a tenner, can't we?"

"He wants fifty."

"Then give him twenty. Alright?"

Rudjord sighs and opens the door for her.

"You're looking good, Maj."

"Thank you."

"Have you been in the sun?"

Maj turns away and laughs.

"We don't sunbathe in Hurdal. We just went on walks. In the forest."

"Were Jesper and Stine with you?"

"No, they only popped up for the weekend. As a matter of fact."

It strikes Maj how hard it is to lie, even if you are experienced. There are always traps to fall into. She has to weigh every word and they are as light as her lire, but still they are heavy to say and could cost her. Besides, she has to remember all her lies; no-one will believe her in the end otherwise. The lie has to stand up to scrutiny. She decides to take Jesper and Stine to Hurdal and in so doing lessen the lie. She can imitate the truth. That is the logic of the liar. Rudjord sighs again and they go in to see Kinck, who is standing by a camera positioned in front of an empty stool. There is a white sheet hanging from the ceiling. Ravn is adjusting the light.

"The boy's in the toilet tending to his spots," he says.

Kinck, Ravn and Rudjord all light a cigarette, finish smoking them and have enough time to air the room too. At length Jostein returns. He has a centre parting now. His hair hangs like short curtains on each side of his bumpy forehead. He stops as he catches sight of Maj, who can immediately see in his eyes that he knows something, he knows where she has been, how he knows doesn't matter, he just does. What does he know? The boy knows everything. It is not possible. She shakes the feeling off, goes over to him and gives him a hug while whispering quickly:

"You'll get twenty kroner from Dek-Rek and thirty from me. Alright?"

Jostein nods.

Maj turns to Kinck and Ravn.

"Let's start then, shall we?"

Jostein sits on the stool and Ravn directs a spotlight on his face. Kinck tells him not to smile. It would be better to look sullen and dissatisfied. Is that a problem? It isn't. It isn't hard for Jostein to look sullen and dissatisfied although he thinks actually it would be better to smile, especially in photographs. Kinck groans and tells Maj to explain the procedure to the lad. He can't be bothered to do it one more time. This picture is *before*. He can smile in the next picture, which is *after*, as much as he likes. Jostein nods. He has understood. He isn't stupid. He has a brain.

"Is it colour?" he asks.

"Only the spots," Ravn answers.

Kinck takes the first photographs. When the light falls correctly it almost looks as though Jostein is a leper. It can hardly be worse. So it can hardly be better. Rudjord, however, is sceptical. The kid mustn't frighten off the customers either. But never mind. Then Jostein changes into a white shirt and puts on a clean blazer which is too tight across the shoulders and back. Jostein thinks it suits him: he is showing his muscles. Maj recognises the blazer, it is Jesper's, the one he wore on May 17th, but she doesn't say a word, she just puts two and two together. Her letter was probably in the blazer. She sprinkles a bit of dry shampoo in Jostein's hair and combs it down the side. Now he not only has to smile, he has to show a tube of Valcrema as well. Suddenly it is hard to smile. It is as if his lips have been accidentally sewn together at the corners. On top of which, there is something Jostein can't quite grasp: he hasn't used Valcrema yet, the spots are exactly as they were before, how can this be *after*? He runs a hand across his forehead to check. Perhaps something has happened in the meantime after all. You can never know. Dek-Rek *is* an advertising bureau. But the spots haven't gone. One of them even bursts with a pop and Maj has to wash the floor before they can carry on. Rudjord gives her twenty kroner and escapes. Ravn adds a filter to the light. Kinck takes four more pictures. Then the job is done. Jostein can keep the tube of Valcrema. He keeps the white shirt as well. In a way it is his now. Wouldn't he like to take the stool too? Kinck was only asking. Or the camera? Jostein can't see jokes today and is about to help himself. Maj pulls him away, puts two ten-krone notes in one pocket and thirty of her own in the other. She feels sullied. She is lying and bribing.

"Have you spoken to Jesper?" she asks.

"He said we shouldn't talk about it."

Maj wants to delve deeper, but refrains, least said soonest mended, instead she says:

"Use the cream every night, just as it says in the instructions."

"Until we do the next shoot?"

"Exactly."

They are quiet for a moment.

"I would've liked to hear Jesper play on the seventeenth."

Maj is so happy. It is another shot of happiness, recognisable and close to hand. These are everyday miracles. She puts her hand on his.

"I'm sure you'll get another opportunity."

"He might not play as well."

"Or he might play better."

Jostein nods and takes the lift down to the ground floor. In Rosenkrantz' gate he is surrounded by shadows. He makes a bee-line for the light in Karl Johan. There he walks as slowly as he can, he *strolls*, with his hands behind his back and suns himself. He bathes in the glory. This is not a small thing. He has never had so much money on him, not even when he fiddled the Christmas stamps for the Red Cross. And what is more, this money was come by honestly. That is why it is worth more. But isn't all money the same? It comes from the same place, Norges Bank, and changes hands in a variety of ways, depending on circumstances. Some people earn it, some steal it, some find it, some win it and some inherit it. In the end, all money changes hands. Perhaps Jostein should get a banana split at Studenten Isbar. He can afford a sundae soda as well and a chocolate milkshake. Or he can buy Turkish cigarettes at Myhre Tobakk, French ones too, maybe both. With a white shirt, a blazer and his spots he doesn't need ID to prove his age. Jostein decides to take a seat at Nille, which has just opened. The bells in the City Hall tower chime a sonorous one o'clock, which causes the pigeons in the university square to take off in formations, flapping their wings behind the benches where the pensioners sit with bags of breadcrumbs in their laps. The waitress stops at his table. Jostein orders a Coca Cola in a glass, without a straw. Straws are for girls and pygmies. He fancies an open shrimp sandwich too, but makes do with the drink for the time being. While he is waiting, however, he gets cold feet. When the waitress returns with the tray, he has changed his mind. He doesn't want a Coca Cola either. He doesn't want to waste money. Drinking Coca Cola without a straw at Nille is squandering money. If he is thirsty he can drink water from the tap. The waitress wants the money anyway. Jostein objects: the bottle isn't even open. She can sell it to someone else. She objects: he has used her time. Jostein counters that he hasn't drunk anything: How else would she have spent her time? The waitress can't be bothered to listen to any more from this petulant brat who, by the way, has so many spots on the top storey that he could be used as a control tower at Fornebu airport. Jostein rambles happily through the Palace Gardens, the blazer hooked over his shoulder from his middle finger. This is how to do it. Not only does he earn money, he saves it too. This is what he does with money. He saves it. So he has twice the amount. For every krone he doesn't spend his value increases. He decides to be miserly from now on. But when he dies he will give half his fortune to the Red Cross, just for devilry, and keep the rest himself. He pops into Trier bak Slottet to buy a maths exercise book. He could have borrowed a sheet of squared paper from his father, but he doesn't want to bother anyone else and especially not his father. He wants to be a self-made man, a doughty loner. And a maths book is an investment, unlike Coca Cola, which is only a refreshment. A refreshment is soon finished. An investment grows. That is how the world has to be seen: short term and long term. The former is good. The latter pays. A maths book is like Jesper's sheet music, except that Jostein has to write the tunes himself, in kroner and øre, and at the bottom the profit should sound like a round of foot-stomping applause. Leaving Trier bak Slottet, Jostein, two kroner and fifty øre worse off short term, but richer long term, sees the flower shop in Skovveien and is drawn in that direction. It is an enticement he cannot control. It controls him. Jostein Melsom wants to buy some flowers he can lay on Elisabeth Vilder's grave. He isn't quite sure whether this is an expense or an investment. It is neither. It is eternal love. The assistant persuades him to buy a wreath. A wreath is the right choice. Then he walks all the way to Vestre cemetery and starts hunting. Jostein knows: today he is important. In Vestre cemetery everything leads its own life. The dead have plenty of time. Even the squirrels take things easy. Eventually he finds the grave. Elisabeth Vilder has been buried in the shade beside the crematorium. A blue vase containing a dandelion stands in front of the dates that are far too close together: 1942–1957. The funeral took place in silence. The silence still hasn't left. There is also a pair of shoes on the ground. Jostein considers this rather tasteless. It is exactly as though Elisabeth has just kicked them off and fallen headlong. He puts on his blazer and lays the wreath by the headstone. This very act, the act in itself, makes him feel even more formal and tearful. It is the seriousness of life, his life. Jostein barely knew Elisabeth. In truth he didn't know her at all. In this way they are becoming better acquainted. As Jostein moves to stand up, a hand lands on his shoulder, he is spun round and finds himself looking straight into the ravaged face of an inebriate smelling of the top shelf in a vinmonopol.

"Who the bloody hell are you?"

"Jostein . . . Jostein Melsom."

"Melsom as in the butcher in Kirkeveien?"

Jostein feels proud.

"I'm his son."

"Do you know who I am?"

"You were probably her father."

"Was? I *am*. I *am* her father! Can you hear the difference?"

"Yes, you are her father."

"Were you and Elisabeth in the same class?"

"No, I go to a correspondence school."

"Why have you laid that wreath there? On my daughter's grave?"

"Because I was probably the last person to speak to her."

Henry Vilder lets Jostein go and eyes him coolly.

"You spoke to her?"

"Only on the telephone. She rang."

Elisabeth's father laughs, a burst of hollow laughter.

"Why would she ring someone as ugly as you?"

Jostein looks down.

"Actually she was ringing Axel. But I answered the telephone."

Henry Vilder is quiet. The sun is in his eyes. It seems painful, like an operation without an anaesthetic.

"Sorry," he says.

Jostein shrugs. The seams of the blazer groan.

"No problem."

"What did Elisabeth say?"

"Only that she was going to have a bath."

His cheek stings as the flat, hard hand strikes home. For an instant the world is ablaze. Jostein staggers to the side and squats down, ready for more blows, maybe kicks. He is obviously dealing with a man whom grief has rendered insane. But Henry Vilder, bewildered and sober now, gives him his card.

"Drop by some day," he says.

"Drop by?"

"Elisabeth's friends are our friends."

When Jostein finally dares to stand up properly, Henry Vilder has already walked around the crematorium to Borgen Metro station, where he waits on the platform of death for the rest of his life. Jostein studies the card: *Henry Vilder Jr, Imports/Exports*. He should get himself a card like this, with his own name on: *Jostein Melsom*. He could also put *Imports/Exports*, but for the time being he is only a plan in the making, a draft, a negative in the dark room: *before*. *After* hasn't happened yet. He stuffs the card in his back pocket and walks down to Majorstua. In the shop his father turns his back on him and is barely or not at all interested in hearing any news from the advertising industry, on the contrary, he considers it embarrassing that his son will have his photograph appearing in magazines in this way. On the other hand, his mother is intrigued by everything, from the roots of his hair to his fingernails.

"What a long time you were!"

Jostein shrugs.

"It's not just taking a snap, you know. You need lighting and planning and so on."

"You got some Valcrema though, did you?"

"A tube."

"Just one?"

"It's enough."

His mother goes closer.

"Have you used it already? Your cheek's so red. Or is that the sun? There."

"Don't touch. Please."

"And the seams of the blazer. They've split. Why did you absolutely have to take Jesper's? Your tweed jacket is much—"

Jostein moves away and catches sight of Stine passing with her satchel on her back like a snail shell. He opens the door, tears off the blazer and throws it to her.

"Your mamma's home."

Stine runs home, stops in the hall and is about to shout. But she doesn't. She hangs the blazer on a hook, puts her satchel in the dining room and goes into the kitchen, where Jesper is sitting and reading his music. He has put Harald Sæverud behind him, but he hasn't come to the end of Satie. He likes the parts where there is more silence than music. Stine perches on the edge of the chair and can't sit still.

"Isn't Mamma home after all?" she says.

"At work."

"But she's really back?"

Jesper chuckles.

"Yes, let's hope so. Really back."

Stine leans over towards her brother.

"How can you learn it by heart?"

"Learning it by heart is easy. It's the rest that's hard."

"Are you going to Enzo's?"

"Why do you ask?"

"Because you're reading music."

Jesper puts it down.

"I read music all the time. Apart from when you disturb me."

"Am I disturbing you?"

"You do all the time."

Stine goes to stand up, her face at half-mast, but Jesper holds her down.

"When Mamma comes, don't ask her loads of questions and no fuss, alright?"

Stine nods.

"Why not?"

"Because there's no point asking questions if she doesn't want to tell us herself."

"Eh?"

Jesper groans and has a sudden urge to move out or go to sea, preferably both.

"You and Jostein can get married," he says.

"Yuk. With all those spots. Why?"

"Because you both ask loads of questions."

Stine stares at the clock.

"Shall we cook before—"

Jesper doesn't let her finish.

"Today it's Mamma's turn."

Then they hear her and go quiet. She is quiet too, quiet and slow. She takes such a long time. It takes her longer to go from the hall to the kitchen than from Rome to Fagerborg. At last she appears in the doorway. Stine runs over. Both of them burst into tears, cry and laugh, but mostly they cry. Jesper is glad he is sitting with his back to them. There should be a law against crying in the kitchen, gymnasium or dressing room. He puts the sheet music in his bag so that it won't get wet. Maj finally lets go of Stine, dries her tears and almost shouts, as if she is on the stage in an opera and not their kitchen in Kirkeveien:

"Are you hungry?"

But Maj doesn't wait for an answer. She just asks Stine to fill the biggest pan with water and put it on, rushes into the bedroom and returns with a flat packet full of sticks.

"Spaghetti."

As soon as the water is boiling she puts these sticks in the pan and waits. Jesper sets the table and acts as if he is not at all interested, but in the end he is drawn to the stove to see: spaghetti boiling. Soon the sticks begin to bend in the water until the froth covers them. After eight minutes Maj strains everything through a colander, shakes it and pours the soft writhing snakes into a bowl.

"Al dente."

They sit down. Maj dollops a pile on each plate and adds a knob of butter on top, which melts at once and runs slowly in all directions leaving yellow stripes. Jesper has forgotten the spoons. Maj fetches three and passes them around. Are they going to eat with a spoon? She explains.

"You can either put a bit in your mouth and just suck up the spaghetti or roll it around your fork like this."

Maj shows how this is done. It seems easy.

"But the best way is to use both your spoon and fork. That's how Italians do it."

She shows how this is done too. It seems more difficult. You have to hold your spoon tightly in your left hand and twist the fork as the spaghetti winds round naturally, so long as you do it properly. Stine can't do it. Jesper can't be bothered to try and raises his knife.

"Can't you just cut the worms into bits?"

Maj glances at him, suddenly fearful.

"Yes, of course. You can eat this as you like. But at any rate it has to be hot."

They each eat spaghetti in their own way.

They say it is delicious.

While Jesper and Stine tidy the kitchen Maj goes back to the bedroom and unpacks. It is odd. She doesn't have to wash any clothes. Don't her clothes get dirty in Rome? Or did she wash them there? Afterwards Stine sits in the dining room and does her homework, sort of. Jesper does the same, more or less. Everything is sort of. The world is out of tune. Then Maj finally comes out with her presents. She gives Stine a pair of sunglasses. They are like the ones Sophia Loren wore in "The River Girl". Stine tries them on. Everything is dark and wonderful around her. She looks at Jesper.

"You look cool," he says.

Stine never wants to take the glasses off. She is going to wear them in class, in the playground and the shower. She is going to wear them in bed. Then her sleep will be deeper and her dreams will change sides and support her.

Maj gives Jesper some sheet music.

On the top page it says: *Dallapiccola*. It is the name of the composer. Jesper has never heard of him. He looks at his mother.

"Thank you."

"It's not me you should thank."

Jesper goes to his room and closes the door. He misses having windows. He wishes he had a window to stand by. There are only walls in the hall. It is a cell. He longs for a window so that he can see who is coming. He longs for doors he can lock. For a second he can't breathe. The hall is no longer a cell but a lift. Everything moves downwards and he moves at the same speed until he is back on the floor, between the same walls, and he opens the music book: *Musica par tre pianoforti*. The notes are strange. They don't look like anything he has seen before. They hang in clusters or they are far apart. He tries to find a melody, but can't see one. A letter falls to the floor. Jesper picks it up and sits down on the sofa bed. It is from Enzo Zanetti:

Dear Jesper, my boy, my hope. I'm staying in Italy and I won't return to Norway. My days in exile are over. So we will never see each other again. However, you will be in my thoughts and perhaps you will give me a thought when you have nothing else on your mind. My mood is one of great sorrow and great happiness. My heart is beating in time again and the notes are in tune, if in a minor key. Your mother said that your playing on May 17th drew tears from the eyes of the audience. This is what I've always known. You won't impress anyone. You will move them. Soon you will be beyond me and therefore I have no more to offer. But look closely at Dallapiccola. When you can play him, go to another teacher. His name and address are at the bottom. Take care of your hands. Take care of yourself, my boy.

Your Enzo

Jesper's first thought is that now he can ask Enzo Zanetti what a devil's piano is. If anyone were to know it would be him. Then he hides the letter in the "Ballad of Revolt", puts it in the bottom drawer and another thought strikes him: Now Enzo has finished repairing and will become a plot-owner in Italy. Most people want to own their last plot where they were born. After Jesper has finished thinking he takes the Dallapiccola with him into the dining room, places the notes on the piano and has to wind down the stool to sit at the right height. Has he grown since he last practised or is the ceiling lower? Stine hasn't taken off her sunglasses yet. It is on the tip of Jesper's tongue to say that wearing them indoors is not that "cool", unless it is a restaurant or a bar, but that is a long way off for Sophia Loren Jr. So he doesn't. Stine can just wear the sunglasses. Mamma is sitting by the window stitching the seams of the blazer that have come apart. The light around her is airy and weightless, with a touch of green, like a gentle wind slowly wafting through the room. Jesper starts playing *Musica par tre pianoforti* by Dallapiccola. It is only sounds, clusters of sound and single notes, unexpected and outrageous. Stine removes her sunglasses. Mamma looks up from her sewing with a sweet smile. The music reminds Jesper of snowfall and umbrellas.

The last meeting before the summer holidays was at Fru Mimi Nielsen's. One or two reps from all the Oslo departments were present, as well as Dept Head Galtung and of course Frøken Henriksen, Fru Bull, Frøken Olga Larsen, the chairman of the Red Cross in Oslo and a Search and Rescue rep. Fru Lund represented Fagerborg department. The Search and Rescue man gave an excellent talk on their work and structure. Fru Mimi Nielsen also gave a very lucid talk about the Red Cross in general, including some of its history. Herr Backer talked about his journey to northern Norway with Erling Steen for the inauguration of the Red Cross clinics up there. He described the dismal conditions, which fortunately would now improve. The population there was grateful. Finally, Fru Mimi Nielsen had arranged a very amusing and informative game of Twenty Questions all about the Red Cross. The prize for the winner came in the form of chocolate. Afterwards a wonderful selection of open sandwiches was served with coffee.

HMM

Jesper looks at the name and address again – *Finn Martins, Keysers gate 8* – stuffs the letter in his pocket and turns to Trude.

"I'll ring the bell."

"You do that."

"That's what I said. I'll ring the bell."

"Do it then."

"What if he isn't at home?"

Trude laughs.

"We-ell. He won't be able to answer, will he?"

Jesper raises his hand closer to the dented nameplates and worn buttons, but withdraws it at once.

"Perhaps it's better to ring his doorbell inside?"

"If we can get in, yes."

"Or perhaps it's better to ring here first?"

"Don't you want to meet him?"

"Or send him a letter?"

"Or is it that you don't dare?"

Trude regrets these words as she speaks them. She has an inkling she can't quite articulate: if Enzo Zanetti was like a father to Jesper, as was her impression, this will be the second time he has to find a new one. Perhaps he doesn't want to tie himself to anyone? Perhaps he doesn't want to tie himself to her either? She kisses him fleetingly on the cheek and leans against the door. It is open. Finn Martins lives on the third floor. Paint is peeling from the walls. The plaster on the ceiling is crumbling and falling over the steps as white powder. There are 118. On every landing there are coloured glass panes that turn the light in the stairwell dark red, almost burgundy. It is reminiscent of snow at sunset. Rumour has it that Finn Martins is famous, but completely unknown. Yes, that is possible too. He composes music nobody wants to play and, even less, hear. Some say this is a pity. Most, however, are profoundly grateful and kneel in gratitude. Finn Martins' music has neither rhythm nor notes, you see. Cats are more classical than he is. The sole redeeming factor, again according to hearsay, which circulates in bars, in butchers' shops, in waiting rooms and school playgrounds, is that Martins used to play double bass in his day for the Oslo Trade Association, where his father was the conductor. If only the son had stuck to the bass. They stop on the third floor. Jesper can't dither any longer. He rings the bell. After a good while a pair of slippers approaches, the shuffle isn't hard to hear, and a round face above a black dressing gown peers out. Jesper gets straight to the point.

"My apologies for the disturbance, but Enzo Zanetti has recommended you, Herr Martins."

Finn Martins rubs his eyes and asks:

"Has that lounge pianist recommended me or you?"

Oh, shit, they must have woken Finn Martins during his nap. But it is only three o'clock. Who has a nap at three? Who has a nap before three? Even worse: they have disturbed Finn Martins while he was at work. Perhaps he had been in the bathroom composing? Or perhaps he simply hadn't got up yet?

"Both," Jesper answers.

Jesper gives the letter to Finn Martins, who turns to Trude.

"Do you play the piano too?"

"No, I've just strung along."

"Merciful God."

Finn Martins asks them to take off their shoes and leave them outside. Only then will he let them in. In this apartment, in a run-down block from the previous century, everything is modern. The walls are bare, the lamps resemble sculptures and the light they cast is as white as the walls, and there is a clock in every room.

There are no curtains over the windows, only narrow blinds. The furniture is futuristic: low and flat. Even the door handles are modern. They are impossible to hold and so all the doors are open. The rest is geometry. Nothing is superfluous. By the time they reach the study, where the grand piano is, Finn Martins has read the letter and gives it back.

"I don't usually take pupils," he says.

Jesper looks down and is basically relieved.

"Alright. That's a shame."

"But as this is Enzo Zanetti. The sly fox. What did he teach you anyway? Operatic chestnuts in gravy?"

"Satie."

"Sentimental circus music. What else?"

"Sæverud."

"Romantic tearjerker. Did you sit in for him at the Bristol?"

"No."

"Have you got the Dallapiccola with you?"

"Yes."

Jesper takes the music from his bag.

"Surprise me," Finn Martins says.

Jesper reflects for a moment, afraid to fall, puts the notes back, passes the bag to Trude, sits down at the grand piano and plays *Musica par tre pianoforti* from memory. Afterwards there is complete silence. Then Finn Martins says:

"Hmm."

No more is said. He just scribbles down a time and another day on a scrap of paper and passes it to Jesper, who puts it in his pocket. The first lesson lasted three minutes. The audience is over. They find their own way out. They put on their shoes. There are just as many steps down. Keysers gate is just as dirty. But the racing ambulances briefly rearrange the dust in the air. Jesper thinks: Enzo Zanetti lived between the church and the fire station. Finn Martins lives between the main library and the Rikshospital. He has no idea where such thoughts are leading him. Trude holds his hand.

They walk to Studenten Isbar. Jesper pays for a strawberry milk-shake with two straws and they find a window seat facing Karl Johans gate.

"What do you think it meant?" Jesper asks.

"What did what mean?"

"The hmm."

"Not easy to say."

"Hmm. I think he wasn't sure."

"Anyway, you got another lesson."

"I reckon it'll be even shorter."

Jesper looks outside. People are scurrying past. They are mostly men in hats and coats with a briefcase under their arms. All the things they have to hurry for: lunches, meetings, the tram, the vin-monopol, the weather forecast, the lottery, wages, births, they have to hurry for everything, their lives are all about being in time for something and the only thing they arrive early for is their death, but never their own funeral. Something like that. He says:

"I might give up school."

"Why?"

"Why not?"

"Because it's stupid."

"Because I don't need all the shit we learn."

"How can you know that?"

"German verbs. Geometry. Vaulting in the gym. Handball. When am I going to need them? It's an obstruction. It's getting in the way."

"In the way of what?"

Jesper sees a young child drop his ice cream on the step and start bawling.

"Most things."

"Don't you like our class either? Are we in the way too?"

"I didn't say that."

"What else would you do? Just play the piano?"

"Just?"

"Do you think you can make a living from that?"

Jesper shrugs, sucks up the last drops and says:

"Hmm."

"Hmm?"

"Wilhelm Kempff definitely makes a living from it. And Robert Levin."

Trude manages to find a pink drop of froth at the bottom of the tall glass, there is always one more in a strawberry milkshake, but eventually it comes to an end too. Then she also looks outside, at the shadows drifting past in the light of the green sun above Studenterlunden woods.

"Do you think about Elisabeth sometimes?" she asks.

Jesper isn't quite sure what to answer.

"Now and then."

"Now and then?"

"Actually, I don't, no."

"Nor me. Isn't it strange how quickly everything comes to an end?"

All of a sudden Jesper feels heavy and uneasy.

"An end? Surely it doesn't finish?"

"Or how quickly we forget?"

They walk together through the Palace Park, but when Jesper goes to kiss Trude before they part company in Riddervolds Plass, it doesn't happen quite as he had imagined. She jerks back with her neck, not much, yet enough for him only to brush her cheek with his lips. Then she sets off down Skovveien without turning; Jesper heads in the opposite direction, along Josefines gate, and turns round several times. He is still uneasy, perhaps even more so. Did he do something wrong? It is easier to play Dallapiccola blind-fold than live a blameless life, even if it is only one day. Unfortunately he meets Jostein by Marienlyst. He is sitting on a bench trying to get a tan in the setting sun. Or maybe he is studying the crossroads where he was hit by a trolley bus. It still can't be healthy.

"Haven't you got rid of the spots yet?"

"I'm working on it," Jostein says.

"I reckon they're worse."

"It's just a transitional phase before my forehead is spot-less."

Jesper sits down next to Jostein and is actually happy to have something else to think about.

"You didn't say anything?"

"What about?"

Jostein has to lean closer as Jesper lowers his voice.

"About my mother."

"What would I say about your mother? There's nothing to say."

"That's precisely what I'm saying. There's nothing to say."

Jostein straightens up again and squints at Broadcasting House.

"Classy sunglasses Stine's got, by the way."

"Have you seen her?"

"Hard to miss."

"You haven't been bothering her, have you?"

"Bothering her? Of course not. Why would I bother her?"

"She doesn't like spots."

"Wish I had some sunglasses like hers."

Jesper chortles.

"You can afford them, can't you? Now that you're famous?"

Jostein laughs even louder.

"Are you mad? Haven't got enough money to go to Rome and buy sunglasses."

EXTRAORDINARY BOARD MEETING

Maj Kristoffersen has barely rung the bell before Dr Lund opens the door. He is wearing shorts and a singlet and is probably about to run around the globe again. He bows, without catching her eye, and lets her in.

"This isn't going to be easy," he says.

Maj laughs.

"Don't kill yourself then," she says.

"I wasn't thinking about me."

Dr Lund shakes his head and the door slips into place after him. Maj can see she isn't the first to arrive, even if she is a little early. Coats are already hanging in the hall. She is the last. She brushes her hair and goes into the living room. The board is waiting. There is something in the air. No-one looks at her, apart from Fru Lund, who says:

"Take a seat, Maj."

"Has something happened?"

"Just take a seat, please."

There is no room on the sofa, where she normally sits for board meetings. She has to make do with a kitchen stool on the other side of the table and sit opposite the ladies, who are finding it difficult to look her in the eye. Maj turns to Fru Lund.

"Has something happened?" she repeats.

"You're probably the best person to answer that."

Maj studies her feet, which are still swollen from all the narrow Italian pavements.

"What do you mean?"

Fru Lund takes a deep breath.

"The worst of this, Maj Kristoffersen, is not that you lied about being in Hurdal. Nor is it that you travelled to Rome with a dubious man. The worst is that you left Jesper and Stine alone at home."

Maj sits quietly and lets the words sink in, but it is as though she doesn't hear them.

"He's not dubious," she says.

Fru Lund leans forward.

"What did you say?"

Maj sees the trail it is impossible to hide: when Jostein found out, he told his mother and in the butcher's shop there is no rumour too small, and this is a big one, it is a fillet steak of a rumour, it is a bad reputation. Nevertheless, she asks:

"How do you all know?"

Fru Lund gives a brief chortle.

"Never you mind. You should concentrate on how you've put us in a very difficult spot."

"This has nothing to do with you."

Fru Lund smacks the table, the coffee service jumps and the ladies recoil.

"This definitely does have something to do with us, Maj Kristoffersen! How can members have any confidence in the board if the treasurer can embark on such an irresponsible course of action while turning her back on her children?"

"Jesper is old enough to look after Stine."

"I don't think you should stoop so low as to defend your actions. That only makes things worse."

The silence deepens. No-one touches the coffee. No-one helps themselves to the loaf cake. But looks are exchanged, inaudibly and almost imperceptibly. Maj looks up and can see that everyone is dying to find out how it was, how it was in Rome.

"We had separate rooms," she says quietly.

Fru Lund is on the point of banging on the table again, but refrains and instead her fingers point at Maj.

"Don't you dare! We simply don't want to hear about this. Isn't that right?"

Fru Lund turns to the ladies on the sofa, who wring their hands in their laps and nod. Maj looks down again.

"I just wanted—"

Fru Lund interrupts her.

"Don't add lies to your indulgence. Until Oslo Red Cross informs us otherwise you're suspended from the board."

"Oslo Red Cross? Is that necessary?"

"If Fagerborg department suffers a loss of moral standing, it's also a case for Oslo Red Cross and accordingly the Norwegian Red Cross."

It is Maj Kristoffersen's turn to smack the table, but she doesn't have the strength, she is numb, empty, only her heart is working inside her, beating hard, thumping, she could die at any moment, exactly like Ewald, she could die from the inside.

"Then I'd prefer to stop," she says.

"It isn't up to you."

Maj rises to her feet.

"I won't be coming back anyway."

Fru Lund has also stood up while the ladies on the sofa – Frøken Schanke, Fru Skjelkvale and Fru Endersen – remain seated, white-knuckled and tight-lipped, and the room is filled with great sorrow. Maj can't remember how she got out to the street. She just runs for the bus, even though she had no intention of catching it, she steps on board, pays and sits right at the back. She closes her eyes. Her heart is still pounding. She doesn't know if she is ashamed or furious. She is both. She is furious and ashamed. All Fagerborg knows about her. She has been to Rome with her son's piano teacher. Can you sink any lower than that? It will be talked about in hairdressing salons and shops, on street corners and platforms, at Smør-Petersen's and Melsom the butcher's and around the tables in the Valka and Larsen restaurants. Is there no end to her fall? Soon the rest of the city will have heard about it. Maj Kristoffersen is suddenly in Frogner Plass. The bus carries on down Thomas Heftyes gate. The exhaust fumes expelled in dark clouds mingle with the lilacs by the entrances to the flats. Some boys are laughing. Are they laughing at her? They are sitting on a box in front of the West End sign, pointing, with nothing else to do but laugh. She looks down. She has stepped on a dog turd – it must have been from a Great Dane at the very least. The mess oozes out from under her shoe, like when you press your fork down on top of a millefeuille. She tries to scrape it off on the kerb. The boys are laughing even louder. They are howling with laughter. There isn't usually much entertainment in Frogner Plass on an evening like this. Now there is. Maj can't stand it anymore. She kicks off her shoes and leaves them. She leaves them behind and crosses Frognerveien. In any case, it is good to be rid of her tight shoes. She breathes through her feet. She can hear the laughter behind her. She can hear the whoops. She crosses the tramlines and almost breaks into a run, barefoot and crying, the last stretch up steep Nordraaks gate. She rings the bell and has only one hope left: that Olaf Hall doesn't open the door. It is Margrethe. She ushers Maj into the kitchen, telling her to take slow, deep breaths, and pours them both a liqueur.

"I've finished with the Red Cross too, now," Maj says.

Margrethe sits still for a moment listening.

"He's downstairs in the shop every evening. Luckily."

They taste the liqueur, which is sweet and thick, almost like honey.

Maj hides her face in her hands, not breathing out but groaning.

"What have I done? What have I done?"

"You're a fool, Maj. What on earth were you thinking of?"

"I don't know. I—"

"Oh, yes, you do. You were thinking of yourself. You should have been thinking about Jesper and Stine, but all you could think about was yourself."

"I wasn't thinking. Not at all. Now don't you get angry with me as well."

Margrethe drains her glass.

"Did they cope while you were away?" she asks.

"Yes, they were so good."

"Excellent. But you could have asked me."

"They'd tidied the flat and washed up and . . ."

Maj starts crying again. Margrethe goes to find a pair of shoes and pours more liqueur into the much too small glasses.

"You'll have to learn to live with it," she says.

"With what?"

"The shame, Maj."

"My God."

"All you have to do is turn your back."

"That's easy for you to say."

Margrethe smiles, but she is sad too because she is thinking about Jesper and Stine, and especially Stine. Can they turn their backs on this?

"No, it isn't easy for me to say, Maj. I've turned my back on so much that soon there'll be nothing left."

"Sorry."

"But how was it in Rome?"

Maj lets her hands fall and looks at Margrethe.

"It was the best week of my life," she says.

When Maj returns home Stine's sunglasses are on the floor in the hall. Both lenses are smashed.

Fru Esther Andersen informed us that the emergency depots were being checked. Some minor rubber items and batteries would be replaced. Schools have applied to the Red Cross for some resources with regard to the teaching of First Aid. Fru Lund suggested donating a box of materials to each school to strengthen our contact with head teachers and to make it easier for us to call on schools when we need children to sell stamps, for example.

The Red Cross would like to recruit new takers for the First Aid courses. They cost 10 kroner for 24 lessons.

At the end of the meeting we were shown a nice little enamel Red Cross pin. It can be ordered through Frøken Henriksen for 4 kroner.

Maj Kristoffersen has been suspended while her case is being discussed. In the meantime Fru Lund is acting-treasurer.

THE SUNGLASSES

Jostein is sweating like a pig. He is walking along Slemdalsveien, past the famous functionalist houses, which resemble enormous, white building blocks with windows as big as walls. He passes through Vinderen, where men in light-coloured shirts are sitting in the backyard at Jeppe drinking beer. He passes the Hippodrome, where two horses are chomping grass. The tram comes from Majorstua, Jostein can catch it in Ris and take it the rest of the way, but Jostein has become a skinflint, a real skinflint, and prefers to remove his tweed jacket and find some shade on the pavement. In fact, he is not sweating like a pig. Pigs don't sweat. They are just hauled to their deaths and afterwards they hang upside down without any regrets. At least Jostein won't have any regrets about things he hasn't done. He still has Henry Vilder's business card in his pocket. He finds the house in the cul-de-sac behind the school, opens the gate and strolls through the untidy, neglected garden. Winter has ravaged it since his last visit. He rings the bell. It is almost the following summer before Henry Vilder opens the door.

"I've come to visit," Jostein says.

Henry Vilder looks as ravaged as before.

"Visit? Whom?"

Jostein shows the card, as though he has to remind this man who he actually is, he is *Mr Imports/Exports*. Henry Vilder manages a faint smile and lets him in. They stand in the dark hallway. The staircase to the first floor is dark too. The reason is quite simply that all the curtains have been drawn and no lights have been switched on. But there is something else, a smell, of stagnant water, remnants of food and ash. Why doesn't Henry Vilder say anything?

He just stands there, silent, lost, behind the harrowed face sagging over a faded collar.

"I was knocked down by a bus in Kirkeveien," Jostein says.

"Oh?"

"Yes. Many years ago."

"Right."

"That's why my hearing's not so good."

"I didn't say anything."

"I know. I heard."

Henry Vilder smiles again and goes into the living room. Jostein follows him. There is a bottle on the table. A glass lies on its side next to it. The ashtray is full. Henry Vilder opens the curtains and it is as though the garden falls through the window into the room with all its weeds and foliage. He has to shield his eyes. Then he turns.

"What are you actually here for?"

"You said Elisabeth's friends are your friends. And—"

Henry Vilder raises a hand.

"What was your name again?"

"Jostein Melsom."

"It seems you take everything literally, Jostein."

"Didn't you mean what you said?"

"I meant it. But apparently Elisabeth didn't have any friends."

"Has no-one come here?"

"Only Trude and Jesper from her class."

"I know them. Jesper's my best—"

"But that's a while ago. And they only wanted to return her blasted shoes. And then her mother decided they should be on her grave. What do you think about that, Jostein? A pair of high heels on a grave?"

"I think it's odd. But they were the shoes she was wearing at the party."

Henry Vilder goes over to the table, lifts the empty bottle and puts it down again. He stands with his back to Jostein.

"If I understood you correctly, you spoke to Elisabeth after she'd come back that night?"

"I came here too."

Henry Vilder turns slowly, his face distorted and shiny.

"You were here?"

Jostein averts his face, afraid he will receive another slap, and it will undoubtedly be more stinging than the last.

"Only outside. I rang the bell. But Elisabeth didn't open up. She didn't open the door. And I just went away. I'm very sorry, Herr Vilder."

The slap is not forthcoming. Instead Henry Vilder places a hand on Jostein's shoulder and tears begin to fall. He remains like this until his crying is over, if indeed it will ever be.

"Don't be."

"I am anyway."

Henry Vilder wipes his face with the tail of his shirt.

"And now tell me why you really came."

"I'm looking for a summer job."

"Is it summer already?"

"I think so."

"Did you have anything in mind?"

"I'll do whatever I'm given."

Henry Vilder opens the terrace doors.

"It might be best to find something you don't need good hearing for."

"My hearing's better now."

"And you look as if you can handle hard work."

"I've worked at Oslo Slaughterhouse."

"Why did you stop?"

"I'm studying."

"To be what?"

"Rich."

"What about starting in the garden?"

They walk onto the terrace facing the back of the house. To the left is a swimming pool, empty, apart from the leaves that have gathered in piles at the bottom. They fetch some tools from a shed by the fence: a rake, a fork, a lawnmower and shears. Suddenly Jostein's courage deserts him.

"Are you going to help?" he asks.

Henry Vilder laughs, and it strikes him with a certain sadness that this is the first time he has laughed since his daughter died and whenever he laughs now he will also think it will be the last.

"No, Jostein. I'm going to sit in a deckchair on the terrace and breathe in a bit of fresh air."

"Right."

Jostein takes off his top and starts raking. He has to rake before he can cut the grass.

"Haven't you forgotten something?" Henry Vilder asks.

Jostein leans on the rake and has the sun in his eyes.

"Do you want me to clean the pool first?"

"Wages, Jostein. Or do you work for free?"

"No, I hadn't planned to. This isn't a calling, you know."

Henry Vilder laughs again; that is twice in one day.

"Then we'd better decide if you should be paid by the hour or results or have a fixed price. Negotiations have begun."

Jostein gives this some thought.

"What will you pay me an hour?"

"What did you get at Oslo Slaughterhouse?"

"Six kroner."

"I'll give you five."

"What's the fixed price then?"

"How many hours will it take for you to finish?"

Jostein looks around. It is impossible to say. You never finish a garden. By the time you approach the end, leaves are already falling where you started.

"It could take all summer."

"What about two hundred kroner?"

"Two-fifty."

"A hundred now and one-fifty when the job's done."

"One-fifty now and a hundred afterwards."

"You drive a hard bargain, Jostein. But that's fine."

They shake hands.

Jostein rakes for the rest of the day until he is dead on his feet.

But Henry Vilder does exactly what he said he would. He sits in a deckchair on the terrace inhaling fresh air. He might easily have been dead. At half past four Jostein approaches the corpse.

"I'll be back tomorrow."

Henry Vilder gives him 150 kroner.

"Bring a packed lunch and a peaked cap with you. I can give you some juice."

"Thank you."

"Why don't you work in your father's shop?"

Jostein counts the money and puts it in his back pocket.

"He doesn't pay very well."

"That's the problem with family businesses, Jostein. What you regard as a job, your father sees as a favour."

"Exactly. And I can't be doing with that anymore."

"Don't be too hard. Doing others a favour can pay in the long term."

Jostein nods, *in the long term*, this is how he should think, not in the short term, but he worked this one out on his own ages ago.

"I'm happy to do you a favour," he says.

"Then don't work too fast."

"Don't?"

"Yes, I'll lose money."

This thought – how Henry Vilder can lose money if he works fast – preoccupies Jostein all the way down to Majorstua, it makes no sense, but with 150 kroner in his back pocket and a hundred more in the offing Jostein can basically think what he likes. Outside Samson he bumps into Stine and has something else to think about. She isn't wearing sunglasses. She seems unhappy and angry. Jostein wants to treat her. It might pay off in the long run.

"Are you alone?" he asks.

"Mamma's in Krogh getting my sunglasses repaired."

"Have they broken already?"

"She can wear them. I don't want them."

"Why not?"

Stine turns away. Jostein has to walk all the way around her.

"Why not?" he repeats.

"My mother's a tart."

Stine pinches her mouth so tight it is a line, while a tear falls from the corner of one eye. Jostein leans closer.

"What did you say?"

"I didn't say it."

"Who did?"

"Someone at school."

"Who's the someone?"

Stine looks down.

"Tor. Gunnar. Stein. Ida."

"Ida? Girls as well?"

Stine nods.

"Everyone's saying it. That Mamma's—"

"Shh! Are they in your class?"

"No. They're in the seventh."

Jostein straightens up and sees Maj coming out of Krogh, the optician's. She stops in front of them, gives the case containing the sunglasses to Stine, who doesn't want it, but Maj doesn't notice because she turns to Jostein, who asks before she has a chance:

"When's the next photograph?"

"Have you been putting on the cream as I said?"

"Every night."

Jostein parts his fringe and it is not exactly an uplifting sight that meets Maj.

"You'll hear from them," she says.

"Will I get fifty kroner then as well?"

"Now just give over, Jostein."

"I was only wondering."

"Perhaps you should start wearing a peaked cap?"

"Lots of people say that."

They cross the road together and choose the cool side of Kirkeveien. Melsom is standing outside his shop sticking a poster to the window. He turns to Maj.

"Do you think Jesper would like to come with Jostein and me to Copenhagen this summer?"

"Oh, my goodness. Copenhagen?"

"I suppose you're used to grander horizons than that?"

There is silence for a moment. Maj looks at the poster: *Leg of mutton, half price*. Perhaps she should buy some for lunch. Stine pulls at her hand.

"I'm sure he would," Maj says.

The butcher turns his white cap around 180 degrees and faces his son.

"We can go to Copenhagen, buy some meat and come back the same day. Can't we, Jostein?"

"What?"

"I'll borrow the caretaker's car and then we can drive to Copenhagen and buy some meat."

"I'm afraid I can't."

"Can't?"

"I've got a job."

"What do you mean? You work *here*. With *me*."

"No, I don't. I work for Henry Vilder. Imports and exports. That's something, that is."

Melsom pushes Jostein into the shop and closes it for the rest of the day. They can hear the racket in the back room; it sounds like a yelling and a groan. Maj seriously wonders if she should check, but changes her mind. You should be concerned, but you shouldn't interfere. Stine lets go of her hand as they walk the last part, where they have walked so many times that they can do it blindfold. You keep walking straight or follow the noises: the dogs, the church bells, the Virginia creeper, the buses, the screaming kids, the pigeons and the postmen.

"Don't you want to wear the sunglasses?" Maj asks.

Stine just shakes her head.

"You don't have to be fed up that Jesper's going to Copenhagen. Because you know what?"

Maj mentions it now: they are going to Hurdal, all three of them, as soon as possible. So that her lie, the thin cover-up story, the cosmetic narrative, will be true, a bit late, mind you, but anyway. As time passes and the years merge into one, what happened first and what happened later won't matter anymore.

"We're going to Hurdal as soon as school's over."

"That's not why I'm fed up," Stine says.

"Why are you then?"

They round the corner of Gørbitz gate and can hear the sounds of Dallapiccola from the open, first-floor, sitting-room window and most people in Fagerborg agree that even the Polish interval signal sounded better. Stine stops and looks up.

"I don't think he's going out with Trude anymore."

The Red Cross bazaar will be held from September 6th to 16th. We drew lots for tables and Fagerborg has no. 7 with Lilleborg and Torshov. (Table 7b is against a pillar and the idea is that Fagerborg should have this side to hang up the coat despite the fact that we drew 7a.) Lilleborg's and Torshov's prizes will be silver teaspoons and a coffee service. I informed the Lilleborg rep, Fru Løfsgaard, that we would have a coat, a doll's pram and sugar/coffee to avoid duplicating prizes at the same table.

LINE CHANGE

The following morning Jostein exchanges a fifty-krone note for four tenners, five krone-coins and ten fifty-øre coins at the Kreditkassen in Majorstua. The cashier subjects him to close scrutiny, but says nothing. Is this a young criminal visiting the bank? Is this the start of a robbery? Then he recognises the boy, it is the son of the butcher in Kirkeveien, he is a bit wild, but quite harmless. He was involved in some jiggery-pokery a few years ago apparently, selling stamps for the Red Cross, but has pulled himself together since. But what about his black eye? That didn't get there on its own. When Jostein emerges he carefully pulls down the cap over his forehead and first of all goes into a telephone box. He finds Henry Vilder's number in the directory, inserts a coin and rings. Fortunately it is free until the person at the other end replies. It is free for some time. Then Henry Vilder picks up and it starts costing.

"I'm afraid I'll be late today," Jostein says.

"That's fine. Come when you like."

Jostein is disappointed.

"You can manage without me?"

"I'll do the best I can."

"Right."

"But on Midsummer Eve I'll need some help."

Jostein puts down the receiver. No money is returned. They have finished talking.

However, Jostein knows this much about accountancy: he can write off this fifty øre as an expense. Expenses are another way of saving. Afterwards he goes into the station toilet where there is an empty sixty per cent alcohol bottle on the shelf above the sink.

Jostein sees himself in the mirror. His left eye is glued together like a smooth, black envelope. It doesn't hurt anymore. Actually it is better when it does. At least the injury has some meaning then. But the peaked cap is classy: *Oslo Slaughterhouse*. He was allowed to keep it when he packed in his job. "I'm on my way," Jostein says. In the waiting room he catches sight of the weighing machine. He already has a card. On his it says: *You will go far*. His name is You-will-go-far Melsom. Then he goes down to Majorstua School and stops at the gates. The bell rings. Soon the playground will be full. It is the penultimate day before the summer holidays. Some of the children are skipping. Some are throwing marbles. Some are just happy. He can't see Stine anywhere. Perhaps she has been kept in during the break. It is not Stine he is looking for. He walks over to the drinking fountain. Some children turn their heads after him. Some laugh. There is silence. He says to two boys:

"I'm looking for Tor. Or Gunnar. Or Stein."

As quick as a flash, the boys in shorts say:

"Have you got a beef with someone?"

Jostein is feeling smart and invincible.

"They'll soon find out."

The boys point.

"Tor's the tallest of them."

Jostein walks over, stops in front of the tallest boy, thinking this should actually be Jesper doing this, defending his mother and sister. However, Jesper has to think primarily about his posh fingers and so Jostein has to step in. Everyone should have a pal like Jostein, thinks Jostein, but only Jesper has.

"Tor?" he asks.

Tor nods and all attention in the playground is focused on this mismatched pair.

"Yes?"

"What did you say?"

"I said yes. My name's Tor. Are you going to the school kitchen?"

Jostein revels in being the only person to know what will happen next.

"No, why?"

"I was just thinking that—"

"What did you say?"

"Nothing."

Tor suddenly becomes suspicious and retreats. All shits become suspicious sooner or later, even if they understand nothing, or maybe that is why. Jostein realises that he is spending too long on this job, even if it is quite a delight to drag it out for as long as possible. He follows Tor and stops at what he considers a suitable distance.

"Can you say hi to Gunnar, Stein and Ida and tell them I'm going to kill them as well if you bother Stine Kristoffersen anymore?"

Jostein aims at the base of his nose and throws only one punch. It is like hearing a dry branch crack. Tor sinks with a groan, holding his face as blood trickles between his fingers. However, the crunch as he hits the ground is louder. Elsewhere the sound has been switched off. Jostein walks to the gates into Sørkedalsveien. A man in a brown smock, armed with a broom, runs over. It is Løkke, the caretaker. He tries to restrain Jostein, who handles him with ease. Ex-teacher Løkke is no more than a pesky fly on his shoulder. Jostein crosses Sørkedalsveien. At the station he meets Jesper, who is catching the Metro to town.

"Are you skiving?" Jostein says.

"Music lesson. I've got permission. It's the summer holidays the day after tomorrow."

"Are you coming with us to Copenhagen?"

Jesper shrugs and nods at the same time.

"Have you got a job with Henry Vilder?"

"I'm responsible for his property."

Jesper can barely meet his eye under the stupid Oslo Slaughter-house cap.

"What a bloody sight you are," he says.

Jostein lifts a hand as if to hide his gummed-up eye.

"Hope it'll be fine for the next photograph."

"How did you manage that then?"

"Becoming Vilder's right-hand man? Just asked him."

"I mean the shiner, you twit."

"Tripped."

"Very likely."

Jesper turns away, but Jostein won't leave him in peace.

"It wasn't Pop's fault, I swear. It was just an accident."

"Don't think I fancy going to Copenhagen after all."

"Then I won't either. Be a pal. Please. Come with us."

"Do you think your father's a pal?"

"He didn't mean it. Word of honour."

"What did he mean then?"

The train is approaching the platform. It is from Holmenkollen. Jesper and Jostein have to go in opposite directions, to Finn Martins and Henry Vilder respectively, and Jostein has to cross the line and catch the train on the other side. And suddenly I feel like going with them both. I want to be the conductor on all lines, east, west, through the city and up the mountains, under the ground and far, far away. I don't want to lose sight of either of them. I want to see how they get on. I don't want to wait and be the last to know. But I also have to choose. This is my regret. I am strapped for time. I can't do both. For this reason I am seeking advice from the reader. Who would you follow this morning on June 20th, 1957? Jesper Kristoffersen or Jostein Melsom? If it is Jesper, you will have to take pot luck with a music lesson in Keysers gate held by the serialist and twelve-tone phantom, Finn Martins, the man with the moon face, and you will probably have to listen to his world-weary lines, a way of speaking common to all cynics, at least Jesper will. If, on the other hand, you go for Jostein, there will probably be more action because the playground fracas has set off a long sequence of events which will eventually catch up with both him and his father, the butcher in Kirkeveien. You can already hear the sirens, first the ambulances, then the police, they come from every corner of the town, but the light they cast has the same speed. The train stops and Jesper moves towards the doors opening in the front carriage. Jostein is also busy. Soon they will be after him. That is a racing certainty. Have you decided? Do we agree? Shall we join the train to town or shall we quickly cross the line to the other platform and travel west? There may be more chance of drama by choosing the latter, but how can you know? A piano lesson can be as fateful as an arrest. One word can have a greater impact than a well-directed punch. I know that. It is harder to portray a child tying shoelaces than the starry firmament. I used to write to remember. Now I write to forget. I have written this before. Every word on paper is a step closer to death. But like me you also dream about standing by a major set of railway points and directing all the lines onto a single track: Jostein makes a decision. He runs after Jesper, pays the ticket collector, is given a transfer ticket to his next life and sits down beside the only pal he has in the world as the carriages disappear into the tunnel and the lights start blinking in the ceiling and the glow of cigarettes in the smoking compartment hover in slow arcs.

"Where are you going?" Jesper asks.

"With you, of course."

"Aren't you supposed to be looking after Vilder's property?"

"No rush."

"You're bluffing. You don't work for Vilder."

Jostein shows him the fee, 150 kroner minus the telephone expenses and transport.

"Do you believe me now, eh?"

"What have you done to your hand? Did you hit your father first or afterwards?"

Jostein puts the money back in his pocket and looks at the sparks between the window and the tunnel wall.

"It'll be fine," he says.

They get off, still underground, and come up in the centre of Oslo, in the middle of the city's premium locality, with all the targets in range: the Royal Palace, the university, Nille restaurant, the National Theatre, Ibsen, Bjørnson, Studenten Isbar, the Musikkforlag shop, Victoria cinema, Myhres Tobakk, Bennets travel agency, Musikkhuset, the Grand Hotel, Stortinget and last but not least the Freia Confectionary clock above Egertorget, the sweet, luminous time, which is already four minutes to ten. Jesper is in a rush. Jostein is hard on his heels. It is impossible to shake him off.

"I can carry your bag for you," Jostein shouts.

Jesper doesn't dignify him with an answer.

He stops outside the entrance in Keysers gate and turns to Jostein, who has become breathless and dispirited over the short distance.

"The new teacher isn't at all like the Italian, so you'll have to wait here, alright?"

"How long will you be?"

"How long do you think an hour's lesson lasts?"

"Why did you come by Metro?"

"Why what?"

"You could've walked down Pilestredet and you would've saved the money. It wouldn't have taken any longer either."

"Because I walked with Stine to Majorstua."

"Why did you walk with Stine to school?"

"Because she told me some kids were bothering her. And now I haven't—"

Jostein interrupts.

"Not anymore."

"Not anymore what?"

"They won't be bothering her anymore."

Jesper catches a glint of triumph in Jostein's halved gaze while the door buzzes and opens although no-one has touched it. Jesper sprints up the stairs. Finn Martins is standing in the doorway, arms crossed, not wearing a dressing gown, fortunately, but a pair of khaki trousers up to his armpits. He doesn't need to look at his watch.

"If you still want to be my pupil, may I ask you to be punctual?"

"Sorry, but—"

Finn Martins raises his index finger.

"No buts. Music is time. So don't waste my music."

Jesper takes off his shoes and they go in. It strikes him that the apartment appears uninhabited. It is more like an exhibition. He sits at the grand piano. It also seems uninhabited. He plays the third movement of Dallapiccola's *Musica per tre Pianoforti*. Finn Martins sits on the windowsill and lights a cigarette.

"Have you got rid of your company?" he asks.

"Company?"

"The girl you brought with you last time. I don't remember her name."

"She only came the first time."

"Good. Emotions are overrated. Don't forget that."

"How do you mean?"

"Do you know who were the most sensitive people ever?"

"No. Who? The Red Cross maybe?"

Finn Martins laughs, but not for long.

"The Nazis. They were all emotion. They didn't have room for anything else. They felt so much they were evil through and through. Now from the top."

Jesper plays the third movement again, but is unsure whether he should play it differently. He only knows he doesn't want to play it like a Nazi. Finn Martins drops his cigarette out of the window.

"Better. But think of the piano as a machine. You only have to feed it with your fingers and get sound back. Do you understand?"

"I think so."

"No, I don't think so, Jesper. You see it takes a long time to appreciate that the keys are democratic and music is more closely related to mathematics and geometry than to your heartbeats. What was her name again?"

"Trude."

"Women like pianists, Jesper. It's something to do with their hands. But they can also bring bad luck. Women, that is. Just look how it turned out for Zanetti."

Jesper doubts Finn Martins has any appeal to women, however many hands he has and however elegant they are.

"What happened to Zanetti?" he asks.

"He left his wife and children and was gone for years. The children are probably adults by now. But now he's finally come to his senses and is back with them."

"Has Enzo got family in Italy?"

"All Italians have. He wouldn't have been a great pianist anyway. But he was good enough for his own little purpose. He never put a damper on the atmosphere. I'll give him that. Shh!"

Jesper has no intention of saying anything. He has enough to think about. A wife and children in Italy? He doesn't know whether to be happy or disappointed. He just feels cheated. It is unbelievable. What about his mother? Has she been let down too? Finn Martins slips off the windowsill and comes closer.

"Listen to the mechanical sounds," he whispers.

Jesper tries to listen, at any rate he sits still. There are the sounds of doors, footsteps and dustbins. There are sirens, car horns and trams. There are ships, cranes and locomotives. There is Enzo Zanetti repairing his family. There are water pipes, radios and bells in the City Hall tower. Have they gone wrong? They shouldn't be ringing now.

"What can you hear?" Finn Martins asks.

Jesper knows what he can hear: lies.

"Noise," he answers.

Finn Martins laughs.

"We aren't trying to imitate the world's sounds, Jesper, but the ideal sound. My God, what's that?"

Finn Martins isn't laughing anymore and walks with short, swift steps to the hallway and tears open the door. Jostein staggers in. Jesper sits at the piano, ashamed and relieved. He doesn't object to an interruption, but would have liked to be interrupted in a different way. Finn Martins returns empty-handed.

"There's a monster here. Says he's waiting for you."

"I told him to wait outside."

Finn Martins sighs.

"But now he's inside. We can't work like this, Kristoffersen. Don't you trust me or are you so lacking in independence that you need someone to look after you?"

"I couldn't get rid of him."

"Anyway, the lesson's ruined. I can't stay calm under such conditions. I get emotional."

Jesper rises to his feet and packs up his music.

"I'm sorry."

"For next time choose three sounds from Dallapiccola, one in each movement, and then we'll discuss what they mean. You can also go to Musikkforlaget and buy Prokofiev's 'Love for Three Oranges'. Can you remember that?"

Jesper nods.

"Is it really true that Zanetti has a family in Italy?" he asks.

Finn Martins lights another cigarette and for a moment it is as if the smoke is seeping out from under both trouser legs, which end in mid-calf above a pair of braided sandals.

"Zanetti was a benign liar, as most lounge musicians are. In the same way that they play what audiences want to hear, they also tell people what they want to hear. He liked to talk about his loneliness and his exile and especially women liked what they heard."

Jesper finds Jostein in the hallway and bundles him down the stairs and into Keysers gate.

"Bloody hell, what were you doing inside?"

"Are you coming with me to Henry's?"

"Henry's? Are you on first-name terms as well?"

"Be a pal, will you?"

"I told you to wait outside, didn't I? And you lumber in through the door."

"Wasn't my fault he opened it."

"Are you stupid?"

"Be a pal, will you?" he repeats.

"I have to drop by school."

"We can go to Steen & Strøm and buy something."

"Why? Perhaps you should go to casualty? Or to the Rikshospital? I'm sure they can change your head there. Mine too, by the way."

Jostein laughs and removes his cap.

"We can swap heads. How would that be, eh?"

Jesper sets off walking. Is everything you don't say a lie? His stomach aches just thinking about it, his stomach aches and he is furious: Enzo has a family in Italy. That isn't the Enzo he knows. He knows a different Enzo. Zanetti has tricked him. How many people can one person be? How many Jespers are there? Is he a no-one with Finn Martins, number one when he is with Trude, number two when he is with Jostein and at least number three when he talks to his mother? He can't bear to think about her. He doesn't have the energy. She will have to do the thinking herself. He prefers to think: Who am I in other people's eyes? Who does Trude see in him? Even more stomach ache. His heart hangs from a clothes peg on a washing line of jealousy. And he doesn't even know if there is someone to be jealous of. Jesper stops outside Musikkforlaget in Karl Johan.

"Do you think everything can be as it was?" he asks.

Jostein is wringing his peaked cap with both hands, as if it were a sponge he was holding and where a short while ago there was a look of black-eyed triumph on his miserable face, now there is utter fear.

"Why are you asking me that?"

Jesper goes into the shop. Jostein sticks to him, the way he will stick to him for the rest of his life, and life seems as cramped as a telephone box.

"Why are you asking me that?" he repeats.

"Forget it."

"Forget what? What should I forget?"

"Fine. Then let's say you've forgotten already."

But when Jostein sees the sheet music the assistant lays on the counter, he bursts into raucous laughter. Then he insists he will pay. It is the least he can do. He has money. He is investing for Jesper. No, he is investing *in* Jesper. When they re-emerge on Karl Johan Jostein is still doubled up with laughter.

"Love for three oranges! Are you going to play that? Three oranges? Do you want some bananas as well?"

Jesper can't be bothered to answer. Instead he asks:

"What's up with you, apart from the fact that your father gave you a shiner?"

The Freia clock above Egertorget says half past eleven. It will soon melt in the sun and run down the front of the building and between the cobblestones. The hours are Melkesjokolade. The minutes are Japp. The seconds are a bag of Twist you can stick your hand in. Perhaps Henry Vilder owns the clock. Jostein feels a sudden urge to spend all his money, as quickly as possible. He wants to splash out. He has nothing to lose anyway. If he doesn't spend it, it might be taken from him and confiscated. He could be fined. Perhaps he will have to pay compensation to the victim's family? The victim? Not bloody likely. They can go to the vinmonopol. The assistants at the one in Storgata turn a blind eye. Jostein has heard rumours. They can also get someone to buy booze for them.

"I'm living on borrowed time," Jostein says.

Jesper almost has a giggling fit. Such stilted, high-flown words don't fit into Jostein's mouth, but there is something heart-rending about his tone that holds Jesper back.

"What do you mean?"

"I can't tell you."

"Why not?"

"Because then you'll be an accessory."

Jesper just shakes his head and lets Jostein keep his secrets. He wished everyone would keep their secrets. Life is easier like that. There isn't so much for others to bear.

"Shall we go home?" he says.

"Don't feel like it."

"Nor me," Jesper says.

The two boys stand outside Musikkforlaget. People walk past them from all directions, an endless stream, but at some point it has to end, it can't carry on, apart from in the hour between four and five in the morning, then Karl Johan is deserted and dark, unless Old Shark or a lost hotel guest appears in the shadows from the cranes that stand stretching their necks in Akers Mek. No-one notices anything. What would they notice? If they did notice anything it would be Jostein's black eye, but it isn't the only one in town. It is more conspicuous that the other boy is carrying a bag, a thin leather briefcase, perhaps he is an errand boy for one of the shops, or perhaps he is just a poser. They are nevertheless two normal boys with all their distinctive qualities and on this day they are more distinctive than usual. Their history is about to be re-written. But there are limits to how long they can hang around in Karl Johan kicking their heels before they are arrested for vagrancy and sent to Jæren to do forced labour. They walk home. But at the crest of Norabakken, where Jesper would carry on up Pilestredet to Fagerborg School, Jostein wants them to walk the last bit together, it is a detour, but surely it doesn't matter if Jesper gets back late when he is already late, there is something Jostein has to tell him, you see, there is something on his mind, it is important.

"Only if you bin that cap," Jesper says.

Jostein chucks the Oslo Slaughterhouse cap into the nearest garden – he has never liked it anyway – but he doesn't have a chance to say anything. As they round the corner of Kirkeveien there is a police car outside Melsom's shop. Jostein comes to an abrupt halt and his mind goes blank. Jesper can see that, the blinds have fallen in Jostein's face, he suddenly understands what Jostein meant by living on borrowed time; in every other respect he understands nothing. Then Jostein makes a dash for it. Across the intersection, and the number 20 bus almost runs him over for a second time. If it had, he would definitely have been given a memorial plaque. But he reaches the pavement unscathed and carries on down Marienlyst. How far should you run when you are escaping? Where should you hide when there is nowhere? The police officers have had their eyes on Jostein for a long time. One of them takes up the chase. Jostein is not a fast runner. He is brought down, dragged to his feet and taken back with his hands tied. All of Fagerborg stops what it is doing and watches Jostein Melsom. Haven't they always said that boy will go off the rails one fine day? Now he is on the skids. Jesper hurries after the runaway and the police officer. Inside the butcher's shop his mother is sitting by the cash till weeping into her apron. His father turns the sign in the window round: CLOSED. If only it could have said: CLOSED BECAUSE OF ROBBERY. Now it is closed because of their son and Melsom doesn't have a clear conscience either. He has offered the officers the use of his office so that Jostein doesn't have to be taken to the police station. However, the father isn't allowed to be present during the interview. He has to console Fru Melsom in the meantime, and that is an impossible job, or talk to Jesper, if that can be of any consolation. It isn't. Would it help to give the officers a leg of mutton each, to pour oil on troubled waters, as it were, a butcher's clumsy gesture? The younger of the two closes the door and leans against it, as though wanting to be sure Jostein won't do another runner. The other officer, Roar Aksnes, a veteran of Møllergata 19, the main police station occupied by the Gestapo during the war, gets straight to the point, it is an open and shut case in his opinion, he only needs a confession and barely that.

"Jostein, you punched Tor Halvorsen this morning, didn't you?"

"No."

"No?"

"It wasn't me."

"Why does everyone say it was then?"

"You'd better ask Tor Halvorsen."

"That's not so easy at the moment, you know. I'm afraid to say he's in a coma at Ullevål Hospital."

Jostein is about to say he didn't hit him *that* hard, it was just a slap, but catches himself at the last minute and watches his life disintegrate into ruins; he didn't know this was how it would turn out: all his dreams down the plughole.

"A coma? I really hope he recovers."

"He banged his head as well. When he hit the tarmac. But we've spoken to approximately 140 pupils who were in the playground at the time of the incident, in addition to Løkke, who was your class teacher, and everyone says it was you who punched him. Why would they do that, I wonder?"

"No idea. They saw wrong."

"You were wearing a cap with Oslo Slaughterhouse written on it."

"Was I? I don't remember. I don't work for them anymore."

"How did you get your black eye by the way? Did Tor Halvorsen hit you first?"

"No. I did a ski jump in Frogner Park. And fell."

"A ski jump, Jostein? It's June now."

"I think it was in April."

"The black eye's recent, Jostein."

"Now I remember. It was the day spring came."

Inspector Roar Aksnes is beginning to be weary.

"Why did you try to run away?"

"Because my father's innocent."

"What did you say?"

"Because my father's innocent," Jostein repeats.

Roar Aksnes has an inkling that he is dealing here with two cases and he would prefer not to know about one of them, yet he has to ask:

"Did your father hit you?"

Jostein looks down, determined not to cry.

"No."

"That's fine, Jostein. But it *was* you who hit Tor, wasn't it? Can we at least agree on that?"

Jostein has crossed a line and reached a point in the logic of denial where he is no longer in any doubt. What he is denying doesn't exist. What he is denying, he didn't do. That is obvious. *No* and *not* are the only words in this magic morality. And if Tor Halvorsen simply doesn't wake up from the coma and dies before he says anything, Jostein is free and innocent. For a moment he calms down. Life is back on the rails.

"No," he says.

Roar Aksnes sighs.

"You called Henry Vilder and said you weren't going to see him. Why?"

"How do you know that?"

"Oh, Jostein, oh, Jostein. We know almost everything. But what else have you been doing this morning?"

"I've been with Jesper."

"Is Jesper covering for you?"

"No, he had a music lesson. He plays the piano."

"So Jesper isn't covering for you?"

"He doesn't know anything."

"What doesn't he know?"

"Anything."

"So we don't need to talk to Jesper?"

"No. He's only played the piano."

"And you?"

"I waited for him."

"I basically don't care what you say, Jostein. What I do know is that hitting someone smaller than you is cowardly. And I would never have thought you a coward, a ski jumper in Frogner Park and a man who slaughters pigs."

Jostein becomes uneasy.

"Smaller?"

"Tor Halvorsen's in the seventh class, Jostein. And you, you attend a, what do you call it, a correspondence school? It's still cowardly."

Jostein stands up.

"He wasn't smaller. He was at least a head taller than me. I had to . . ."

Jostein goes quiet and sinks back down. Inspector Aksnes smiles in the sad way he does and feels no pleasure.

"Why did you punch him?"

"I'm not telling you."

Jostein hides behind crossed arms.

The inspector lays a hand on his shoulder.

"That's fine, Jostein. Now you'll just have to hope Tor wakes up. Otherwise it's Bastøy for you."

They leave Jostein in the back room and go into the shop. The mother has finished crying for the moment, but there are more tears where those have come from. Jesper is standing by the door and has a clearer understanding now of why Jostein said Stine wouldn't be bothered anymore. He feels like shouting it aloud: Jostein's right! He says nothing. Melsom slowly pushes two packets across the counter. The younger officer is about to take one, but Roar Aksnes stands in front of him and meets the butcher's uneasy gaze.

"Jostein's fine and has made a clean breast of it," the inspector says.

The butcher nods, relieved and desperate.

"It's only a little cervelat and ham. For Midsummer Night."

Roar Aksnes leans closer as he pushes the packets away.

"And don't you touch your son again. Do you understand?"

Jesper opens the door for the officers. They get into their car and drive off the pavement and round the corner by Ole Vigs gate.

On the other pavement there are still people standing and watching: housewives, schoolchildren, pensioners, shoe-soling experts, chemists, shop assistants and layabouts. For a moment Fagerborg has come to a standstill. Then there is nothing else to see. Then everyone goes back home or to where they were.

When it is quiet, however, you can hear Jostein sobbing in the back room.

Board meeting at Fru Lund's. We decided what we would have at the autumn bazaar: one suede jacket, one scarf and tartan skirt material, one lovely woven basket of wool and knitting needles, one wheelbarrow with toys and a large doll in rompers.

THE BONFIRE

We all have a debt to pay. Enzo Zanetti owes Maj and her family a proper explanation and he is unlikely to find one. Maj owes the Fagerborg department of the Norwegian Red Cross an apology, at least she ought to bow her head and show deep remorse. It is not certain she will. Jesper owes Trude a visit and perhaps she owes Jesper one too. So it is a while since they have seen each other. They don't even know what has come between them. We are seldom in balance. We always have outstanding debts. We prefer to wait for others to restore the balance and hope that in this way we can escape. Not even Stine is guilt-free. She regrets smashing the sunglasses, but if she had the chance she would do it again. Fru Melsom's guilt is that she looks away when her husband is unable to control his temper and takes it out on his son. This time, however, he is unable to apologise to Jostein; he is ablaze inside. I am in debt to my characters. It isn't freedom of expression that makes me write; it is the oath of silence. And, Jostein, he will soon be in debt to the whole world. He is not only living on borrowed time. He is living on a loan. He will probably have to grovel for the rest of his life. He will especially have to grovel to Tor Halvorsen. But Jostein doesn't want to. It is more Tor Halvorsen who will grovel, if he wakes up from the coma. He will grovel to Stine. The only debt Jostein can make good is what he owes Henry Vilder. Jostein will have to pay back the money he cannot work for, if he is sent to Bastøy, the prison island in Oslo fjord. Jostein's honour remains intact. He has cried. One eye has cried. Now he is out of tears. He is on the Holmenkollen line. It is Midsummer Night. Those who end up on Bastøy rarely return, at least not unscathed. He has heard rumours about the maiden's bower, the iron bed everyone has to lie in for the first night while the oldest boys piss on you and the guards turn their backs and laugh in the darkness. Jostein doesn't care. It doesn't matter. They can do what they like to him. All he cares about is the picture in the magazines. Perhaps no-one will print it now, now that he is on the skids, now that he is a *persona non grata*. He feels like crying again, but he doesn't, he steels himself. He gets off at Slemdal and makes his way to Vilder's property. Henry is sitting in a deckchair on the terrace watching the wispy, white clouds drifting past. Sometimes they resemble animals, perhaps an elephant, a giraffe or a dog. The next minute a cloud can take the form of a face, but he doesn't recognise whose. Henry Vilder beckons Jostein closer.

"I want you to sweep all the grass into the pool."

Jostein says nothing.

Henry Vilder sits up straight.

"Didn't you hear what I said?"

"I did."

"You didn't bring your cap?"

"Chucked it."

"Perhaps you won't need a cap today anyway."

Jostein passes him a handful of notes and coins.

"There you are. That's the fee minus one day and travel expenses."

Henry Vilder doesn't look at the money but at Jostein.

"The police came here yesterday asking about you."

"I know. Sorry."

"What have you been up to?"

"Nothing."

"Nothing? You'll have to lie better than that, Jostein. That won't help."

"I punched a boy in Marienlyst school playground."

"Why? Had he done something to you?"

Jostein can no longer stand upright. He sinks to his knees and starts sobbing again.

"And now they're going to send me to Bastøy. Now I'm done for. I'd rather die now. I won't even be allowed to come here. Oh, what have I done?!"

Henry tentatively lays a hand on Jostein's head and feels the heat surging through the boy. He can feel the rhythm of fear. It isn't wild and uncontrolled, only strong and remorseless. Henry Vilder is also on the verge of tears. He has to hold his breath and swallow. Then he withdraws his hand and it is as if he is still carrying Jostein's heartbeat.

"There's always a reason for what we do," Henry Vilder says.

Jostein slowly struggles to his feet.

"It was because he was harassing my best friend's little sister."

"In what way?"

"I can't tell you."

Henry Vilder picks up the money and gives it back to Jostein.

"Make a start on the leaves, will you?"

Jostein rakes all the leaves into the pool. He has no idea why. It doesn't matter. He has nothing to lose. Sooner or later they will come for him anyway. When he dies he will at least have some money on him. Henry Vilder disappears and returns with a box of Swiss chocolates and a glass of juice. Jostein drops the rake and goes over to him.

"Bastøy?" Henry Vilder says.

Jostein drinks the juice and helps himself to a chocolate.

"That's what the police said. I'd go to Bastøy. If Tor Halvorsen doesn't come out of the coma."

"Did you hit him hard?"

"He must've banged his head on the tarmac as he fell."

"So you only wanted to teach him a lesson?"

Jostein turns to the pool containing leaves instead of water.

"He shouldn't have called Stine's mother a tart."

"And Stine's the little sister of your best friend?"

"Yes. I think he deserved it. Not to hit his head on the ground though."

Henry Vilder is quiet. The sun emerges between the clouds, pushes the shadows away and bathes them both in white light. Then he says:

"Relax, Jostein. I'll get you the best lawyers there are. And now I need a hand inside the house."

Jostein follows Henry Vilder, who makes a couple of telephone calls, then goes upstairs to the first floor, continues down the corridor and stops at the last door. He turns to Jostein and it is as though Jostein can see right down to the wreckage at the bottom of Henry Vilder. He opens the door. It is Elisabeth's room. Everything is as she left it. A fragrance greets them: girl. What are they going to do here? What does he want Jostein to help him with? Jostein daren't ask. He waits. He waits and looks: pictures of actresses on the wall – Greta Garbo, Rita Hayworth – a gramophone, records in a rack – Tommy Steele, Pat Boone, Nat King Cole – a sofa bed, shelves of Nancy Drew mysteries, Hvem Hva Hvor almanacs and an English–Norwegian dictionary, on the floor a dress Jostein recognises from Axel's party, it was the one she wore on the last night of her life. Then she took it off and died. Jostein thinks: would Elisabeth have cut out the picture of him and hung it on the wall? He has to support himself against the door frame. It is too much. Henry Vilder picks up the dress, rolls it up, opens the window wide and throws it out. He beckons Jostein closer again. Jostein goes over to him. For an instant the red dress hangs in the air, it is like a dance, then it plummets and lands on the leaves in the pool. Henry Vilder smiles.

"Now let's deal with the rest," he says.

What they can't throw through the window they carry down: the sofa bed, the desk, two chairs and finally the heaviest item of all: a make-up table with a marble top. Jostein wonders how much all of this cost, hundreds of kroner, he calculates, maybe thousands, they are throwing away a fortune, they could have sold it to the scrap merchant in Astrids gate. Jostein stops midway down the stairs. This isn't scrap. This is Elisabeth's things. It is her personal effects.

What they are doing is wrong. They should stop. They ought to make a museum, Elisabeth's museum. Jostein says nothing. Henry Vilder looks at him across the oval top.

"Have you had enough?"

Jostein hasn't had enough. They carry the make-up table out and hurl it into the pool. Some neighbours on the other side of the hedge are standing and watching. No-one says a word. Henry Vilder doesn't care anyway. When they go back to Elisabeth's room it is almost empty. Jostein can barely grasp what is happening. All traces of her are being erased. They put the last objects into the wastepaper basket: two crayons, a lipstick, a May 17th ribbon and a brand new single by Elvis Presley: "Heartbreak Hotel". Jostein catches sight of a vanity mirror, in the corner amid the dust; quickly he slips it into his pocket, not to steal it but as a keepsake. When Henry Vilder considers there is nothing left to throw away he lays his hands on a photograph of her mother, in other words his wife, standing on a diving board and waving, in the days when there was water to dive into and her wits were intact. Even this he wants to jettison. He throws the wastepaper basket out of the window and closes it. Afterwards he fetches a jerrycan from the garage, empties the petrol into the pool, flicks his lighter into life and drops it. Flames immediately leap into the air. Then they sit down on the terrace, Henry Vilder in the deckchair and Jostein on the doorstep, and watch the fire burn. The neighbours have gone. They are standing behind their windows. It surprises Jostein that it is so quiet, there is no roar, no noise, just black smoke wreathing the garden and an acrid smell that no longer reminds anyone of the girl who once owned this bonfire: a girl who took her own life. A thought strikes Jostein and is gone in the time it took to think it: *Just as I was beginning to get to know her.*

"The stuff that won't burn we can collect later," Henry Vilder says.

Jostein takes a chocolate, which has almost melted.

"How do you get rich?" he asks.

"Get up early."

"How early?"

"Before the others, Jostein."

Henry Vilder leans back and watches the smoke drifting away and disappearing above the treetops. When the clouds appear one of them resembles a face and he immediately recognises her features.

"Now Elisabeth's in heaven," he says.

FRIENDS OF PATIENTS

"I was just thinking about ringing you."

There is a silence at the other end, a semblance of doubt.

"Were you?"

"And you know what that means, don't you?"

"That I rang first?" Trude says.

It is Jesper's turn not to say anything for a couple of heartbeats. At length he says:

"I was thinking more along the lines of two minds with a single thought. To ring, I mean."

He can hear himself how unconvincing he sounds. Fortunately, Trude asks a question before the situation becomes too embarrassing.

"Haven't you been on holiday yet?"

"No. Where to? And you?"

"I'm ringing from Galdhøpiggen."

Jesper believes her. He believes everything she says. He thinks: I should have called her first. Now it is too late.

"Is there a telephone up there?"

Trude laughs.

"I'm at home, alone. Are you coming?"

If Jesper is coming?

He is already on his way. And he was there ages ago in his mind. His thoughts merge into dreams. And dreams are only a preparation. It pays to dream in detail. But his mother stops him. She is standing by the window and pointing.

"Is that a bonfire or a fire, do you think?"

There is a pall of black smoke hanging over the forest edge

behind Ris church. Jesper merely shrugs. He hasn't got time, but stands staring anyway. If it is a bonfire it would have to be pretty bad wood. And where do you draw the line between a bonfire and a fire?

"No idea," he says.

"I think it's a fire. People are so careless. There should be a law against bonfires except alongside the fjord. Margrethe invited us to Nesodden by the way, but I said no. Was that a mistake?"

"Nope."

Jesper glances at his mother and can't see any difference. Doesn't she know that Enzo is married in Italy? Doesn't she know that he pulled the wool over her eyes, just as he did with the other women who fell for his fingers, accent, musical chestnuts and the glint in his eye? He feels like asking, asking her point-blank, but he doesn't. Sons shouldn't ask their mothers such questions. He looks at her again. Of course she knows. That is why she came back alone. A siren, perhaps several, can be heard in Majorstua.

"What did I say?" Maj says.

"About what?"

"There's a fire. Can't you hear?"

Jesper is about to leave, but his mother stops him again.

"It's a long time since we've seen Trude, isn't it?"

"That's why I'm going to see her now."

Jesper's mother lets him go with a laugh.

"Hurry up then."

Jesper takes the kitchen stairs. Stine is skipping in the yard. She is alone and skipping. Every swing of the rope sounds like a whiplash between the abandoned house-fronts. She stops when she sees Jesper. The rope settles around her ankles. It is a long time since Jesper has seen his little sister smile.

"What are you grinning about?" he asks.

"Nothing."

"Are you grinning at me?"

Stine shakes her head.

"Ida from the class has asked if I want to make a bonfire and grill sausages in Huk."

"That's nice, isn't it?"

"Yes."

"I could cycle there with you."

Stine smiles again.

"I'm not going."

Then she continues skipping and Jesper counts the jumps, ten, thirty, fifty, all the way down to Solli Plass, where he loses count and walks as slowly as he can approaching her house. Trude lets him in. There is already a smell of holiday in the apartment. It is quiet.

"Mamma and Pappa are in Galdhøpiggen," she says.

"But not you?"

"I'm here."

They drink tea in the kitchen. Trude is only wearing a big, white shirt that reaches down to her knees.

"Shall we cycle to Ingierstrand to see the fires?" Jesper asks.

"Do you feel like it?"

"Not really."

"Why do you ask then?"

He places his hand on hers, but it doesn't respond.

"Are you going to Galdhøpiggen too?"

"Gotland. With Mamma. If she comes down from Galdhøpiggen."

A great fear washes over Jesper: Gotland boys. Gotland is full of Gotland boys. And Gotland is probably so small that she won't be able to get away from them.

"What do you do on Gotland?"

"Eat vegetables and go for walks in bad weather."

Trude starts washing up. Jesper finds a tea towel and dries. There are only two cups, two plates and two teaspoons, so it doesn't take long. Jesper dries as slowly as he can.

"Is your house help on holiday too?"

Trude nods.

Afterwards Jesper helps her to lay sheets over the furniture in the lounge so that the material doesn't fade over the summer. But the sun doesn't reach as far as the sofa against the wall anyway and so what is the point? Is light damaging, given enough time? They extend the last sheet and let it fall over her father's armchair and it reminds Jesper of cemeteries, graves, marble, silence, the devil's piano and Satie. He doesn't have to think like that because as Trude turns, her long shirt becomes almost transparent and he can make out her figure, an uninterrupted soft curve, a silhouette that never ends. Isn't she wearing anything underneath? Jesper has to pull himself together. He has to take this *piano*. He has to take this devilishly *piano*. Perhaps it is precisely death and music he should think about so as not to drop his mask or lose face. She moves a little and is gone. Then he feels a gentle draught. She has opened the window. The curtains swirl up from the wall as though the whole apartment is capsizing, while he is standing steadfastly on the spot. They go into her room. It just happens. Jesper thinks: *It just happens*. But there has been a tangled knot of lines, chances, conversations, dreams and delays that have led to precisely this point. They lie on the floor. He unbuttons her shirt and she doesn't stop him. He wishes she would so that they could just lie like this; it is more than good enough. Jesper is afraid, afraid to do something wrong, it would take so little, he imagines. He hasn't got a rubber either. He can't even remember where the packet is, in another jacket, in another season. He can't stop now. He lays his hand on her stomach; her skin is smooth and warm. He slips his hand inside her knickers, she stirs, is it to let him have easier access? He feels, with two fingers, as gently as he can, while listening to her, should he be hearing something now, something deep, something unprecedented, should he be breathing heavier to show that he is excited? He thinks about musical notes. He is thinking too much. Should he lie on top of her now? Do you ever learn this by heart or is it like a new composition every time? Suddenly she pushes him away and turns her back on him. He catches a glimpse of a line of blood running down her thigh. Has he hurt her? She sits up and puts the white shirt between her legs.

"Do you think I'm disgusting?"

"Disgusting? Of course you aren't. Why do you say that?"

Trude sits up and pushes the shirt between her legs. Jesper strokes her back. But she doesn't want him any closer.

"Why didn't you say anything?" she asks.

"About what?"

"About your mother not being on a business trip."

Jesper sits up too. This is all going too fast. How can she ask about that now of all times? But perhaps it isn't precisely now. Perhaps she has known for a long time.

"How do you know?"

"My father's a journalist. Have you forgotten?"

"Is he going to write about this too? Fagerborg widow leaves her kids while she goes on holiday with son's music teacher?"

"Now *you're* being disgusting."

"You aren't disgusting."

"Anyway, I was only joking. You take everything so literally."

"Were you joking?"

"It wasn't my father. Everyone knows what your mother did. Pappa only knows what no-one else knows."

"Right."

"I thought we were supposed to tell each other everything."

"I'd been intending to tell you."

"You'd been intending to ring as well. Is intending all you can do?"

Jesper looks down and tightens his belt.

"If that's how you see things . . ." he says.

Trude looks down too, at the crumpled, soiled shirt.

"Sorry."

"Perhaps it's best if I go?"

Jesper stands up and again has this feeling: *It just happens.*

He repeats himself:

"Perhaps it's best if I go?"

Trude doesn't move.

"See you in the autumn then."

Jesper stops in the doorway hoping she will tell him no, they will see each other the following day, the day after that and also the day after that.

"OK. See you in the autumn. Have a good summer."

"You too."

Jesper finds his own way out. He leaves with a heavy heart. The light is a torment. The holidays already lie in front of him like a slow nightmare, days that drag, mind in a spin, the same again and again. Where do things actually go wrong? Is it in the cards from the very outset, waiting only for the right moment? It is unbearable that everything is written down in advance, everything is pre-determined and the only freedom we have is to change clothes. Jesper stops again in Vestkanttorget. There is neither ice nor gravel there now, but sand, sand as far as the eye can see, a desert in the middle of the city. And he has this whole square to himself. It doesn't help. There is never enough space for the lonely person who has been rejected. This is how he feels, lonely, rejected, and it surprises him that it not only hurts, there is something significant about it too, something in which he can almost find repose, a kind of elevated sorrow. Then he isn't alone after all. The refrain comes to him: *In the winter it moves by sleigh, While in the spring it rolls on wheels.* There is Old Shark sitting on the bench beneath the faded lilacs and Jesper is reminded of everything that isn't elevated, but dirty and low. Shouldn't it be the other way around? Shouldn't it be Old Shark who reminded him of what was elevated, while Jesper was the dirty, stooped one? Nevertheless he hurries on, away from this song he can't get out of his head. It follows him. It is a broken record. However, when he reaches Majorstua he has something else to think about: there is a black Mariah parked in Valkyriegaten and from the front seat steps none other than Jostein Melsom, who closes the door and shakes the hand of an officer through the window before it drives off. This evening is unbelievable. Then

Jostein catches sight of Jesper, but can't even be bothered to cross the street, it is too great a detour for Jostein Melsom, who is so in love with himself that he could have found a summer job as Færder lighthouse. Jesper goes to meet him.

"What have you done now, eh?"

"Well, what have I done? Only some business with Henry Vilder."

"Business, eh? And afterwards the cops drove you home?"

"More or less. Can't tell you everything, I'm afraid. Confidential. But this much I can say – Bastøy will have to do without me this time."

"How do you know?"

"Henry Vilder made a telephone call and pulled strings. All the charges have been dropped with immediate effect."

"Give me one good reason why I should believe you."

Jostein produces a compact, at first sight it looks like a shell, but when he opens the shell, there isn't a pearl inside but a mirror. He lowers his voice.

"Henry Vilder gave me this. It belonged to his daughter. The late Elisabeth Vilder."

"And what are you going to do with a mirror?"

Jostein shrugs, unwilling to find the energy to answer such a crass question and puts the compact back in his pocket.

"And you?"

"Me? What about me?"

Jostein grins.

"Have you been fighting as well?"

"What do you mean? Have I been fighting? Of course I haven't."

"Why've you got blood on your piano fingers then?"

Jesper looks down and only sees it now. His fingers are rust-coloured. He will have to go home and have a wash. He sticks both hands in his pockets and sets off. Jostein follows him, scenting something or other.

"Can't tell you everything, I'm afraid," Jesper says.

"Why not?"

"Confidential."

"What did you say? What is?"

"Oath of confidentiality."

Jostein shoves his face into Jesper's and is wild-eyed.

"I know what it is! You've—"

Jesper puts his rusty paw over his mouth.

"Does all of Fagerborg have to know?"

Jostein squirms, sinks to his knees and is almost sick.

His mother appears in the middle of Kirkeveien waving a bunch of flowers. Jesper helps Jostein to his feet and they walk towards her. She is also wild-eyed.

"Tor Halvorsen has come out of the coma. Thank God."

Jostein wipes the back of his hand across his face and spits.

"It's Henry Vilder we have to thank. He made a call and pulled strings."

Fru Melsom turns to Jesper.

"Who do you think we should thank?"

"The doctors."

"What is absolutely certain now is that you and Jostein should go and visit him."

Jesper takes a step back.

"Me? I have nothing to do with this."

Fru Melsom takes a step closer and her expression changes.

"If your mother hadn't travelled to Rome with that scoundrel none of this would've happened."

Jesper tries to grasp this chain of events, in which one thing leads to another, but is unable to find the starting point that triggered everything, and once again he has to acknowledge that there are no beginnings, only processes.

"How do you know that?" he asks.

Fru Melsom tosses her head and says almost the same as Trude.

"Everyone knows, Jesper. Fru Lund said. They can't tolerate that sort of thing in the Red Cross."

She gives the flowers to Jostein, who is scowling in all directions.

"Aren't visiting hours over?" he says.

"Don't you try it on with me. Off you go!"

Then Fru Melsom gives Jesper a little packet of smoked ham so that they both have a present for Tor Halvorsen.

She watches the two boys walk away and in her own God-fearing way she is anxious, angry and grateful. But when they reach the top, where the pungent smell of the Shell garage on the corner clears their minds, she can't see them anymore and they can do what they like.

"Feel like some smoked ham?" Jesper asks.

"Not after you've touched it. Besides, I've eaten Swiss chocolate."

"That's why you were sick."

Jesper throws the packet over the cemetery fence.

"But you can give Trude the flowers," Jostein says.

"Trude's on holiday."

Jostein throws the flowers the same way. They scatter in the air and fall in a yellow shower on the closest graves. Then they go to Ullevål Hospital. Tor Halvorsen is still in the emergency ward, but has been moved to a room with two beds. They have to wait in the corridor. Jostein starts getting nervous again.

"Hope his parents aren't there."

"He started it."

"Actually he did."

Jesper places his hand on his friend's shoulder.

"So thank you. Stine was invited to a barbecue today."

Jostein wriggles away from under his hand.

"Can't you wash your hands, eh? At least one of them."

Jesper finds a toilet, where he washes both hands. Yes, it does look like rust. The water turns almost brown and runs slowly down the plughole. There is nothing to dry your hands on. He wipes them on his trousers. As he comes out he sees Fru Lund. She is sitting beside a bed knitting. An elderly lady is lying in the bed with her eyes closed. She is asleep or dead, perhaps both. It occurs to

Jesper that it is impossible to move around Fagerborg without bumping into someone you would rather avoid, especially from the Red Cross. And he knows at once, even though he doesn't quite know why, that he has to get away. He simply has to get away from Fagerborg. The insight is overwhelming. It shakes him. It is probably the biggest thought Jesper has had so far: he has to get out of Fagerborg. He would like to sneak past Fru Lund, but then changes his mind and goes in to see her. It is time to clarify a couple of issues. She lays the wool and needles in her lap and looks up.

"You shouldn't talk badly about my mother," he says.

Fru Lund places a finger to her lips and nods towards the bed.

"Perhaps you could be a friend of a patient too, Jesper."

"A friend?"

"The Red Cross needs young friends too. Think of all the lonely people here without any visitors. It's a good deed that costs so little and achieves so much."

Jesper almost loses the thread and has to repeat himself.

"You shouldn't talk badly about my mother."

Fru Lund sighs.

"I don't talk badly about Maj, Jesper. How can you believe that? As I'm sure you know, since you've brought the subject up, she's made things difficult for the Red Cross and herself. And for you and Stine."

"She hasn't made anything difficult for us."

"I appreciate that you're defending your mother, but I'd prefer not to—"

Jesper interrupts her.

"She went to Rome to meet Enzo Zanetti's wife. That's all."

Fru Lund forgets to speak in a low voice.

"Wife?"

"And family. I was supposed to go as well. But I couldn't take time off school. Just for your information."

The patient has woken up and starts to cry. Fru Lund wipes her face with a soft serviette and looks at Jesper again.

"What are you doing here?"

"I'm also a friend of a patient," he says.

Jesper rushes back to Jostein.

They sit for a while waiting.

"What was it like actually?" Jostein asks.

"What was what like?"

"Fucking, of course."

"Would you like to say that a little louder?"

"Fucking."

"We didn't get that far."

Jostein is silent. Then he says:

"If Elisabeth hadn't killed herself we could've done it."

Jesper has nothing to add and he would rather not ask how Jostein had found his way to that idea. He can have that one all to himself. It shouldn't be shared with anyone. A nurse comes to a halt in front of them and says that Tor Halvorsen is able to receive visitors, even though this is out of hours, but they can't stay long. It doesn't matter. This won't take long. They go into his room. First they have to pass a patient who definitely needs a friend, and a good one. Both his legs are in plaster and hanging from wires in the ceiling. Tor Halvorsen doesn't exactly look happy when he sees them. He looks more as if he would like to make a quick exit, but he doesn't have the strength or the opportunity to do that.

"We're your patient friends," Jesper says.

"Oh?"

"From the Red Cross. It's great that you're conscious and well."

Tor Halvorsen relaxes a little and scratches at the bandage.

Jostein pushes Jesper aside and leans across the bedhead.

"So that we can beat you up again."

They run out and don't stop until they reach the top of Kirkeveien. There is something special about being here, between the smells from the cemetery and the petrol station, seeing the gentle curve down to Majorstua, and the buildings on either side, to the left the old facades, to the west the modern blocks with a refuse shaft system and a lift. But it is above all the light you notice. It merges with its surroundings as if it is the pavements, the tarmac, the bricks and the balconies that are shining. Jesper thinks that that is why it doesn't help to hang a sheet over the city when it is holiday time; it will fade anyway because the light comes from below and casts its lustre over everything.

"Your hearing's pretty good these days," he says.

"At least in my left ear it is. I mean in my right."

The birds are still fighting over the smoked ham among the graves. Along the fjord, which you can glimpse if you stand on tiptoe or climb the fence by the gate, you can see the fires burning brighter as darkness falls. It is Midsummer Night. Jesper wraps an arm around Jostein and they walk slowly back.

"Think I'll go with you to Copenhagen after all."

"Oh, shit, now I am happy."

PHEW!

Melsom the butcher has borrowed a Volvo PV 440 from the head chef at Larsen restaurant and at 04.25, on Friday, July 2nd, before anyone has risen, apart from the paper boys, shift-workers, dustmen, tramps and those who never go to bed, they head for Copenhagen where they are going to make meat deals, among other things, as Melsom puts it; what the other things are he won't reveal for the time being. That kind of information is reserved for beyond the Norwegian border. Fru Melsom has made them sandwiches for the whole trip, there and back, and filled two Thermoses with coffee, so that they won't need to pay for food on the journey, otherwise it wouldn't have been worth the effort, not only do you have to struggle with driving on the left in Sweden, but the Swedish krone can also deliver the *coup de grâce* to a Norwegian butcher. Accordingly you have to pass through this back-to-front and in many ways unpleasant and arrogant country as quickly as possible, preferably without stopping. It is all about the Danish currency now. Maj, for her part, has contributed fruit and macaroon cake, while Jostein has a secret store of chocolate, not Swiss this time, but Henry Vilder's most exclusive confectionery: dark and Belgian. They drive down Kirkeveien, across the Majorstua intersection, to the left at City Hall square, past the railway station and it is only when they finally come out onto Mosseveien, alongside Oslo fjord, that the trip, or *business* trip, begins in earnest, even if it is only after Svinesund that they will be put to the test. Jostein and Jesper sit at the back so that Melsom won't be disturbed by having someone next to him, and he doesn't need a map-reader anyway. He has studied the route rigorously beforehand. It is: Oslo–Helsingborg, the ferry to Helsingør and then *gerade aus*, as they say in Germany, even if you are in Denmark, to Copenhagen. Melsom, however, is perfectly capable of disturbing the passengers on the back seat. As a butcher's apprentice before the war he learned a song from a meister from Fyn, who maintained he was the only man in Scandinavia who could find a word to rhyme with *pølse*, a sausage. Melsom sings in broken Danish: *En pølse skal serveres med føl'se*. A sausage has to be served with feeling. It is important to stress – and drop – syllables, *følelse* to *føl'se*, in a Danish way, otherwise the rhyme doesn't work. Jostein slumps back into the hard seat and turns to Jesper. Jostein's eye is no longer black, but green.

"How do you say meat in Danish?" he asks.

"Don't know, but I'm sure you do."

"Yes, I do. It's *kød*. Same as *prick* in Norwegian! With a long ø."

Melsom isn't singing anymore. He turns into the Hvervenbukta layby and parks.

"You're living dangerously, Jostein. Just so you know."

"You too."

"What did you say?"

"Nothing, Pappa."

Melsom is quiescent for a good while with his hands on the wheel. Then he turns to the boys on the back seat and he has something on his mind.

"As we three men are travelling together we should talk like men, shouldn't we?"

Jostein slumps down even further. Melsom hasn't finished yet.

"So there's one thing we mustn't forget. Whatever we say stays between the three of us. Are we agreed on that? Are we, Jesper?"

Jesper nods and glances at Jostein, who is chewing and can't speak anyway. They wait for Jostein's father to say more, something ground-breaking, something illuminating, something that will make their lives easier or cast a new light on existence. He doesn't. Instead he takes a sandwich from the hamper beside him without asking if Jesper would like one. He is immersed in his own thoughts. They drive on to Svinesund, to the Swedish border, where shady dealings go on, as they always do at borders: smuggling, pornography, black market, espionage. They fill up with petrol in their homeland, check the oil and wash the windscreen. A man in a Swedish uniform stamps their passports. It is actually easy to escape from Norway. They are directed into the left-hand lane. They are abroad. Being abroad means you have to drive on the wrong side of the road. Jesper thinks: Is this getting away? No, if you want to get away you have to do it alone. Now he has half of Fagerborg with him. If you want to get away you have to leave your baggage.

They drive through Sweden without saying a word, apart from the butcher, who at regular intervals shouts to himself: Keep left!

They make it to the ferry.

In the middle of the Øresund Jostein is sick, even though the sea is like a pond. He hangs over the railings and blames driving on the left. He isn't seasick; he's carsick. Jesper laughs and points to the chunder floating in the water.

"Belgian Congo," he says.

Then they are in another foreign country: Denmark. Here at least they drive on the correct side, but Danish bikes are black and square, their postmen wear red jackets and the light between the tall trees along the road speaks a different language: fluent sun. They arrive in Copenhagen at 14.53. Melsom has an address: Warehouse 4b in Nyhavn. He finds the place, tells the boys to stay in the car, tells them not to ask questions or answer any enquiries, and goes in. When he returns he isn't alone. Two men are carrying a box, which they put in the boot and hide under a grey blanket. Melsom shakes their hands, gets back into the car and drives to Kongens Nytorv and parks there. Now they all get out of the car. The smell of the nearby canal mixes with exhaust fumes and Danish pastries. A little girl lets go of her balloon and it rises into the air like a slow, yellow satellite. For a moment the whole town is still looking up at what will soon disappear. The girl starts to laugh. A thought strikes Jesper: She doesn't cry when she loses something; she laughs. He has to turn away. He doesn't know why. It moves him. It moves him so deeply. He catches a lift down inside himself. It has been a long time. He feels dizzy and has to lean on Jostein, who wants to try Danish red sausages. After all, it is two and a half hours since he spewed up. This is out of the question. Melsom has several addresses. The job isn't done yet. Besides he wants to go home before it gets dark. And then Jostein can finish off what is left in the hamper if he likes, or perhaps he has more sweets he doesn't want to share? They walk down Strøget. The shop windows here are bigger than in Karl Johan in Oslo. Everything is more expensive too. Even the tobacconist is by royal appointment. Imagine if Melsom the butcher were by royal appointment to the Norwegian court! Perhaps King Haakon would have done his shopping in Kirkeveien and bought his cervelat there. Or Jostein could have delivered it to the Royal Palace. Then Jostein would have been the royal purveyor. They have to go to Magasin du Nord. Steen & Strøm is just a contemptible kiosk by contrast with Magasin du Nord. Once inside, they can't even see where the floors end in this spiral of balconies; it is like an endless floodlit snail shell. If Jesus ever returns it will have to be on an escalator in Magasin du Nord. Melsom has an exclusive errand here he has to run. They agree to meet an hour later, exactly where they are standing, between the perfumery and the customer help desk. They synchronise their watches. It is 15.48. Melsom pats the boys on the shoulders and heads for the exit again. Jostein and Jesper stand watching. After two minutes Jesper has lost sight of Jostein. He is nowhere to be seen, at least nowhere near him. Jesper takes the escalator up to the next floor and enters the *Teenagers' department*. On the wall there is a picture of Tommy Steele. Perhaps he can buy something for Trude. At the record bar there are small booths, a bit like telephone boxes, except that you are not supposed to talk in them, but listen to music: on the glass doors it says *Only for LPs and 45s*. The girls sitting inside and listening have wavy hair and broad belts tightly buckled around their waists. They are in danger of being strangled. They move their lips and remind Jesper of fish, fish gasping for air, girls trapped inside an aquarium; that is what they are. He can't bear to think about Trude. Perhaps she sees him as a failure. The world is full of boys better than him. The girls wave to him. Are they calling for help? No, they are laughing. The world is full of girls too. This is no comfort. It is Jesper who is trapped inside an aquarium. He is the one who should shout for help. He is the one struggling and gasping for air. He could buy a rubber ring or a snorkel. He can't see Jostein anywhere. He takes the escalator up a floor. Between the floors a figure comes down towards him. He is going in the wrong direction. He is walking so fast he is standing still. It is a clown. He is wearing a white outfit, a tall white hat, his face is also painted white, while his mouth is red, in a broad grin resembling a wound because his real lips form an arc pointing downwards, like a child's confused grimace as tears begin to flow. Or perhaps it is vice versa; perhaps it is the red smile that is real. It is Pierrot in Magasin du Nord. In his hand he is holding the yellow balloon. Jesper can't see the string on the end. They approach each other. As they meet, the clown stops and is taken upwards, backwards, beside Jesper. They accompany each other briefly like this. But the yellow balloon remains in the middle of the escalator, in the same place. Pierrot laughs soundlessly. The thick layer of make-up cracks. From these cracks, or openings, green hair grows, thin strands, like the edge of a lawn. Then he starts walking again, more slowly than the metal steps are moving beneath his oversized shoes, yet he is faster. He raises a hand, makes a grab in the air and pulls the balloon down, to the applause of the customers. Jesper falls off on the third floor and when he stands up he is in the ladies' department. He sees it at once: the blue dress Maj tried on in Steen & Strøm. He goes closer. The dress is on offer here and costs only half the price, but what good is that when he has no Danish money?

"Are you going to buy it for Trude?"

Jostein lays a hand on Jesper's shoulder.

"What do you think?"

"You can't afford it."

"Where've you been, eh? I was looking for you."

"And so you worked out I'd be in the ladies' department?"

"You're right by the way."

"Right about what?"

"I can't afford it."

Jesper is about to go, but Jostein holds him back.

"I can."

He takes out a wallet smelling of freshly slaughtered hide, opens it and runs his index fingers quickly over a wad of Danish hundred-krone notes.

"Have you robbed a bank or what?"

"Just changed it. Do you want to borrow some?"

"It's not yours."

"Why have I got it in my wallet then, eh?"

"Just tell me where you got it?"

"Henry Vilder. Advance."

"For taking care of his property? I thought you'd already had one advance."

"I'm a trusted employee, Jesper. Just so you know. And we think long term. Do you want to borrow some or not?"

An assistant comes over to them, with a stiff smile.

"Well, boys, are you hatching a clever plan or are you studying our underwear?"

Jesper only understands half of what she says and, to be on the safe side, points.

"I'd like that dress."

The assistant's facial expression changes.

"Ah, I see. Cool Norwegian men on a visit. You mean the blue one."

"Yes, the blue one."

"That's a really, really good choice. But can you afford it, young man?"

Jostein leans closer to Jesper, sweating Danish mustard.

"What did she say?"

"Have you been eating red sausages?"

"Why does she ask that?"

"I'm asking you."

"I had four."

"And you've been drinking beer too."

"I'm not drunk."

"She asked us if we can afford it."

"Only if she can knock a hundred kroner off."

Jesper turns to the assistant, who has crossed her arms.

"What's it going to be, boys?"

"Could you knock a hundred Danish kroner off?"

"I'll have to think about that. By the way do you need any knickers or bras? Or nylons perhaps?"

"No, I don't think so."

"Good. What size do you want?"

"Size? I have no idea."

The assistant inspects Jesper and pulls down the blue dress.

"This should fit anyway. You can follow me to the changing rooms. Are you coming?"

Jesper gives up. If this is going to be so difficult he may as well drop the idea.

"I've changed my mind."

"That's a shame. We've got it in green as well."

"It's the blue one I don't want," Jesper says.

The assistant hangs the blue dress back up.

"And now I think you should go down to the teenagers' department and look at girls of your own age."

Jesper and Jostein take the escalator down. Jostein is in fact happy about the deal that didn't take place, but mostly on Jesper's behalf.

"Think of all the money you've saved. The interest too. And a krone saved is a krone earned."

"Did you learn that from Henry Vilder?"

"No, I worked it out it in my own little head."

"You hadn't been intending to charge me interest, had you?"

"Hadn't I? Borrowing money isn't free. I could've put the money you didn't borrow in the bank and it would've gained interest."

"I'm your pal, Jostein."

"Exactly. And we aren't going to fall out over money. Five per cent interest on nothing is nothing."

"Five per cent! I'm bloody glad I didn't buy that dress."

"But think how happy Trude will be when you tell her you'd been thinking of buying her a dress."

Jesper lets Jostein muse on this calculation of his in peace. An hour has already passed. An hour in Magasin du Nord passes faster than elsewhere, it takes only forty-five minutes, sometimes no more than forty, and neither of them has bought anything to prove they have been there, all they have is their thoughts. Jostein was considering buying a record by Harry Belafonte for Elisabeth, but wasn't sure how to pronounce his name in Danish. Jesper wants to say words to the effect that there are no record players in heaven, but refrains, it isn't funny anyway, it is rather macabre and he feels sorry that his friend has these thoughts, so he shuts up. They wait by the customer desk. It is Melsom who doesn't show up on time.

"You should clean your teeth," Jesper says.

"Why?"

"Otherwise your father will notice you've been drinking beer."

"Do you think so?"

"And if he doesn't, the customs officers will. And then your father will definitely notice."

"Do you imagine I have a toothbrush on me?"

"Then you'll have to hold your breath all the way through Sweden."

Ten minutes later Melsom comes rushing in, not from the food section, but through the swing doors. His shirt is dark with sweat. He has filled up with petrol. The car is outside. They follow him out and sit at the back. They drive home. It is the same route, but the other way around: the ferry goes from Helsingør to Helsingborg. They eat what is left of the food in the hamper and Maj's cake. You still have to drive on the left in Sweden, but at least they are looking at what was on the right-hand side this morning. Jostein has to sit at the front or else he gets carsick. It is a lovely summer evening, a broad sky and light. The wind is combing the fields, which extend all the way to the horizon. Insects splatter against the windscreen. Occasionally Melsom has to stop to wash off the corpses. It occurs to Jesper that the windscreen looks like Jostein's forehead. He has also walked through a storm of insects splattering against his hairline. The sun sets behind a forest, with no difficulty at all, but it never gets completely dark. There is always a kind of melancholy about journeys home, a weariness that almost resembles happiness. It is a chord that Jesper already knows, even if it is the first time he has returned home. The clock on the dashboard jumps. It is sleep playing tricks on them. When they wake up, time and place have moved on. Melsom keeps himself awake with cold coffee. A kilometre before Svinesund he turns into a lay-by, parks and tells the boys to listen carefully. This must be the man-to-man chat at last and Jesper and Jostein do what they have been told.

"Don't you two say a word if we're stopped at the border. Have you got that?"

The boys nod.

"Don't breathe a word," Melsom reiterates.

"Why would we be stopped?" Jostein asks.

"Because the customs officers do spot checks. In all probability we won't be stopped, but if we are, you mustn't say anything, not even if you're asked a question. Leave it all to me. And it's also important you act naturally."

Jesper leans forward between the seats.

"Naturally, Herr Melsom?"

The butcher is beginning to tire.

"Yes, simply act as you normally do. Imagine we've just been on a little summer trip to Copenhagen."

Jostein stares at his father.

"Haven't we?"

"That's exactly what we've been doing."

Melsom raises a hand in a pally, egalitarian way, which impresses the boys.

"All for one and one for all."

Jesper leans back in the seat and closes his eyes. Jostein takes a deep breath and holds it. Melsom drives so slowly over the last part that it is just as if their homeland is disappearing into the distance. At length they find themselves in a queue. The customs officers take an Opel to one side. The officers let a VW through. They inch forward.

"You didn't buy anything, did you?"

Jostein shakes his head, still holding his breath.

Fortunately there is no customs to pay on petrol.

Melsom rolls down his window and hands his passport to the officer, who glances at it and hands it back while taking a quick look inside the car.

"Nothing to declare?"

"Nothing. Just the boys."

Melsom laughs heartily and rolls up the window as the officer waves him on. At that moment Jostein lets out his breath, it sounds like a happy Judgement Day *phew*, and Melsom doesn't quite manage to get his front wheels into Norway before the officer waves again, but this time it is to go back. The officer leans closer.

"What did you say?"

Melsom stares straight ahead.

"Me? I didn't say anything."

"Did someone else say something then?"

"My son might have. He says a lot of strange things. He damaged his hearing in a terrible accident a few years ago."

The officer glances at Jesper, then at Jostein, while keeping his eyes fixed on Melsom the whole time.

"Let me ask you once again if you have anything to declare."

"No, unless the boys have brought anything with them, but I know they haven't. I trust them implicitly."

"Switch off the engine."

"Switch it off?"

"Just do what I say."

"I have done nothing but."

"You have another chance. Have you anything to declare?"

Melsom switches off the engine. It is so quiet, much too quiet. He looks down. The inside of the car is boiling hot. Jostein has a terrible thought: his father has pissed himself. And he has never loved his father more than at this moment.

"Maybe the odd thing or two."

The officer orders all of them out of the car and tells Melsom to open the boot. He does so. The officer tells Melsom to remove the blanket. He does so. Melsom can pack his job in as a butcher and start working as a conjuror. Underneath the blanket there is not one box but three. The officer calls for reinforcements. They break open the lid of the biggest box. In it there are 180 cans of Danish pork loin. In the next box there are nineteen kilos of sirloin packed in plastic. In the last box there are two bottles of cherry liqueur, a bottle of Aalborg aquavit, a carton of Pall Mall and a pile of Kongelig Dansk chocolate boxes.

"Just help yourselves," Melsom says.

This comment isn't well received.

The customs officers carry the boxes into an office and Melsom has to accompany them. Jostein and Jesper have to wait, which they do without protest.

"Do you think he'll come back?" Jostein asks.

"No, they'll execute him twice. First in Sweden, then in Norway. For being so stupid."

Jostein pushes Jesper, who falls to the ground and looks straight into the furious face of his pal and starts laughing, because he is reminded that this boy is advertising Valcrema in women's magazines. Jostein gets even crosser and is about to stamp on him. Jesper rolls away and gets to his feet, terrified for a second as he can see that there are no holds barred with Jostein. He brushes down his trousers and shirt. Jostein looks away. Melsom comes back, alone and empty-handed. They get into the car. Jostein wants to sit at the back. They drive into Norway. Melsom grips the wheel tightly. It is all white knuckles, speed limits and sunset. He says nothing. There is nothing more to say. There is more not to say.

"Perhaps Henry Vilder can make a call and pull some strings," Jostein says.

Melsom turns into a forest path and this time he tells everyone to get out of the car. Jesper goes first, Jostein is slow and reluctant. At length Melsom slams the door and rummages for something in his pocket. Jostein cowers with his arms in front of his face and his voice is more like a groan.

"If you hit me, you'll go to prison too."

It is as though his father melts at the last minute, misunderstood and unhappy. He lifts his hand again, slowly, nervous about any movement he makes, nervous that he might do something wrong. In the end he produces a can of Danish ham. That was all there was. Nothing else. They sit down on a log and roll open the thin, sharp metal lid. The pink meat is in a kind of shiny jelly and doesn't seem very appealing; on the contrary, it looks unpleasant. At least they can agree on that, travelling home from a not altogether successful business trip to Copenhagen. They are hungry as well. They eat with their fingers. Actually it tastes quite good. They have rarely tasted anything better. Darkness begins to fall from the forest behind them. For a time the fields of crops stand bent in the dark blue. An aeroplane crosses the sky, northwards, to Fornebu airport, pulling a soundless white stripe through the summer evening.

"We won't tell Mamma about this," Melsom says.

They bunch closer together on the log. There at last was the man-to-man chat. *We won't tell Mamma about this*. Now they are no longer tourists. They have returned from afar to their own lives.

YKSI, KAKSI, KOLME

Stine looks up at the aeroplane as it banks over the rooftops in Fagerborg, hanging so low and on its side that she only has to put out a hand to touch one wing, while Maj can't take her eyes off the shadow moving between the clothes lines at the back of the yard and it is only when it has gone and it is quiet again that she realises the sun has gone down behind Kirkeveien, and where did the shadow come from? It is Fru Lund. She has a knack of suddenly appearing from nowhere. Maj is embarrassed, not only because of their previous meeting, but because she has her washing hanging on the line after eight in the evening.

"I'd forgotten the time," she says.

Fru Lund laughs.

"It's summer."

Maj drops the pegs into her apron pocket, folds the last shirts and puts them in the laundry basket that Stine is holding with both hands.

"Yes, it's quiet."

"Are you going to stay at home?"

"We're going to Hurdal for a few days. The house is there. And you?"

"We're going to the mountains. And I have a conference in Helsingfors."

"Finland?"

"Yksi, kaksi, kolme. Do you know what that means, Stine?"

Stine shakes her head.

"It's one, two, three in Finnish. Say it after me. Yksi, kaksi, kolme."

"Yksi, kaksi, kolme."

"There you are. Now you can speak fluent Finnish."

"Yksi, kaksi, kolme," Stine repeats.

Fru Lund straightens up.

'It seems I was a bit hard on you last time, Maj. I couldn't have known, of course . . ."

Maj turns to Stine.

"Take the clothes upstairs, will you? I'll be up soon."

Stine waddles over to the kitchen stairs, opens the door with her foot, balances the laundry basket on one knee and darts inside. Maj asks:

"What couldn't you have known?"

Fru Lund looks around and suddenly regrets coming here. There was no rush. It could have waited until after the summer.

"Has your childhood home been empty since your parents died?"

"A neighbour pops by."

"It's handy to have good neighbours. Perhaps people look after one another better in the country?"

"What was it you couldn't have known?"

"That Enzo Zanetti was married and had a family in Italy. You could've said."

Maj hears every single word, but they don't reach her, they veer off, they are incomprehensible. Is Fru Lund still speaking Finnish?

"And he isn't even from Solferino. He was probably fooling us all. He's from Bellagio. A tiny village by Lake Como. Did you go there too?"

"How do you know?"

Fru Lund hesitates for a second and looks away.

"Brun, the manager of the Bristol, told me. Zanetti was employed there for a number of years, as you know."

"Yes, he played the piano there."

"And that puts the matter in a different light, don't you think?"

Maj shrugs.

"In what way?"

"If not a good light, then at least a better one. The element of doubt may be to your benefit."

"What doubt?"

"We don't need to go into detail, Fru Kristoffersen, but there are many ways of travelling with a man, aren't there?"

"Now I'm with you."

"Good. And of course you may be welcome back on the board."

"I may not wish to go back."

Maj starts walking towards the kitchen entrance, but doesn't arrive. She walks, but makes no headway. Even though she isn't carrying anything, only some pegs in her apron pocket, she can barely lift her legs. Every clothes peg weighs a ton. Whatever happens she mustn't turn, she must not turn. Yksi, kaksi, kolme, she says to herself. And if Stine is standing by the window and waiting, she mustn't notice anything, no-one must notice anything, fortunately most people are on holiday, only Fru Lund can see her, unless she has already gone, and Stine, if she is standing by the kitchen window, she is probably waiting there. The sound of the gravel beneath her feet sounds like a landslide. The door finally closes behind Maj, it is impossible for her to remember walking the last part. She sits down at the bottom of the narrow, brown staircase, at the lowest point of all daily grinds, hides her face in her hands and draws all sound into her heart. She can see the room in Pensione Astrid, and Enzo moving the bedside table from between the beds and pushing them together. Then she stands up, grabs the handrail and slowly ascends to the kitchen. It is better now. It is over. Stine is still standing by the open window and looking at the sky, which is empty and blue.

"Do you think they saw us?" she asks.

"Who?"

"The passengers in the aeroplane."

"Oh, no, it was going much too fast."

"I think it looked slow."

"If a plane went to Hurdal it would take only a minute and a half."

"What kept you?"

"Are you hungry?"

"Maybe Jesper's brought us something back from Denmark."

"So long as he comes home safe and sound, I'll be happy. Don't you think? And now you have to go to bed soon."

"We have to iron the clothes first."

"Hurry now."

Stine closes the window and turns. Her face changes. It distorts. It is impossible to see if she has burst into laughter or tears. Barely coherent, she asks:

"What have you done, Mamma?"

Maj is listening to the birdsong from the Virginia creeper and it reminds her of the drawings hanging over the two beds that became a double in Pensione Astrid, a bird with red wings, which is first a songbird and then resembles a carrion bird, she is incapable of answering, she just falls and cannot fall any further.

What have you done, Mamma?

Stine is laughing. She points at her.

"You look like a hedgehog."

Maj looks down. The clothes pegs are attached to her apron, dress, stockings, even on her fingers she has some. She doesn't remember this. She doesn't remember doing this. It is as though she has walked through a swarm of pegs that have attached themselves to her. The apron pocket is empty. She laughs. She laughs with Stine and begins to remove the pegs; she pulls them off and fills the bag on her stomach with these dead, wooden birds.

"Well, I never," she says.

Then they take out the ironing board and wedge it between the refrigerator and the worktop so that it doesn't move. They have to wait until the iron has warmed up. Soon it is glowing and Stine is allowed to try, even though the iron, when it is on, is the most dangerous object in the house, more dangerous than the knives in the drawer. You can burn yourself before you realise, and not only that, you can burn down the whole block of flats too, and the fire can spread and ultimately destroy the whole of Fagerborg. It has happened before, in other places, entire towns have burned down, because of an iron, and an iron is supposed to repair, not destroy. The iron is hot enough. Maj stands behind Stine and watches, ready to intervene, but Stine is good, she even manages the collar and sleeves of Jesper's shirts, and she doesn't forget to sprinkle water on every item of clothing, a light drizzle, so they won't be scorched. Maj leans against Stine, and for a moment it is she who is keeping an eye on Maj, who is thinking simply and naturally, for that is where our images come into existence, in that which is simple and natural: if only she could iron out the bumps in life, if only she could iron away the wrinkles around her mouth, if only she could iron out the nights in Pensione Astrid on the banks of the Tiber. Stine has finished and pulls out the plug. They fold the clothes and leave them in the laundry basket for the following day, if the following day dawns. They have supper, but neither of them is hungry. Jesper hasn't returned yet. Stine goes to the bathroom first. Then it is Maj's turn to get herself ready. She stands in front of the mirror. Why should she get herself ready for the night? She will be alone in bed. She won't even dream. She starts to cry and holds both hands over her mouth. The wrinkles have spread to her eyes, a slow fire spreading across her face that won't go out until she dies. She switches off all the lights, but it isn't dark enough, the summer light still suffuses the rooms. She can't sleep. It is a long time since Ewald lay beside her in bed. She thinks about him and distance vanishes. She can't keep him away. Is that smell salt pastilles or beer? She folds her hands. There will never be a man in her bed again. There will never be a smell of salt pastilles or beer. And she will never be with a man again. How often will she have to think about this before she can finally forget it? She has to think about something else. She thinks about sewing machines. What can you say about a Singer sewing machine that hasn't already been said? Singers are the real McCoy. Singers are a housewife's best friend. How corny. It is so *yesterday*. Besides, it isn't true. A sewing machine can also be an enemy, a reminder, a sore point: it reminds you of everything that is coming apart. Maj thinks about Enzo after all, he also needed to repair now and then, but it was still good to be in his repair shop, for as long as it lasted, she felt at home in the gentle melancholy, the laughter, the slow pace. Singer machines never break down. That isn't true either. Everything that works can break. *Singer machines fix your bad conscience*. Then at last Maj hears Jesper arrive. She wants to get up and make him something and he can tell her about his trip. She stays where she is. It is too much. All the nights she has to sleep alone hold her back. She hears Jesper go into the kitchen and drink a glass of water. She is aware of every sound and knows exactly what they mean. Now he is rinsing the glass and putting it in its place. Now he is taking a few raisins from the packet in the larder. This is the flat's very own vocabulary. It is their language. Then he goes in to see Stine, who has already woken up – Maj hears the springs of her mattress creak in that special way. Jesper is singing something to her, a strange song: *En pølse skal serveres med føl'se*. Stine laughs and tells him she has learned some Finnish while he was away. Then they whisper together, brother and sister. Maj breathes more lightly. It is easier. They are a family. They are still a family.

PIKE

First of all they have to go down to Majorstua, catch the Metro to Nationaltheatret, continue with the tram to Storgata and then walk to Ankertorget, where the bus station is, between the church spire, the silos and the chimneys. And they still haven't started the journey. Now the main thing is to find the right bus so that they don't end up at the stonemasons' holiday camp by Løten. It is further to Hurdal than it is to Copenhagen. Jesper can remember the last time he was there, when he caught the train to Dal and his grandfather picked him up. He also remembers a pike lying so still in the water that it resembled a suitcase. Now there is no-one to pick them up, their grandparents are dead, and so they have to take the bus. The departure bays smell of sun and exhaust fumes; it is headspinning and wonderful. Maj asks the drivers, who doff their caps and point to the next bus, it is always the next one to Hurdal, and at last they find the right bus, scramble on board and Maj pays as the driver produces long tickets from a machine like a little organ that rings with the sound of change and coins, there is no music. Jesper stows their rucksacks on the shelf. Stine wants to sit with him, but Jesper prefers not to be disturbed. There have been enough disturbances already. He has two sets of sheet music with him – Prokofiev and Debussy – which he will read on the journey. He finds a free seat at the back, which is not that difficult as they have the bus to themselves. No-one else but the Kristoffersen family is going to Hurdal on this July morning. Stine and her mother sit at the front of the bus. Then they leave Oslo, northwards along Trondheimsveien, over the Sinsen intersection, past the blocks of flats in Grorud, and after Gjelleråsen they are already in the country, there are forests, fields and green, sleek ridges as far as the eye can see, apart from Mortens kro, civilisation's last outpost, where they have sandwiches and home-made jam. A couple gets on there, but they are only going to Gjerdrum. Jesper doesn't manage to read the music anyway. The notes dance in front of his eyes. If only he could play them as they are. He knows what it is called when the notes are unreliable: improvisation. A thought strikes him, it is too early to think it, and it is exactly as though he is thinking at the same time that he isn't ready for this thought, it is too sudden, he should wait for it or the thought should give him more time. Love is also notes that don't stand still. Love is also improvisation. He suddenly feels ill, leans against the window and finds a certain calm in the bangs against his forehead as the bus goes over a pothole or a cattle grid and that happens all the time. He falls asleep and dreams: the bus skids off the road, rolls down a slope and lands in a hollow alongside some wrecked cars, stoves and broken grand pianos. Then it turns out it is only a bus stop and Trude is waiting there, suitcase in hand. Jesper wakes with a start. Stine is poking him. The bus has stopped.

"Are we there?"

Stine shakes her head. Jesper looks up; they are by the church at the southern end of Lake Hurdal, which is shallow in the summer. The driver is sitting on the footboard in the shade with his cap on his knees. It doesn't matter if he does an extra stop when there are no other passengers, and anyway he is ahead of schedule, besides it is nice to do decent people a favour, and last but not least he can have a cigarette. Maj waves to Stine and Jesper. They get out and follow her into the churchyard. There is a lot of space between the graves. There is more room in the country. In towns, space is at a premium. Maj's parents lie directly to the north of the chapel. They haven't got a proper headstone, only a worn, flat slab bearing their names and dates. That was how her father wanted it. He didn't want any adornment on the grave. Back in 1938 when he was making new steps in front of the house he found a flagstone he kept to one side and made it clear that this was the one he would lie under, he and Esther, when the time came. Jesper imagines this gravestone is one step in a staircase. Where does it lead to? Do the dead go up or down? It depends. It depends on the individual's life. Maj tidies the earth and grass where they have been sitting. Stine takes Jesper's hand. They can't keep the driver waiting any longer. He has finished his cigarette. They hurry back on board the bus, which has a flat front and is called a bulldog for this reason, and drive on to Jeppedalen, where they alight. There they do some shopping in the Co-op store. Jesper looks around. Copenhagen looks more like Oslo than this does. This is quite different from Magasin du Nord. This is getting away, he thinks. This is abroad, not Denmark. We don't come from the country. We come from abroad. The goods in the shop smell of turpentine and the bread is hard. Stine takes his hand again and is clingy today. They buy no more than they need, plus a bit: a bag of Twist, which is half price, it is so old, but the sweets still taste good, according to the cashier. Maj knows her. Perhaps they were in the same class at school. Perhaps they were neighbours, or both. Jesper only notices now: his mother is dressed differently, not only because she has to sit on a bus for half a day, but mostly because she is *back*. The conversation, as the till lady cashes up the items, is slow and painful.

"Been a while."

"It has indeed."

"And your husband passed on. He wasn't that old?"

"No, it was much too soon."

"Your parents hung on for a long time though, despite everything."

Maj doesn't know quite what this *despite everything* means. Probably it is just a way of speaking, a heartfelt sigh.

"Yes, despite everything," she says.

"Are you going to keep the house?"

"I have no other plans. Why do you ask?"

"I was only asking. It's empty."

Stine suddenly lets go of Jesper's hand and takes a step forward.

"I'm going to live there," she says.

Maj laughs, happy to be interrupted.

"You'd better wait until you see it."

The till lady laughs as well.

"I sort of recognise your lad, but your daughter's new."

"It's the first time she's been here."

Stine says her name and curtsies. Jesper puts the shopping in his rucksack. Maj pays.

"And your husband?" she asks.

The till lady, whose name is Astrid Nordbråten, rummages for change in the drawer.

"I'm afraid he can't drive you."

"That isn't what I meant."

"He's still working at Mathiesen's. But there'll soon be no forest left."

"Surely there are enough trees."

"But no forest."

Maj takes the change she is due. They promise to drop by the shop. Both know this probably won't happen. Jesper sees that and it hurts: the reunion is only an even greater distance. It doesn't help to change your clothes. It doesn't help to resemble who you once were. You don't anyway. He shrugs on the rucksack. It takes almost an hour to walk up to Rud, where Maj's childhood home is, in shadow as two o'clock passes. The lawn is cut. The garden is well-tended. The key is under the flagstone. They walk in, Maj first, Stine next, Jesper last. It is like walking through a portal to another era, or to the ante-room of the kingdom of the dead, because you notice it at once. Those who lived here are not away on holiday. They have departed for good. That is why the house is also dying, the colours are fading, the curtains are coming apart, a floorboard is loose, there is a drip somewhere, the damp is making the wallpaper bulge, darkness has settled, until the house falls down and light comes in, but it is no home at any rate, it might take years and in the end nature has taken over. Maj draws a sharp breath and slaps a hand over her mouth. Now she feels like crying. She doesn't though. Instead she sets about cleaning up. It isn't dirty. It is just neglected. Jesper and Stine help as well. She puts the milk and the food in the larder and wrings the cloths. Jesper changes the water. After they have finished it doesn't even smell of apple cake anymore. The house can begin to live again, but only for a short while, the time they will be there. The sky has clouded over, the way it usually does on a late afternoon in July in Hurdal, before the wind sweeps the clouds away and allows the evening sun to hang above Rudsetra, where it bathes the steep mountainside in dark yellow, as though someone has rubbed mustard over the spruce needles. They eat in the kitchen: sausage and potato cake. On the wall there is a pike attached to a piece of wood. Jesper can't remember if it was there last time he came. He remembers all the rest: the clock, the embroidery, *Home Sweet Home*, the plate decorated with the Norwegian flag and the confirmation picture of his mother – she is standing in front of the church, wearing the traditional costume and looking so serious she seems to be on the point of fainting. But he can't remember any pike. At any rate it is dead, a metre long and could well be an alligator with its sharp, flat jaw, had it not been for the fact that it had probably been caught in Hurdal. There are no alligators in Hurdal, only pike. Now Jesper can see that his mother resembles Stine, this is how he views the chronology, the mother looks like her daughter, on that May day in 1934 when the photograph was taken.

"Can you sing that song, Jesper?"

Jesper turns to his mother.

"Which one?"

"The one about sausages."

"I don't know any song about sausages."

"Yes, you do. The one you sang to Stine. Melsom taught you it, didn't he?"

Jesper had been trying to forget the butcher's humorous line. But no chance. His mother made sure of that. What was worse was that she had been listening. He can't think straight. If you sing in Fagerborg everyone can hear you. This sours his mood.

"Would you rather sing about pasta instead?"

Maj collapses over the little kitchen table by the window, where the lower half is covered by a thin curtain to impede prying eyes. Jesper feels remorse, but doesn't know what to say. Stine does.

"Jesper had been about to buy you a dress."

Maj looks up.

"A dress? For me?"

Jesper blushes.

"It was only that blue dress you tried on at Steen & Strøm."

Maj rests a hand on his.

"Did you really remember that?"

"Yes."

"Where did you see it?"

"In Magasin du Nord."

Maj is suddenly frightened and suspicious.

"You weren't going to steal it, were you?"

Jesper pulls his hand away.

"Are you crazy? I said buy. Jostein had some money."

"You should never borrow money from Jostein."

"Right. Why not?"

"You should never borrow money from anyone. Your father was very firm about that. Ewald never borrowed any money. Getting into debt is a disgrace."

Jesper has to laugh.

"Yes, he only lent money to everyone else."

"He *treated* people, Jesper. And that's different."

"Treating means you don't get back the money you lend them."

They can hear the wind driving past in a calm, regular arc. But it isn't the wind doing the cleaning. It is the treetops nearby sweeping the sky with pointed, green brooms that reach into every nook and cranny. They go out onto the stoop and watch the darkness open. There is still some light in the windows up in Rud. Then it too is extinguished and the farmhouse disappears into the night that is waiting by the hay-drying racks. Some sheep are grazing on the slope between the barn and the gate. They look like clouds that have descended. A bell rings and the sound billows through the grass.

"Ewald was much too nice," Maj says quietly.

They go back inside. In the country you go to bed early and wake even earlier. You become tired in a different way from in town. Time seems to lie deeper. It takes longer. Stine is going to sleep in Maj's old room on the ground floor. Maj will take her parents' room, while Jesper has the attic room where he slept on the previous visit. What had been large and high before seems cramped now. The ceiling slopes down over his face. Perhaps he won't be able to breathe. Nevertheless he drops off at once. There are no dreams. His sleep is heavy and regular, except when he is woken up. It is Stine. She is standing in the middle of the floor with a duvet under her arm.

"Can I sleep with you?" she whispers.

Jesper makes room for her. She creeps into his bed and makes herself as small as possible.

"And you're thinking of living here?"

Stine closes her eyes.

"Yes."

"And you don't dare sleep alone?"

"Only tonight."

"Only tonight? Who will you sleep with if you move here, eh? Do you think anyone will come with you to this wilderness?"

"Don't know."

"But I do. No-one will. And you'll have to sleep alone. Do you dare?"

"Don't know, Jesper."

"Did you see the pike in the kitchen?"

"The fish?"

"Yes, the fish. It can swim under the ground. And when it can't breathe it sticks up its snout for air."

Stine laughs.

"Snout?"

"Yes, the pike snout. Keep well away from it. But pike are happiest in the cemetery. They clean the bodies."

"Yuk."

"Can you sleep now?"

Stine opens her eyes.

"Didn't you think about buying me something in Copenhagen?"

"You've got everything."

"What for example?"

Jesper doesn't answer and moves closer to the wall.

"I'm tired. If you're going to stay here, don't make any noise."

Stine is still for a few minutes.

"Is it really true that Jostein got into a fight for me?" she asks.

Jesper has no desire to talk about this.

"Would you rather sleep with the pike?"

Stine shakes her head.

Then both of them fall asleep.

Next time Jesper wakes he needs the toilet. You pee more in the country. He crawls across Stine without waking her. It strikes him that we resemble one another when we are asleep. In sleep we share a face. He tiptoes down the stairs in his underpants and leaves the house. It is getting light. The sun is lifting the shadows from the forest. He stands behind the shed and pisses. It is good to piss outdoors. He pisses for a long time and it is dark yellow. When Jesper turns he sees a man sitting on a folding chair in the middle of the garden. He is wearing blue overalls and rubber boots. His face is like a pair of bellows and as brown as leather. He is puffing on a cigarette. He has combed his dark hair with water. Beside the chair there is a zinc bucket. In his hand he is holding a piece of string that goes down into the grass. It is the Gnome.

"I keep an eye on the place," he says.

All the light that collects on this plot, the way snow also falls precisely here in December, makes Jesper appear even paler and thinner than usual or perhaps that is only an effect of his white underpants. He gleams in a matt, dry way. He takes a few steps closer.

"Are you waiting for my mother?"

"There's no rush."

The Gnome's hand twitches, the line quivers and he begins to pull, it takes time, the ground is deep, but eventually a giant appears between his feet, a pike, at least twelve kilos, it is green and the teeth in its jaws are snapping. The Gnome stamps on the pike's neck, there is a loud crack and he throws the body into the bucket while the blood, which borders on a black colour, flows into the grass, where ants and other insects gather for a feast.

At that moment Maj appears on the stoop, cup of coffee in hand, shielding her eyes; she seems young and cheery, her clothes are light, her hair hangs loose onto her shoulders, she is barefoot and laughs.

"We don't need any fish today, Nils. We're leaving tomorrow."

"Why did you come here then?"

Maj walks over to him with the coffee.

"Thank you for looking after the house."

The Gnome blows onto the coffee, takes a sip and puts it down.

"I don't only look after the house."

"Don't you like it?"

"City coffee."

The Gnome stands up, takes the chair in one hand and the bucket in the other and wanders off. Maj turns to Jesper, as though she has only noticed him now.

"Aren't you going to get dressed?"

She carries the cup inside. Jesper stands surrounded by the glistening, verdant grass. Then he dashes up to the first floor. Stine is sitting on the edge of the bed, bent over and uncomfortable. She has to pee too. Jesper remembers what his father once said: "Men piss. Women pee. Ladies go to the ladies. Men go to Sirkus Sjumann."

"Can't you come with me?" Stine asks.

"Go with you? Is there anything to be afraid of?"

Stine can barely sit still. She whispers:

"The pike."

Jesper laughs and puts on his shirt and trousers.

"Relax. There are no more pike."

He accompanies her outside and stands guard by the door with the heart on, even though it can be locked from inside with a big hook. The sheep no longer look like clouds but soap bubbles. The farmer walks along the line of haystacks feeling the hay. For an instant the world is soundless. The sky, low and blue, has muffled everything. Then Maj shouts from the kitchen window. At last Stine has finished, washes her hands in a bowl and dries them on the grass. As they eat breakfast Maj plans the day and it has to be done carefully: they have to go round to greet everyone, and this has to be done in the right order, otherwise some people will be offended. Jesper is reminded of the song: *Gøy på landet, gøy på landet, sånt no' ha'ikke vi i by'n.* Fun in the country, fun in the country, we have nothing like that in town. Jesper thinks of all the things they don't have in Fagerborg: outside toilets, pike, sheep with bells, gnomes, farmers, haystacks, hay and a flagstone over a grave. But is that fun?

"I'm not going with you," he says.

Maj looks up.

"Of course you are."

Jesper is in no doubt: he has to rid himself of these songs; he can't carry them around with him for the rest of his life, he has to drop radio request programmes, morning prayers, children's hours, church services, the City Hall bells, applause and the eternal whistling every morning, sentimental pop songs that call to mind jelly and syrup, he simply must stop listening to things that bother him. Things that don't bother him are: wind, traffic, waves, rain, hammer blows, sirens, interval signals, cash tills, railway track points and snow.

"You can say hello from me," he says.

"What's the matter with you?"

"I'm going to read music."

"You're on holiday, Jesper."

"And I'm going to read music."

Stine laughs.

"He's just going to think about Trude."

"I'm bloody not. Shut up."

Maj stands up and bangs the table.

"You do not swear in this kitchen. Is that understood?"

Jesper turns to the curtains. If you can't see in, you can't see out either.

"Sorry."

"And no-one in this family tells someone to shut up. Say sorry to your sister as well."

Jesper glances at Stine, who doesn't meet his gaze.

"Sorry."

Maj sits down again and rattles her cup.

"What's the matter with you?"

"Nothing."

"Nothing? And yet you talk like that? I thought we were going to have a nice day, but it seems you don't want to be part of it."

She is quiet and her expression changes.

"Have you got a headache?"

"No."

"Sure?"

"Yes."

"Absolutely sure?"

"It's my head, isn't it? And if you ask me once more it definitely will ache."

Maj feels like hugging Jesper and Stine, but she can't reach around both of them.

"So we're friends again," she says.

They clear the table, rinse the cups and plates and save the hot water for later. Jesper goes up to the attic room and stands by the window. Soon he sees his mother and Stine walking out to the road. Stine has a ribbon in her hair. His mother has also dressed up and is carrying a small, green bag over her arm. What does she keep in it? What do you carry in a handbag in the country? A torch? A packed lunch? A gun? First they visit the farmer, who leans against his scythe and doffs his cap. His face is in two halves. The forehead is as white as a bandage while the rest is a suntanned underhung jaw. Stine curtsies. Maj proffers a hand. For a moment they all turn to the window where Jesper is standing. He lies down on the bed and starts on the Prokofiev. The notes have calmed down, but his thoughts are bounding away. They are improvising. They are spinning from Trude's blood to the handball goal and on to Enzo Zanetti's repairs, Jostein's hearing and Magasin du Nord, where they divert to Elisabeth Vilder's high-heeled shoes and finally land on the pupils who died during World War II, to end up back with Trude, but it is not the blood Jesper thinks about this time, it is the future and it strikes him: the future shouldn't be so damned long. Then he hears a motorbike approach and roar past. Motorbikes don't bother him either. As the mind-numbing noise is about to disappear down the hill to Lake Hurdal, it returns and stops outside. Jesper goes over to the window. A cloud of yellow dust hangs over the road. As it dissipates the motorbike is visible, green and low-slung, with two seats, but there is no-one sitting on it. Jesper's brain short-circuits: motorbikes don't ride themselves, the way that some pianos play themselves. Then there is a knock at the door. He runs down and opens it. A young man is standing on the step and he is also wreathed in dust. It has stuck to his sweaty skin, which looks like coarse sandpaper. Otherwise he has black hair, a tattoo on his upper arm, and is wearing a white T-shirt, jeans and clogs.

"Saw people were staying here," he says.

"Yes, people are."

"So I thought I'd just check they weren't the wrong sort."

"No, it's just us. The Kristoffersen family."

"Lots of tramps around, you know, and if they see an unoccupied house, they can't restrain themselves."

"What do you mean?"

"They vandalise and steal and leave a calling card in every room."

"I'm Jesper."

Jesper passes him a hand. Perhaps he shouldn't have done. Being polite comes at a cost. It might be the last time he plays the piano with two hands. His fingers are almost crushed.

"My name's Bror."

"What?"

"Bror as in brother, but with a capital B."

Jesper gathers what is left of his hand.

"Is that your motorbike?"

"Fancy a ride?"

"I haven't got a helmet."

"Nor have I."

Jesper closes the door, walks over and straddles the pillion seat behind Bror, who twists the throttle. The gravel beneath them is sent flying, but they don't move from the spot. The sheep, however, have run off and the farmer is standing with his back to them, barely casting a shadow. Bror is holding back. He is restraining the power that is bursting to be unleashed. It sounds like thunder. Then he lets everything go, the motorbike rears up, Jesper hangs onto Bror and they are off. They leave the noise they have created behind them and vanish into a zone where there is no sound or time, only light and wind. Jesper isn't a blupper anymore and he isn't a petrol-head either. He is Glenn Gould breaking the speed limit over the Hurdal variations. The sun rushes closer. At the crossroads he glimpses Stine and his mother, but they are hardly likely to catch a glimpse of him. Bror turns into a narrower road, closer to the camp-site, slows down and stops. Jesper is as stiff as a chair. Bror laughs, lights a Blue Master and passes the packet to Jesper. He takes a cigarette and Bror flicks a shiny lighter. The first drag makes Jesper feel dizzy. A forest fire starts in his head. They lie down on the grass. The sheep have come to heaven. They amble past lazily and roll down the Misberget slope on the other side of the lake.

"On holiday?" Bror asks.

"Only for a couple of days. And you?"

"On leave."

"Military?"

"Sea."

"Where?"

"Hamburg, New York, Rio, Sydney, Amsterdam, Aberdeen and Stavanger."

In Jesper's ears this sounds like a song and it is a song that bothers him in a different way: it attracts him.

"What do you do on board?"

"Mess boy. And you?"

"Me?"

"You're the one who plays the piano, aren't you?"

"How do you know that?"

"What do you think of the machine?"

"It's great."

"Basse Hveem rides one."

"Who's Basse Hveem?"

"Only the greatest Norwegian speedway rider in the world."

"Oh, him, yes."

Bror laughs, gets up, takes a cloth from his back pocket and cleans the mudguards.

"Horex Resident. 350 cc, 6,500 rpm, lamella clutch, four-speed gearbox, foot-shift and chain-driven. Bought it in Stavanger and rode it back."

"Do you live here?"

"Are you thirsty?"

Jesper treads on the cigarette end in the heather and gets back on the pillion. Bror rides past the campsite, which is like a Red Indian camp with pale-faced chiefs, continues along a narrow road into the forest, turns left by a a pole holding a crooked postbox that could equally well have been a bird box, and soon the road is no more than a rutted track leading to a disused farm. This is where Bror is at home when he isn't at sea. A tractor is rusting in tall grass. Big tyres lie strewn around as though they had just rolled here from all over the place and tipped over. A wheel-less car has ended up on its roof and looks like a dead turtle. Two red towels are hanging from a clothes line to dry. A pig has been tethered to a post and is walking in a circle of mud. Jesper thinks about Jostein. The pigs at Oslo Slaughterhouse are better off than this hog-tied sow. The barn has collapsed in the middle. The farmhouse has also seen better days and they must have been sometime in the previous century. A black cat is lying on the windowsill. Behind all this you can make out the northern end of Lake Hurdal. The water glistens in the sun. A man emerges onto the doorstep. He is wearing black trousers, a white shirt and a waistcoat with a golden chain. His hair is grey and lustrous. He looks out of place. He looks out of place with all the neglect around him. Bror goes over to him. Jesper follows. The man studies his watch and puts it back in his waistcoat pocket.

"Weren't you going to kill her today?"

Bror wipes his forehead with the back of his hand.

"Jesper's going to help me, Far."

"Jesper?"

"The Kristoffersen lad."

The man, who is Bror's father, turns to Jesper.

"You're the Kristoffersen boy, are you?"

His accent is askew and broken, a different kind of Norwegian, peppered with Swedish words and intonation from the underworld.

"I suppose so," Jesper says.

"The Kristoffersen boy who plays the piano?"

"Yes, I suppose I do."

Bror just smiles and isn't of much help. His father takes out a pipe and hangs it from the corner of his mouth.

"Which pianist is better, do you think – Robert Levin or Wilhelm Kempff?"

Jesper is surprised; he can't believe his ears. He would never have thought anyone would know these names in the country and especially not on this run-down farm.

"Wilhelm Kempff," he answers.

"Good for you."

"Good?"

Bror's father lifts his cold pipe and proffers a hand.

"I'm Far."

"Sorry?"

Bror laughs.

"My father's name is Far. And my sister's name is Søster. Just so you're in the picture."

Jesper looks around, but doesn't see any sister.

"How do you know I play the piano?"

Far goes into the house and returns with two knives: one long and pointed, one short and broad. They follow him to the round stone behind the barn. Bror pours water on it and starts cranking the handle. The stone whirrs around like a wheel. Far lays the first blade against it, lightly, holding the knife as gently as though it were a flower, and the sparks fly in an arc from the steel. Then he sharpens the second one and passes it to Bror; it is the short one. Far turns his attention to the pig, which has stopped walking. This one at least appears to react. It knows it is going to die in a little while. It is sure. It jerks at the chain. It wants to flee. Its eyes are big and pale. They are trembling. Bror takes off his shirt. Now Jesper can see what is on his shoulder, inside a blue anchor: *Mor og Far*. Jesper feels a sudden urge to go home. Bror wraps his arm around him.

"You have to hold her," he says.

Bror stuffs the knife inside his belt, takes off his shoes, loosens the leash from the pole and starts pulling this tub of lard through the mud. Jesper has to help him. It is impossible. Half a ton of pig resists. Far shakes his head and walks back to the house. Bror straightens up. Jesper hopes this is over now. Jesper hopes the pig will be allowed to live after all. Far comes into view in the window.

He is gently lifting down the cat. Are they going to kill it as well? Bror looks at Jesper.

"Far loves animals," he says.

"Does he?"

"He doesn't want puss to watch us killing the pig. It'll give him nightmares."

When Far comes back he is wearing a rain cape and rubber boots. He stands in front of the pig, ready with the slim-bladed knife. Bror pulls the sow's head back with one arm; in his other hand he has the short knife. Jesper holds what he can of the fat pig. It happens so quickly. He doesn't see what they do. He doesn't even see who does what. He sees only blood streaming from the pig's neck and feels the animal slump beneath him, without noise, abandoned. It isn't Jesper that has let go; it is the pig that has. Far goes down on his knees and closes the pale eyes. It is as though he is extinguishing light. Bror puts his knife back in his belt, walks over to the rusty tractor in the tall grass, sits on the seat, pulls a few levers and brings it back to life. He drives closer and pushes the carcass into the tumbledown barn. Far follows him. Jesper stands in the mud, and only now does he see that his trousers are covered in blood, his shirt is covered in blood, he is covered in blood, blood and mire, and it smells sweet, it is a kind of steam, which he has known only once before, at home in Fagerborg, and he knows at once that the deaths of animals and humans are similar. Bror comes out of the barn, alone, the knife has gone too, and he leads Jesper around the house. There is a shower on a pole. The hose pipe is attached to a pump by the well. Bror removes his trousers and finally stands naked in the mud that makes everything on this farm site seem even more derelict, apart from Bror, who is lithe and tanned. Jesper does the same. They are both naked. Bror pumps the water, detaches the shower head and sprays Jesper. It is freezing cold. It is good. He wakes up. He wipes off the blood. Then Jesper takes the shower and sprays Bror, who stretches out his arms and slowly rotates as the blood runs down him. Afterwards they wash their clothes in a bowl. When they walk back around the house there is a bathing costume on the clothes line as well, in two parts, a yellow bikini. Jesper is suddenly shy and starts to feel the cold. Bror unpegs the towels and passes him one. Jesper wraps himself in it. Bror laughs and hangs their clothes on the line.

"Now I suppose the Kristoffersen lad is thirsty," he says.

Jesper hears a whine, it is terrible and heart-rending, it seems as though he is the only person to hear it, the pig's delayed whine. Bror just ties the towel around his hips and heads for the front door. It is everything that hasn't been articulated. It is everything that burns inside. It is everything that is left hanging in the air. It is everything you can't get rid of. It is even worse: it is everything you can't do anything about. Jesper hurries after Bror. An older woman, large and square, wearing a headscarf and a flowery dress, is sitting in the kitchen reading a book by Joseph Conrad – *Heart of Darkness* – which she doesn't put down. She must be Mor. Bror puts out two glasses, finds a full jug in the refrigerator and pours a dark-brown, almost black liquid. Then he pushes to the side a trapdoor in the floor, clambers down a short, steep ladder and returns with a handful of ice cubes, which he drops carefully into the glasses so as not to spill anything. They each take a glass.

"Iced coffee," Bror says.

Jesper drinks, at first it is bitter, soon it is pleasant and in the end he has never tasted anything better. He would like to say so, but there is a girl in the doorway; her hair is black and falls onto her shoulders like fresh curtains. She is holding the cat in her arms and watching Jesper in a way that leaves no doubt, head tilted, forehead creased, a little smile: she saw him naked and now she is deciding whether he amounts to anything at all, this Kristoffersen boy with a red towel around his waist, an abducted and shy matador.

"Søster," she says by way of introduction.

Her bra is wet and forms two dark ovals under her white top. Jesper looks elsewhere. Mor jumps up with surprising ease.

"I suppose you're all hungry now?"

She takes a loaf out of the oven. The crust is golden. She places it on the kitchen table, where there is already brown cheese, jam and butter. The aroma fills the room and it is no longer as lifeless as Jesper felt it was. There is wonderment. There is strangeness. There is hunger. Søster lets go of the cat and passes him a knife. Everyone gives each other a knife in this topsy-turvy circus. Jesper has to start: he has to kill the freshly baked loaf. He has to use all his strength to cut through the top, but then the knife slides through and the crust falls away. The loaf is dead. The bread can be eaten. The loaf is alive. He cuts another slice. The butter melts as soon as it touches the bread. The strawberry jam is equally runny. Jesper takes a bite and it becomes part of him. Mor smiles and combs her daughter's hair.

"You shouldn't swim on your own," she says.

Søster tosses her hair.

"Why not?"

"Someone might come."

"And so?"

"You know. There are lots of hungry men."

"But no-one will find where I am anyway. It's behind the cliff."

Søster turns to Jesper. Her eyes, which he thought were brown, are green. Or perhaps they change colour according to whoever they see? They turn green when they look at Jesper. Bror stands between them.

"Fancy listening to some decent music?"

Mor stops him.

"You two get dressed first."

They go outside to the washing line. Their clothes are already dry. They change and go back in, to the sitting room this time. The walls are covered with bookshelves. Jesper sees names such as Edith Södergren, Pär Lagerquist, Henrik Ibsen, John Steinbeck, Karin Boye and Hans Christian Andersen. Some of them he knows. Most he doesn't. On the floor there are piles of old newspapers and magazines. Søster is sitting in a rocking chair eating a slice of bread.

She has nothing on it; it is just bread. Jesper sits on the sofa and dare not look her way. He counts books instead. It is a whole library. It would take many people to read all this. Bror places a record player between them, puts on an LP and lowers the stylus onto the grooves. The sound isn't much good, with all the dust and clicks, but the music impacts on Jesper at once and equally surprisingly there are only a piano, bass and guitar. He is envious. He is outright jealous. It is so easy. It just swings. There are no depths it has to plumb. Now he knows. This must be the devil's piano. Brother passes him the LP cover. It is Oscar Petersen. *That Old Black Magic.*

"Why didn't you buy Elvis instead?" Søster asks.

"Elvis who?"

"Don't mess about."

"Because Elvis is a flash in the pan."

"He is not."

"But Oscar is eternal."

"You could've bought an Elvis for me."

"I do everything for you, sister Søs. But I'm not doing Presley."

The music glides into an empty groove. Sister turns her green eyes on Jesper, who rises to his feet abruptly.

"I've got to go home," he says.

Bror lifts the stylus.

"I'll take you."

"No need."

"You won't find the way."

Søster sits thumbing through a magazine.

Mor is waiting in the kitchen with a paper bag. She gives it to Jesper. It is the rest of the loaf. It is still warm. He bows, but by then she is already sitting with her back to him and reading her novel, *Heart of Darkness.* Is there a link between black magic and the heart of darkness? Are both equally alluring? Jesper has no time to give this any thought. He follows Bror into the yard. They get on the motorbike. Far is standing by the crooked barn door smoking his pipe, as immaculate as ever, while the cat rubs against his polished shoes. Bror chooses a short cut through the forest, under the power lines, down to the Co-op, where he comes to a halt.

"Can you find the way now, city boy?"

Jesper slides off the pillion, stiff and bow-legged, and can't seem to find the will to go.

"Where did you buy the record?"

"In New York. Where else?"

"Yes, where else?"

"In Bleeker Street."

"Bleeker Street? What's it like there?"

"Women, music. But the music is probably not to your taste. Or the women?"

"How do you know?"

"Relax. I bought it in Karl Johan. In Musikkhuset."

Bror pats Jesper on the shoulder and heads north, back to the campsite. It takes Jesper roughly twice that time up to Rud, even though he doesn't have to drag Stine, his mother and the luggage with him, only half a loaf, wrapped in grey paper. His mother is standing at the gate when he arrives. She is very chatty. He would prefer not to talk to anyone and walks past her. She runs after him.

"Where have you been? Tell me where you've been."

Stine is lying on a blanket on the grass, but the shadows have long fallen over the grass and she struggles up and looks at her brother.

"Have you been on a motorbike?" she asks.

"Maybe."

Jesper goes into the kitchen and puts the loaf on the worktop. Stine stops in the doorway and gapes at him. Maj doesn't give him any peace either.

"Then it *was* you we saw!" she almost shouts.

"So?"

"Don't you be difficult with me, Jesper. I was worried about you. *We've* been worried about you, haven't we, Stine?"

Her voice is low.

"Yes."

Jesper laughs.

"Worried about me? Do you think anything dangerous can happen in Hurdal?"

"Who were you with?"

"Bror."

Maj comes closer and lowers her voice.

"Bror? The boy on the farm?"

"Is it a farm?"

She spins round and points.

"What's that?"

"A loaf of bread."

"Where did you get it?"

"From his mother."

"Have you been to their house as well?"

"Of course."

Maj goes over to the worktop, takes out the bin from underneath, throws the loaf in and takes a deep breath before saying:

"Never go there again."

"What are you doing? That's bloody great bread."

Jesper goes to take out the loaf, but Maj stops him.

"Did you hear what I said? Do not ever go there again."

"Why not?"

"Because I told you not to."

Jesper is about to answer, but he has had enough. He bounds up the stairs to the first floor in two steps. Maj hears his door slam. She turns to Stine, who is still standing where she was, sad, almost sullen, as she tends to be when anyone raises their voice.

"He'll come back down soon enough," Maj says.

But Jesper doesn't. It starts raining. The forest is a grey wall inching closer. Jesper doesn't even come down when they have dinner: new potatoes with butter and pork rissoles. Maj asks Stine to take a portion up to him and ask if he wants strawberries for afters. Stine carefully carries the full plate up the stairs. Maj sits at the

kitchen table. There is always some unease. There is always something to rue. There is always something you are not looking forward
to. Whatever she does she will have regrets. Is it possible to make
amends, to do something so good that everything will go back to
how it was? How do you do that? How do you repair what is broken
in a person? Because there is something broken in Maj. She has
had her spirit crushed, there is some corrosion in her heart, which
is spreading, not only in her, but also in those closest to her:
Jesper and Stine. That is how it feels. She closes her eyes. Enzo
Zanetti used to put it this way: *I'm repairing.* But that was only
when he had been drinking a little too much and his hands were
shaking the following morning. She opens her eyes, goes to the bin,
retrieves the loaf and puts it on the worktop. It isn't warm now.
There is only the waft of a certain aroma, a taste, as sweet as vanilla.
She spews up, vomit gushes from her mouth, sick, tears, snot,
everything is liquid. She manages to run a cloth across the floor
before Stine returns with the plate, which is untouched. Maj takes
a deep breath.

"Wasn't he hungry?"

Stine puts down the plate and shakes her head.

"Didn't he want any strawberries either?"

"No."

"What was he doing?"

"Lying in bed."

"And reading music?"

"No, humming."

"Humming? What?"

They are both silent, listening, but hear nothing, only the rain,
the summer rain on the roof, and this sound, light and short-lived,
yet still enduring, makes Maj cry. It reminds her of other days,
other times, when she was whole and could stand face to face with
the forest and everything in it, without giving ground, without
any hesitation. It reminds her of another happiness, which wasn't
earned, it was just there, like a gift, a feature of life. She wonders

when it left her, when nothing could be taken for granted anymore. She wonders when she had to earn everything.

"We can take some strawberries up to him," Stine whispers.

Maj wipes her tears on her apron.

"Let's wait a little."

They eat strawberries and wait.

Has Stine still got the gift? Can she take happiness for granted?

Maj has a sudden urge to ask, but refrains at the last moment. If you ask that question, you have already marred the happiness.

At eight o'clock it stops raining. For an instant the light is bright and cold and you can count every spruce needle in the forest, which isn't a wall after all but a busy sky. Animals and shadows cross paths. It is like autumn. Then the evening is back to its usual self, matt, melancholy, beautiful in its own way. Maj can't bear to have the pike on the wall anymore. She stands on the chair, unhooks it and takes it to the shed. Nils cycles past. She waves. She has forgotten to tell them not to call him the Gnome. His name is Nils. That is his name. He raises an arm as well, almost loses control of his bike and has to hold the handlebars with both hands. Maj watches him. Everything in the distant past catches up with her for a moment. It is good. It hurts. Then Nils, whom everyone calls the Gnome because he is kind and has powers, rounds the bend and is gone. Maj goes back in. Stine is in the sitting room flicking through an old magazine. Maj cuts a thick slice of bread, puts on some brown cheese and takes it up to the first floor. She stands outside the attic room. She can't hear anything now either. She knocks. No-one answers. She opens the door. Jesper is lying in bed with his hands behind his head.

"Aren't you hungry?" she asks.

"Dunno."

Maj chuckles.

"You don't know?"

"Haven't checked."

"Check then."

Jesper checks.

"No, seems I'm not."

Maj puts the plate on the bedside table anyway.

"I meant what I said," she says.

"What did you say?"

"We shouldn't be impolite or anything, that's not what I'm saying, but we shouldn't socialise with them either."

It's Jesper's turn to chuckle.

"Socialise? Who with?"

"You know what I mean."

Jesper closes his eyes, hears his mother sigh and the next time he can be bothered to open them his mother has gone, fortunately. It is dark. He switches on the wall lamp. It is ten past twelve. For a moment he is unsure. Has he been lost in thought in the meantime? Or has he been asleep? He can't remember dreaming. It doesn't matter. He takes a bite of the bread. But it has lost its flavour. It is no longer magical. It is ordinary. He can't swallow it, goes outside and spits the mouthful into the pile of rubbish by the shed. Before the night is over an animal will have eaten it. What kind of animal? Jesper has to think hard. A fox? Do they dare come so close to humans? The sheep? They are in pens. And elk probably wouldn't bother with anything so small. So it must be rats. Rats would like bread. There are rats in the country too. What about pike? Do they suddenly appear from the ground and sink their jaws into half-chewed bread? No, birds would find the crumbs first. That is how the loaf will go to heaven. He can't get "That Old Black Magic" out of his head. As soon as it is over, it starts again. Does it bother him or is it a blessing? He doesn't know yet. He has a piss in the grass. It is wonderful to piss in the open at night. It is raining. He hurries back to the attic room and tries to read the music. It is no use. The notes lie still on the lines, but he can't hear them, all he hears is "That Old Black Magic", not Prokofiev. Someone knocks at the door. Jesper sits up in bed. It is already light. It has stopped raining. Stine peeps in.

"Toilet's free," she says.

Jesper washes his face in the bowl on the small, round table with the marble top and ornate brass feet. The water is lukewarm and lifeless. A swarm of midges have drowned and are lying on their backs. He goes down to the kitchen, which suddenly seems empty, as if they were also about to leave the house, even though Maj is standing at the stove and waiting for something to boil.

"If you absolutely have to wee outside, please do it *behind* the shed where no-one can see you."

"Did someone see me?"

"Yes, someone did. Don't think just because you're in the country that you can do whatever you like."

"Was it the Gnome spying on us?"

"His name's Nils. And he doesn't spy on people. By the way, it wasn't him. You should say sorry."

"Sorry? Alright. I'll just wash my hands first."

Maj turns to him.

"And don't talk to me like that."

"What is actually the matter with you?"

"There's nothing the matter with me. You should just behave properly. That's all I'm asking."

"It's boiling over."

"And keep away from those people."

"I know you were suckered in Rome, but don't take it out on us, alright?"

The slap hits Jesper before he has finished speaking. It stings. He turns away. Maj drops her hand. Stine grabs the pan of milk at the last moment. Everything happens at once. That is how Jesper experiences it. The words, the actions and the regret co-exist in the same moment, like a large, intricate sound for which there are no notes. He runs out, through the garden and shuts himself in the toilet. He pushes the lid to the side. The hole stinks. He takes aim and pisses. Afterwards he tears a page from the newspapers lying there, yellow and stiff, and dries round the edge while holding his breath so as not to faint. But he can read the date: November

21st, 1949. Twenty-eight Jewish refugee children die in a plane crash in Hurumlandet. Why can't Jesper remember that? He was a child himself then, perhaps the same age as those who died. When does your memory start to work? Is it only when you know you are going to die? He drops the paper in the foul-smelling darkness and replaces the lid. Then he sees what is missing from the kitchen: the pike. It is hanging here, directly above the faded picture of King Haakon. Jesper lifts it down. A name has been burned on the board to which the pike is attached: *From Nils*. Who do you give a pike as a gift? Who wants a stuffed pike? He takes it back to the kitchen. Maj and Stine are having breakfast. He leaves the pike on the worktop, washes his hands and sits down. After a while Maj says:

"I had been going to bake you a cake today, Jesper."

"Great stuff."

"Chocolate cake."

"Even better."

Maj sighs. Soon she will be sighing non-stop.

"Do you mean what you say or are you just making fun of me?"

Jesper turns to Stine.

"Remember to take a piece home for Jostein."

Stine pulls a long face and imitates her big brother's way of speaking.

"Right. And you take a big piece for Trude."

"That's nothing to do with you, schwesterlein."

"Or you."

Maj still hasn't finished sighing and leans across the table.

"Now you two make peace. Let's all be friends."

They are silent. Then Stine lets out a little sob.

"I didn't start it."

"No-one started it," Maj says.

Jesper stands up, pats Stine on the head and goes out again. Maj follows him.

"Where are you going?"

"For a walk."

"Don't go to—"

"I'm just going for a walk. OK?"

"Can't you take Stine with you?"

"Nope."

Jesper opens the gate and sets off down the road where the dust has settled after the rain. Behind the low curtains in the other houses he can make out faces. A dog runs along the field on the right collecting the sheep that have escaped. The same farmer is resting against his scythe and watching him. Jesper is unable to interpret what he can see: is it displeasure or friendliness? Perhaps it is something quite different. He raises a hand and waves, just to be on the safe side. The farmer doesn't move a muscle. On the bend he is out of sight. Jesper can make out Lake Hurdal between the trees. The next moment it is gone. The sun rolls up Mistberget at a furious speed and hangs at the top until it bursts and light spreads across the whole sky. The dust rises all around him. He reaches the Co-op and runs past, but changes his mind, goes back in and buys two small Cokes, changes his mind yet again and keeps only one. Astrid Nordbråten, Maj's old school friend, cashes up on the till and gives him his change. Jesper wants to go; she wants to chat.

"Do you like it here then?"

"Yes, it's great."

"Maybe there's not so much to do here as in the city?"

"Not much to do there, either."

"You play the piano, don't you?"

"Yes, I do."

There is a short pause in the conversation, or the interrogation, before she continues:

"You've been on a motorbike now anyway."

Jesper takes a step towards the door.

"I was only on the pillion."

"You should be careful."

"What with?"

Astrid Nordbråten, who seems much older than Maj, perhaps

because of the blue coat and kerchief, perhaps because of the smell of turpentine, is less forthcoming all of a sudden.

"You shouldn't butcher animals in the wrong season," she says.

Jesper opens the door with his foot.

"Thank you for the Coke."

Astrid Nordbråten laughs.

"It was you who paid."

"Thank you anyway."

"Shall I open the bottle for you?"

"No need."

Jesper hurries out and follows the path through the forest. It becomes narrower and narrower and culminates in a field of ferns. He has to plough his way through. Some of the ferns reach up to his shoulders. They drip water on him. From the ground, or underneath the ferns, which are always in shadow, a damp, sharp chill rises, the way that dust specks rise in heat. When he is through the field, the lake lies in front of him, long and slim. Only a buzzard disturbs the peace, a shiny back that is just visible. Jesper looks around. Further down there is a rock face that plummets into the water. Is that the cliff? He walks by the forest edge. A swarm of flies follows him like a restless buzzing shadow. His feet get tangled in the heather and twigs. There is no point trying to creep up on someone here. Jesper stops again and listens. He has no intention of creeping up on anyone. Nevertheless, he knows he ought to turn back. He shouldn't be here. He should have stayed in Oslo and practised. He could fall and break his fingers. He could fall, smash the bottle and cut an artery. But he doesn't hear anyone. Jesper can't hear anyone and everyone can hear him. He should have stayed in town and rung Trude. He continues past a pile of rocks. One comes loose and ends up in the water. Jesper crouches down. It is even quieter now. This is like a plan. The noise he makes is being assessed by the ensuing silence. The sun is burning his neck. Then Jesper hears something after all. But he doesn't know if it is only inside his head or somewhere else. It is "That Old Black

Magic". This is something he doesn't understand: how magic, black magic, can be so light. It is magic in action. His head is empty and quiet. The music must be coming from somewhere else. Jesper moves in that direction, towards the cliff, and sits on his haunches. There is nothing inside him, everything is on the outside and it is drawing him closer. Søster is lying by the water's edge on a large flat stone. Her bikini is still yellow. Her back is tanned and smooth and forms a hollow for drops of water to collect in. She has tied up her wet hair so that her neck and shoulders can also get the sun. Actually she doesn't need to sunbathe. She is tanned enough. Perhaps she just likes sunbathing. The towel she is lying on is white. Jesper can't see a record player anywhere, only a small bag. Now he can hear it. The music is inside him after all. It is too late.

"Come on over," Søster says.

Jesper clambers down. She is lying in the same way as before. He doesn't know where to look. He dare not go too close. He sits on a rock some distance away and feels he has to say something.

"So this is where you sunbathe?"

Søster looks up, supports herself on her elbows and smiles.

"Haven't you got any trunks with you?"

"No, shit, I forgot them."

When she is lying like this, Jesper can see her breasts, there is almost no gap between them, and her skin is golden brown there too. Years and years may pass before he can stand up again.

"Doesn't matter," she says.

"What doesn't?"

"Forget it."

Jesper looks around. The forest forms an oval wall making the cliff and the rocks around it resemble an amphitheatre with the water as the stage.

"Does Bror go to sea or is he only bluffing?"

"Why would he do that?"

"Do you always answer questions with a question?"

"Do you always ask so many questions?"

"Just wondering."

"He'd really like to be a chef on land. In Oslo. There aren't any restaurants in Hurdal. There's nothing in Hurdal. He's been looking for a job everywhere. Hope he finds one. Then he can look after me too."

"Why?"

Søster takes a round, blue Nivea jar from her bag.

"Because he gets seasick just float fishing in Heggtjern pond."

"I mean why would he look after you?"

"What do you think?"

Søster unscrews the lid, inserts two fingers, digs deeper and starts to cover her arms. It takes her a long time. It is hard to spread the thick, lumpy suncream evenly. Jesper can't take his eyes off the slim, white strip around her wrist where her watch had been. Now he has to say it:

"Would you like some Coke?"

"I thought you were never going to ask."

Søster sits up, screws the lid back on and leaves the jar in the sun. Jesper goes closer. He regrets not having let the woman in the Co-op open the bottle. In fact, it is already warm. He gives it to Søster, who puts it in a pool to chill. Jesper sits down on a corner of her towel.

"What's the time?" he asks.

"Haven't you got a watch?"

"It's not working."

"Are you in a hurry?"

"Forget it," Jesper says.

Søster looks down and springs to her feet at the same time.

"I've lost it. I must've lost it when I was swimming."

She wades into the water, slips on the slippery stones, dives down and comes up again.

"Help me then, you sissy."

Jesper is confused, he hesitates; he really is a sissy. Then he tears off his shirt and socks, but not his trousers, and starts swimming

399

in the dark, cold water, where it is hard to stay afloat. He takes a deep breath and dives down to the bottom. It surprises him that the water is lighter the deeper he swims. He would have been so happy to find the watch. He would have been so happy to see it shining in the seaweed below and to hand it to Søster. But he doesn't see anything. For an instant he sees her. She glides past him, quite close. Jesper needs air. He turns and follows. They wade ashore. His jeans weigh at least a ton and get tighter and tighter.

"Are you sure you were wearing it?" he asks.

"Perhaps it's at home."

"Perhaps a pike's eaten it."

Søster laughs again.

"Do you always swim in your jeans?"

"Only in fresh water."

"They'll dry faster if you take them off."

She kneels in front of him, grabs the legs and pulls. This isn't right. Jesper knows that. It's not right and this is how it should be. It shouldn't be like this and it is right. Afterwards she hangs his jeans over a withered branch behind them, opens the cold, dripping Coke with a hair slide, takes a gulp and passes it to Jesper. There are no more than two and a half gulps in a small bottle. Then they lie beside each other on the towel. If only you could tear an hour out of time the way you do a page from a calendar or from a newspaper, everything would be fine. Everything isn't fine. It strikes Jesper that your conscience is the most zealous, irritating and oppressive of all feelings, worse than falling in love, envy and jealousy all rolled into one. Your conscience is the biggest of all emotional intrusions. It starts working before anything at all has happened. Still nothing has happened, apart from him lying in his underpants beside a girl in a bikini he barely knows. They have also drunk from the same bottle. Otherwise, though, nothing has happened. Jesper's mood lightens. It takes so little.

"Actually, how come . . .?"

Søster appears to be laughing at him. Jesper sits up.

"Did I say something stupid?"

"You talk like the radio. Actually, how come . . .?"

"The radio? Yesterday I was the Kristoffersen lad. In fact, my name's Jesper."

"Sorry, Jesper. I didn't mean to make fun. Are you angry?"

Søster runs her hand along his neck as he lies down, a bit further away from her this time, thinking that the people who have the worst consciences are good, but why do they do what gives them a bad conscience?

Jesper starts again.

"Actually, how come everyone in Hurdal seems to know that I play the piano?"

"Because Nils knows."

"You mean the Gnome?"

Søster is not best pleased.

"Don't call him that. He's my uncle."

"But how does Nils know that I play the piano?"

"Doesn't he look after your house for you?"

"Yes, he does. So?"

"Perhaps he just likes to keep himself informed. He once went out with your mother."

"The Gnome? You're kidding."

"His name's Nils. Relax. It was a hundred years ago. Are you angry?"

"Why would I be?"

Jesper closes his eyes and sees only the dead pike in front of him, crucified on a crooked piece of wood.

"I bet you've got a girlfriend in Oslo," Søster says.

A cloud parts the light into two. Where the shadow falls, Lake Hurdal breaks up into small, choppy waves that together make a noise evoking memories of carpentry classes. Jesper lies on top of her. At first she tries to push him off. She tries several times. He is stronger. Then she lets him in. She is willing. He can do whatever he likes. Afterwards the light is full again, but duller, not as bright, and the water is calm and quiet. They lie beside each other. The rock beneath them is rough and sharp. Søster has pulled the towel around her.

"I knew it," she says.

Jesper stands up and feels his jeans. At last they are dry. As he turns to Søster he spots her watch and it is not the fact that she probably knew it was there the whole time that makes the biggest impression on him, it is the time itself gleaming so clearly up from the bottom of the bag: twenty-two minutes past twelve.

"What?"

"What?"

"What did you know?"

"That you're just a bloody city boy."

Jesper pulls on his jeans, balancing on one leg, hops to keep his balance and topples backwards into the undergrowth and feels the short, sharp branches scratch his back, it feels like whiplashes. He lies there, ashamed and frightened. Søster stands above him, still wrapped in her towel; she passes him a hand, smiles and helps him to his feet.

"Bror is going to give you a beating now," she says.

MATERNAL LOVE

Fru Melsom is the first to see them: the pictures of her son in *Norsk Dameblad*. She sees them at the hairdresser's in Jacob Aalls gate, where she has an appointment every year, at 9 a.m., on August 19th, to have a perm after the summer, so it can see her through at least to Christmas. And in 1957 her hair is especially flat and dry, with split ends, as a consequence of her husband's bad mood since he returned empty-handed from Copenhagen. He has been impossible to live with. But it was the hairdresser, Fru Steen, who noticed them first because she gets the magazines a day earlier than other people, on Mondays, so that they can be laid out ready in the salon for Tuesday morning. She points to the picture under *After*, and in it Jostein looks like a grown lad, a real man, in a white shirt open at the neck with a cool smile.

"I hardly recognised him."

His mother doesn't either, as the last time she clapped her eyes on her son, this morning in the kitchen, less than half an hour ago, he still had a forehead covered with spots and looked more like the picture under *Before*, before using Valcrema. There he is sullen and pimply. Nevertheless she is proud and her heart softens because it is as though she has been given a glimpse of a kind future, the man Jostein is going to be.

"Let's hope he can keep his feet on the ground," she says.

Fru Steen is washing her hair.

"If I know your family well, he will."

"But they do whatever suits them, young people do."

Fru Steen trims the ends, rolls up her hair and attaches curlers.

"It's fantastic that Valcrema can work so fast," she says.

"What do you mean?"

"I saw Jostein the other day, in Majorstua, and then I thought he still had some spots on his forehead. But I may have been mistaken. I probably was."

"There's so much you can do with photographs nowadays, isn't there?"

"Yes, there certainly is, but it's an awfully good photo anyway."

Then Fru Steen pushes the domed hairdryer closer to Fru Melsom, who is still holding the *Norsk Dameblad* in her lap. And although it has been said often enough, I am more than happy to take the liberty of repeating it anyway: these round capsules that are lowered over hairdos make the mothers in Fagerborg look like astronauts, and this is their own, private space trip into the unassuming universe of beauty, which is without men and deception. But this time Fru Melsom cannot enjoy the slow ascent from the summer's negligent torpor. She has to go home as fast as possible, before Jostein leaves to see this Henry Vilder, who has put some whims into Jostein's head. Now the correspondence course isn't good enough. Now it is the school of life that counts. School of life, I ask you! As if it hurt to be able to add and subtract a little as well. What is more, isn't it ungodly to appear in a vulgar magazine which only serves up superficial pastimes such as fashion, film and gossip? Isn't pride one of the deadly sins, exhibiting yourself, on top of everything else, in a false light? Fru Melsom dismisses these thoughts, she hasn't been that godly herself in recent weeks. It isn't at all easy to be godly in the summer. Godliness belongs to winter. Nor is it easy to be pious with an introverted man who never gives you more than vague intimations. She began to skip prayers, first in the morning, then in the evening, until it all came to a head between her and God at the beginning of July; they simply agreed to take a break, perhaps they can find their way back to each other at a later opportunity. Fru Steen pushes the hairdryer aside. The space voyage to beauty is over. It is taking longer and longer with every year that passes. Fru Melsom sighs, but consoles herself with the thought that at least she doesn't need to exert herself any longer. Those days are over. She doesn't want to be seen anymore. She pretties herself up purely for her own pleasure. Melsom the butcher stopped showing any kind of interest ages ago and she has no plans to try and tempt him. She pays and takes a copy of Norsk Dameblad as well. Then she scoots home and first goes up to the flat. Jostein is still sitting in the kitchen studying the telephone directory. Was he going to call someone? No, not for the time being, but Henry Vilder told him it was important to have contacts. If you have them, you can find your way around the corridors like a fish through water.

"Which corridors?" his mother asks.

Jostein eyes her condescendingly.

"I'm afraid you won't understand this, Mamma. But if Pappa had had the right contacts in Svinesund he would never have been stopped."

His mother forgets to take off her coat.

"Was Pappa stopped in Svinesund?"

"We-ell."

"Was he trying to smuggle? Answer me now, Jostein!"

Jostein continues to flick through the directory.

"Actually, everyone's stopped in Svinesund," he mumbles.

His mother goes closer to him.

"So that was why he came back empty-handed and had only a half-eaten Toblerone with him?"

Jostein looks down, he has come to G, soon he can contact the Norwegian Prime Minister, Einar Gerhardsen, but what good is that now? He speaks in an even lower voice.

"I promised Pappa I wouldn't say anything."

"Don't you worry, my boy. Besides you haven't said anything. Now let's forget it."

Jostein's mother lays the Norsk Dameblad in front of him. He looks from one picture to the next, Before and After, After and Before. Then he looks up, bewildered, confused, while pointing to After.

"Haven't I got spots anymore?"

His mother is unsure how to handle this.

"At least not in the *After* picture," she says.

"But are they better than *Before*?"

"Yes, definitely."

"But not as good as *After*?"

She chooses her words with care.

"No, not quite yet."

Jostein is immersed in deep thought. Then he goes into the bathroom. There, in the mirror, he can see with his own eyes that one picture is lying. There is still a bumper crop of redcurrants on his forehead. Dek-Rek might just as well have swapped them round so that *Before* became *After* and *After Before*. He goes back to the kitchen, rolls up the *Norsk Dameblad* and stuffs it in his pocket.

"Are you going to see that Henry Vilder again?" she asks.

"I'm going to talk to whoever is responsible," Jostein says.

He hasn't time to wait for the Metro, so he walks down Bogstadveien, through the Palace Park, across Karl Johan and in the university square he meets Trude, who has been to Tanum bookshop to collect the new school timetable. Jostein doesn't really have any time to stop, but he can show her the new advertisement now that they've happened across one another. He opens the *Norsk Dameblad* at the right page. Trude leans closer.

"That's you, isn't it? Wow."

"Before and after," Jostein says.

Trude scrutinises his face.

"Before and after what?"

"Are you taking the mickey?"

"Of course I'm not."

"Well, it seemed like it."

Jostein closes the magazine and makes a move to leave. But Trude holds him back.

"Have you seen Jesper?"

"Lots of times."

"Don't mess around. I'm not taking the mickey."

"Not since we were in Copenhagen."

"Have you been to Copenhagen?"

"On a business trip."

"Is he in Hurdal?"

"Stine and his mother are home at any rate. Should I say hi and pass on a message if I see him?"

"Maybe."

Jostein notices that Trude, whom he doesn't really know, even though she is the girlfriend of his best pal, seems depressed and unhappy and she is usually optimistic and full of beans. For a moment he is almost sorry for her and immediately feels better.

"By the way, Jesper was thinking of buying something for you in Copenhagen," he says.

Trude glances up.

"Oh?"

"At Magas . . . Magazine doo . . . anyway, a bloody big shop."

"Magasin du Nord?"

"Exactly. That's the one."

"What was he thinking of buying, Jostein?"

"A blue dress in the women's department."

"A blue dress?"

"Right."

"Why didn't he buy it then?"

"Because it was so expensive and he didn't want to borrow money from me."

At last Trude smiles and gives him a quick hug.

"I'll probably see Jesper tomorrow. If he hasn't changed school. Or given up."

"Then you can say hi from me too," Jostein says.

Jostein lopes down Rosenkrantz' gate and in the lift up to Dek-Rek he hatches a plan he intends to follow. He walks straight into Rudjord's office without knocking. The MD is sitting behind a desk and carries on signing a pile of papers, probably contracts worth several thousand. He doesn't bat an eyelid. It is hugely annoying.

But it is also educative, if you can view it as such, and Jostein has learned to do this, little or nothing passes him by. This is the lesson he learns in MD Rudjord's office: Never allow yourself to be caught off guard, and if you do, under no circumstances show it.

"Happy with the pics, Jostein?"

This is also a blow. He, Jostein Melsom, was supposed to open the negotiations.

"You took only one photograph," Jostein says.

"That was all we needed."

"It's a con."

Now at last Rudjord puts down his pen and gazes at Jostein.

"Please do not use that word."

"Which one?"

"The c-word. We never use it. Never. Do you understand?"

"If it isn't a con, what is . . .?"

"There, you said it again. We obviously have a serious communication problem, Jostein."

"So what is it then?"

"Advertising."

Rudjord signs the last documents. Jostein ventures a step closer. At least he has to carry out the last part of his plan, even if the first went down the tube. He takes a deep breath and launches himself.

"I want another fifty kroner or I'll tell all."

Rudjord does four more signatures, then he looks up.

"All? What do you mean by that, Jostein?"

"The cream doesn't work."

"How do you know?"

Jostein lifts his fringe.

"Look at my forehead. It's even worse."

Rudjord prefers not to and gives the matter some thought.

"Unless it's you, Jostein. Maybe you don't work. Have you considered that?"

Jostein is confused. There is so much he hasn't considered. Most things simply haven't occurred to him yet. He sticks to his guns, however.

"I'm in the permanent employ of Henry Vilder," he says.

Rudjord raises one eyebrow.

"Chocolate Vilder?"

"Among many other things."

"How is he?"

"Not bad by and large, Rudjord. But he's good to me."

Rudjord takes out his wallet and opens it.

"What about a compromise?"

Jostein is on his guard.

"A what?"

"A compromise, Jostein. We meet in the middle. It happens all the time in business."

It is Jostein's turn to give the matter some thought. He says:

"Not exactly in the middle, a bit before, as there was no *After*, I reckon."

Rudjord gives Jostein thirty kroner.

"Let's say this transaction remains between us and this matter is now off the agenda for ever, as I hope your spots soon will be?"

Jostein nods slowly while counting the three notes another time and intuits, without knowing quite for sure, that he has the upper hand.

"If it is to remain between us, I need five more."

Rudjord throws a five-krone coin to Jostein.

"You can find your own way out, right? After all, you found your way in."

Rudjord sits back behind his desk and when he looks up the infernal youth has gone and the door is left open. Maj Kristoffersen appears in the doorway. Has she lost weight? She seems unkempt, almost ungroomed. This is not like her. He beckons her closer.

"Has Jostein been here?" she asks.

"If it is our spotty friend you're referring to, yes, he has certainly been here. Please, would you mind closing the door?"

Maj does so and stands beside it as though wanting to be able to beat a quick retreat if necessary.

"So it *was* him I saw. Did—?"

"Let me put it like this: we will, I think, *never* use him again. He really is a tough cookie."

"Yes, he can be a bit wrong-headed. His hearing's not so good."

Rudjord stands up and laughs.

"That wasn't my impression. But at least I do have to admit the boy has a certain talent in the noble art of business negotiation. He's gone to a good school with Vilder."

"Vilder? *That* Vilder?"

"Yes. Henry Vilder. Who lost his daughter. Suicide. We shouldn't talk ill of the living, but he's a cynic of the worst order. Is everything alright, Maj?"

"Yes. And you? Did you have a nice summer?"

"Sadly there's too much nature in the mountains. Are you sure?"

"We went to Hurdal, all three of us. And Jesper was in Copenhagen. Only for one day though. Tomorrow he starts school again, fortunately. It'll be good to get back to normality. That's what I think."

Rudjord waits until Maj has finished speaking.

"Are you sure everything's alright, Maj? You seem . . ."

"I've been thinking about the Singer campaign. And I have a suggestion. I—"

"Maj . . ."

"I don't think Singer should sign off when the machine has been bought and paid for. They should offer the customer a home service, help with maintenance, inform them about new technology and generally let the customer become a member of what we might call the Singer family."

"The Singer family. I like that."

"I know this is as much a business model as a campaign, but nevertheless. I think it's worth a try."

Rudjord gazes at this unusual woman who generates more

ideas in the course of a morning than her husband had during the eight years he was employed with the agency.

"Now I understand why you look a little windblown, Maj. It takes a lot out of you to come up with such genius. I'm a bit dizzy myself. And now we deserve a drink."

"It's a bit early for me. I—"

"Nonsense. We shouldn't let these moments pass unheeded."

Rudjord walks over to the drinks cabinet and pours two whiskies. Maj has to grab the back of the chair. Is it so obvious? Can people see the state she is in? She lets go as Rudjord turns and passes her a whisky. They clink glasses. He drains his in one draught. She just sips. It burns her tongue. She doesn't like spirits. Then Maj does the same, empties her glass, she has nothing to lose. She shivers. Rudjord laughs and re-fills their glasses.

"Do you know what this means? It means Dek-Rek can probably run a campaign for them for years."

"Yes, and we'll become members of the Singer family too."

"You've taken the very words from my mouth. *Skål!* I'm really looking forward to telling them about this. We'll simply blow them away."

Maj empties the next glass and gives it to Rudjord, who for a moment, to his surprise, thinks she wants even more.

"May I be so bold as to ask for a few hours off?" she says.

"Take the rest of the day. My goodness. And tomorrow too. Just make sure you have the minutes ready for the Saturday meeting."

Maj leaves, closes the door after her, fetches her coat from its usual place and nods to the men, who are sluggish and suntanned after the summer or whatever. She can't remember taking the lift down when she is standing in Rosenkrantz' gate and a taxi has stopped by the kerb in front of her. She slides onto the back seat, tells the driver to go to Nordraaks gate and rolls down the window. The next moment they are outside the house at the top of the hill. The driver turns to her for the fare. She gives him enough, without waiting for any change, and walks through the garden, where autumn is so plain to see: the apples ripening. The door to the antiquarian shop is closed, there is no light on. Perhaps they are still in Nesodden? She rings the bell by the other door, too weak to tidy her hair or dry her tears. She isn't crying, though. It was the wind. Someone is at home anyway. Margrethe opens the door.

"I'm pregnant," Maj says.

Margrethe ushers her into the kitchen and they sit at the table.

"What did you say?"

Maj looks up.

"You've got a nice tan. You look good. Wish I did."

"Are you pregnant, Maj?"

"I haven't had a period for three months. And I'm not that old."

"Rome then."

"What else?"

Maj quickly places a hand over her mouth and looks down again. Margrethe leans across the table.

"Olav isn't at home, so you can talk freely."

"Yes, Rome."

"How is it possible to be so stupid?"

"I know. I know, Margrethe. How is it possible?!"

"My dear friend, have you been drinking?"

"Rudjord gave me a whisky."

Margrethe gets to her feet.

"You didn't say anything to him, did you?"

"You're the only person who knows."

"You don't know for sure yet."

"Oh, yes I do. I know."

Margrethe sits back down. They are silent. Then she says:

"You said it was the best week of your life."

"Does that have any significance now?"

"You're the only one who can judge that, Maj."

Maj hides her face in her hands.

"I'm over forty."

"You said just now you weren't old yet."

"And he has a family in Italy."

"What? A family?"

"Wife and children. Always has had."

"Did you know that?"

"Not until I got back home."

"The shameless swine! He's been living the life of a gay bachelor and then he has the audacity to invite you—"

"Stop it. It's my fault. Mine. I should've known."

Maj didn't think she could sink any lower. She could. Her life is over, life as she has known it. Margrethe takes both of her hands in hers.

"Do you want the child?"

Maj is unable to raise her gaze.

"Do I have any choice?"

"Yes, you do, Maj."

AUTUMN AND SUMMER GARDENS

Jesper is walking past the mayonnaise factory and Manfred's bakery. He has his hands in his pocket and his fists clenched. He has made up his mind. He is going to finish with Trude. Finish? He doesn't even know if they are still together. He is with another girl. He isn't with anyone. But he has been with someone else this summer. He can't lie. Is it lying if you don't say anything? Is omitting to tell the truth also a lie? How long can you live with such a secret? Jesper stops. He hasn't just messed things up. He has done something hurtful. He will never drink Coke again. Industrigata is a vale of shadows. He glances over his shoulder. Is Bror after him? Will he be casting glances over his shoulder for the rest of his life? Jesper carries on down Bogstadveien, where those fortunates who have a tan display it. They carry their holidays like a mask. Sirens tear them from their dreams for a few moments. It was only a false alarm and they find their place in the future again. Jesper is dragging the past after him. He changes his mind. He will walk to Jørgen Moes gate, between the church and the fire station. It interests him: what does a place look like after you have left it? There isn't even a detour. All roads lead to Trude. He hastens his pace. The fire engine is reversing into its spot in the immense garage; the hoses are being rolled up. The clock on the church tower says ten minutes past seven. Otherwise he can't see any difference. The pavements are the same, the cobblestones too. He goes into the hallway of the block. Now he can see a difference. Enzo Zanetti's name is no longer there. It has been removed. That is how it is. If you have let down another person you lose your name. No-one can shout your name anymore. You are alone for ever. You won't find your way home. Jesper shouts anyway: *Enzo!* No-one can answer either. He runs out, but not fast enough to catch the tram in Holtegata. It makes no sound on the sharp bend by the school. Perhaps someone has oiled the rails. Perhaps the world has lost its sound. He walks through Urra Park instead. Someone is following him. He daren't turn round. There are two of them. He can tell by their footsteps, the rhythm. The ground reverberates beneath him. The white clouds move faster. They are gaining on him. Perhaps they are also just out for a walk. It is possible. Everything is, perhaps. Nothing is sure. What was it Søster said? Now Bror is going to give you a beating. Jesper will have to hide. He will have to go so far away that no-one can follow him. But they are still behind him when he gets to Riddervolds Plass. Jesper ups his pace. Those behind him do the same. They aren't out for a walk. By Vestheim School he takes a left and walks through the abandoned plot at the bottom of Oscars gate, a short cut to Solli. He is making a trap for himself. He should have kept to more crowded areas. He knows. Nevertheless this is what he is doing. He is making a trap for himself. And he has time to think: it was already made a long time ago. He is just walking into it. Jesper stops. He may as well get this over and done with. Otherwise he will have to wait for the rest of his life. One holds him from behind; the other comes round and stands in front of him: Jesper has never seen the boy before. It isn't Bror. Perhaps they are his gang. Perhaps they are boys he has sent. He can probably send people all over the world to deliver a beating. But the boy looks more like some greasy slalom skier from Røa. However, he has a good punch on him. Jesper tries to wriggle free. The blow doesn't hit his nose, but his left eye. Jesper remains upright, not unaided, because he is being held. The boy holding him says:

"Break his fingers."

The slalom skier hits him a second time, in exactly the same place, his eye. This is probably just the warm-up.

"If you touch my cousin one more time, you'll die," he says.

Jesper can barely speak.

"Your cousin?"

"Yes, my cousin. Do we have to smash your hand as well before you get it?"

"I don't know any cousin."

The boy becomes unsure of himself and steps back.

"Tor Halvorsen. You punched him in the school playground."

"That wasn't me."

"And you threatened him with a further beating when he was in a coma."

Jesper starts laughing. It hurts. He is guilty anyway. Everyone is guilty of something. Everyone deserves something. Now, however, he is even with Jostein. They are quits. He doesn't owe Jostein anything. This is how things happen. Everything is done for someone else. Stine, Jostein, Jesper, Trude. The grip on him from behind slackens. The boys run the other way. Jesper falls to his knees. His eye is leaking down his cheek. That is how it feels. Drips fall to the ground, small, jagged splinters, dust, half of all he used to be able to see is broken, like a mirror. He wishes it had been Bror. Then it would have been over. Now he has to wait. The punishment is never-ending. He will have to suffer again every single day. He struggles to his feet and staggers over to Solli Plass. The casual summer crowds give him a wide berth. Faces turn after him as the tram passes; apathetic pigs on their way to the scaffold. He can barely see. A car screeches to a halt in Bygdøy allé. The driver rolls down his window and gives him an earful. Eventually Jesper finds Inkognito Terrasse. Outside the entrance to Trude's place there is a lorry. Her father is sitting in a chair and giving directions to two men carrying a desk between them. It is heavy; they can hardly swing it onto the back of the lorry. Jesper holds the corner of his shirt over his eye and would prefer not to meet the correspondent who interviewed the Shah of Persia. Is he moving out? Or is he just taking his desk with him to where he is going to work? Jesper can't work this out. Pain is a wall his thoughts are beating against. They can't break through. They can't make any progress. Now he can ask

Trude's father what the devil's piano means. No, he should ask Old Shark. He knows. *In the winter it moves by sleigh, While in the spring it rolls on wheels.* Jesper walks round to the other side of the house where he can see Trude's room. He throws a stone up at the window, misses by four metres, tries again and only hits when he doesn't aim. He hides behind the hedge and waits. Then Trude is there. She looks out. Jesper ducks down when her mother also appears. Trude draws the curtains and turns to her.

"I don't want to move."

"Please, Trude. I thought we'd agreed."

"*You* agreed."

Her mother goes closer to the window and peeps between the curtains.

"Is there someone out there?"

"I think it was a bird flying into the window."

"Ugh, don't say that. Now I'm starting to cry."

"Couldn't Pappa live in Stockholm and visit us at weekends?"

"No, that's out of the question."

Trude sits down on the sofa bed and swings her feet onto the table.

"I didn't think you cared so much about Pappa."

"What are you saying? Keep your voice down. And take your feet off the table."

"He can't hear. He's swearing at the removal men. Besides, it's my table."

"That was really unkind, Trude. Really naughty of you. How could I not care about Pappa?"

"It just always seems like that."

"Well, I'm not talking about always. No two people love each other *all the time.*"

"Just now and then, as it were?"

"Anyway, it's nothing to do with you. Come on, start packing."

"I'm not packing until I leave. *If* I leave."

Trude's mother sighs.

"Is this Jesper boy the reason you can't tear yourself away?"

"Don't even go there. And I know why you want to go to Stockholm. So that you're nearer to Gotland where you can meditate and eat vegetables and be alone."

Trude's mother sits down on the sofa and wraps an arm around her daughter.

"Either you forget him or he waits until you're back. And Stockholm's not so far away that we can't invite him over."

"I don't know if we're even together."

"Why not? Has he done something, Trude?"

"He thinks I'm disgusting."

Trude's mother laughs and kisses her on the cheek.

"Disgusting? You? Then he'd better think again. Disgusting?"

Trude says nothing and takes her feet down from the table. Trude's mother looks at her daughter and knows. She is too young. She doesn't want to ask, it isn't necessary, but she can't stop herself.

"Have you—"

Trude cuts her off.

"No! And so what?"

Trude's mother knows she hasn't paid enough attention to Trude recently, perhaps she doesn't even pay attention to people she loves, only herself, and wants them to love her even more. She is tormented.

"Pappa's going tomorrow to get the flat in shape. You know how important this is for him. No, perhaps you don't. But he's getting on and won't have many more opportunities abroad after this one."

"I know it's important for Pappa."

"And then we'll follow. In the meantime we can have a little girlie chat."

Trude stands up and throws the sofa cushions on the floor.

"Oh, right. Welcome back."

"Are you going to bed already?"

"School starts tomorrow. Didn't you know?"

Trude's mother goes to the door, hurt, she is forever being misunderstood, and she would so like to understand others.

"Strictly speaking, you don't need to. Go to school, I mean. But perhaps you really want to. What do I know? I know nothing of course."

"I'd like to say goodbye to the class, alright?"

"What, Trude?"

"Tell them I'm leaving."

Trude's mother turns and smiles.

"Yes, you do that. Then we can go to the school garden and pick some food for our long trip."

Trude looks up.

"Do you always have an ulterior motive?"

"No, why?"

"I want to be left in peace."

The door closes.

But Trude doesn't have any peace. She lies awake and tries to define her feelings, but they won't let themselves be defined. The following morning her father has departed with the desk and the first load. Her mother is making tea and has her back to her. The music on the radio is cringeworthy. Trude gives her a peck on the cheek and goes. She doesn't bump into Jesper. She doesn't see him in Jacob Aalls gate either and he isn't in the playground. All she sees is the others. New gangs have formed. Friends have changed sides. Girlfriends have switched allegiances. This is the long summer's doing. Summer is everything that has happened since school. But she can't see Jesper. What do the others see when they see Trude? What do they think has happened since they last met? That Jesper has broken up with her? Why can't they think that it was she who broke up the relationship? The bell rings. Trude waits until she is the last in the playground. He still hasn't come. Then she goes to her new classroom and has to take pot luck with a desk, one in the middle row. It is the only one free. She smiles at the others, is given a hug, Axel whistles, everything is as before, nothing is the same. It is as she thought. Jesper has finished with her. And he didn't even bother to tell her. She places the timetable in front of her. The door opens. For a moment she thinks it is Jesper. It is Ramm, their teacher. Everyone stands up. He stands by the desk and surveys the class. He is suntanned and even thinner. Soon there won't be any holes left on the belt around his waist. Otherwise, though, he seems to be back to his old self. He has been in Germany for two months in the heatwave to help the country get back on its feet.

"Cologne cathedral," he says, "Cologne cathedral didn't receive a scratch in the war. It sought refuge in heaven with all its spires as the bombs fell and the town lay in ruins around it. Give that some thought, dear students, and let that be a sign to you. Is anyone missing?"

Axel puts up his hand.

"Alf Iversen isn't here."

"Who?"

The class laughs.

"Jesper Kristoffersen, sir. It's his version of *auf Wiedersehen*."

"You don't need to explain old witticisms to me, Axel. Has anyone had any contact with him?"

Everyone turns to Trude, who looks down at her empty timetable.

"Perhaps he's at home, practising," she says.

Ramm nods.

"It's nice that you want to spend your last days with us, Trude. And if Auf Wiedersehen comes we'll have to fetch an extra desk for him. Who's the class monitor?"

Trude puts her hand in the air.

Ramm nods and carries on.

"There are dark clouds on the horizon, however. King Haakon's eighty-fifth birthday was celebrated quietly on the third of August because of the state of His Majesty's health. We have to be prepared for the worst."

At that moment there is a knock at the door and everyone looks in that direction. It is Jesper. He has his bag slung over his shoulder, as is meet and proper, and he is wearing sunglasses. But for all that he doesn't seem particularly cool. Standing there with his eyes hidden behind the dark, crooked glasses, he looks more like a halfwit. Ramm moves towards him with his arms outstretched.

"Let's give our pianist a round of applause."

The girls clap; the boys bang their desks.

Jesper looks at Trude, a shadow in the middle row, but he can see only part of her. She isn't clapping. He should take that as a sign and about-turn. It isn't even a sign. It is obvious to everyone: she won't clap for him. Besides, there are no desks free. He should never have come. He should have stayed at home. He is surplus to requirements. He is done for. He is an outsider. What else? He has even got a medical report to say that he is sensitive. What is he doing here in such a state?

"And now you can take off your sunglasses, Kristoffersen."

"I'd prefer not to."

"You'd prefer not to? Can you give us one good reason why not?"

Jesper has to think on his feet.

"It's a free country," he says.

"Don't abuse the language. There's a difference between liberty and taking liberties. You'll have to think of something better."

Jesper is on shaky ground.

"I have a right to wear sunglasses."

Ramm laughs heartily.

"A right? You're misusing words again. To be more precise, you're trivialising them. Do you understand? A right has to cost something. Hungarians and Yugoslavs have the right to talk about rights. Do you understand?"

He turns to the class.

"Can anyone help Jesper with a good argument?"

Axel would like to contribute.

"Perhaps he's just trying to look tough. Or he's lost his mind?"

Scattered laughter.

Ramm examines Jesper again.

"Is there anything in what Axel says? Are you following some American fashion and trying to make yourself appear interesting?"

"No."

"So you've lost your mind?"

"I damaged my eyes while I was practising in the summer."

"I see. And how can a pianist damage his eyes?"

"He can fall off his stool. Or have eye strain."

Ramm sighs and takes a step closer.

"Would it help if we drew the curtains?"

"I doubt it."

Ramm, to be frank, doesn't quite know what to believe. He is sceptical, but gives Jesper the benefit of the doubt. He would like to snatch the wretched glasses from him, but controls himself. Furthermore, Ramm likes Jesper, as indeed he likes all his pupils, Ramm wants nothing but the best for them.

"Is the intention perhaps that you should also wear women's glasses?" he asks.

This is a brilliant start to the school year. The whole class laughs, no, not quite the whole class. Trude doesn't. Jesper doesn't. All of a sudden he loathes Ramm. His friendliness is no more than barely concealed preening; cheap jokes cannot disguise the arrogance. Jesper takes a deep breath and places a hand on his brow.

"Women's glasses? I didn't realise. I can barely see. But thank you for telling me."

"Take a seat."

"There aren't any."

"You can see that much then?"

"I still have some night vision."

Ramm turns back to the class, weary; he has a sudden sense that he is being treated like an idiot, that his affability is being confused with weakness and fawning, in short, this is all taking too long. For a moment he has to think about Elisabeth, he has to think about her to retain his composure, that is how it is now, he has to think of the worst to keep himself on the rails. He clears his throat.

"Can anyone help Jesper go and get a desk?"

Trude stands up and heads for the door. She also receives a round of applause and shouts of encouragement. Jesper leaves his bag and reluctantly follows her down to the resources room in the cellar. She switches on the light and eyes him.

"Have you lost it or what?"

"What do you mean?"

"Wearing sunglasses. In school."

"They're Stine's. I couldn't find any others."

"They're broken too."

"They've been repaired."

The desks are stacked against one wall; the chairs against the other. Trude takes one of each. Jesper sits down. The chair is too high. Or the desk is too low. He might also have gained a few centimetres in height. Anyway, it is all wrong. Trude changes the chair. It is better, but it isn't good.

"Have you had a good summer?" she asks.

"I went to Copenhagen with Jostein and his father."

"Jostein says hi."

"Have you met him?"

"Yes. Great pics in the women's magazine. Or at least one of them."

"His father was caught smuggling in Svinesund."

"You weren't, though?"

"Me? No. Why would I be? It had nothing to do with me."

Trude sits on his lap.

"Not even a blue dress?"

Jesper doesn't know what to do with his hands.

"No. What do you mean?"

"Jostein told me."

"What about?"

"He said you almost bought a blue dress."

423

"Bloody Jostein. The big mouth."

"So it's true?"

"I almost bought it for my mother. OK? She wanted one like it years ago. But it was too expensive. Anyway, I didn't know what size she was. Because she's been depressed this summer and has put on weight."

"Right."

"I don't think she's *that* fat."

Trude is sitting on his lap, completely still, and now she doesn't know what to do with her hands. Then she does. She removes his sunglasses. His left eye is gummed up and swollen. It can't see. It looks like a ripe plum with a split skin.

"What happened?"

Jesper turns away.

"Bumped my head against the hot-water tank in the bathroom."

"Very likely. Now tell me, Jesper. Did someone beat you up?"

"I was attacked in Oscars gate."

"What were you doing there?"

"Does that matter? Nothing."

"Who did it?"

"No idea. Some gang."

"Did they steal anything?"

"No."

"Why did they do it then?"

"Perhaps they think I'm no good at playing the piano?"

Is this the flippancy he inherited from his father, the humour that kept Ewald Kristoffersen afloat? No, he is just acting the part. He is bluffing. Flippancy isn't part of Jesper's make-up, it isn't in his repertoire; on the contrary, he suffers from worry, remorse and a conscience, which is made of heavier material, like the lead on fishing lines. Trude can hear it from miles away.

"Are you frightened?" she asks.

"Why?"

"Your heart's beating."

"Thank goodness."

"I can hear it from here."

"Well? You're sitting on my lap, aren't you?"

"I think you should go home, Jesper."

"What about my bag?"

"I can get it and tell Ramm."

They stand up. Jesper puts the chair on the desk with the legs pointing upwards. It is a symbol of absence, skiving, holiday and death. Trude carries all the furniture up the stairs. He watches her. Her skirt reaches down to her knees. Her calves and ankles are thin and tanned in her white shoes. Her hair has bleached in the sun. He puts his sunglasses back on as she disappears around the landing and her footsteps sound like soft thuds down the corridor above him. When she returns she is carrying his bag.

"What did you tell Ramm?"

"You have to go to the doctor's. Do you promise me you'll go to the doctor's?"

Jesper nods and takes the bag.

"And you?"

"Yes, what about me?"

"Did you have a nice summer?"

"Maybe I missed you."

"Maybe?"

"But not anymore."

Can Trude see it in him? Is everything you have done, and especially what you have done wrong, visible? Is it written all over his face in thick letters? Yes, she can. It is obvious. He can see by her expression that she can.

"Me too," he says.

"Me too what?"

"Maybe I missed you."

"But not any longer?"

"*I* didn't say that."

Trude takes a step closer, but changes her mind and stops.

"If you're trying to hide something, those stupid sunglasses are not helping," she says.

For his part, Jesper can't get out of his mind the time the watch at the bottom of Søster's bag showed: *twenty-two minutes past twelve*. All the watches in the whole wide world show twenty-two minutes past twelve. Now he can hear his heart beating too. And now he could ask her what the devil's piano is.

"I've been with another girl," he says.

Trude stands motionless, her arms down beside her.

"Been with another girl?"

"In the summer holidays."

"Why are you telling me?"

Jesper loses the thread.

"Why?"

"Are you doing it just to be nasty?"

"You said we should tell each other everything."

Trude raises a hand, hesitates and strokes Jesper's sore cheek with a finger. It would have been better if she had slapped him. Then she runs back to the classroom. Jesper drags his bag into the schoolyard, where the sky has clouded over in the meantime. He regrets every single word he said. All words come out wrong, however right they are. Why didn't he tell her he loved her? Loved? Has Jesper the right to use that word after this summer? Is he even worthy of articulating it in his mouth, he wonders in his youthful earnestness, and this is what he has inherited from Ewald, not flippancy, not the jargon, not the advertising, but the earnestness, which wasn't given the chance to manifest itself in his father and which the son has the bad habit of revealing. Are making love and falling in love the same thing? We use the same language when we lie as when we tell the truth; we just move the words around. When we play out of tune it is the same notes as always; they are just in a different order. Jesper feels like chucking his bag in the drinking fountain and screaming at the sky. He feels like tearing out the rest of his eye and stamping on it. Instead he continues to Kirkeveien and down to Melsom the butcher's. The Valcrema advert is framed and hanging on the short wall in the window. Many people stop to examine it more closely. And then it is only a hop and a skip into the shop. This is Jostein's idea. He has so many. Some wags hung the same pictures on the nearest lamp posts, but swapped round the *Before* and *After*. Jostein tore them down this morning.

"The sunglasses suit you," Fru Melsom says.

"Mm."

"Maybe you'll get your picture in a magazine one day."

"Maybe."

"But there's no sun now, Jesper. It's raining."

He doesn't need to look outside to know it is bucketing down. He can't actually remember when it started.

"Is Jostein in?"

Fru Melsom glances towards the office, where Herr Melsom is doing the accounts after a poor holiday, and lowers her voice.

"Jostein's at Henry Vilder's in Slemdal."

Jesper goes home. He is drenched before he even gets that far. He keeps his sunglasses on. He likes the idea of sunglasses in the rain. No-one is at home. The flat has its own sound, an echo of the summer light, which makes the rooms smaller, and smallest of all is his room, the hall. There is barely space for the sofa bed. Soon there won't be any space for him. Nevertheless, he is relieved, almost brimming with confidence. The sounds haven't left him after all. But just as quickly he is dejected again: what should he do with them? He drinks a glass of water in the kitchen, where there is a message for him: *Promise me you'll go to Dr Lund with that eye! Mamma.* Everyone is nagging him. It is suffocating. Everyone is nagging him from all sides. He can't move his arms. He can't breathe. He goes into the sitting room, looks up Henry Vilder in the telephone directory and dials the number. It takes quite a while before anyone answers: an impatient drawl he hardly recognises.

"Vilder here."

"Is Jostein there?"

"Who am I talking to?"

"Jesper Kristoffersen. Jostein's friend. I delivered Elisabeth's shoes to your house at that time."

Henry Vilder puts the receiver down beside the telephone and walks onto the terrace. The rain is passing. Jostein is standing by the pool with a net on a long pole and catching leaves. They have already begun to fall in Vilder's garden and it is still only August. It is the first autumn in his life. It is eternal. It has come to stay. And this youth, Jostein, will be there for ever with the net.

"It's for you," Vilder shouts.

Jostein drops the pole and hurries over to the terrace. He is heavy-limbed. He is carrying too much weight. What is it we say? He has been "eating the profits". He will have to give up sweets. It is no good being podgy in this company. If you want to make it in this life you have to be as fat as Ollie or as thin as Stan, never somewhere in the middle. You will get nowhere. The middle is the quietest place in the world. And then he will have to get rid of those spots. He can't walk around gentlefolk with that forehead. He would frighten the living daylights out of them. Jostein is good to have, but bad news for your appetite.

"For me?"

"Yes, for you. That's what I said. You should never ask someone to repeat a message, however incomprehensible it is."

"Sorry."

"And you can tell your friend if he doesn't introduce himself the interlocutor has the right to hang up."

Jostein runs into the living room and forgets to take off his shoes. Henry Vilder sighs and looks up at the much too clear, blue sky. He is suddenly gripped by a desire for what he has hitherto despised and looked down on, the middle, ordinariness, meals and sleep, the happy medium that shines at us from birth until death. He clenches his fists behind his back and digs his nails in his palms.

"You're crying, Vilder."

Jostein is in front of him again. Vilder wipes his eyes with the back of his hand.

"Tell me something I don't know."

"I have to ask you for some time off."

"Why's that?"

"My best pal's in a fix."

"That's a good enough reason, Jostein."

"Thank you."

"But first you have to do me a favour."

"What is it?"

"Come with me to visit Elisabeth's mother."

Henry Vilder spruces himself up: white shirt, blue blazer, light-grey trousers and suede shoes. Jostein will have to go as he is. They walk down to Vinderen Psychiatric Clinic without saying another word. Fru Vilder is playing badminton with an elderly nurse in the garden. Badminton is said to be good for patients. Henry Vilder sits down on a bench some distance away watching her. Jostein sits beside him, as noiselessly as he can. Fru Vilder is wearing a grey outfit. Her movements are heavy and slow. She rarely or never hits the shuttlecock and doesn't have the energy to pick it up either. The nurse has to do that. She shows no signs of impatience. She is wearing the clinic's white uniform. Fru Vilder serves and misses. The nurse ducks under the net again, grabs the shuttlecock and pats it not too high, not too low, back to Fru Vilder, who slowly draws her racquet through the air with both hands, but hits nothing but the still light and consigns it to the shadows beneath the trees. It is the woman he met as a young student at Oslo Commerce School, later married in Ris church and with whom he lived for a whole world war, who never uttered a single complaint, not even when they didn't have any further children after Elisabeth. Instead they gave their daughter all their love. Perhaps it hadn't been enough. Perhaps their love had been too little. Now she is a different person. Now she has gone too. But what Henry Vilder pays most attention to is the garden. It is still green; the lawn, the hedge and the treetops are green. The leaves aren't falling. In this garden it is always summer. Summer has got stuck here. Summer is the middle of the year. You cannot get any closer to defining it.

"Wait here," he says.

Henry Vilder walks down to the badminton players, who drop their racquets and leave the shuttlecock on the grass. First he greets his wife, Elisabeth's mother. It is like a meeting between two old acquaintances who haven't seen each other for many years. Then he chats with the nurse, who gives him her racquet, and while the bereaved couple start to play, at the same slow tempo, with the same lack of purpose, she approaches Jostein, glares at him and says firmly:

"Come with me."

Jostein is unwilling.

"I'm not crazy," he says.

"No, you've only got loads of spots. Come with me."

Jostein follows her, despite his reluctance, into the stately building, more reminiscent of a palace than a nuthouse, just like Gaustad. Perhaps it is to make the nutters believe they are kings and queens. But then the nutters would only become even nuttier. They continue down a staircase and along a corridor. There is a smell of green soap, or something stronger, maybe lye, medicines or petrol. In one room there are three men standing around a carpenter's bench. This must be the woodwork room for the nutters. There is a woman in a bed, held fast with straps, singing a Christmas carol in August. The nurse stops at the last door and turns to Jostein.

"By the way, we don't use the word *crazy*."

"What do you say then?"

"Lost."

"Is that all?"

"And then we try to bring them back home."

The nurse opens the door and lets Jostein into a kind of laboratory. Along the walls there are glass cabinets full of jars and tubes. In the middle of the floor there is a chair. He sits down. The nurse lifts his fringe and studies his forehead at close distance.

"Will you be able to bring Fru Vilder home?" he asks.

"That's the question."

"Where is she lost?"

"Inside herself, Jostein. Have you had these dreadful spots long?"

Jostein is thinking: If my mother or father died, perhaps both of them, would I be as sad as Fru Vilder? He cannot imagine this. But if Jesper, or Stine, died, yes, he would also end up getting lost, and much further away than just inside himself.

"For a year. And three weeks."

"And you've squeezed them?"

"What else should I do?"

"Leave them alone."

"And then I used Valcrema."

"That's not much use."

"The advert said it worked."

"Don't believe adverts. They generally promise more than they can deliver."

"No-one knows that better than me," Jostein says.

The nurse doesn't ask for any elucidation of this comment and goes to a cabinet, takes out a variety of tubes and containers, pours a selection into a dish and stirs. Then she returns to Jostein, tells him to close his eyes and smears an ointment over his forehead, which at first smarts, almost burns, but then feels mild and soothing, like a hot bath, and cools him down, so much so that he is almost asleep on the chair. The nurse puts the rest of the ointment into a jar with a screw top and gives it to him.

"Rub this onto your forehead every day until there is none left. Don't squeeze the spots. That will only make them worse. And don't eat too much chocolate either."

"I'll tell Henry. He's the one who gives me the treats."

"Are you a friend of the family?"

"I'm with Elisabeth."

The nurse, the stiff, old lady who has spent half of her life working with the dark side of human nature, turns sharply to Jostein, on the point of saying something, and then refrains. She has heard worse. If, however, he says it again, she will have to give him some guidance. They go back to Vilder, who is waiting on the steps, alone, with a racquet in each hand. He passes them to the nurse. Then Vilder and Jostein accompany each other down to the street. The white shuttlecock is left on the grass.

"What did it cost?" Vilder asks.

"What did what cost?"

"Think about it. The treatment of course."

"Nothing."

"Did you ask?"

"No."

"How can you know it's free then?"

"I didn't pay anything, did I?"

Vilder sighs and waves away an insect.

"Don't let people work for you free of charge, Jostein. You'll only make enemies. You owe them a favour. And you must always have more friends than enemies."

"Of course."

"But let it go this once. After all, it was in her working time and she's paid by the hospital while I entertain my wife, who is her patient."

"She gave me an ointment as well."

Vilder lights a cigarette and looks up at the same sky that is never the same.

"Did the nurse say anything about her?"

"She said she was lost."

"Lost?"

"And they're trying to bring her home."

Vilder blows smoke up into the light and drops the half-smoked cigarette to the ground.

"I don't think she wants to come back home, Jostein."

"No?"

"She's too far away."

"It's not certain that she's so far away."

Vilder grinds the cigarette under the tip of his shoe and stands for a while in the shade from the green park.

"Now you've done me a favour," he says.

Vilder gives Jostein two tenners, takes off his blazer, slings it over his shoulder and walks towards Vinderen. He might have a beer at Jeppe's bar. He might buy a new racquet in the sports shop, one that is lighter and easier to hold. He could also do both. Jostein shoots off in the opposite direction, past the Norwegian Railway School and Vestre Aker cemetery, which is so steep that the dead have to clear the paths themselves in winter. Then he turns down Kirkeveien, between the blocks of flats, and over to Gørbitz gate, where Jesper opens the door for Jostein before he has a chance to ring. They sit in the kitchen. Jostein is about to ask him about his shiner, but Jesper is quicker out of the blocks again and speaks in such a low, secretive voice that Jostein has to stretch across the table.

"They're after me, Jostein."

"Who are?"

"I can't tell you."

"Why not?"

"Don't ask me. Please."

"Is it the Frogner gang?"

"No."

"Who is it then? The Blacky gang?"

"I've fucked a girl in Hurdal. But that wasn't why."

Jostein sits up straight, crestfallen and fed up.

"Do you fuck all the time?"

"Of course I don't."

"What does Trude say to that?"

"And what did you tell Trude about the dress I showed you in Copenhagen?"

"I just said what happened. You were thinking of buying a dress for her, but you didn't have the money."

Jesper hides his face in his hands.

"Shit, shit, shit."

"Was that wrong too?"

After reflection Jesper seems to be in a better frame of mind: Trude was only pissed off because he said the dress was for his mother. She couldn't see anything in his face after all. He places his hands back on the table.

"You shouldn't tell others what we talk about," he says.

"Why did you fuck a girl in Hurdal?"

"Why?"

"When you have Trude. That's not right."

Jostein suddenly seems older, different at any rate, it must be the summer coming between them, turning us upside down.

Jesper is silent before answering.

"Because she wanted me to."

Jostein is silent too.

"How do you know?"

"Because. Don't ask so many bloody questions."

"What is it actually that you want to tell me? Have you put her in the club too?"

Jostein bursts into loud, oafish laughter.

Jesper hides his face in his hands again. He hadn't thought about this. He had forgotten to consider the worst possible scenario. And if the worst possible scenario becomes a fact he might as well bury himself. In that case, he will be either dead or a farmer in Hurdal.

"She has an older brother," he whispers.

"Was he the one who punched you?"

"Not this time. But maybe next time."

"Just because you fucked his sister?"

"They might break my fingers. Just as they did to Enzo."

"Did he fuck a girl in Hurdal too?"

"Only the chambermaids at the Bristol, you fool."

Jostein is reflective for a minute.

"I'm glad I'm not you," he says.

Jesper leans closer.

"You have to help me, Jostein."

"How?"

"Beat them up."

"What did you say?"

"You heard. Beat them up."

"Beat who up?"

"Her brother."

"You said them."

"There might be more of them."

Jostein is silent again. Then he stares at his pal, who seems more tormented than ever. It is not only his black eye, it is his whole body; he has the shakes.

"As a matter of fact, I'm no longer active in that field. I'm Henry Vilder's right-hand man now. I'm a businessman."

They hear Maj arrive. She is back too early. Jesper puts a finger to his lips. Jostein nods. They sit in silence. Maj doesn't see them until she is standing by the worktop gulping down water.

"Have you been to see Dr Lund already?" she asks.

"Not yet."

"Not yet? Why are you home from school then?"

"Why are you home from work?"

Maj sits down with them and sends Jostein a desperate expression.

"Can't you talk some sense into him?"

Jostein becomes nervous, wondering if he should affect some hearing problems.

"I truly don't know, Fru Kristoffersen."

She laughs mirthlessly.

"Last night he comes home from handball training, despite the fact that he said he would never play handball again. Someone elbowed him in the eye, not that I can understand how that would happen, and now he won't go and have it looked at."

"People are always getting injured playing handball, Fru Kristoffersen," Jostein says.

"You don't need to keep saying *Fru Kristoffersen*."

"Sorry."

Maj examines Jostein more closely, who is becoming increasingly nervous about saying the wrong thing, because she doesn't seem to be in a very good mood today, more the opposite, and she herself could do with a good combing and ironing. She isn't *presentable*. And Jesper isn't much help either. He is immersed in his own misery across the table and appears to have given up. The black eye is watering: purple, almost black, tears quiver on his cheek. The Kristoffersen family is at a low ebb. Maj continues to stare at Jostein.

"There's something about you," she says.

"Me? Not as far as I know. I haven't done anything."

"Now I know what it is."

"What is it?"

"The Valcrema has finally started to work."

"Do you mean it?"

"I do. It won't be long before you're exactly as in the advert."

"Before or After?" Jesper asks.

Maj turns to him, furious.

"Go and see Dr Lund now. Or do you want me to go with you? And you're not taking Stine's sunglasses. Is that clear? My God."

"Can't I just pop up to see Bjørn Stranger? He's supposed to be a doctor as well."

"He saved my life anyway," Jostein says.

"No, you can't. I don't want you to have anything to do with him."

Jostein gently places a hand on her shoulder.

"I'll go with Jesper to the doctor's, Fru Kristoffersen."

The boys get up and file into the hallway. The telephone rings. Maj dashes into the sitting room and takes the call. She dashes everywhere, as though rushing will turn back time and change her life. Maj hears the door slam and footsteps on the stairs. It is Margrethe on the telephone. She is speaking in a low voice, assuring Maj that she is still safe. How can you be safe? How can you know that you are choosing the right course of action? What are you left with after you subtract? What do you have if you add? She says she is sure. She whispers so as not to hear herself. No-one must hear. She is sure. Margrethe says she has set up a contact. It should take place next week. They ring off. Maj walks over to the window, calm now, quite calm. She watches the boys crossing Kirkeveien. Jostein will soon be as tall as his father, Jesper is thinner; he has become lean this summer. She starts to cry. She can cry when she is alone. She wishes that Jesper would turn and wave. Then he does. Her thoughts can reach him. Her thoughts touch him. He turns and raises an arm in a brief greeting. Maj imagines that the block of flats is a ship and now she is sailing away from everyone she loves. She waves. Jostein does the same and turns back to Jesper as they reach the entrance to Dr Lund's surgery.

"What's up with your mother actually?"

The waiting-room door is open. They sit down, each on a flimsy chair.

"Dunno. Don't want to know either."

They wait.

After some time Jostein says:

"There are two things I'd like to say to you, Jesper."

"What is it now?"

"First, you must never have more enemies than friends."

"Do you think I'm daft?"

"No. Why?"

"Do you think I want fewer friends than enemies?"

"How many have you got?"

Jesper hesitates, but it doesn't take long to count them up.

"One."

"And how many boys attacked you?"

"Two."

"There you go."

"Where?"

"You've got more enemies than friends. And second, never let anyone work for you free."

"Do you want some money for helping me too?"

"I'm only saying you shouldn't let people do you favours."

"Why not?"

"Because then you owe them something."

"Forget it. I can manage."

Jostein laughs.

"No, you can't. You wouldn't hurt a fly."

"Funny man."

"Besides you have to take care of your fingers. You can't fight with your hands behind your back."

Dr Lund finally opens the door and lets Jesper in. Jostein would like to accompany him, but he isn't allowed to. Jesper sits at the desk while Dr Lund stands up and examines him visually.

"You got a straight left, I see."

"Yes. Something like that."

"Did you put up a good defence?"

"I didn't have the chance."

"No-one will die from a black eye. It'll pass."

"My mother sent me."

"But you'll have to learn to defend yourself, Jesper."

Dr Lund clenches his fist and shows him a classic guard, shoulders up, head low. Then he leans across the desk and squeezes Jesper's eye a little, fetches a bottle of disinfectant and dabs away blood and pus. Minor beauty mark, but the eye will heal, he says. It's a fabulous muscle. Jesper has a revelation as Dr Lund is washing his hands. It comes to him in the form of a memory: the time Ewald took him up the clock tower in the City Hall. What he remembers best is not the loud chime, but the view of the harbour, Akers Mekaniske Verksted on one side and the America boat on the other. And in between lay the fjord that vanished in a haze beneath the sky. Was that why his father took him up the tower, not for him to hear, but to see?

"Is everything we say here confidential?" Jesper asks.

"Do you mean, have I taken the oath?"

"Yes. Sort of. Have you?"

Dr Lund sits down and looks at Jesper.

"Yes, I have. Unless the patient confesses to a serious crime."

"You won't say anything to my mam?"

"No, I won't say anything to your *mam*. Is there something you want to tell me, Jesper?"

Jesper is lost in thought for a moment, then rises to his feet and opens the door a fraction. Jostein is still there.

"You won't go, will you?"

Jostein looks up, shakes his head and says:

"And there was one more thing. Always say your name on the phone. Otherwise I'll hang up."

Jesper closes the door and Jostein can hear them talking inside, but he can't make out any words. They are speaking in such low voices, at least Jesper is. Anyway, he doesn't care. Instead he places his hand carefully, as carefully as he can, on his forehead, and can feel that it is smoother than it was this morning. The ointment is working already. He is almost happy. Soon he will be ecstatically happy. He has the jar in his pocket. Tomorrow he will rub in a bit more and then it won't be long before he is exactly as in the *After* picture, and the *Before* is finally a distant memory. What do you know, I got rid of my spots at the nuthouse, Jostein thinks.

HANDS

Dek-Rek is celebrating: Rudjord has signed a contract with Singer Sewing Machines. It means work for everyone for at least a year, probably more. Pop goes another cork, the champagne is flowing, it is the least they can do. It is going to be a long night. Tomorrow they can have a long lie-in. Tomorrow I can have a long lie-in, Maj thinks. Either she hears the City Hall bells chime four or someone is going to give a speech. She fetches her coat and takes the lift down. No-one notices. She has a sense of déjà vu. This day comes from an old calendar. She walks around the corner to the Grand Hotel and finds a taxi. It is an Indian summer. But the sun shines with a different glow and she isn't fooled: it is September. She asks the driver to take her to Markveien in Grünerløkka. Once there, she pays and gets out. She notices it immediately: there are different smells on this side of the city, different colours, more shadows. She hears the City Hall bells again. She isn't far away. You are never far away in this city. Ewald is following her. Half an hour has already passed. But the sound is different here; it is as though a beggar is in a backyard playing an organ grinder. She hasn't experienced this day after all. It is new. It doesn't exist yet. She can still retrieve it and start again. She walks across the street and into Beckers café. The men in the darkness lift their gaze for a second and carry on drinking. It can't be one of them. She sits by the window. The waiter gives her a menu. She asks for a glass of water. The waiter shrugs, leaves the menu and fetches a glass. She takes a gulp. She drains the glass. The door opens. In the sudden light from outside she recognises him. His coat reaches almost to the floor; as he raises his hat the thinning hair shines like a halo. When the door closes, she sees who it is:

Bjørn Stranger. She tries to hide, but then realises it is her he is looking for; it is him she is going to meet. Bjørn Stranger comes over to her table and sits down.

"I've had a word with Margrethe," he says.

Maj looks down.

"I see."

"I know you would prefer that someone else do this, but right now I'm the only person who can help you."

"I trust Margrethe," she says.

"You'll have to trust me too."

The waiter comes to their table and fills her glass from a jug. Bjørn Stranger gives him five kroner and waits until they are alone.

"You'll have to trust me too," he repeats.

"That was expensive water," Maj says.

"You don't need to worry."

"Worry?"

"Like all doctors I'm subject to the Hippocratic Oath."

"Even when you break the law?"

Bjørn Stranger laughs.

"Especially then. But I don't think we should speak about this. There's so much else we can speak about."

Maj looks down, it is much too warm in here for a coat and the cigarette smoke is making her eyes smart.

"I just want this over and done with," she whispers.

"Third month?"

"Soon be the fourth."

Bjørn Stranger looks at his watch and places two pills on the menu.

"In half an hour it is too late to have regrets."

"I don't have any."

"You can't know, Maj."

"Are you trying to talk me out of this?"

Bjørn Stranger shrugs.

"It's just what we say. So that I can also have a clear conscience."

"You too?"

Maj opens her bag and takes out a long, blank envelope. Bjørn Stranger stops her at once.

"Please, not here."

Maj closes her bag, swallows both pills with a draught of water and contemplates this young man, he is still a boy despite his thinning hair, however much he combs it, and his cheeks sag below his pale eyes.

"What are they for?" she asks.

"They're sedatives. They'll start working in about twenty minutes."

They sit in silence. Then Bjørn Stranger stands up and makes for the door. Maj follows him. The light is brighter, perhaps as a result of the pills or the darkness where they were sitting. They continue around the corner, still without speaking. Bjørn Stranger comes to a halt by an arched entrance in the side street.

"Now you can give me the money."

Maj hands him the envelope containing the banknotes, and again this jogs a memory. It reminds her of the Christmas bonus at Dek-Rek; this is Bjørn's autumn bonus. He stuffs the envelope in his inside pocket.

"Aren't you going to count it?"

"I'm sure there's no need."

Maj freezes, a shiver runs down her spine. Bjørn Stranger puts his arms around her. She closes her eyes and lets him.

"Is this where it happens?" she whispers.

"On the first floor. Ingunn Olsen. Her name's written on the door."

"Aren't you coming in?"

"No, it's not necessary."

"What happens afterwards?"

"You walk up to Birkelunden, take a taxi home and go to bed."

"Has it gone by then?"

"It will have gone in the course of the evening or night. If you bleed profusely or you're in a lot of pain, tell Jesper or Stine to fetch me."

Maj is incensed.

"I don't want them involved in this."

"Then come on your own, if you can."

Bjørn Stranger lets go of Maj, watches her enter through the archway and disappear into the shadows of the backyard. He waits to be sure she hasn't turned back. Everything is quiet and normal. The smell of dustbins mixes with that of meals being made on the upper floors. Then he strolls over to the banks of the Akerselva and sits down on a bench. He opens the envelope and counts the notes, ten of them, a little fortune, no, an immense fortune, if he views it soberly. He puts the money in a purse and stuffs it down the lining of his coat where he has had a special pocket sewn for personal possessions. He takes out a hip flask, checks his surroundings and has a gulp. Then he screws back the top. He can control himself. His hands aren't even shaking. Why should they? This is just an organised accident he has stage-managed, it is his little performance. And if you have regrets all you have to do is make another child. That is all it is. Child? There is no question of a human being before the twenty-eighth week. Until then the foetus is a foreign body, a germ, fungus. He laughs: *a non-being*. When does a human become a human? He takes another swig after all. All this talk about a soul. It torments him. Is the soul there before the human being? Is the soul, which has neither shape nor weight, waiting to be clad in flesh and blood? Or is the body there first, like a container for the soul? He remembers that his mother – when she was in a good mood – would come into his room, take his pencil case or whatever came to hand as she passed, raise it to the ceiling in a grand gesture and proclaim: *To be or not to be, that is the question, Bjørn!* There is nothing in between. It is either . . . or. And the soul is where memories and conscience can unfold. In addition, he may have done the world a favour. He may have prevented a new Hitler from growing up, or at least an Italian gigolo. Bjørn Stranger laughs. A hand grabs his shoulder. He looks up; the constable looks down.

"You are not allowed to sit here drinking."

Bjørn Starnger stands up.

"I saved the life of a boy in Kirkeveien," he says.

"But that doesn't permit you to sit here drinking."

"And you can't talk to me like that. I—"

"I'm talking quite normally. And if you don't move along now, I'll have to take you in a vehicle and you know what that means."

Bjørn Stranger bows imperceptibly, spins on his heel and crosses the bridge. He is loath to spend a night in the Hole. Beneath him flows the filthy river that splits the city in two. Drunks and bums sit on one bank. The constable tries to move them along too, but they loiter on the brown grass. Bjørn Stranger hurries on. He isn't like them. He is going to take that bloody police officer to court. He catches a taxi to Majorstua, pays generously and gets off outside Melsom the butcher's. He fancies a steak. The shop is closed. It is past five o'clock. The hams and legs of mutton hang from hooks behind the counter. A fly is locked in. It is a summer that has been captured in September. Then he sees the picture of the boy, Jostein, in the window, an odd photograph, he is almost unrecognisable. It must have been torn out of a magazine. The face is smooth, like a mask, a death mask, and Bjørn Stranger remembers the post-mortems during his medicine studies, the corpses, grey and abandoned, so *unlovely*, especially the women, they just lay there on the table at their disposition. He feels like throwing up. It says *After* beneath the picture. Why is there no *Before*? What comes before *After*? He continues walking along Kirkeveien, unwell, empty, and this day had started so well. At least he has done a good deed. Of that he is sure. As he rounds the corner by Gørbitz gate Jesper comes out of the entrance. He has the flat briefcase under his arm. So he must have a piano lesson. Bjørn Stranger would like to say that he can practise any time on his grand piano, it is at his disposal, but Jesper seems to be in his own world and doesn't notice him. He barrels along in the opposite direction, hoping, please God, that Bjørn won't follow him. He can't bear to listen to him prattling on about how he must come up and play for him. Bjørn Stranger is beginning to resemble the Hurdal bus: a bulldog face. Jesper mustn't think about Hurdal. He has more than enough on his mind. He thinks about his black eye. It will pass. It is a minor injury. But every day he is afraid of bumping into Bror or his pals. He stops in Bislett, looks around, and chooses Sophies gate instead of Pilestredet. He runs across St Olavs Plass thinking he is being followed. He slinks along the wall by the Rikshospital, so as not to be seen by anyone *he* can't see. It isn't only his room, the windowless hallway, which is shrinking. It is the city as well. Soon there won't be any space for him. When he finally reaches Keysersgate unscathed, he is already worn out. He removes his shoes, goes into the living room and plays Claude Debussy. Finn Martins sits on the windowsill, dressed in a black robe, listening, body half-averted while gazing downwards, as though he is enjoying this posture of his.

"The melody's dead," he says.

Jesper tries again, Jacques Ibert this time.

"The melody's dead," Finn Martins repeats.

Jesper drops his hands into his lap.

"Am I playing so badly?"

"I'm talking generally, Jesper. Don't take it personally. After the atomic bomb the melody is dead and it's futile trying to resurrect it. Any attempt at harmony is blasphemy. We can throw everything we have learned hitherto on the scrapheap and discover new music. Is there something the matter, Jesper?"

"No. Only that I'm playing badly."

"You don't seem to be concentrating. Did you hear anything at all of what I said? Or are you thinking exclusively about your poor black eye?"

"The melody's dead."

Finn Martins jumps down from the windowsill.

"Isn't it fabulous?"

"What is?"

"The fact that the melody's dead. Imagine all the possibilities that gives us. We can start from scratch, from a *tabula rasa*. We've already begun!"

"But if the melody's dead, aren't the notes too?"

"Now you're mixing things up, Jesper. The melody's dead, but not the music. Shall we give Prokofiev a last chance?"

Jesper plays "Love for Three Oranges". Afterwards there is a silence, but only on the outside. He can still hear "That Old Black Magic" inside his head. It is a melody. Why isn't it dead? He would certainly like to kill it, but he can't.

"I'm not getting any better," he says.

Finn Martins stands behind Jesper and lays his hands on his shoulders.

"I've arranged a test lesson with Agathe, so she can decide what's best for you."

"Agathe?"

"Yes, Jesper. Old Agathe. She will decide. Sooner or later there is a moment of truth. For you it will be tomorrow."

Jesper is given a notelet with the time and address, and he takes a different route home, through the Vor Frelser graveyard, past Sankthanshaugen and over to Alexander Kiellands Plass, where he thinks he sees someone looking for someone who could be him. There is no peace for Jesper. He ducks behind a dustbin and holds his breath, his heart pounding so hard that the leaves on the last, slender trees in the middle of the intersection are falling. It is a false alarm. It was just someone going to Tranen to drink more beer before autumn arrives in earnest. Jesper carries on up Geitmyrsveien. From there he can nip behind the Norwegian School for Veterinary Science and sneak over to Fagerborg unseen. Someone calls his name, however. He gives a start. It isn't Søster. Nor is it Trude. Trude is kneeling by one of the furrows in the narrow vegetable plot in the school garden and doesn't see him. It is her mother, shouting and waving a carrot. Jesper knows already. Wherever you go there is always someone whose attention you can't escape. Yes, this town is too small. He opens the gate and dawdles over to them. Trude is still busily working on the ground. Jesper doesn't have much idea about horticulture and can't tell whether she is planting or earthing up, harvesting or sowing, but it is definitely potatoes. Her mother removes her gloves and throws them into a basket already brimming with vegetables.

"You look like an office wallah with that briefcase under your arm," she says.

"I've been playing the piano."

"You look like an office worker anyway. You should get a shoulder bag. That would suit you much better. When's your birthday?"

"Soon."

"Did you hear that, Trude? Jesper would like a shoulder bag for his birthday."

It is still mild even though it is September. It is what they call an Indian summer. It comes every seventh year. The sun is casting its last rays, a red fan which makes the leaves rustle. Trude's mother draws the back of her hand across her brow and leans over to Jesper.

"Don't tell anyone I'm here. I'm not allowed in."

"I won't say a word. Aren't you allowed in?"

"I'm sure you can understand why. I don't go to school. I'm scrumping."

She laughs and pokes Trude with the tip of her boot.

"What is it with you two? Can't you even say hi to each other?"

Trude straightens up, wearily and awkwardly, and when her eyes finally meet Jesper's, he is looking down.

"Hi," she says.

Jesper shrugs.

"Hi."

Trude's mother waits, rolls her eyes, but not a squeak comes from either of them.

"Was that it?" she asks.

Trude also takes off her dirty gloves and her hands shine in the darkness the Indian summer has left behind.

"Mamma, please will you—"

"No, I won't. I can't stand any more conflict. There's enough conflict in the world as it is without you two arguing."

"We aren't arguing."

"Oh, I know an argument when I see one. Believe you me. And if you don't make up here and now, one of you had better go home and have a good think. And I want you two to walk together. And I'll tell you something, Jesper. Are you listening?"

"Yes."

"You just pull yourself together."

At any rate, Jesper pulls the bag up under his other arm.

But she hasn't finished yet.

"I know this is difficult, but it's not the end of the world. You could at least say goodbye properly."

Trude gives Jesper a hug. It is only for appearance's sake, the hug, it is what friends give each other, friends who have fallen out too, for that matter. But he shifts his weight to the left so that for an instant he is standing closer to her. She whispers:

"Thank you for being so honest."

Then Jesper walks back to the gate facing Kirkeveien. Trude carries on digging. They don't know yet, but I can tell you: they won't see each other for many years. And during this period, when things really get tough, Jesper will remember her hands shining in the school garden one September evening.

Thank you for being so honest?

Jesper doesn't run back home. Now he is longing for someone to attack him. He is longing to be beaten up. Sadly, he is allowed to walk unmolested. But as soon as he closes the kitchen door after him, finally in safety, he knows something is wrong. Stine is standing by the refrigerator with a glass of milk in her hand.

"It's for Mamma," she says.

Jesper drops his bag.

"What's the matter with her?"

"She's ill. She wants some milk."

"Ill? What's wrong?"

"She came in a taxi and went straight to bed."

Jesper takes the glass, strides through the flat, stops outside her room and knocks. No-one answers. Stine has burst into tears. He opens the door. His mother is in bed, on her back, with her face averted. There are no lamps lit. They go into her room in the pitch dark. Jesper puts the milk on her bedside table.

"Shall I call Dr Lund?"

She sits up, her face is shiny and moist, her hair stuck to her forehead.

"You will not call anyone."

"Alright."

"I just feel a bit nauseous. It'll pass. I don't want you two to catch it."

She slumps back down, exhausted, holds the sheet with both hands and grips it tight. Then Jesper sees the blood, a stain on the linen, it is like a red blot on crinkled blotting paper. He is embarrassed.

"I'm going to ring Dr Lund."

"You're not ringing anyone. Do you hear me?!"

Once again she tries to sit up, using her elbows; she speaks slowly and softly.

"What are you doing with a medical certificate, Jesper?"

"A medical certificate?"

"The one Dr Lund sent you."

"Have you been opening my post?"

"When it's from Lund, I do."

"You're bleeding, Mamma."

"What are you doing with a medical certificate?"

Jesper takes a step back. He doesn't recognise her voice; he doesn't recognise the eyes beneath the sweaty forehead or the pale but burning cheeks.

"I have to do a piano test for Agathe."

"For whom?"

"She's the person who decides who makes it and who doesn't."

"And for that you need a medical certificate?"

"Yes, I do. Was I healthy?"

"Yes. A clean bill of health."

"Not even sensitive?"

She smiles, her grip on the sheet relaxes and at last she looks like the person she is: only their mother.

"Then Jesper will have to practise. Won't he, Stine?"

Stine nods and is the first to leave. Jesper follows her and closes the door slowly, reluctantly. Maj slumps back into bed, puts her hand in her mouth, bites and groans. They mustn't hear. She is being lacerated. The bed sheet is warm and thick with blood. Instead she hears music. Jesper is playing Satie. It is a long time since he has played this piece. It is getting better now. The music is doing her good. Jesper goes back to the beginning. She is bleeding. Blood is flowing out. She stops bleeding. She dare not examine the blood. It is only blood. She knows that. There is silence. Stine switches off the lamps in the flat. Maj can see that by the strip of light underneath the door, which opens a fraction. Jesper peers in. She pretends to be asleep. He closes the door. The pains return, in her back, her hips, the bouts last longer and longer. For one pain-free moment, she thinks just that, it is a free moment, for pain is work, pain is overtime, she takes two tablets, washes them down with milk, retches and falls asleep. She wakes up in the middle of the night, confused, she is cold, cold and sweaty. So it must be morning. The dustcart drives past. Why doesn't it stop? The sheet is stiff and thick with blood. She can't have been bleeding for a while. She assumes it is over. She has no pain. The lights in the flat are on. The usual sounds make her feel good too, a tap running, quick footsteps, drawers being opened and closed, it is everyday life, which has to continue. It is her children. Maj wants to get up and go out to them. She can't. Stine opens the door, shy almost, and asks whether she wants any breakfast. Maj will get up soon and make her own breakfast. That's nice of you, Stine, but don't worry about me. You have to go to school. Go on. Footsteps on the stairs, light, heavy, heavy, light. Maj drifts off into a doze. She wants to stay there, unsuspecting and free. She hears Satie again. It isn't a dream. She wishes it were. It is Jesper playing in the sitting room. Why is he at home? Is it a school holiday? What is this one called? At that moment things begin to move again. There is a butcher inside her, chopping. She puts a hand in her mouth. How much blood can she have? It takes longer to lose a child than to have one. She rolls over onto Ewald's duvet. She soils his clean linen. A strip of light along the floor cuts the darkness into two.

"Mamma?"

Maj doesn't have the energy to turn.

"Mamma?" Jesper repeats.

He can just make her out. She is lying on the wrong side of the bed. She seems calmer, as far as he can judge. But there is an acrid smell in the room: sweat, piss. He can't let her lie in bed like this. If she isn't up by the time he is back, he will have to air the room. If she isn't better he will have to call someone.

"I'm off now."

Jesper closes the door, grabs his bag, and then changes his mind. He leaves it where it is. He doesn't need the notes. Today he will play from memory. He puts the medical certificate in his back pocket. He goes downstairs and stands in Gørbitz gate momentarily at a loss. Which route should he take? He decides on Kirkeveien. At least he has a good view there. He can see if anyone is coming. No ambushes are possible in Kirkeveien. To ambush him you would have to be standing in an arched gateway or lying behind a hedge in Suhms gate. He passes Marienlyst where a first class is being taught the rules of the road by a constable wearing a bandolier and white gloves. The Priests' Church shimmers in the clear air. Fru Melsom waves to him from inside her shop. Should he tell her? Should he say his mother is ill and needs help? Only the fake picture of Jostein is in the window now. The birdbrain demanded that the *Before* picture was removed. But now he looks like the lie, he doesn't have any more spots, and so it all boils down to the same thing. Jesper wants it to as well. He wishes that everything that was before didn't exist, not even the *now*; he wants only a future that has no connection with yesterday. He waves back and hurries on. In Majorstua he jumps on a tram. No-one from Hurdal goes by tram. He pays and takes a seat at the back. It is the tram he used to catch to go to see Enzo Zanetti, when he caught the wrong one, mind you, the one that goes past the Salvation Army building, Majorstua School, Frogner stadium and Vigeland Park and turns off by Frogner Plass, at the bottom of Kirkeveien, and heads east, ignoring the line down Bogstadveien, up to where the track forks in Holtegata and from there through Briskeby. He gives a start whenever he hears a motorbike. He can't distinguish their sounds. The young man who can hear differences between renderings of the same note can't tell the difference between a Honda and a scooter. *In the winter it moves by sleigh, While in the spring it rolls on wheels.* How do you get around in autumn? You walk, on rubber soles. Fortunately there aren't many motorbikes in this part of town, so it is all the worse when one comes along. It might be Bror. Søster might be on the pillion. The whole family might be after him. In Fredrik Stangs gate he spots Olaf Hall and Margrethe. They are walking arm in arm over the pedestrian crossing and stop in front of the green Narvesen kiosk, where newspapers are hanging on a stand by the window. It strikes Jesper that he has more or less forgotten about them, certainly the man. Margrethe seems old and fragile, she is holding on to the arm of Olaf Hall, who is thin and pale, the antiquarian book dealer's face is already a bound edition, thank God they don't see Jesper, and if they had he would have been well past them anyway. He gets off at Solli Plass and remembers the address he was given by Finn Martins: The Piano Academy, the K.N.A. Hotel, on the corner of Cort Adelers gate and Parkveien. It is the hotel owned by the Royal Norwegian Automobile Club. Only people with a driving licence can stay there and it is the only hotel in Oslo with a garage. This is where Jesper has to do the test. He enters the lobby. The lighting is muted, a dark yellow. The receptionist looks up. Finn Martins has already arrived, wearing a grey double-breasted suit jacket with a handkerchief in the chest pocket and a plaid bow tie. He is more nervous than Jesper. In fact, Jesper isn't nervous, not about this anyway.

"No music?" Finn Martins says.

"I can manage without."

"Up to you."

They take the lift to the fifth floor. There are mirrors all over the place. It is impossible to see where one starts and the next one finishes.

"Besides, the melody's dead," Jesper says.

Finn Martins stamps on the floor as the lift comes to a halt and the door slides open.

"Don't take everything so literally, sonny. I'm getting tired of it. Improvise a little."

"I thought you meant it."

"Of course I mean it. But you still don't have to take it literally."

"Alright."

Finn Martins holds Jesper back for a moment.

"And don't take everything personally either."

"What do you mean?"

"Agathe shoots from the hip, as they say, or reads straight from the score, as we musicians prefer to say. She can be ruthless, but she's also openly enthusiastic. And if she is enthusiastic, we take it personally. If she's ruthless, we don't."

"What do you reckon?" .

"I reckon we'll take it personally."

They walk down the corridor and stop at Room 611. Finn Martins knocks. A sombre voice answers: *Come in.* Finn Martins takes a deep breath and opens the door. Room 611 is a suite. On the walls hang signed photographs of famous composers, conductors, singers and musicians. At any rate Jesper can see Wilhelm Kempff, Herbert von Karajan, Kirsten Flagstad and Harald Sæverud. She has Sæverud's autograph. He walks closer. It is the same hand that wrote the music to the "Ballad of Revolt". Jesper tries to see a connection, but can't find one, they are two different signatures. Above a make-up table there is also a picture of a racing driver, who is standing with one foot placed on the running board laughing at photographers, a pennant fluttering in the background: *Monte Carlo Rally*. And in the first part of the suite is sitting the woman who must be Agathe. She is wearing a long, black dress, a little hat, black too, with a thin veil fastened at the edge with a silver pin. She is from the previous century, at least. But she fixes Jesper with a sharp, almost funny, stare and beckons him closer. Finn Martins keeps in the background. Jesper stops in front of Agathe.

"You should know that I'm not dressed in black for your sake," she says.

Now Jesper can see the Steinway in the adjacent room.

"I hope not."

"It's for King Haakon's sake. He could die at any moment and I want to be prepared for the occasion."

"Are things so bad?"

Agathe passes him her hand, palm down and fingers bent. Jesper isn't sure if he is supposed to kiss it. He brushes her knuckles with his lips.

"And you're the Jesper Finn took on after our good friend Enzo Zanetti became homesick?"

"Yes. Jesper Kristoffersen."

"What are you going to play for me?"

"Satie's *Gymnopédies*."

"All three of course?"

"Yes."

"Have you ambitions?"

"I'd like to hear what you have to say first."

Agathe looks up and smiles.

"That's the spirit. Away you go, young man."

Jesper walks into the other room, sits down on the stool and starts. The piano has its own sound, fuller, darker, yet more precise than he is used to. Every touch stands out in the stream of notes. He plays "Gymnopédie No. 1". He thinks about rain and the droplets falling far apart. He thinks he plays it well. He can't remember ever having thought that before. Perhaps it is he who is good today, not only the instrument. It is as though he can hear himself for the first time and he likes what he hears. He allows a few seconds to pass before continuing with No. 2. It is shorter, but he increases the tempo, imperceptibly almost, only a light touch of the accelerator pedal in the Satie Rally, where the idea is not to arrive first, but without a scratch, without any damage to the bodywork. He slows down at the bends. It is as if he is learning it there and then: the art of hesitating. Nevertheless it is in "Gymnopédie No. 3" that Jesper understands the composition. Each piece is a door into the same room. It could be the hall in Kirkeveien: coming from the hallway you see everything for the first time. If you come from his mother's bedroom you will notice the shadows. If you come from the pantry it is the colours that catch your eye: brown, red and light green. This thought makes Jesper happy. And the thought that a thought can make him happy makes him even happier. He plays flawlessly. But playing without any flaws isn't enough. Anyone can do that. You have to play *properly*. Jesper cannot imagine that he is doing anything but playing properly. Then he lifts his hands slowly and there is silence in the suite. Finn Martins is still leaning against the wall. Agathe is sitting on her chair.

"I'd like to hear No. 1 again," she says.

Jesper plays it for her. He is unsure for a moment whether he should change anything, especially with the left hand, he could press harder and in that way emphasise the rhythm and still retain *the hesitancy*. A thought strikes Jesper: I am thinking too much. Thinking isn't the same as concentrating. It is the opposite. He plays the last bars even more slowly, with an even harder touch, and rests his fingers on the keys to draw the sound out. It lasts quite a while. Agathe beckons to him. He goes over to her. She takes his left hand.

"That is absolutely excellent," she says.

Jesper doesn't quite catch her drift, but surely it can't be bad. He waits for her to carry on. She does.

"That is absolutely excellent, for an amateur."

Agathe lets go of his hand.

He shouldn't take it personally.

He walks past Finn Martins, into the corridor, to the lift, into the lift, he presses the button for the ground floor, the door closes and becomes a mirror, he turns away, but there is another mirror there, and surrounded by himself he sinks down through the floors in the Royal Norwegian Automobile Club hotel. And it is only now, now that the verdict has fallen, the worst of them all, *for an amateur*, that he can see how much this meant, it meant everything, now it means nothing.

The melody is dead.

Jesper Kristoffersen shouldn't take it personally.

The lift stops and the door glides open again. He has gone too far. He has ended up in the garage. He walks among the elegant sports cars parked there, low-slung, open-top vehicles, with mud and crap on the windscreens still. He can see his reflection in the bumpers. He has to walk around a pillar to find the exit. He emerges. He can see the rear of the university library. Trude lives in the street below. The windows in her flat are vacant, there are no curtains, even the potted plants on the little balcony have gone. He waits. He can also walk round and throw some more stones at Trude's window. Then he can tell her he has stopped playing the piano. But no-one will open the window. Trude's window is somewhere else now. Everyone has gone. He runs up to Solli Plass, spots a free taxi, scrambles onto the back seat and tells the driver to go to the Seamen's House. The taxi driver wants to see his money first. Jesper shows him two banknotes. The driver's scepticism is temporarily assuaged. He drives down to the city centre, to Wedels Plass. Jesper pays, receives his change and gets out. It isn't hard to find. A huge gable wall announces SEAMEN'S HOUSE, NORWEGIAN SEAFARERS' UNION. The wind is blowing; it pulls and tears at him. Rain and leaves sweep past. The Norwegian flag flaps as the rope thwacks against the pole. It is September. A sign by a door says: RECRUITMENT OFFICE, GROUND FLOOR. Just like Agathe, the bloody fossil who anticipates sorrow and wears black before King Haakon has even died, Jesper has also made a decision before a decision has to be made. He has known without knowing. He has to get away. He already has the medical certificate in his back pocket. He hears the City Hall bells chiming close by. He can see the view from the clock tower: the fjord, which is the sea's arm, and at the very end the fingers pointing into the distance. He goes in. There is a queue at the counter, young men in big boots, jeans rolled up at the ankle, leather jackets and greased hair, lined up, patient and restless; these are young men who want *out*, the same as Jesper. They seem aloof and experienced, but if you look more closely, you know they are also just novices who will soon be in the top bunk calling for mamma. Jesper thinks: Perhaps I will meet Bror at sea? But the ocean is bigger than the city and so the chances are slimmer. He sees a notice on a board: *Proposals re war pensions for seamen who contracted diseases during the war.* Perhaps Old Shark can move from the ski jump in Frogner Park to a bedsit in Grønnegata 19? It is Jesper's turn. He hands over his medical certificate and is given a pencil and two forms to fill in. He sits by the wall. It doesn't take him long. He has finished before the others, but doesn't automatically go to the front of the queue. Different rules apply here. There are at least eight people in front of him. The names are called out. In the corner there is a kind of indoor telephone box. He walks over, inserts a few coins and rings home. He is relieved when his mother answers. He asks before she has time to say her name:

"Are you OK?"

"Yes, I'm up and about."

Her voice sounds weary, breathless.

"Shall I do some shopping?" he asks.

"I think we have what we need. Thanks."

"Is Stine at home?"

"She'll probably be here any minute."

"Me too, Mamma."

"Did you do the test today?"

"Yes."

"How did it go?"

"Fine."

"I knew it would. What's all that racket? Where are you, Jesper?"

"I have to ring off now, Mamma."

Maj hears someone call his name, *Jesper Kristoffersen*, in the background as the line goes dead. She drops the receiver, slumps down and has to hold on to the sofa. This is never-ending. It has got stuck. There is only blood. Soon she won't have any more. Then she is sent reeling backwards by another contraction and is lying on her back, forcing her hips up in an arc, banging her hands on her stomach, and there is some movement inside, at last there is some movement. She manages to turn and crawl into the bathroom, fasten the hook on the door, tear off her clothes and squat astride the toilet bowl. It is moving, she is dilated, the first blood on the white porcelain, then she presses a bit more, closes her eyes and the last she hears before she faints is the brief, dull splash of something falling into the water. When she comes to she is lying semi-naked next to the bathtub. There is blood everywhere. She will have to clean up. That is her first thought. There is a packet of Pep on the shelf. She struggles to her feet, finds a cloth, takes the packet, she is going to clean and wash up. She will be doubly happy. Then she remembers she hasn't pulled the chain. She has to do that first. She can't stop herself looking: there is a lump floating in the red water. She pulls the chain. There is a knock at the door.

"Mamma?"

Maj leans back against the wall and can barely talk.

"I'm having a bath, Stine."

"Are you alright, Mamma?"

"I'll be out in a mo, my love."

"There's someone ringing at the door, Mamma."

"Just say I'm not in."

"You're in the bathroom though."

"And don't let anyone in."

Outside there is silence. Then the doorbell rings again. Maj sinks down to the keyhole in the bathroom door and watches Stine running into the hallway. She still hasn't taken off her satchel. Maybe it's Jesper, Stine thinks. Maybe Jesper has forgotten his keys, or lost them, it doesn't matter, so long as it is Jesper. Jesper can come in. She opens the door. It is Fru Lund.

"Mamma's not in," Stine says.

Fru Lund looks down at her and smiles.

"Sure she isn't just sitting by the phone? Because it's been engaged for—"

"Yes, she's having a bath."

Fru Lund laughs and hands an envelope to Stine.

"Could you give her this when she's finished? It's notice of a Red Cross board meeting. Do you know what that means?"

Stine nods with a serious face.

"Yes."

Fru Lund takes a step closer and peers inside.

"Is anything the matter, Stine?"

"No."

"Are you sure everything's alright?"

"Yes."

Fru Lund listens for a moment, then retreats onto the landing.

"And can you also tell your mother we need her for the autumn bazaar. We simply cannot manage without her. Could you say hello from me and pass on the message?"

"Yes, Fru Lund."

Stine closes the door and takes off her satchel. She hears water running in the bath. That calms her and makes her feel happy. Then she goes into the sitting room, lifts the receiver hanging by its cable, almost to the floor; she has to use both hands, places it against her ear and for safety's sake says what she has been taught, Kristoffersen family here, hello, and she makes a big effort to get the R right, she almost throws herself into it, Kristoffersen family here, hello, the way she will do not so many years hence when she has to say revolution, the Rolling Stones and the Red Front. But there is no-one, there is no-one at the other end, only a soft hiss from all the lines criss-crossing the city and connecting them in a lonely and reassuring network. She gently cradles the receiver.

The bazaar was inaugurated in the presence of Princess Astrid. Of our ladies Fru Lund and Frøken Jacobsen were present. Our tombola opened on September 9th and closed on the 13th. Only a week later King Haakon passed away. The Fagerborg department of the Norwegian Red Cross organised an open meeting in the Parish Hall two days after the magnificent funeral. We would have liked Trude Hagen and Jesper Kristoffersen, whose performances had met with such success on May 17th, to speak and play for us. It would also have been appropriate to let youth have its sway. But Trude Hagen has moved to Stockholm with her parents and it has transpired that Jesper Kristoffersen has gone to sea. We therefore had to make do with the chairman reading Nordahl Grieg's "We Shall Come Again". Fru Maj Kristoffersen, who is back at her post of treasurer, informed us that the tombola produced an income of 537 kroner. Lean pickings, one has to say.

LARS SAABYE CHRISTENSEN is the author of novels, poetry and short story collections. His international breakthrough came with *Beatles* (1984), since translated into many languages, and for *The Half Brother* he was the winner of the Nordic Council Literature Prize in 2001. *Friendship* is the second in the *Echoes of a City* trilogy.

DON BARTLETT is the acclaimed translator of books by Karl Ove Knausgård, Jo Nesbø and Per Petterson. His translation of Roy Jacobsen's *The Unseen*, the first in the Barrøy series, was shortlisted for the Man Booker International Prize in 2017.